Also by Robert Flynn:

North to Yesterday

In the House of the Lord

The Sounds of Rescue, the Signs of Hope

Seasonal Rain and other stories

Wanderer Springs

A Personal War in Vietnam (a memoir)

When I Was Just Your Age (with Susan Russell)

The Last Klick

A NOVEL BY

Robert Flynn

BASKERVILLE
PUBLISHERS, INC.
DALLAS • NEW YORK • DUBLIN

This book is a work of fiction. Names, characters, places and incidents are either the product of the author's imagination or are used fictitiously. Any resemblance to actual events or locales or persons, living or dead, is entirely coincidental.

BASKERVILLE Publishers, Inc.
7616 LBJ Freeway, Suite 220, Dallas TX 75251-1008

Parts of this book appeared in *Seasonal Rain* and are reprinted with the permission of Corona Publishing Company.

Library of Congress Cataloging-in-Publication Data

Flynn, Robert, 1932-
The last klick: a novel / by Robert Flynn.
p. cm.
ISBN: 1-880909-21-9 (lib. bdg.) : $21.00 ($27.00 Can.)
1. Vietnamese Conflict, 1961-1975--Journalists--Fiction. 2. Journalists--United States--Fiction. 3. Americans--Vietnam--Fiction.
I. Title
PS3556.L9L37 1994 93-45618
813'.54--dc20 CIP

Manufactured in the United States of America
First Printing, 1994

For Deirdre

Saigon

It was a standard patrol. Single file through the wire at first light. Lock and load weapons. Single file under trees hung with burned out flares. String out along the ravine, around the crater left by a mine. Single file across the rock-bottomed creek. Fan out through the ville and check the hootches. Single file through the bamboo. Spread out across the paddy. Single file through the treeline. Fan out through the ville and check the hootches. Single file across the river. On line through the grass. Close in around the ville and check the hootches. Two files around the hill. Two trails through the bush. Link up at the cemetery. Single file back to the wire. Unload weapons. Single file through the wire before dusk. Check in grenades.

It was routine except that one of the men killed a Viet Cong. Sherrill O'Connell, reporter for REAL magazine, interviewed him when they returned to the base camp. The killer was sitting with his helmet and rifle between his knees, his back against a sandbagged bunker, a cigarette in one black hand, a beer in the other. Sweat clung to his forehead and dripped from his smooth black chin. O'Connell made a note that he was animated, exhausted, bewildered. "God damn," he said.

O'Connell sat beside him. "What's your name?"

"You going to write about me?"

"Maybe."

"The Army calls me Cletus Harvey but don't write that. Write me down as Spike." Sherrill made a note. "And don't say I'm skinny. My mama don't like that. Say I am wiry. And don't make me out baby-faced neither."

Sherrill wrote ". . .the look of a little boy who has just been bitten by his own dog."

"Where are you from, Spike?"

"North Carolina. Don't say I'm a hillbilly. Say I am a mountain man."

Sherrill wrote down "mountain man." "What did you do in North Carolina?"

"Went to school. Played second base. Worked in a feed store. Don't say I swept floors."

Sherrill scratched through "mountain man." "I understand you killed a man today."

"I wasted a Charlie. Hit him right in the neck." He pointed at a spot just below the corner of his jaw. "He didn't even scream. Blew the whole side of his head out."

"Was it your first kill?"

"Hey man, this was my first patrol. My first shot. Hey, I ain't even been shot at yet. I fired the first shot I heard. The first gook I seen I killed. Hey, if I kill somebody every day I'll kill three hundred and. . .God damn."

"How long have you been here?"

"I got here yesterday, man. The day before that I was in Ban Me Thout. The day before that I was in Da Nang. And the day. . .or the night. . .hey, how long was we in Da Nang? Anyway, the day before that I was in. . .I was in. . .fucking California. And the day before that, man, I was home.

That's. . .let's see, that's one, two, three, four days. If I get one every three days I'll have a hundred by the time I DEROS. A hundred and twenty one. . .or two. Jesus. God damn."

"What was the patrol like?"

"They all said it was a slide. They said we was skating. This was just to get me ready for the humping I'll have to do later on. Man, it kicked my ass. I ain't never been so hot. I could hear my heart beating in my head. 'How far we come?' I said. 'About ten klicks.' Ten klicks. Hell, I can run ten klicks."

"When did you first see the enemy?"

"We was taking a break, all crapped out along the trail in this little clearing, and I walked back in the bush to drain my lizard, and I seen this dude with a rifle. He wasn't much farther than that piss tube over there. Hey, I said, because I didn't want to shoot no friendly. I didn't even know what the enemy look like. Then he aimed his rifle at somebody and there wasn't nobody for him to shoot but us, so I shot him. Wet on myself too, but I had my pecker out. Hit him right in the neck. He just stood there and. . .blew out the whole side of his head. Don't say I pissed on myself."

"Wet his pants," Sherrill wrote in his notebook.

The killer threw away his cigarette and lighted another one. Sherrill made a note that he was wearing a high school ring. It looked new. "I probably saved somebody's life. He was the enemy and I did what I'm supposed to do. I don't feel. . ." He wet the corners of his mouth with his tongue. "I'm sorry that he had to die, but he didn't have to point that rifle."

"He had to die because he's the enemy of freedom," Sherrill said.

"I reckon I could have told him to chieu hoi."

"But the world's a better place because you're here."

"I'm just doing what folks told me to do," the killer said, showing his teeth.

Sherrill wrote, "'Just doing my job,' he said with a smile," and closed his notebook. Others had slowly gathered to watch the interview and when it was over they closed in to congratulate the killer. "Don't tell my mama I did something wrong," he said to Sherrill. "I promised her I wouldn't shoot nobody."

Sherrill made a note to call the story, "The Promise." A boy had to break his pledge to his mother to bring peace and freedom to a troubled land. He scratched through that and wrote, "Doing the Job."

"Hey, blood brother, heard you zapped a cong," said a huge black machine gunner, slapping hands with the killer and going through an elaborate handshake. Sherrill noted he was the kind of black one had rather meet in a living room than in an alley.

"Killed the motherfucker my first shot. Hit him right in the neck," he said, pointing a finger at the spot. "I only been here a week. If I kill somebody every week. . .fifty-two people. Minus one for R&R."

"There it is. Come the revolution we gonna be needing you."

"Real fine, soldier," said a sallow, pimple-faced lieutenant. He looked to Sherrill like a poster-boy for a campaign against self-abuse. "You saved my life. They always go for your officers first. Thank you muchly."

"I hit him high. Right in the neck." He pointed at the spot. "I was aiming at his chest."

"You saved your leader and now he is going to look after you."

"Thank you, sir."

"There is no color between us. Check it, trooper. No color."

"Yes sir."

"That's affirm."

"God bless you, son," said the deep-throated, short-legged chaplain. He seemed to be all head and chest, a man who spent more time in the chapel than in the hospital or the field. "Sometimes it is tragically necessary to kill in the defense of one's life or family or national honor."

"Yes sir."

"Are you a Christian, my son?"

"Yes sir," the killer said, making the sign of the cross.

"Are you Catholic? There's a Catholic chaplain."

"No sir, I'm Baptist. I don't know why I did that."

"Well, God forgives Baptist boys who kill the enemy. Have you asked for forgiveness?"

"I ain't had no time."

"Then get your sierra together, soldier," the chaplain said in an attempt at jovial amiability. He laid a fat hand on the killer's head and pushed until the head was bowed. "And while you're praying, thank God for preserving your life to this very hour." He looked up and saw the others watching. He stared until they lowered their heads or walked away. "And pray for free world forces everywhere."

Some of the men prayed and others looked around in embarrassment. One of them, wearing the crisp new uniform and the white, unlined face of a newby, prayed with a fervency matched only by the intensity with which he picked his nose. "Hear the prayer of thy children, O God," the chaplain intoned. "Make us strong that we may continue thy fight against the forces of godless communism. We pray in the name of Jesus who died for us all."

"I hear you're not cherry anymore," said a joyless kid with three hundred days behind his eyes. He had a grenade pin in his bush hat, love beads around his neck, jungle sores on his arms and Ho Chi Minh sandals on his feet. He looked like a supposer to Sherrill, a man who chewed his mind instead of his nails, a man who would always have a month to go. Even if he got back to the world his tour would never be over.

"I saw him before he saw me. Hit him right in the neck."

"That old papasan has been taking shots at us ever since I been here. He never hit anybody though. Glad it was you that got him and not me."

"You think I shouldn't have shot him? What am I supposed

to do, let him shoot my buddies? How am I supposed to know who to shoot and who not to shoot?"

"Sorry about that, hero," he sneered.

"Hey, tiger, got you a dink," said the sergeant, a hulking lifer who had more malice for his own men than for the enemy. "Going to get some more tomorrow, right?"

"God damn. Right," the killer said, wiping his mouth with the back of his hand and swallowing whatever was welling in his throat. "Kill the motherfuckers."

"Outstanding. The lieutenant said you didn't have to go out tomorrow, but I knew a blood like you would want to get with the program. We're going into Indian country. And some of you fuckers are going to die."

"God damn."

Everybody had left except Sherrill and the fervent nosepicker who had been hanging around the edge of the crowd. He squatted beside the killer. "What's it like?" he asked. "I'm going on my first patrol tomorrow."

The killer leaned back against the sandbags and looked up at the first stars. "Jesus God, I'm going out tomorrow. Three hundred and sixty days to go. Ain't no way."

"I hear you killed a Victor Charlie."

"Three hundred and sixty more days. God damn."

"Were you scared when you went out? I got to know."

"Don't say I was scared. Say I was. . .say I was careful."

"What's it like to kill somebody? Did you know you could?"

"I seen him and I shot him. Blew out the whole side of his head. For a minute he just stood there. Like he was surprised. He just stood there and I says, son of a bitch I done a bad thing. I thought he was going to turn and look at me like I done a bad thing. I seen stuff blow out the side of his head but he didn't fall and I says, son of a bitch I missed him. And I was scared. And glad. And awful. And then his rifle dropped and he just. . .he didn't fall, man, he just sank. He just sank down. I heard him, man. I heard him snapping his teeth."

"What if I can't do it? What if somebody gets killed because I can't do it?"

"I heard him snapping his teeth. And I saw his face. He was real, man. He was. . .my daddy killed people in Germany. But I didn't know they were real. They were Nazis."

For a while no one spoke. The mosquitoes came in waves and behind them a mortar coughed. A flare popped high in the sky and hung sizzling beneath its tiny parachute, blotting out the stars.

"You going to chow?" the nose picker asked.

"I ain't hungry," the killer said.

"You coming to the hootch?"

"I may lay out for a while. I don't want to hear nobody snoring and clicking their teeth."

The newby left to find his own accommodations. The killer lighted a cigarette and blew smoke upward at the sky. "He was just a little guy," he said. "Just a little old man."

Sherrill waited, offering himself to the mosquitoes as a kind of penance.

"If you write about me, say I wish it had been somebody else," the killer said. "Say I wish it had been folks I ain't even heard of."

Sherrill went back to the empty hootch they had given him and worked on the story by the hissing light of a Coleman lantern. Then he lay down on the soiled mattress, using his flak jacket for a pillow. He had gotten what he had come for, a story REAL would buy. After so much failure, a success. Why didn't he feel elated?

He was homesick. That was part of it. He missed Jennifer. Honest, direct Jennifer, everybody's friend, the kind of girl everyone hugged and no one kissed until he kissed her. She had found beauty in herself and in him and together they had struggled, he to be a writer, she to help and support him, and they had never been apart before.

Jennifer wrote almost every day but her letters rarely reached him at remote bases like this one, instead were scattered across Vietnam, every place he had been or said he was going to go. When he got them they were in haphazard bunches with huge gaps in time and information. Some of the gaps he never filled.

He was also depressed. Writing for REAL had not brought the satisfaction he had expected. He didn't know why he had to write. He did know he was not happy or complete without a private stage in his head where people born in his imagination danced his yes, lived his death, and gave voice to his dreams. But writing for REAL was less satisfying than writing fiction and he hadn't been able to write a novel since Marie died.

His first novel was going to be about his father, a Texas farmer, who had died when Sherrill was thirteen. The book was going to explain why his mother and father lived in separate spheres, their lives touching but never merging, why life seemed so full and people so empty, and it was going to enlarge the lives of those who labored under mutual disapproval.

He had intended the dying father to leave a last message to his son. For months Sherrill had struggled with the father, a self-righteous, sententious puppet, until one day the character emerged as a fur trapper who built a raft to carry the fruit of two years of lonely, back-breaking work. The raft overturned in the river, the hides were lost along with his supplies, and his leg was broken. Desperate, he bound the bones together, and with a makeshift crutch, attempted to reach help. Finally, mad with hunger, pain, loss of hope, and the smell of his putrefying leg, he left a message to whoever found him.

In his last hours the trapper went from rage at the Creator who had given him fragile bones in a hostile environment, to acceptance that he like all men must die, to hope that whoever discovered his bones would recognize how courageously he had struggled and how bravely he had died, to the understanding that life was struggle unto death. With his last strength he scratched in the rocks, "What did you expect?"

Sherrill wanted the reader to know what the trapper understood, that he had done only what was expected of him and that the trapper had the same expectations of those who found his bones. The critics saw none of that, but praised the book for its nihilism and warned readers that it was a painful book to read, a warning readers took to heart.

In his second book, a young cowboy traveling across the Texas prairie with his bride was attacked by a small band of Comanches. He explained the hopelessness of the situation to his wife. She asked him to shoot her to spare her being captured by the Indians. He, following the conventional truth of his day, honored her request, intending to die beside her. Unaccountably, the Indians left.

Troubled that he saved his life by killing his wife, he turned to the nearest settlement for judgment. There he was viewed as a hero. "By God, it took a man to do what you did. I'm not sure I could have done it." Desperate for their approval he was unable to believe them. He traveled to another town, going from bar to bar, telling his story. They agreed that it was a hard test of manhood, but he did what was right. In the town was a young woman who had been an Indian captive and was an outcast because she had had an Indian husband.

The cowboy fell in love with her. In an intimate moment she confessed to him that she missed her dead husband and her life as an Indian. If that was true then he hadn't saved his wife from a worse fate. Everything he believed about men, about women, about right was a lie. The cowboy struck her, called her a whore and a liar and became an implacable Indian fighter because they caused him to kill his wife. His life was a lie but it was a lie he could live with.

Most critics dismissed the book as a western. The few who reviewed it complained that he never showed the cowboy tracking down and killing Indians. One critic deplored the fact that Sherrill, who had shown promise, chose to write about an idealized American past rather than expose himself to modern ideas and problems such as nuclear war, hunger, poverty and bigotry.

Sherrill was stung by the reviews. He didn't write westerns. He had considered writing the book about a man who killed his wife to save her from a Nazi concentration camp, only to meet a survivor who said the camp was better than death. The husband then became an implacable hater of anything German. It didn't work.

It wasn't the setting that was important but the idea that people conformed to standards that they knew were lies—Southern politicians who pretended that slavery was benign, industrialists who pretended that child labor was uplifting, lawyers who clung to pretensions of justice long after their practice had become haggling over the division of dollars. The readers saw none of that. No critic mentioned his ideas.

Sherrill was unhappy that his books were misunderstood, but he was not discouraged. The small college where he had been teaching gave him tenure. Jennifer was delighted; now they had roots, security and they could plan Marie's future. The money from his books went for Marie's dancing lessons, braces, the best health care money could buy and her future college expenses.

Then Marie died without warning. Without preparation.

The first time he had seen Marie he had believed Jennifer had given him a perfect thing. When he held her and looked into her eyes he saw all the approval, all the recognition he would ever need. He had never particularly wanted to be a father, but when he held his child in his arms and her tiny hand curled around his finger he knew he would die to defend her, would give up anything he possessed to make her smile. He was surprised at the fierceness of the paternal instinct in him.

"How is she?" Jennifer had asked. Jennifer looked proud,

and shy and a little frightened at what she had done.

"She's perfect," he said, shaking her gently so that her eyes opened and her tiny mouth moved. He wasn't frightened at all. "She's perfect." But Marie hadn't been perfect. She had been doomed the moment she was conceived, prone to perish. Thirteen years. He did not understand why it had happened to him. He had been a good man. He had worked hard. He had followed the rules. Unknowingly, he had blamed Jennifer.

Jennifer found comfort in routine. She found comfort in friends. She didn't find comfort in him and was unable to cope with his absence, if not in body then in mind. Writing shut her out. She wanted to be part of everything he did, to go everywhere he went. She wanted to make love and lie in her feelings all day with him beside her.

He couldn't talk to anyone, least of all Jennifer. The pain in her eyes made his own pain more unbearable. "You're shutting me out," she said. But he wasn't shutting her out; he was trying to save himself the only way he knew by curling into his pain, giving himself to it so that out of his pain something might come because there was nothing they could do for Marie, and nothing they could find to do for each other.

Jennifer wanted to be a mother again. She wanted to hold a baby, to hold life in a manageable size. He never wanted to know that much of pain and loss again. He wanted to write a book that would keep Marie alive forever. It was the only way he could save her, the only way he could hold her. In time he came to believe the book could save him as well. He would create something that would last, something not as vulnerable as a child.

He tried to write about the simple beauty of Marie's short life, but the little girl who emerged from his pen was bloodless and so precious that he had disliked her himself. Every plot he devised was maudlin, with the world's most beautiful child asking, "Daddy, why must I die?" Everything he wrote was sentimental and trite. He believed he would never be able to write again.

Another might have found comfort in the students, but Sherrill saw them wasting the life that his daughter had been denied. He was revolted by their frivolous complaints. Why did they have to read about Greek gods that no one believed in any more? Why did they have to write papers about values as seen by Tolstoy or Kafka? Why couldn't they have their own values and ideas? Why couldn't they write the way they wanted to write? It was a time when dissent was respected and language was not.

In his despair, Sherrill turned to Alvord Lindly. Lindly was the best paid and most popular professor on the campus. He entertained classes in his home and students were free to drop by to discuss politics over a drink or a joint. Although Sherrill didn't know why, Lindly admired him and was the only person on campus who had read Sherrill's books.

Lindly was quick to point out Sherrill's flaw. "You have no ambition," he said. Sherrill was shocked. Of course he had ambition; he feared he was too ambitious. "If you had ambition, you'd write something so shocking, so outrageous that people would have to notice."

"I'm not going to write something I wouldn't read," Sherrill protested.

"See, no ambition," Lindly said.

Sherrill re-read the reviews of his now out-of-print books looking for inspiration. An obscure magazine called REAL had named his second book about the wife-killer and Indian fighter the best novel of the year. It troubled Sherrill that they had understood the book no better than the critics that disliked it, but at least they had recognized its quality. "Sherrill O'Connell brilliantly describes the courage and conviction that has made this nation great, the courage and conviction that has carried our men to the shores of Vietnam."

The idea, born of desperation, sprang into his head full grown without the gestation or maturation that allowed him to trace its processes or to explain it, even to himself. He would go to Vietnam. He didn't know what was so appealing about the idea except that it was different from anything he had done. Far from his problems at home. He had lived a sheltered, even guarded life. That's why he had nothing to write about. He had loved steadfast, dependable Jennifer, but it hadn't been enough.

He wrote REAL magazine that he wanted to be their reporter in Vietnam, enclosing a copy of their review of his book. Fred Stone, editor of REAL, had read neither of Sherrill's books but had read that Sherrill idealized the American past and was pleased that Sherrill was not a journalist. "We're not sure what kind of stories we're looking for but we know the kind of man we want," Stone said. "A man who will stick his nose in it and tell us whether it smells like fish or figs. This is not a news magazine. We don't have big buck accounts and big name writers. What REAL has is guts. We know whose side we're on. We know who the bad guys are and we're not afraid to say so."

REAL would advance the money for his airfare and expenses in return for three stories and would pay him for each additional story. That seemed reasonable to him. REAL wanted someone to write about real heroes and the job they were doing winning the war. He saw no problem with that. His politics was to do what was right and helping people was always right. That there might be other ways to help them had not occurred to him.

He tried his idea on Lindly first. He thought Lindly would admire his daring and ambition.

"Nobody cares about Vietnam," Lindly said.

"You have to care," he said. Lindly was louder than anyone in denouncing America for not jumping into war in 1939 and saving the Jews, but he admired Switzerland's neutrality and cared nothing about the Vietnamese. What kind of morality was that?

"Let them fight their own war," Lindly said.

"They have been fighting for years. The French didn't last thirty days in World War Two."

"We were saving French culture, the French language, the French people. Nobody gives a shit about Vietnamese culture and if they want to kill each other, good riddance. Don't go, Sherrill. Nobody on this campus is going to see you as a hero. Nobody in this country either."

The conversation with Lindly made it even more difficult to explain to Jennifer and when she questioned him he became defensive. "Why?" she asked in the insistent way she had. Jennifer, ordinarily the most reasonable of women, understood nothing he said.

"To get ideas for the next book."

"You don't even know what the next book is going to be."

He didn't even believe there was going to be a next book. "That's why I'm going, to find the next book."

"You don't have to go to Vietnam to find a book," Jennifer said in that logical way she had of ignoring the obvious in favor of the rational.

"REAL will pay me for writing about Vietnam. Nobody else cares whether I write or not, not even you." Since Marie's death they had not been able to talk without rancor and determined misunderstanding.

"You're a novelist, not a reporter."

He struggled with and regained control of his anger. "While I am there I will also get stories I can use in a novel." He recognized the patronizing simplicity that was effective with his college students.

"If you want to quit teaching I'll get a job," Jennifer said. "I'll support us until you decide what you want to do, or write a book or whatever. I've done it before."

"I have a year's leave of absence," he explained. It was an unpaid leave but he had a job when he went back to the school. "REAL is going to pay me for the stories I write so you'll be okay."

"And what am I supposed to do while you're gone?"

"Whatever you want to do," he had exploded. For years she had complained she never had time for herself, that she was always taking care of Marie or him. "Here's your chance to do whatever you want to do."

"I don't want you to go, Sherrill. Please don't leave me." She cried.

He sat down and lifted her into his lap the way he used to do. He held her close and kissed her tears and stroked her hair. "I have to go," he said. "I have to." He believed he did.

She thought he was deserting her, but he didn't intend it that way. He was desperate to save himself, his career. He would go to Vietnam, write his stories, maybe gain a little recognition, a little respect, and come back home with enough experience of suffering and death and grief to write about the death of a beautiful and beloved child.

He explained the budget he had worked out. She would live on their savings while he wrote the three stories to pay back the advance, then she would start getting a check from REAL for each additional story. "You'll be fine for three months, four if you stretch it. If you haven't gotten a check in four months, you'll have to borrow money on the house."

"What will you be doing?" she asked.

"I will be working on the stories," he said with the exaggerated patience he used on students who asked a question he had already answered. "I should be able to do one story a month. Maybe one a week. I'm talking about an extreme case where it takes me longer than I expect."

"So you could be gone longer than three or four months?"

"I have a year's leave of absence. I have to get enough stories for us to live on. Some of the stories I can write after I get back."

He had left for Vietnam believing he was separated from Jennifer only by miles and some mutual pain that distance and time would heal. And by her obstinate refusal to understand why he had to go to Vietnam. What neither he nor Jennifer had considered was that REAL might not like the stories he wrote.

"Your first story is a piece of cake," Stone had said. "Just tell us what it feels like to be in Vietnam, walking proud and kicking ass."

What it felt like was being a tourist. He had arrived in the sweltering heat wearing the wrong clothes, speaking the wrong language, and carrying the wrong money. The telephones at Tan Son Nhut were useless and the bank was closed for the day. At the Caravelle he found REAL had not made reservations. At JUSPAO, Joint U.S. Public Affairs Office, he discovered he had to get Vietnamese accreditation before he could get MAC-V accreditation. At Vietnamese press headquarters he learned that his visa was good for only three days and he had to go to Immigration on Vo Tahn to get a visa for a longer stay.

After several trips between Immigration, the Vietnamese press agency, where he filled out the same form ten times because they had no carbon paper, and JUSPAO, Sherrill had gotten an extended visa, a Vietnamese press card, a MAC-V press card, privilege card, ration card, and two non-combatant I.D. cards to be surrendered to the enemy if captured. The I.D. cards described him as 73 inches tall, 175 pounds, red hair, gray eyes, Protestant, blood type O, forty years old, a reporter for REAL Magazine. The photograph revealed an ambiguous man with broad intelligent forehead over small, intense eyes, and a ragged moustache above an uncertain mouth. A professor masquerading as a journalist.

Vouchers in hand, he rose early for the day's excursion, a helicopter assault with blazing rockets, machine guns pouring streams of tracers, frightened men running to cordon off a village. One dead man. The arrest of three suspects. An hour from the hotel, he was in a smoking hamlet as remote as the moon and as accessible as a helicopter. He was given a tour of the village, shown the captured VC suspects, and allowed a camera session with the dead man. All conducted by courteous, experienced, English-speaking tour guides. "Those are theirs over there, these are ours here."

He had taken three rolls of film, one roll on the dead man alone. The dead man was on his back in the paddy, one foot stuck in the mud holding his knee up, his head resting on the conical straw hat as though it were a platter, aura, halo. Sherrill took photographs trying to suggest each.

He shot pictures with the village in the background, a water buffalo in the background, a helicopter in the background. Everyone had ignored the dead man so he led them over and posed them: U.S. soldiers, Vietnamese soldiers, women, children, alone, in groups, standing over the man, squatting beside him, pointing at his wounds.

He jostled the other tourists for the best view, and exchanged tidbits of information. "Did you get that mamasan over there with the burned arm?" "What speed are you using for napalm?" He flew back to a shower at the Caravelle and dinner in Cholon.

The tourist seemed the proper metaphor for the war—traipsing around the country, some as vagabonds, others on expensive junkets, rubbernecking, taking pictures, spending hard cash on trifles, being gulled by native chiselers, neither changing nor being changed by the country or the people, leaving behind nothing of value but tokens and film wrappers and the remains of a hundred picnics in the grass.

REAL had not accepted "A Tourist in Vietnam." Fred Stone had not liked the tone that trivialized suffering and death. Perhaps Stone was right. The merchandising of the war troubled Sherrill; everyone he met had a story to tell or to sell. He would find a story that REAL liked and he would write it without turning it into entertainment.

Seeking an ethical viewpoint with which to frame the war, he had interviewed a chaplain, but the chaplain did not want to talk about ethics. The chaplain wanted to talk about agents. He was writing a biblical novel about people who never got hungry or horny, never felt tired or discouraged, and he wanted advice on getting it published.

"Why are you writing this?" Sherrill asked.

"America needs heroes," the chaplain answered.

Sherrill reported it straight-faced.

He interviewed a sniper team. "We're part of the morale factor," one said. "Uncle Ho tells these guys they're going to be big heroes with the peasants. They have to dodge bombs and patrols in Laos, and when they get here they have to hide in the jungle and steal food from the peasants. Then one day one of their buddies drops in his tracks before they hear the shot. Welcome to Vietnam. We pick up diaries off the dead that say that half their outfit is lost to bombs, disease, snipers before they ever go into combat. We see guys wandering around because their unit was wiped out and they've gone crazy. We used to pick them off. Now we let their own guys take care of them."

He had accompanied a patrol that was to pick up the team. From a thousand yards the sniper had shot a VC courier. The team alerted the patrol that a woman was also on the trail. The woman eluded the patrol. When the patrol reached the dead man, the point turned the body over, luckily turning it away from him, because the woman had left a grenade beneath it. The point got three cuts on his face, one of them puffing his upper lip so he looked like the victim of a schoolyard fight, and his arm was torn and dripping.

Someone handed the lieutenant the contents of the dead man's pockets. A package of American cigarettes, malaria pills, and a photograph of the courier surrounded by smiling American officers. In the background was a plastic Christmas tree. The lieutenant handed the photograph to Sherrill. "Fucking spy," he said.

"Jesus, look at my flak jacket," the point said, half laughing, half sobbing. His friends laughed with him, pointing at the bits of metal embedded in the jacket. "Jesus, look at my finger." One finger dangled loosely from his hand. "They killed my finger." His friends laughed hysterically.

"You're supposed to be a marksman," the lieutenant screamed at the sniper. The lieutenant was a dark Italian whose body seemed too small for the energy it contained. The helmet was bouncing on his head. "You sit on your ass while Charlie steals the papers and boobytraps the body, and probably the trail we have to take back."

"It was a woman," the sniper said.

"That's damn decent of you," the lieutenant screamed. "Sit up on the hill and decide who you prefer not to kill. Let her kill us stupid sons of bitches that have to hump these trails. Sharpshooter, you are walking point so you can pick up any presents she left for us, and if she doesn't get your ass, I'm going to. I'm going to see that you're down here on the trail with us guys who do more dying than deciding."

Sherrill wrote the story so that the reader would recognize himself as one who did the deciding while others did the dying.

Stone rejected the stories. "I recognize irony and figures of speech and all that pussyfooting by people afraid to speak their mind. I'm not interested in it, and fifteen years as editor of REAL convinces me that our readers aren't either. What I am interested in is what the readers of this magazine want. It's my job to give it to them, and if you want to write for REAL, you had better find out what it is.

"Men do not read REAL to be educated; they already know what they think. We cater to those who think a certain way. We give them adventure. We poke their noses in reality—hot, steamy jungles, bomb-cratered countryside. 'Bullets tattered the air and stitched the bamboo wall behind which I crouched.' We make them feel good about themselves and we make them feel good about America."

Sherrill had been stung by the rejection but amused by Stone's idea of reality. He had never read REAL, believing it to be a cheap skin, crime magazine. He paid Harry Tompkins twenty dollars to find copies of REAL. Tompkins, a free-lancer who supported himself between stories by selling girls, drugs and information, claimed he could get anything if the price was right and Sherrill put him to the test; REAL was a disposable magazine. Harry found six back issues. Sherrill studied them.

In each issue was a crime story with a woman as either the killer or the victim; a special report—three of them dealing with homosexuality: "Reds Blackmail Gays to Gain Secrets," "Homosexuals are Invading Our Campuses," and "Are the Courts Soft on Homosexual Offenders?" A fourth article examining assassination discovered that all known assassins were latent homosexuals.

There was a series on the triumphant male: REAL stories of a road contractor who outsmarted crooked politicians, one of them a woman; a baker who kept his store open despite threats from the mafia, gaining the respect of his young wife; a middle-aged lumber retailer who rescued a coed from drug-crazed hippies and was rewarded with her love: all written in the conversational style that pretended to be the way guys talked when there were no dames around. No imagery. No subtlety. No wit.

There were ads for guns, war souvenirs, trusses, girls in nude poses and books that offered to unlock the mysteries of science, religion, ignition systems, gambling, owning your own business, making your own beer and seducing women. There was a page called REAL Facts—a scattering of unrelated items with editorial comment provided by photos of a female nude who expressed amusement, dismay, shock—and a photo essay of nudes entitled REAL Beauties.

REAL believed might meant right and even when it didn't it meant money. A strong America meant military power to protect business interests anywhere in the world. That power had been sapped by "liberals." REAL hated liberalism, something associated with women, artists and queers.

After reading REAL Sherrill almost gave up; he wasn't sure he wanted to be published in the magazine. He wanted to go home, but he couldn't go home with nothing after coming all this way at this expense. He paid fifty dollars to Harry Tompkins for a story.

"I wanted this one for myself; this one is going to win a Pulitzer," Harry said, telling Sherrill of an American doctor who was quietly running a civilian hospital near Tuy Hoa. When a nearby village suffered heavy casualties in an accidental bombing the doctor opened his hospital to all of them, filling the wards and corridors with wounded and dying. In his anger, he refused military assistance, worked more than twenty straight hours saving lives, then fell asleep exhausted. He awoke to find that two of the wounded had been placed in an out-of-the-way office where they had died forgotten. Several peace and health organizations were calling the doctor a hero and petitioning for official recognition, maybe even a Nobel Peace Prize. Back in the closet were two patients who had died of neglect.

"REAL will love it," Harry said. The doctor represented most of the things REAL detested. He was an educated, holier-than-thou, pacifistic do-gooder who was being beatified by the liberal press and REAL could expose him as an egg-headed, limp-wristed bleeding heart. But Sherrill did not want to write the story. As fiction the idea intrigued him—a good man who by protesting the evil he saw around him gained the applause of the world and lost his self respect. But the doctor was real, the injured were real, the neglected patients were real. In fiction he would be the doctor. In REAL he would be the judge.

Sherrill paid ten more dollars for the name of an American who was living in Viet Cong territory in the delta. He was certain that if he could get a good interview REAL would take it. All he had to do was to go into the countryside alone.

He had flown into the little strip in the middle of Ca Mau. It was essential that he get the story and get back to Ca Mau before dark. It was vital that as few people as possible know about his trip into the countryside. He went to the crowded market along the river that was thick with sampans. He waved away the cyclo drivers who wanted to pedal him around town in their pedicabs. A small, wry-faced man led him to a battered, unreliable looking Renault, opened the back door and gestured for Sherrill to get in. Sherrill looked at the crowd. Their faces were blank, some secret behind their eyes, an unseen smile on their lips.

The Renault bumped down the narrow street with children running alongside holding out their hands. Sherrill expected one of them to throw a grenade. They drove past Vietnamese soldiers guarding a bridge in their sleep and were in the bush. Weeks earlier Sherrill had given up seeing scenery, instead looking for ambush sites and likely places for snipers and mines. It looked bad. The road was empty, the rice fields deserted.

They came to a hamlet encircled with barbed wire and sharpened bamboo stakes. There was no sign of life. The driver stopped at the barricade and killed the engine. No one came out to open the road. The cooling engine ticked. Flies buzzed. It was so quiet Sherrill could hear his skin crawl.

The driver turned and raised his arm. Sherrill jumped, expecting to see a pistol in the driver's hand, but he appeared to be asking for instructions. Sherrill wanted to turn back. To screw up his courage he flagellated himself for failing his talent as a writer, for failing his child. Only the belief that he was a coward because he had fled Marie's tube-entangled body enabled him to press on.

The driver got out, opened the barricade, and they drove through the hamlet past hootches, urns, straw mats, a gas can.

There were no people, no chickens, no ducks, no pigs. The driver opened a barricade on the other side of the hamlet; what appeared to be a banner fluttered from a pole.

They passed a deserted watch tower and the road ended in a huge puddle of water. Through the trees Sherrill could see thatch roofs. He got out of the car and waited but the driver did not move. Sherrill walked along the muddy path, waded into the water, followed a trail that led to a footbridge hung on poles driven into the mud. On the other side, houses on stilts hung over the river. A wrecked gunboat rusted in the water. Sherrill was relieved to see people although he was not sure why. No one looked at him and that was more frightening than the curiosity in Ca Mau.

Among the sampans Sherrill saw a young American. He sat down beside the man who was mending nets and saw that he was slight, red headed, with no fingers and burn scars up both arms and across his chest. Fascinated, Sherrill watched him work using only the web between his missing thumb and fist.

"Get away from me, you bastard," the man hissed.

Sherrill was stunned. "I'm a reporter—"

"Go, please go." The man was crying. "You're going to get me killed." Sherrill looked over his shoulder expecting to see VC. "They know I'm here. I'm no threat. But if you write it's so safe an American can live here they'll kill me. Now go. Get the fuck out of here." The man had not looked at Sherrill.

Sherrill stared at the rusting gunboat. Water lapped at a hole in its side. He had risked his life to get there and getting back was likely to be as dangerous. REAL would take this story. It had everything—courage, patriotism, pathos. Squatting beside the American was a lovely Vietnamese girl holding a red haired child. He needed the story but he knew he couldn't write it.

Without a word he got up and walked across the bridge to the car, forcing himself not to run, not to look over his shoulder. The driver sped away without urging while Sherrill prayed the engine would not fail or the cracked tires explode. The lower the sun got on the horizon the more Sherrill wanted to get his hands on Harry Tompkins's throat. He was going to get his fifty dollars back if he had to choke it out of Harry.

The watch tower was still deserted but the barricades had been replaced across the road. When Sherrill saw that, only the wide expanse of the rice fields prevented him from jumping from the car and trying to hide. The driver stopped but refused to get out. Sherrill got out, expecting to be blown apart by a boobytrap or sniper's bullet, expecting the driver to race away without him. They passed through the hamlet without incident or sign of life and reached the safety of Ca Mau at dusk.

Sherrill lay sleepless on a grimy mattress in a barren hootch at a remote base camp remembering the failures. REAL would buy this story of a young American who killed the first VC he saw. He turned on his side and thought of Jennifer, hoping to dream about her. From this distance he could see her clearly, clearly recognize his need for her. He thought of how she would greet him when he came home. He would catch a cab to the house and walk in the door. She would have a spoon or brush in one hand, wearing a robe and she would fling herself into his arms and cry, and say she missed him, and he would untie the robe and gently open it so that it no longer separated them. . .

He dreamed of Marie. She was somewhere in the house crying, "Daddy, Daddy." He searched everywhere for her, tearing the rooms apart. "Daddy, Daddy," she cried. He woke himself calling her name.

When he finished the story of the young killer he handed it to a soldier heading for Da Nang and the Freedom Bird home. The soldier would mail it to REAL when he got back to the world.

Sherrill attended a kind of funeral on a raw hilltop called Barbara. A chaplain, distinguishable by his cleanliness and sense of urgency, read a service, prayed over a portable altar and the departed who had already gone to a better land, and left after masking his clear eyes behind sunglasses. The rites had lacked both body and substance and were nothing he could write about.

He caught a helicopter to Chu Lai where he joined a plane load of photographers for a medal ceremony for some pilots. To avoid the photographers interrupting the rituals, or the formalities getting in the way of camera angles, the exercise was staged—a medal was pinned on a man until the photographers were satisfied they had documented the moment, then the medal was returned to the box. After the photographers left with the pictures that would be shown in America as the event, the ceremony was held with military decorum and sanction, but without photographic record.

After the ceremony Sherrill talked to some of the pilots, the kind of heroes REAL was looking for—brave, uncomplicated, modest, and enjoying their job. Everything seemed to be fun from the volleyball games in the hangar, to the cangun shootouts, to flying.

Canguns were made by removing ends from C-ration cans and taping the cans end to end. A tennis ball was slipped in one end, lighter fluid was squirted into the other and ignited. The ball was propelled with enough force to get a man's attention at twenty meters. Every man had a cangun and there were shootouts between the fast movers, prop jockeys, scope dopes, prop tops, herky jerks, and trash haulers. After which everyone went to the officers club to get roaring drunk.

While waiting for the targeted stage of drunkenness, they demonstrated maneuvers with their hands, sang ribald songs, and played practical jokes like setting one another's boots on fire with lighter fluid.

One of the pilots had been decorated for successfully

penetrating a storm in Laos and bombing a bridge after the rest of his flight had turned back. "I think the asshole should have been court-martialed for endangering his aircraft and that of his wingman. He risked four lives and two multi-million dollar airplanes to bomb a fucking $500 bridge. It's his wingman who should have gotten a medal for staying with him."

Another pilot had been decorated for an airstrike that broke up an ambush. "You have to get a clear picture of what the situation is and what you're going to do, and you have to hold the picture no matter how bad the information is," he said to Sherrill. He was tall, thin, with frank brown eyes and little worry lines around his mouth. "We had to plan the mission in the air in bad weather with people shooting at us, and grunts, artillery and helicopters all talking at the same time. And I naped a ville. Two canisters on main street." He demonstrated his pass over the village.

"A board of inquiry said I wasn't at fault, that I had bad information. I burned a lot of people and I'm never going to forget that, but I have a great bunch of guys to help me live with it. When I leave here I'm never going to know people like this again."

Sherrill looked at the great bunch of guys singing and yelling, helping each other through the night of their boyhood.

"When you have a picture you have to hold it no matter how bad the information is. This ain't Camelot. I bet Camelot wasn't Camelot either. I bet Lancelot knew there wasn't any Camelot and went right on killing dragons, screwing Guinevere and looking for the Holy Grail because it was the only picture he had."

Sherrill called the story "The New Lancelots" and portrayed the pilots as good, brave men doing their job with honor and skill, trying with napalm and five-hundred pound bombs to kill what their information told them was a dragon.

A new operation had started and he climbed into a Huey designated "Scarface Two." The floor of the chopper was sticky with blood. Fighting had been going on since before dawn but seemed to have temporarily stopped. The helicopter had spent the morning bringing in the wounded and was now returning for the dead. Medevac requests had an order of urgency from emergency, to priority, to routine. This was a routine medevac. The grunts called it "permanent routine." "Scarface Two, this is Charlie Two actual. We have numerous permanent routine, Hill 342, over."

The Huey touched down beside the bodies that were wrapped in ponchos and lined up for the long ride home. The rotor wash whipped the rubberized ponchos, blew debris into the faces of the dead, and made flags of the tags attached to their boots.

A battery of photographers was taking pictures of the sweating, cursing men who loaded the bodies into the helicopter, not without feeling, but in repudiation. The bodies were something alien to be whisked out of sight as quickly as possible. The loading crew alternated between ignoring and glowering at the photographers who uncovered the bodies, stood in the door of the helicopter, kneeled on the ground, looking for a fresh angle.

Sherrill turned away, repelled not so much by the scene as by the symbolism. He had seen too many inductions, initiations, graduations, each with its efficient directors and intrusive recorders. Tying a tag on a young man's boots and throwing him into the chopper was too much a travesty of handing him a diploma and shoving him into the forgetful world. Sherrill had done one, now he was witnessing the other.

When Scarface Two lifted off, the loading crew collapsed on the ground to doze or smoke a little apart from the dead while waiting for the next helicopter. The sun was white and inescapable. The landing zone was on a barren limestone ridge with wooded peaks rising above it. On another ridge an artillery battery was digging in, one of the guns already firing, the bang and echoing thump chasing each other through the valleys. Smoke rose from one of the peaks. Far below was the muddy Song Cha Nang and more smoke.

Sherrill had no idea what was going on; he looked at the landscape to avoid looking at the dead. Everyone seemed to be avoiding the dead now, even the photographers. Having exhausted this opportunity, they were waiting for a ride to the next. Except for the landscape and the dead it didn't seem like war—it seemed like late night in a train station.

It occurred to Sherrill that what was missing was women—women to cry, to make the futile humanizing gestures of arranging clothing, patting down hair, wiping dirt from faces. Women seemed to know what to do, reacting as instinctively to death as to childbirth. When Marie died, Jennifer had cried with each woman who came to comfort her, talked about the weather with each man and let the children know that it was all right that they forgot for a moment and laughed. She had listened to the simple-minded homilies while he had stood stupid and alone, hating them for their little lies. Hating himself that he could not make her immune to death, hating a world in which a child's death was as trivial as television.

"Did she die suddenly?" they asked. He didn't know. Her life of thirteen years had been so short and her death—it had taken her three days to die—had seemed its own lifetime. He said nothing, and unable to bear the sympathy in their faces he had turned his back on them.

He had turned his back on everyone, even Jennifer. Only Jennifer suspected. The others told him how well he was doing. Back in the classroom. Writing again. He was an inspiration to them, they said. They were amazed at how strong he was, how much he could bear and still behave as though nothing had happened.

Five men struggled up the hill carrying a sixth in a poncho. Sherrill wondered why one of them didn't carry the packs and rifles, leaving four to carry the dead man, but they all had a hand on the improvised litter. Seeing the photographers they skirted the landing zone and one of them held up a hand and warned, "No pictures." The photographers looked at each other and sat back down. The faces of the five were drawn and grimed and they stumbled with fatigue as they heaved their burden past the neat row of bodies on the LZ. "Put him there on the end," one of the working party yelled at them.

"We'll take care of this one," said the black man carrying the foot of the poncho. They carried the dead man well past the LZ to a level bit of ground where they dropped him without ceremony, threw the corners of the poncho over him, and sat down beside him.

Not knowing what he was going to do or say, Sherrill walked over and sat with them. They looked up, marking him an intruder. They looked murderously uncertain and he said nothing. A helicopter came in to pick up more litters, stirring up a mini-tornado of dust, and they shut their eyes and bowed their heads over the dead man.

Sherrill examined them. Beneath their helmets, uniforms and the dust and grime of battle there was little to distinguish them. One was black, one white although at the moment his face was red from exertion and sunburn. One wore love beads and had written "love child not war child" on the cover of his helmet. One was thick, droopy eyed, with a tattoo on his muscular arm. "Death Before Dishonor." One was nondescript.

When the helicopter left, they opened their eyes. They did not look at him. They did not look at anything. "How far do you think we come?" asked the black man who had a naturally upturned mouth that made him look cheerful despite his weariness.

"Same distance we got to go back," said whitey, whose white eyebrows and the long white hairs on his upper lip stood in contrast to his red, peeling face.

"Fuck it," said love child. "It ain't real."

"Who was the poor bastard anyway?" asked death before

dishonor.

"Some fucking polack from Oklahoma."

"Lay off the fucking polacks," said love child.

"How could he be a fucking polack if he was from Oklahoma?" asked nondescript. There may have been a trace of L.A. in his voice. Lower Alabama.

"You think you have to be an Indian to be from Oklahoma, shithead?" asked death before dishonor. "When was he zapped?"

"When we crossed that ravine," whitey said. "Hey, maybe he didn't finish his smokes." He pulled back the poncho and started going through the dead man's pockets. Sherrill did not look directly at the dead man although the face was unmarked. He knew the body was a mess. He knew by the smell the sun cooked out of the poncho. "Fucking Salems," whitey said. "Nobody but a fucking polack would smoke these fucking Salems."

"Lay off the fucking polacks," said love child.

"That ain't right," said death before dishonor. "Taking things from a dead man."

"He don't have no use for them," said the black.

"If it was me I'd want you guys to have them," said nondescript, wetting his lips.

"Fuck it," said love child. "It ain't real."

Whitey took a cigarette and passed the pack around. "His name is Kersnowski," he said, examining the dog tags. "Hey, he's a fucking Protestant."

"How can he be a fucking Protestant if he's a fucking polack?" asked nondescript.

"Lay off the fucking Protestants," said love child.

Another helicopter came in and conversation stopped as they ducked away from the noise and dirt. On take off, the rotor wash blew the poncho off the dead man and Sherrill turned his head from the sunken eyes and gaping mouth. "Don't he look young," said whitey, covering him again.

Whitey looked both eighteen and forty.

"How old are you?" asked the black, smiling his perpetual smile.

"Eighteen, but I been here nine months." He took off his helmet and examined the numbers written on the cloth cover. Those above seventy-three had been marked out. "Seventy-three more days," he said. "Seventy-two and a wake up."

"Seventy-one not counting today," said nondescript.

"Today counts until tomorrow," said whitey. "I don't mark off a day until it's light enough to see green. That's how I know I ain't in hell."

"I thought this was hell," said death before dishonor.

"If you die it's hell," said nondescript.

"If you don't die it's hell," said whitey.

"Fuck it," said love child. "It ain't real."

Another helicopter came in spraying them with grit. "Did you talk to him?" asked death before dishonor when the helicopter was gone.

"Just when he was dying," whitey said.

"What did he say?"

"He said mama. What the fuck do you think he said? He said doc, doc, I'm dying. He said Jesus, save me."

"Why did he say Jesus if he's a fucking Protestant?" asked nondescript.

"Fucking Protestants believe in Jesus for christsake," said the black man.

"Lay off the fucking Protestants," said love child.

"It's the fucking Jews who don't believe in Jesus," reasoned nondescript.

"Lay off the fucking Jews," said love child.

"Are you a fucking Protestant or a fucking Jew?" asked nondescript.

"What the fuck it is to you?" asked love child.

"It ain't nothing big, pecker breath."

"Then shut the fuck up, motherfucker."

"The only mother I ever fucked was yours, fart face."

"My mother is fucking dead, maggot turd. You fucked a fucking corpse."

"No wonder she was a dry fuck. Jesus, if she hadn't been so ugly I would have kissed her."

"Does that fucking polack have another fucking Salem?" asked the black.

"Fucking polacks are queer for fucking Salems," said whitey, going through the man's pockets again while Sherrill stared at the ground.

"At least he's going home," said love child.

"Fuck that shit. I'd rather stay here the rest of my life than go home like that," said the black.

"If you stay here the rest of your life you will go home like that, numb nuts," said nondescript.

"Stick it up your ass," said the black.

"I can't. When it's hard it won't bend and when it's soft it won't go in."

"When was you ever hard?" asked death before dishonor.

"The last time I saw you eat a banana, cunt face."

"You ain't seen nothing until you've seen a fucking brother eat a banana."

"Lay off the—"

"Hey man," the black said, putting a hand on love child's shoulder. "This one's on me. Lay off the fucking brothers," he said to death before dishonor. This time the smile was grim and deliberate.

"Shitcan it," said whitey. "We got a dead man here."

"What are you going to do when you get home?" asked nondescript.

"I'm going to keep my head down," said whitey. "Them fucking pacifists back in the world will blow you away for being in fucking 'Nam."

"Lay off the fucking pacifists," said love child.

"Not me," said the black. "I'm going to hump the Statue of

Liberty. I can't wait to get my teeth into them tits."

"What I would give for some pussy," said nondescript.

"What I would give for some pot," said love child. "Mary Jo Warner." He tasted the words with his mouth.

"What I would give for tomorrow," said whitey. "Seventy-one days and a wake up."

"Hey, I'm a one digit midget," said nondescript. "Nine more to go."

"Yeah, nine months," said whitey.

"I don't think you ought to talk about going home in front of a man who is done gone," said love child.

"I don't think you ought to talk about going home in front of a long timer like me," said death before dishonor. "I still got ten months to go."

"Jesus," said nondescript. "That's three hundred days."

"Fuck it," said love child. "It don't mean nothing."

"Hey. You men," someone shouted from the LZ. An officer had come in on one of the helicopters, fresh from Chu Lai. His uniform was not only clean and starched, it was new, his boots polished. "We'll take care of the KIA. You get back to your outfit."

Nondescript rose slowly to his feet, raising his rifle at the same time, but not exactly pointing it. "This is our outfit," he said. "We didn't even get to say goodbye to the others and we're going to see this one off."

The officer glared, opened his mouth, hands on hips. Nondescript's rifle moved slightly in his direction. "I want that body on the next chopper," the officer said, then turned and walked away.

"Fucking officers, they got no respect for the dead," said nondescript.

"Lay off the fucking officers," said love child, but his heart wasn't in it.

"Let's have one last cigarette before we go," said death before dishonor.

Whitey uncovered the body and took out the pack. "Last two," he said.

"Leave him one," said death before dishonor.

Whitey looked at the circle of faces. The black nodded. Nondescript shrugged. "It ain't real," said love child.

Whitey took out one cigarette and replaced the other in the man's pocket. He lighted the cigarette, took a drag and passed it around the circle. Sherrill could hear the wap wap wap of a helicopter and the officer was glaring at them but no one moved until the cigarette had made its circle back to whitey who field-stripped it, sprinkling the tobacco on the ground, rolling the paper into a ball and throwing it away. The filter he slipped into the dead man's pocket with the cigarette pack.

They stood up, picked up the poncho, and braced against the swirling wind and dust, they ran to the settling helicopter and lifted the man aboard. Not wanting to hang around, Sherrill scrambled into the chopper, careful where he put his hands and feet, trying to stay off the bodies and out of the way of the loading crew. As the helicopter lifted off, he looked out the door to wave goodbye and saw the five men standing at attention, their eyes and mouths tightly closed against the dust, their uniforms flapping in the gale.

In Chu Lai, Sherrill wrote their story. There was so little they could do for the dead man, so little time to mourn for themselves, but they did what they could. He wrote the story for them. And for Marie because he grieved her anew in the fall of every sparrow. He wrote the story because the war could not be understood without pain. It could not be told in heroic slogans.

Sherrill made an abortive trip to Phu Cat then returned to Saigon for a letter from REAL accepting his stories. There was no letter.

While waiting in Saigon for REAL's acceptance of his stories, Sherrill tried to write the book that was going to keep Marie alive in all her ages. The baby who tightly held his collar and pulled at his moustache. The toddler who ran to him and hugged his leg, looking up with unconditional love. The child who stood beside him, tightly holding his hand, bravely smiling goodbye on that first day of school. The girl who stole a look at him while she waited for the music to begin for her dance recital.

Now he knew enough about suffering, about death and grief that he could save her in his book. He worked at the book with a patience and dedication beyond anything he had experienced before and every word was as lifeless as she. Until one day instead of asking, "Why must I die?" she asked, "Why must I live?" He had been startled by that faint throb of life in her and in himself. Fascinated he had watched as she turned into a soldier and the question became, "Why did I live when everyone else died?"

The ideas tumbled over one another. A National Guard Company from a small town, called up and sent to Korea, wiped out in an ambush. Except for one man with an experience he could neither understand nor share, who went home to explain why he lived to the women of the town who wanted to know why their son, husband, brother, father died. It was so beautiful in his mind that Sherrill gasped.

How could the survivor form a story about an unbelievable, inexplicable event he did not understand when there was no one to verify or corroborate? Especially if the others believed they already knew the story. If the military made the survivor a hero because they needed a hero, the press made the ambush a battle because they needed news, and his hometown made martyrs of those who died to palliate their loss and vindicate those lives. Then what happened to his story? Could his hero be certain that his perception, his memory, was in fact what happened?

Marie's death had destroyed Sherill's benign and meaningful world and now he had to construct another. He didn't blame God for a viral infection but he began to doubt the existence of God when his life seemed beyond his or any other control. What he feared was worse than conspiracy or crime; those at least supposed some order, some reason, some meaning. He feared there was nothing. Darkness. The abyss.

Sherrill wanted to put Cassady, the name came to him unbidden, in that darkness, in his stead, to search for one ray of light, of reason. Cassady alone had survived the ambush. The others had died and with them they had taken his identity. He had been a member of First Platoon but First Platoon had ceased to exist. Who did that make him? How was he to explain how he alone survived? Reason demanded to know why. Or was reason the cruelest of man's attainments?

Sherrill looked at his watch, surprised at how much time had passed. He wanted to let Jennifer know he was writing again, that something good had come of his being here. He always talked out his ideas with Jennifer. She listened and through her eyes he could tell when something sounded false or unconvincing. Pushing aside his notes for the book, he got a clean sheet of paper and began a letter.

He told her briefly about the stories he had written but most of the letter was about his book. Maybe he would call it "Pretender Among The Dead" with its suggestion of "pretender to the throne," and because it implied unjustified claim to having survived. The book would begin with the ambush as bodies exploded, limbs flailed in the convulsion and storm that rocked the trucks and caused the ground to shudder. In that first paragraph he hoped to describe the insanity, the derangement of a world that moments before had seemed rational, even safe.

Perhaps two men would survive, one of them severely wounded. The wounded man moaned in his pain and Cassady held his hand over the man's mouth to save both of them, never to know whether he had contributed to his friend's death. Sherrill liked that ambiguity, that vague, pervasive guilt that was such a part of the twentieth century. He sealed the envelope, wondering if Jennifer could understand the insanity, violence, guilt he was writing about. He believed she would after she read the stories he wrote for REAL; he would make that world known to her.

Taking the letter he left the hotel to walk to JUSPAO to check for mail. The mail was always screwed up and the more one moved around the more screwed up it became, but every day he hoped for a letter from Jennifer and to hear that REAL had accepted his stories.

Outside he wilted a little in the afternoon heat rising from the streets and the air that was brown with the exhaust of incessant traffic. He walked across Lam Son Square and pushed his way down Le Loi along the crowded corridor between the street vendors and the parked Honda cycles.

When he got to JUSPAO an NCO told him that Support Command in Da Nang wanted someone to tell their story—hauling food and ammo over the world's toughest roads. Sherrill nodded; REAL would like that story. The NCO gave him the name of a contact and told him that kinescopes were being shown so that the television newsmen could see what footage got on the screens back home and what kind of presentation it received. Sherrill looked in and was startled by the image of the finger-less man in the delta with his wife and child, the river at their back. They smiled, delighted by the attention, while a voice said ". . . among millions of homeless refugees, can one American find peace and a measure of safety?"

What the hell? He had given up that story because the man had feared for his life and here he was posing for the camera, risking his life, and that of his wife and child for thirty seconds on a television screen. Next on the screen was a burning truck and a voice saying, "Highway One north of Da Nang has again become the highway of death."

At the mail room the clerk handed Sherrill his letters. Jennifer had written two of them. Across the miles her handwriting reached out to him. Those last months at home he had not held her much, and then he had held her more with desperation than love. Jennifer had turned to him and he had not been there. He thought of the letter he had just mailed her full of a joy he had not known in a long time as Cassady groped for the answers Sherrill so desperately needed. He was overcoming his anger that Jennifer had given him a gift that was unbearable to lose, had made him vulnerable to that deathless pain. He hoped Jennifer would not resent the world he was creating with Cassady and the peace he found there, the peace of a man whose daughter had not died.

There were also letters from REAL, Alvord Lindly, and his mother. He carried the letters to the press room and sat down at one of the battered desks. He always delayed reading important mail although he was not sure why. He suspected it was because whatever was in the letters was going to change his present in some way, however small, and he was taking one last accounting of it.

He opened the letter from REAL first. Fred Stone did not like any of the stories. "REAL has few black readers," he wrote about the story of a young black soldier killing an old yellow man. "And save your moralizing for your students; they have to listen, I don't." The story about the pilots, that men acted on the information they had, was too negative. The story about the sniper was too complex. "You are not there to make it seem complicated, you are there to make it easy to understand." REAL was not accepting the story about men paying tribute to a fallen comrade because Stone objected to the obscenity in the story and found Sherrill lacking in sensitivity for the feelings of the dead.

Sherrill stared at the letter in disbelief. How could Stone call his story unfeeling when REAL had a monthly crime story revealing intimate facts and using the names of real people? When REAL published photographs of crime victims who were always helpless and usually dead; the women naked and exposed? Stone had ended the letter with a word of advice. "Get out of the whorehouses and into the trenches. There's a war going on there if you can find it."

Sherrill was furious. He had never expected fame or fortune but he had expected through discipline, diligence and perseverance to gain the respect of those who depended on his commitment. Instead, he found himself in the position of a whore. They were not interested in him but in what he could do for them in the way they wanted it done, and the more he gave the less he was respected.

A bell rang and he joined the crowd in the hall pushing their way outside. "Someone called in a bomb threat," said the Marine sentry at the door frustrated that his training and professionalism could be thwarted by anyone with access to a telephone. "Nobody got a bomb past me but we have to clear the building until EOD checks it out."

Sherrill walked across the street to the little park. "Happens two or three times a week," groused an enlisted clerk to whoever was listening. "See these Vietnamese. If there was a bomb in there you wouldn't see them standing around out here." MP jeeps had already blocked off the street and a television crew stood by to film the arrival of the Explosive Ordnance Demolition team in their red jeep and red helmets.

Sherrill recognized the telecaster as the one reporting on the American in the delta. He had short stubby legs and the enormous chest and shoulders that suggested a dwarf or gnome, but his future was in his face. His large head, topped with long flowing yellow locks, had the charisma of a millionaire evangelist and the authority of the only funeral director in a retirement village.

"Scenes such as this suggest the precariousness of the American presence in Vietnam," he intoned, his voice deep and professionally rich. "Once again the Viet Cong have demonstrated that no person, no building, no installation is safe from terrorist attack."

"Once again the Viet Cong have demonstrated that the camera comes when they whistle," said the enlisted clerk.

Behind Sherrill, two young airmen were arguing the merits of their watch bands. "Leather's no good," one of them said. "You stick your arm out to stop a cab and they'll jerk the watch right off your wrist. This band is stainless steel. Ain't no way they're going to rip it off."

"They'll just cut off your hand," said the other. "That happened to a nurse right there on Le Loi. This gook couldn't get her ring off so he just chopped off her finger and ran off with it."

Sherrill looked at the young men. They were the fresh-as-apple-pie American boys REAL wanted him to write about, but they weren't killing gooks in steamy jungles; they were trying to hang on to their watches in downtown Saigon.

When the EOD team came out and the filming was over, Sherrill stopped the television newsman before he got back in the car. "Did you do a story on an American living in the delta?"

"Rick Belk," he said graciously, giving Sherrill a firm handshake. "Hell of a story. Unable to find a job or understanding at home he comes back to the place where he lost his fingers. Great pathos."

"What happened to him?" Sherrill asked. Belk looked at him without comprehension. "Is he okay? Did he leave? What happened to him?"

"I've been in Chu Lai," Belk said. "Got a hell of a story on the bakery. It's so hot they add ice to the ingredients to keep the bread from rising too fast. Fantastic footage. A half-million pounds of bread a month, truck loads of bread. You can smell it for miles, and all these hungry kids come and stand with their faces pressed against the wire. We got fantastic footage of those kids." He clapped Sherrill on the arm, got in the car and they drove away.

"There wasn't any wire around the bakery. And what happened to that guy in the delta," he shouted as the car disappeared down Le Loi. Damn, he should have gotten that story in the delta. Stone would have loved it. He could have written about an American soldier falling in love with an exotic beauty in a war-torn land and refusing to be frightened away by a bunch of Commie gooks. REAL was devoted to male fantasies.

Sherrill went back inside and found the press room deserted. The others were attending the Five O'Clock Follies. He didn't often go. It was too much like faculty meetings where numbers were supposed to prove progress and a new name in the administration represented a fresh strategy.

He looked at the letters from Jennifer. The postmarks were illegible and not knowing which was written first, he opened the top one. "I wish I understood why you were in Vietnam," she wrote. "I wish I understood what writing means to you." How many arguments had ended with Jennifer asking what he wanted? "I want to be a writer," he said. Sometimes she dismissed it as folly (I want to be president), and sometimes as fact (I want to be an American), but always as something extra rather than elemental.

"Sometimes I think I will never understand you, but I believe in you and I know you will succeed." He read the words again trying to hear her as she spoke them matter-of-factly, an admission rather than a boast. "I know what it means to love you and I know what it means to be without you, and I'll wait for you forever. I don't know if I will ever let you out of my sight again. Sometimes I pretend you're here. When I'm in the kitchen, you're in your office. When I'm cleaning house, you're at school. It's only at night when I reach out and you are not there that I realize how much I miss you. If you walked in now, I'd be hiding behind the door."

Once, before Marie was born, she had hidden naked behind the front door and when he walked in, she pulled him to the carpet, undressed him, and playfully seduced him. It was out of character for her and he was both surprised and delighted. Afterwards, she was embarrassed and had hidden her face for fear she had offended him. He held her, teased her, assured her that he liked it. Although she seemed convinced, she was never so bold again. After Marie was born she was more reserved, more cautious, but no less responsive when they were in the bedroom and the door was locked.

Sherrill wondered if Jennifer's passion was in response to something he had written. He couldn't remember anything specific he had said to her and it was impossible to know when her letter had been sent. Postal procedures were both haphazard and miraculous. According to the troops some letters took a week, some letters took a month, some never got there, and for some diabolical reason letters were never received in the order in which they were written. Trying to comprehend what was happening back home by reading letters was like trying to follow a foreign film when the reels were out of sequence and the subtitles out of synch.

He opened Jennifer's second letter. She was sorry that his leaving was such a disaster. She didn't want him to go; she wasn't sure she could ever let him go again, but she understood why he had to prove himself and she knew when he came home everybody would be proud of him. Alvord Lindly had called every day to ask how he was. She regretted she had not understood how good a friend Lindly was. "I still don't trust him, and I don't believe anything he tells me about other people, but I know he genuinely cares about you." He tried to imagine her saying "genuinely" but could not.

Jennifer had never approved of Lindly because Lindly was

twice divorced, relentlessly pursued coeds and school secretaries and was always the first to espouse a cause and the first to drop it. "Lend-lease," Jennifer called him. "A geographical bastard; he doesn't have roots." But Lindly knew his way around the campus, effortlessly garnering promotions, raises, grants, favorable schedules. "He knows how to get things done," the president said. It was the highest compliment he could pay a professor. Sometimes Lindly did things for Sherrill.

Jennifer wrote that she had seen the president at a faculty party and told him how proud she was of her husband and how honored the school should be that he was willing to risk so much that they might know the truth. Good ole Jennifer. She disliked school functions but she went alone to represent him.

She apologized for not having more news but she hadn't been on the campus since the accident. What accident? He turned the page for more information but there was only the wish that he find what he was looking for, followed by her signature.

Sherrill read the letters again, trying to hold on to the momentary closeness and warmth. At first her letters had been tentative, filled more with facts than with feelings. Now her letters were filled with love. Unless he had received the letters out of sequence.

Jennifer was his foundation. Sometimes he complained that she tried to hold him down when he was made to fly, but he knew she wasn't trying to keep him from getting too close to the sun but from falling into the sea. He needed her. He needed her steadfast refusal to leap into joy or plunge into despair. Jennifer was the gravity that kept him in orbit.

When it came time for him to leave for Vietnam, neither wanted to talk of the distance between them or the distance to come but her letters bridged the miles. She wanted him back and he was more determined than ever to turn this separation into something good. Jennifer's faith meant a lot to him. He only wished he deserved it, that he was as sure of himself as she. If Stone had accepted the stories he had written he could go home now. If Stone had accepted just one story. He should have done that interview in the delta. Stone would have taken that one, but he had let someone else get it. Harry had sold it to television.

The letter from his mother had been written more than a month earlier. As usual most of the letter concerned her health, her friends, her activities and could have been written to a stranger. The last two paragraphs were written to her son. The gift shop was doing well but she was thinking of selling it, leaving the town where she had lived most of her life and moving in with Jennifer. "I'll have a new set of insects, ha ha."

He wondered how much of a joke it was. Was her health failing? Had she detected trouble in the marriage and felt mother-called to make things right? Was she asking if he needed help?

"What do you think about me selling the shop?" she asked. Sherrill did not like being involved in her decisions, particularly with the shop. When his father died, Sherrill and his mother had managed to run the farm until his unhappiness had forced her to sell it, give him half the money for college and move to town and open the gift shop with the rest. He still felt guilt about that decision.

"I got a nice letter from Jennifer telling me all about what you are doing. I know you do not have time to write me." Even when he was home Jennifer was the one who corresponded with his mother. Jennifer apologized for his neglect by explaining how busy he was with students and committees. She said little about his writing because teaching and advising were acceptable excuses for not calling or writing his mother. Writing a book was not. It was his own fault, of course, but when he saw his mother he found it difficult to talk to her because he was not the person Jennifer represented him as being.

"I don't know why Jennifer let you go to Vietnam," his

mother wrote, "but I hope you will come home soon and take care of your old mother." His mother held him under the same disapproval she had practiced on his father. She thought she was encouraging him to be his best but he believed he could never live up to her expectations.

Nevertheless, her letter was a whiff of clarity. Only his mother spanned his life and he needed that assurance that in an altering world the bond between mother and child was unalterable, even when she didn't know who he was, or approve of who she thought he was. Their clumsiness in expressing their love for each other had been graced by forbearance. Her letter didn't tell him who she was or what she needed from him, but it told him her love remained the same even though she did not.

"I hope you don't mind what Jennifer has done to the house." He felt a sharp pang of guilt. Jennifer had been forced to mortgage the house because he hadn't written an acceptable story.

He opened the letter from Al Lindly. Incredibly it had reached him four days after being written, unless Lindly had misdated it. Lindly described his activities—changing a grade to prevent a student from being drafted, devoting class time to a high school dropout who believed marijuana should be legalized and war outlawed, teaching I Ching in the Free University, giving class credit for work with anti-war groups, and writing his book, *Doing the Middle Ages.*

Lindly wrote nothing about the house or accident but said he had taken Jennifer to lunch a few times. "You don't mind do you?" Lindly had always attempted to incite jealousy in Sherrill by insisting there was no cause for it. It had never worked. Unaware how pretty she was, Jennifer had not learned to attract the attention of casual admirers. She was unwillingly sexy and disliked clothes that accentuated her figure although she did not recognize why. Even after marriage Jennifer was uncomfortable with her sexuality. Sometimes she came to him wearing neither bra nor panties beneath her dress and then resisted when he tried to make love to her to prove it was not her idea.

Sherrill tried to imagine Jennifer and Lindly having lunch together. Where would they go? Lindly liked student hangouts with cheap beer, loud music and menu on the wall. Jennifer liked bright, neat places with waitresses in frilly aprons. What would they talk about? Lindly changed ideas, jargons, loyalties in mid-conversation. Jennifer weighed everything twice and when she expressed an opinion she lay it down like an ace.

"I'm glad you are finally taking yourself seriously," Lindly wrote. "An artist would prostitute his mother for his art and you couldn't deny Marie cotton candy and a ride on the Ferris wheel. That's why your books lack conviction. You've never before been willing to lay it on the line. But, mon ami, you have chosen the wrong side. And even if it were right it isn't popular. In a war everybody is going to find someone to hate. If they don't hate Ho, then they're going to hate guys like you. Get out, Sherrill. Admit that you made a big mistake and get yourself off the hook."

As always with Lindly, Sherrill was both amused and annoyed. Lindly knew so much and understood so little. It was true he would do anything for Marie. He had climbed trees with her, carried a doll, played house while neighbors gawked. He would have denounced his books, he would have given up writing, he would have laid down his life for her. Did that make him less serious as a writer?

What mistake had he made? He should not have left Jennifer when she needed him, when there were problems at home. He didn't need Lindly to tell him that. He had confessed that mistake to Jennifer and he didn't have to confess it to anyone else. He had rather be writing for a better magazine but none would pay his way. How could Lindly judge his stories when none had been published? Sherrill felt good about the stories. Maybe they wouldn't have been popular but they were honest. The only thing wrong with them was that REAL didn't want them.

He had awaited the letters with such anticipation. Jennifer's letters had brought him comfort and fresh resolve but he was discouraged by the letter from REAL, preferring his expectations, and it irked him that Lindly was no more open-minded than Fred Stone. Absently he picked up a MAC-V teletype report. "HQMACV—During the night, one indirect fire attack was reported against U.S. forces in the Republic of Vietnam which caused no casualties or damage." Words. Words that conveyed nothing of the bone rattling, ear splitting, gut-clenching explosions. If he were given the chance he would help people understand.

He looked up as a woman sat down at one of the desks and began the frustrating process of reaching someone by telephone. "Press priority," she said into the phone. Although they had once shared a flight to Phuoc Vinh she gave no indication that she either saw or recognized him. Despite the fact that she had the figure of a teenage boy and the lean, sharp face of a political agitator, she was invariably referred to as the glamorous Norela Cook, popular with the press because she was exactly what they needed a woman reporter to be.

Norela wrote a syndicated column that was more autobiography than feature—a kind of confessional metaphor for a world view. In one piece she had compared Vietnam to the rape of her teenage son. "He begged me not to tell the police," she wrote. "Unpleasant as such things may be, someone must call attention to them and that is what I am going to do."

There was something desperate in her attempts to establish an identity. Stories of stock market scandals, political intrigues, revolutions in token countries were bumped to back pages to cover Norela's antics— leaving a lipstick kiss on a mirror in the enlisted men's head on an aircraft carrier, hiding herself in an officer's latrine at MAC-V headquarters to eavesdrop on the generals, masquerading as a Tu Do bargirl for an inside story on prostitution despite the handicap of being a foot taller than the Vietnamese girls.

The military distrusted and fawned on her. Wheezy colonels carried her bags up ramps and opened doors, trying to direct her down wrong corridors. In Saigon the male members of the press treated her like a possible lay, in the field like a buddy, and in their stories like a celebrity. Sherrill was intimidated by her bigger-than-life public image. She not only had been front page news, she had appeared on talk shows. He felt sympathy for her because she looked like a woman who had been mistreated by men but survived without rancor, and there was a little-boy-bravado about her that he found both endearing and fragile.

"I want to report the waste that's going on in there," Norela yelled into the receiver and then paused a moment in anger and frustration. "I know it's going on because my paper says it is going on. Now are you going to let me in there so I can get the facts or do you want me to write it without them? Thank you very much."

Here was a reporter who knew what she wanted and was going to get it. Sherrill admired her for the risks she took of making front page mistakes and opening her private life to public judgment while he had been timorous, self-protective. He started to express his admiration but she had someone else on the line. "Hi doll, it's Norela. Doc said for me to give you a call. How much do you need? How much will you have to spread around? Can you give me a name in case he should ask? That's a good name. That's a damn good name. Peace," she said, ringing off.

"Been to Phuoc Vinh lately?" Sherrill asked, to initiate a conversation, hoping she would remember him.

Norela turned to face him. "Who are you?"

"Sherrill O'Connell."

"Well, Sherrill O'Connell," she said sweetly, "get your own

fucking stories." Dropping her notebook into her shoulder bag, she shrugged past two reporters and out the door.

"Don't you know who that was?" one of them asked. "That was Norela Cook. You can't treat her like a reporter, she's a celebrity."

She didn't respect him because he wasn't tough minded the way she was. If he had been, he would have gotten that story in the delta. He left the building. Outside he was engulfed by the noise of the city. He walked down Nguyen Hue, but was so crowded by vendors, beggars, and parked bikes that he took his chances in the street, dodging military vehicles, cyclos, and the tiny blue and white Renault taxis. The gulf between him and Norela Cook loomed large in his mind. She had made mistakes and subjected herself to public ridicule but when she wanted a story she got it. The comparison depressed him. He wasn't sure he could ever be that daring, that reckless.

In one of the crowded side streets, two girls on a Vespa collided with an old man on a bicycle. Sherrill idly watched the girls cry, holding their hands over their mouths, and the old man wail, pointing at his bent bicycle.

"Watch your pockets," someone said behind him as a crowd gathered. He turned to look into the young freckled face of Blair Scobic. Blair had quit his job with a newspaper and left his wife and children for Vietnam. No one knew what Scobic was looking for and only once had Sherrill heard him refer to what he had left. "I got tired of pimping for people who were celebrated because of how much of the world's goods they devoured." Blair was an idealist in a world of hype.

"Hey, Blair," Sherrill said. "What's the foment of the moment?"

"Not all these accidents are real," Scobic said. "I just tried to help a boy who fell off his bike. A gang of kids grabbed my watch and billfold and almost got my camera."

Sherrill nodded in sympathy. There were hundreds of reporters in Vietnam, a handful of them freelancers who, while waiting for the break that would get them a job or buy them a ticket home, scrounged a living illegally changing money, selling information or drugs, or blackmarketing liquor and cigarettes they had bought at the PX with their privilege cards. Sherrill knew that Blair would not change money or sell drugs and if he had lost his cards, he could not get in the PX to buy liquor and cigarettes. "Did they get much?"

"All I had. It wasn't much. My cards. A few bucks."

"How much do you need?" Sherrill got out his wallet and looked at it to avoid looking at Blair, who was trying to keep his face together. Saigon was a tough town for an American without money. Money can't buy success but it can cover your ass with opportunity, reporters joked.

"I've got three stories out," Blair said. "I should hear something this week. Twenty bucks would hold me until then." He didn't reach for the money Sherrill offered. "I don't know when I can repay you. I don't have any stories REAL would want."

"Take it."

Blair took the money and quickly walked away to hide the mixed shame and gratitude on his face. Sherrill looked at his wallet. Safely tucked away was his most prized possession, his airline ticket home. It was his life preserver and he would not go in the water without it. Scorbic had given up everything—his job, his savings and his wife, who took the children and had not contacted him since he had been in Vietnam. Blair wrote only what Blair believed, selling stories to small town papers and obscure magazines. Twenty-five dollars was a good day for him; enough to keep him alive in Saigon but not enough for a wife back in the world.

Sherrill wished he had Blair's integrity, Norela's audacity. He had to try harder. He'd go to Da Nang for that story on Support, find the kind of uncomplicated heroes REAL wanted and write it so they had to take it.

Behind the National Assembly building armless, legless

Vietnamese veterans scuttled about on knees, crutches, platforms set on rollerskates, begging for handouts. Once they had paraded their uniform zeal before generals, politicians, cameras, while flags snapped in the breeze. Now they crawled in pinned-up, cut-off uniforms to exhibit their worth to clerks, orderlies and reporters who paraded to the Brink for an evening meal.

Sherrill had sometimes avoided the Brink to avoid their need, to escape the pity sight of them required. Despite inadequate leadership, arms and pay, they had risked their lives and sacrificed their limbs for a government that gave no pensions or benefits to its wounded veterans. Now they were unable to fight or work and their bravery had been reduced to beggary. Sherrill passed out handfuls of piasters, trying not to see the gratitude on their faces. Those who were able came to attention and saluted smartly as though he were commander of wizened, mutilated boys. He was moved by their continued courage in spite of their circumstances. No matter what Lindly said, helping such people could not be a mistake.

The MP standing at the entrance to the Brink pointed at a jeep against the wall a short distance away. "That's a stolen jeep. We think it may have a bomb in it." Sherrill walked away. Photographers waited behind barrels filled with concrete, around corners of buildings, hoping for a shot of the jeep, maybe the hotel, disappearing in a cloud of dust and smoke.

Sherrill did not have his camera; he disliked carrying it around the city. It reinforced his feelings of being a tourist and it added to his vulnerability to pickpockets. Through eternal vigilance he had been able to hold on to both watch and wallet but in a crowd it was impossible to guard three items with two hands. An EOD team arrived, checked the jeep and drove it away. Sherrill walked past the disappointed photographers, aware that if he had his camera he too would be disappointed. He wanted to get his stories and get out of this place where he was tantalized by the misfortune of others.

On a wall inside the Brink was a newspaper headline about ARVN officers training in the United States. Across the bottom some disgruntled soldier had printed, "Join the ARVN and see the world." In Vietnam "the world" meant America.

Upstairs in the dining room Sherrill looked over the room crowded with reporters and officers. He saw public names and television faces. He was among strangers but worse than strangers; he was among familiar strangers. At one table a colonel argued with Rick Belk. "That firebase was intended to be used only until the operation was over. No flag ever flew there until you gave them one and asked them to raise it so you could get a picture of it coming down so it looked like defeat. That was the only footage that was shot of a successful operation that went on for weeks."

"You know what a firebase looks like," Belk said. "Without the flag there was no picture. If there's no picture, it didn't happen."

Sherrill wove his way through faces that examined him. Was he someone they needed to know? He saw his presence fade from their minds but it didn't bother him the way it once had. These weren't real reporters either, most of them. They were here, like he was, because if you couldn't make it here you couldn't make it anywhere.

Sitting alone was a young reporter who looked like runner-up for the door prize. He had long braided hair and love beads that ended in the parietal bone from a child's skull with a bullet hole through the middle of it. Sherrill sat down and introduced himself.

"You don't look like a reporter from REAL," the man said. His face was slack and he had blackheads as well as an earring in his ear.

"What's a writer from REAL supposed to look like?"

"Rod Reaves," the man said.

"I'm not Rod Reaves," Sherrill said.

"I'm Rod Reaves," the man said without putting down his

fork. Rod Reaves had been at a Special Forces camp for four years, longer than any of the men stationed there, had accompanied small patrols into Cambodia, had been wounded twice and had a personal body count of eight Viet Cong. "Tomorrow I start a story on the SEALS."

Sherrill did not want to spend his life looking at other people's slides, but in this man's carousel every picture was of himself.

They were joined by a sociologist who was studying the sexual deprivation of ARVN widows, and a film maker who was using street children to make a movie that sounded like child pornography to Sherrill. Why had he been so timid? Maybe he didn't know anything about journalism, politics or Vietnamese history but he knew as much as these guys and he had as much right to be here.

After finishing his meal Sherrill stopped for a drink at the Continental terrace bar. He was joined by a man who looked vaguely familiar. "I believe we're fellow novelists," the man said. "Si Hardeman."

Si Hardeman, the television definition of a real person, was everything Sherrill disliked. Stylish, successful, celebrated for the public image he had created, he lived in a world created by the movies, a world imagined by mischievous children. He had no values and no convictions except the belief that having no values made him open-minded. Sherrill didn't respect Si's world but he wanted that world to respect him.

In person, Si seemed not only shrunken but leached. He was small, bald except for a fringe of hair above his ears—his wife had written that she liked to bury his face in her breasts and make love to the top of his head—with damp eyes, and sharp little ferret's teeth.

"I don't remember your name but I believe I reviewed one of your books."

Si wrote a syndicated column that combined book and movie reviews with gossip about best-selling authors and glamorous stars, mental trinkets that passed for thought. He had written the only bad review Sherrill had gotten on his first novel. "It was a good book but it wasn't big, you know what I mean? It couldn't be scanned. You have to be somebody to write a book like that, somebody they're interested in. Maybe if the trapper had been killing wolves. . .people were into wolves then."

"It wouldn't be authentic." Sherrill had researched the book.

"That's why I admire Jack Glass. He has the courage to take liberties with facts, to recreate history. You weren't outrageous enough."

Glass had written the authentic story of a vicious murderer who had died in a shootout with police. He could not get the story published but sold it to the movies, where the criminal was made into a folk hero who battled a corrupt society and was martyred by vicious police. The movie was a hit, partly because Dix Deveraux played the macho role that he was celebrated for, and Glass rewrote the book to conform to the movie image, turning it into a best seller with a photograph of Dix on the dustjacket.

Sherrill, who knew something of the murderer and his victims, was outraged that people would associate the killer with the heroic image of Dix Deveraux. "It was totally dishonest," Sherrill said.

"It was an honest reflection of what people wanted at the time."

"Jesus, Si, you have to have some standards. You can't stoop to everybody's level."

"You call it stooping, but a lot of people think you're too egotistical, too elitist to write what they want to read. At least I'm democratic."

Simon had written a best seller about a political columnist who was pursued by beautiful women but was secretly in love with the wife of the only man he respected, the president of the United States. The lovers had only a brief weekend—which took up most of the book—before being discovered by the CIA who threatened to discredit the president by revealing his wife's infidelity unless the columnist volunteered for a suicidal spy mission. The first lady wanted to flee to a forgotten island where they could spend the rest of their lives in love but the columnist knew a higher duty. He accomplished the mission at the cost of his life, and as he was dying he learned that the president, in forgiveness, had vowed to care for the columnist's invalid wife.

The newspaper syndicate promoted the book before it was published, denying that it was based on actual people or events until everyone was convinced it was. Critics scoffed that the book was "naked commercialism" and that Hardeman was "not afraid to be trite" but gave the book attention. Hardeman's wife, a minor television actress better known for her escorts than her acting, wrote a breathless five part series detailing her life with the sexy, popular, best-selling writer. "I can always tell when he is writing well," she confessed. "He makes love to every woman in his book and every one of them is me."

"She's doing a three parter right now," Si announced proudly. "The loneliness and sexual deprivation of a woman whose husband is in Vietnam; her tribute to the women who have husbands over here and the wives of the POWs."

"How long are you going to be here?" Sherrill asked.

"A week. Two at the outside."

Si ordered another round and handed Sherrill a picture of his wife in a near nude publicity pose that had appeared in magazines and calendars. Sherrill looked at the photograph aware that Si was studying his face. He was embarrassed to be so familiar with Si's wife. "Nice tits, huh?" Si asked. "Got a picture of your wife?"

"No," Sherrill lied. He had a photograph of Jennifer with one hand on her hip, one hand holding a pan, looking dreamily out the window. It wasn't her most flattering picture but he liked it because it caught a wistful yearning he found appealing.

"This is my daughter," Si said. Sherrill searched the photograph for traces of the actor rumored to be the child's actual father. She looked like an ordinary, gap-toothed, bookish nine-year-old. Her mother had written, "Not only did my friends make passes at my usually unsuspecting husband, our daughter asked, 'Daddy, may I see your penis? All the girls at school want to know what your penis looks like.'"

"Do you have any children?" Si asked.

Sherrill ordered another drink before answering. "I have a daughter," he said, taking the easy way out. He did not want to discuss Marie's death with Si Hardeman. He did not want to share that intimacy with a man who had no private emotions.

"Does she have trouble keeping the writer separate from the father?"

"They're the same person." He thought of Marie, nearsighted, serious, asking if she could be a writer too. He had told her she could be anything she wanted.

"That's what I'm saying, you haven't made your face. You have no mystique. Wait until you're famous. Hell, wait until you get home."

He wished that Marie were waiting for him the way she waited for him to come from work every day. Watching for him, but hiding too, timidly awaiting some sign that he was happy to see her. When he held out his arms she ran and jumped into them, burying her face in his neck and laughing. If only he could see her, hold her one more time.

The last time he saw Marie—her body sustained by the tubes and machines that had supplanted her brain—he did not want her to live. He did not draw close, did not touch her, did not hold her one last time and weep. He had slipped away like a criminal ashamed of his crime. Only now could he, sometimes, permit that memory to pass quickly across his consciousness. Permit the fear that despite the doctor's claims, somewhere, somehow Marie knew that he had deserted her. Only now, with thousands of miles between them, could he face his anger that Jennifer had given him a child he was powerless to save and could relinquish only by mutilating himself. Only here, removed from every suggestion that Marie had lived, could he accept that in her death Marie had planted the seed that became Cassady stumbling in the darkness to find Sherrill's salvation.

"I had to tell my daughter that those people in the papers or on television are not her mother and father and she was not to believe what they said," Si said. "The people at home are her mother and father. She's a bright girl. She said, 'Then that girl in the papers is not me.' And I said, 'No, honey, that girl is just someone your mother made up.'"

Sherrill had seen Marie playing with an imaginary playmate. "What do you call your imaginary friend?" he asked her. "I don't call her anything, she's imaginary," Marie said. Sherrill stood up and the world wavered. "I've got to go," he said.

"Mind if I walk with you?" Si asked. "There's something I want to ask you." As they walked along the crowded street, Si outlined his next book about a pacifist sent to Vietnam. When he refused to kill, he was dropped into VC territory where he would be forced to kill or die. Instead, he threw down his rifle and called upon the enemy to be his brothers. The VC took him to their camp where he fell in love with a dedicated Communist.

When they asked him to join them in an attack on his own base, he refused and persuaded his lover not to kill either. They stayed behind and for three days explored all the joys that sex could offer. The pursued guerrillas returned with their wounded. The pacifist and his lover volunteered to care for the wounded while the others slipped away. When the Americans overran the camp they found an American soldier and his Viet Cong lover dead, their arms around each other.

The battle-hardened men were so moved they spared the Viet Cong wounded.

"See, the message is, love is better than hate," Si said as they walked along Lam Son Square.

Sherrill was embarrassed. How many times had he taught *Preface to the Lyrical Ballads?* "It's not true," he said.

"Of course not, it's fiction."

"I mean it couldn't happen."

"It's what people want to happen. Americans and Viet Cong loving each other. It's how people want to see Vietnam. And I'm not ashamed to say, I respect them enough to give them what they want. Your problem is you never watch the soaps."

When she was very young Marie had cried because she thought firemen burned houses. Her confusion was understandable; every time she saw a burning house on television news she saw firemen throwing things on the blaze. "How will they understand what it's like if what they read gives them the wrong picture?"

"They don't want to understand. They want to believe what makes them feel good. That's our job. That's why you have advertising. People want to be reassured that it's good for them and makes them feel better even when they know it isn't true."

"If you spend your time escaping reality rather than learning to see, to hear—isn't that going to be reflected in the way you think and act?"

"If people wanted to understand they wouldn't read me. They wouldn't read REAL either."

As drunk as he was, Sherrill knew that Si had said something important. Men didn't read REAL to understand. Did that make him another Si Hardeman? Another Harry Tompkins doing anything for a price? No, he hadn't written the story about the man in the delta because he wasn't like them. He could help men understand, even those who read REAL.

"The problem is," Si said, pausing to get Sherrill's attention. "Do you think it should be a homosexual or a heterosexual love story? My publisher thinks the time is ripe for a best-selling fag romance, but will the public accept that kind of story from a guy with my macho image, and will they pay to see a queer movie? Unless a book becomes a best seller or is made into a movie you might as well not have written it."

He had risked his life for that story. Rick Belk may have endangered the man but he had risked his life as well. Harry didn't have the guts to get the story so he sold it to whoever would pay. That fucking coward. Sherrill hated him, remembering the nightmare of the deserted village.

"It's even more complicated. There are two actors who want to play the lead. One is straight but can convince anyone he's gay. The other is Dix Deveraux, but he's never come out of the closet. If I go with the straight I can write it either way but if I go with Dix I'm going to have to write it straight because of his macho image. I can get either one but I have to decide which one I want before I write it. So what do you think?"

"Dix Deveraux is gay?" Sherrill's thoughts had been elsewhere.

"That's top secret. Dix is everybody's ideal of the American male. It would ruin his image if people knew."

"How can you ruin his image? Dix Deveraux is an image."

"He's a real person."

"He's an actor, an image on the screen."

"Before he was an actor he was a real person."

"Before he was an actor he was Bill Stump."

"We have to protect people like that."

Si was going to write something superficial about the suffering and terror of others without cost or risk to himself in a calculated attempt to dupe readers into believing what he knew was false, but he had to protect the invented image of a two-bit actor? There was no shame left in the world. There was guilt, personal and collective, pressed down and running over.

There was self-hatred that expressed itself in depression and degradation, but there was no shame. To fail one's intent was painful, even tragic, but to intend something stupid and inglorious was shameful.

A tiny child approached them carrying a tray almost as big as she. "Souvenirs for our children," Si said, picking over trinkets. Si bought a head band that had "Nietzsche for President" woven into the threads. Sherrill picked up a high school ring brought from America.

"Get one of these bands for her to wear it on," Si said, taking another of the bands and poking it in Sherrill's pocket. "Now that I know about your daughter I understand you a little better," Si said. Across the street Sherrill saw Harry Tompkins. "I take little bits of information like that and form a picture of who you are. That's the way a writer works. I see you as a family man . . ."

"Bastard," Sherrill yelled. Dropping the ring, he followed Harry, plunging into the devil's carnival that was Tu Do Street at night.

He went in search of Harry down the narrow street that was bumper to bumper with honking cars and taxis and popping Hondas; crowded with shouting vendors and shrilling bar girls from the Caravelle to the river. There were barber shops, children selling cigarettes, souvenirs and condoms from boxes hung on straps around their necks; massage parlors, the Big Boy Hamburger occupied only by Americans, and a photo shop complete with fake jungle that took pictures of garrison troops posing with Vietnamese girls. One of the girls caught him by the arm. "You pose me, I boom boom." He shrugged past her.

Sherrill wondered if REAL would buy a story on the bar girls. One prostitute was costumed in ao dai as a dainty Vietnamese virgin, another disguised in white chiffon as an American virgin. Others were dressed as cheerleaders and airline stewardesses. A tall girl, who somewhere had a father who had seen France, was dressed in a go-go dancer's red vinyl miniskirt and red high-heeled boots. There were even prostitutes who posed as prostitutes. Dutiful daughters in a male-dominated society, they assisted their families the only way they could, without passion or guilt. They fit none of the REAL stereotypes—the lazy slut, the glamorous call girl, the socialite who loved being degraded by working men.

A small hand caught his and he looked down to see a small boy who, while holding him with a couple of fingers, had managed to get a thumb and forefinger into his pocket and around his wallet. Sherrill grabbed the wallet and the boy twisted away and was immediately lost in the crowd.

"Get anything?" asked a thin, unshaven American in a dirty seersucker suit. "If that little bastard hadn't nicked me for fifty bucks yesterday I'd write this story myself, but I'll let you have it for the fifty. Real money, not MPC." He put out a hand to stop Sherrill. "I've got a guy from the 9th who will swear he shot this gook in the belly and fucked the bullet hole while she was dying." Sherrill brushed past him; everyone had a story to sell. "So he didn't get VD, see. Look, it was tight and hot and she was squirming and moaning. Hell, you know how to write it."

"Where was it?" Sherrill asked.

"Just below the navel. If you shoot them too low you get shit on your dick."

"I mean where did it happen?"

"Jesus, I don't know, some gook village." Sherrill turned away. "Look, if you got some real money I can change it for you. I can get five hundred piasters for it."

Three MPs dragged a young soldier from a bar, braced him against the wall, and took a .45 from him. "I wasn't going to sell it, honest," he said. Sherrill crossed the street to avoid a woman who was defecating on the sidewalk. A dog-eared, middle-aged Frenchman flashed grisly pictures of dead women and children, American heads with genitals stuffed in their mouths, chains made of human ears, child prostitutes, G.I.s shooting up, and dozens of stoic, stunned, angry, frightened Vietnamese faces.

"Tell me what you want and while you write I get you picture," the man said, wagging a scabbed finger. "Woman VC interrogated by Special Forces." The man produced a photograph of a woman being held with her legs apart and a bayonet shoved into her vagina. It was impossible to tell whether the expression on her face was agony or rigor mortis.

Sherrill turned away in disgust, almost colliding with three young airmen who were fighting the only war they had, the war against boredom. "Hey, I got a quote for you," one of them said. "Women are easy to shoot, but kids you got to lead." It was an old joke, best loved by those farthest from the killing, but the three airmen, emboldened by their own bluster, went careening down the street, laughing at the girls and giving mock salutes to the white-helmeted Vietnamese police called "white mice."

Sherrill walked past costumed girls who called, "Hi, lover boy," "Come in, honey," and stepped into one of the bars. The place was crowded with Americans. Except for the girls and the bartender there were no Vietnamese. He found a barstool, ordered a drink, and looked around for Harry. Before the drink arrived, a girl was nuzzling his neck and licking his ear. "I love you too much," she said.

He turned to look at a serious, straight mouthed little girl in what looked like an American bridal gown. She looked eight but was probably eighteen. He found it impossible to guess the age of the Vietnamese; the women looked like children or crones. She kissed him with dry, thin lips and ran a tiny hand from his knee to his crotch. "You buy me one drink."

She had old, tired eyes in a sad little face. Sherrill saw the beginnings of two parallel lines between her brows. He folded two hundred piasters into her fist to buy her a moment's respite from male hands. The hand-me-down eyes did not leave his face as she raised the dress and tucked the money into her cotton panties. Then she slipped down the bar to the next man. "I love you too much," she said, licking his neck.

A young soldier sat down beside him. One look at the taut, sun-browned face told Sherrill this was no Saigon commando. "You a reporter? My buddy got zapped last week. He could have been a fucking lifer because his old man was a general but he wanted to be one of us. He could have been in West Point but he was over here. And when he died his general fucking father had his moustache shaved off and his hair cut and his boots polished. . .He took him away from us. Over here a friend is all you have, and when he goes down you want to be with him. Back home the women take over, and marriage and family. Friendship don't mean shit. But here. . .the fucking general took him away from us. He took him away."

Once he had listened to such stories, sympathized, tried to explain the kind of story REAL wanted. "Wrong magazine," he said. He shoved his way out of the bar and into another, looking for Harry.

"I'm a medic," a soldier said. His face was composed but his fingers trembled. "We got hit bad last month, rockets, mortars, ground assault. I was working in the aid station and we had wall to wall wounded and the only doctor we got flies back to the fucking division hospital leaving me and two other medics. . .I did a fucking amputation. And they're going to give that cocksucker a medal. . ." The man's face had gone tight, and ridges ran across his forehead.

REAL would like the heroic medic amputating a comrade's limb under fire if there were some way to write the story without mentioning an officer who ran.

"I saw an officer chew the tits off a girl. No shit, man. Lt. Zobell, and I want to see his ass hanged."

Sherrill went from bar to bar, brushing aside the prostitutes, brushing off the stories of atrocities, fraggings, waste, told to him by men who would confess any crime, admit any shame, play any role, even an assigned one, to be the subject of thirty seconds on television.

He looked up to see Larry Caldwell who tried to get media coverage for a Rhade orphanage. The Rhades were a non-Vietnamese ethnic minority who lived in mountain villages. The men were recruited by Special Forces to fight the Viet Cong. In retaliation the VC attacked the villages. American missionaries began an orphanage.

Vietnamese soldiers, who held the Rhades in contempt as moi or savages, raided the orphanage stealing food, blankets and medicine. The story, reported by the media, brought an outpouring of aid to the orphanage, and it was moved away from ARVN troops. In its new location the orphanage was attacked by the VC, who killed the staff, burned the buildings, and carried off children. Media coverage brought financial support.

Sherrill had written the story but Stone replied that REAL was not interested in do-good-soup-and-soap religion. "Tell me how the children and missionaries fought off the Viet Cong and we'll reconsider. But don't tell me U.S. Forces can't protect children. And stop flaunting your knowledge. Rhades are Vietnamese, right? Then call them Vietnamese."

The orphanage was moved closer to Saigon and had again been attacked by the VC. "They burned everything. We have to start over," Caldwell explained. "It's another attack, but the reporters say it's the same story and they've already done it."

Sherrill understood. The reporters couldn't keep filing the same story over and over no matter how many times the orphanage was attacked, no matter how much they might want to help.

"There are twenty-eight ethnic groups here and the Vietnamese treat them worse than we do blacks. They won't protect the orphanage. We use the adults as guerrillas but we won't do anything for their rights as minorities. Can't you do a story on that?"

REAL wasn't interested in ethnic problems in Vietnam and Sherrill wasn't convinced anyone else was either. The story was the war—no, the story was the American involvement in the war. The ethnics were a backdrop for stories on Special Forces. No one was interested in their rights or problems. Maybe it wasn't the whole picture but it was all that was likely to be known. "Too complicated," Sherrill said, quoting Stone, and again went in search of Harry.

Sherrill stood in front of the Caravelle, not drunk enough to face his room, too drunk to face the muggers and pickpockets of Tu Do. One of the television networks owned a sedan that they parked unlocked in front of the hotel at night to allow homeless children a place to sleep. Sherrill was trying to count the tangle of bodies, one of whom looked like the boy who had tried to pick his pocket, when he saw Harry Tompkins across the street. "Harry," he yelled. Harry tried to disappear into the crowd, but Sherrill ran after him and grabbed him by the arm. "You son of a bitch, you sold out that guy in the delta. You endangered his family."

Harry showed no sign of understanding. "You wanted the story."

"I risked my life and you sold it to somebody else."

"Just television," he said. "Hey man, they sold the story for you. They got national attention and you're the only one with an in-depth interview. I did you a favor. Hell, you could do a book after the exposure that guy got."

"I didn't do the interview because the man feared for his life." Harry shrugged. Sherrill grabbed him by the shirt. "Give my money back, you son of a bitch, and if something happens to him I'm coming for you."

"He's okay. I promise you he's okay."

Sherrill studied Harry's lying face. How could Harry know unless— "You're still selling that story."

"What we need is a drink," Harry said. "Clear our heads." He produced a bottle and offered it to Sherrill.

Sherrill tipped the bottle back and swallowed, closing his eyes to keep them from tearing. When he opened them he saw Harry's back disappearing around a corner. He chased Harry through the maze of streets, caught him again, grabbed his collar and spun him around. "You bastard, don't you know you'll cause that man's death."

Harry spread his arms in repudiation. "He chose to live there. That makes it a story. Somebody is going to tell it. You can't hold me responsible for what happens to him."

Sherrill knew what Harry said was true and there was nothing he could do to make it right. Frustrated, he shoved Harry again, banging his head against a building. "Give me back my money."

"Jesus, Sherrill, some bastard picked my pocket last night. If I had your money, I'd give it to you." Sherrill shoved him against the wall. "I'd give you a story but all I got is fraggings." Sherrill shoved him again. "Rape. Drugs. I don't have anything REAL will use." Harry offered to let Sherrill buy into an opium deal. He offered him one of his whores. "A week. A month, dammit. Jesus, Sherrill."

Harry sagged against him, his breath hot and foul in Sherrill's face. Harry's teeth were rotting; bastard couldn't afford to get them fixed. Sherrill relaxed his grip and Harry slid down the wall. "I get paid when I deliver the girl," Harry said. "I'll get the money and be right back."

Sherrill leaned against the wall and turned to look at the girl who had appeared from nowhere. Harry had put her in dark makeup and a cotton dress with bright orange and yellow flowers. A scarf of the same material was tied around her head. Despite a padded bra she looked small and undernourished. Sherrill wondered what her appeal was supposed to be and why she was made to look black when there were so few blacks in Saigon. She didn't seem robust or animated enough for universal appeal.

He slid down the wall and took another drink. Unless Harry had sold her to a whole platoon, she wouldn't bring taxi fare. When he turned to tell Harry, he saw that Harry was gone. Good. He didn't want to have to look at him again anyway. Sherrill looked down the long, dark streets. He wondered where he was. In chasing Harry he had gotten confused. The streets were empty. Everyone had disappeared.

Holy shit. He had missed curfew. After ten o'clock nothing moved except police and military patrols. He didn't even know the way back to his hotel. He eased to his feet. He would wait until his head cleared or until a patrol came along and took him back to his hotel. Or arrested him. He wondered what the fine was for curfew violation.

Someone tugged at his arm. He looked down and saw Harry's whore. Her thin, pinched face had resigned itself to being unattractive. She was pointing at a cyclo. Sherrill grabbed the driver. "Caravelle Hotel, you biet?" He got in the cyclo and the girl got in beside him. "Didi," he told her. Get away. She ignored him. The driver pedaled silently away. He wondered if the man was her father, delivering her for Harry. He felt something uncomfortable under his hip. The bottle was all he was going to get out of Harry so he might as well enjoy it. He took another drink.

The damn driver was taking the long way back to the hotel to demand more pay. Sherrill turned to glare, to let him know he understood what was happening. The driver pedaled down a dark, narrow street of crowded hovels that seemed to be leaning against each other and spilling into the street. They were so close to the river Sherrill could smell the slime and debris. Mist rose from the filthy street. Harry had set him up to be mugged. He had to clear the alcohol from his brain and think.

"Caravelle," he yelled at the driver. "Caravelle Hotel," he said to the girl. They ignored him.

He grasped the bottle by the neck to defend himself and did a quick inventory. He was carrying a few dollars, a few hundred piasters, some funny money MPC and his airline ticket home. They could have the money but he would fight for the ticket home. He shook the bottle at the girl. "I cacadow," he said. I kill. She ignored him. He looked at the driver. Were they both deaf?

If he wasn't being set up, where were they going? No one in this neighborhood could afford a prostitute, not even this one. Unless there was a house of prostitution and Harry had sold her. This girl was destined to prostitution from the day she was born. The day she was conceived. Perhaps even the day her mother was conceived.

The cyclo stopped and Sherrill held the bottle like a club, ready to defend himself. The girl and driver urged him out of the cyclo. He got out without presenting his back to them. Sherrill considered taking the cyclo by force but the driver left too fast. He spun around searching for unseen foes. He kept turning, as fast as he dared. He did not want to appear drunk, an easy target. The girl waited to lead him into the darkness.

He wanted to run as fast and as long as he could but he did not know which way to run and the police were likely to shoot at anyone running down the street after curfew. He could not stay where he was. He followed the girl who padded in a strange, flatfooted way as though accustomed to walking on sponge. Down a muddy path between shacks made of packing crates, ammo crates and pieces of sewer pipe, across a stagnant pool of filth, to a house made of sheets of plywood and strips of corrugated steel, with the front fender of a car for one corner of the roof. The girl ducked through a curtain into the doorless opening.

Sherrill waited, unwilling to stoop to enter and present his head as a target. The girl lighted a lantern and appeared in the doorway. He peered inside. There was an old woman and several children lying on plywood on the floor of the single room. Some of the children looked at him with sleepy eyes. Were the children hers? Harry's? Why had she brought him there? She took his hand and led him inside.

The girl moved the children, unrolled a pad and hung a piece of tarpaulin to isolate one corner. Sherrill watched the doorway. If anyone came through it he would hold them off with the lantern threatening to set the place afire. Even in his drunken state he knew that was folly; he would burn with it. When he turned he saw the girl undressing. "No," he said. Harry had taken him again, giving him the girl instead of his money.

Sherrill stared at the doorway. It would be foolhardy to leave; he was stuck until daylight. He picked up the flimsy dress where she had tossed it and covered the girl who was lying naked on the pad. Until Vietnam he had never seen a prostitute, at least had not recognized one, and here he was spending the night with one. He sat down on a corner of the mat and looked at the bottle. He hoped there was enough to get him through the night. He took a drink and blinked as the liquor burned his throat.

He should write this as an example of Vietnamese-American communication. All she wanted was a few dollars and he would give her everything in his wallet to be back in the air-conditioned Caravelle. REAL wouldn't be interested but someday he would tell Jennifer about it, when he was able to see the humor in it.

The girl put her arms around his chest. "No," he said. "Didi."

"You fay," she said. "You fay."

"No biet," he said, pushing her away. She put her arms around his neck and tried to kiss him. He turned, took her by the shoulders, pushed her down on the mat and covered her with the dress. "You didi," he said, raising a hand as though to slap her. He knew his Vietnamese wouldn't make sense to her, but he hoped the upraised hand would.

The girl didn't bother him again and he relaxed enough to lie on his side with his back to her. He knew he was probably in no danger but he watched the door anyway. The mat did not cushion the earth, only protected him from its dampness. He took off his shirt and rolled it up to use for a pillow. He stared at the doorway in the flickering light of the lantern and as always before he slept, thought of Jennifer. He saw her the way she slept, turned to his side of the bed, one arm reaching for him, her hair tucked under her head leaving her neck bare.

In his life there had never been any woman but Jennifer, or any need for one. He missed her; he missed making love to her. It wasn't just the intense, fleeting sensation, although he missed that too. It was feeling good about himself, feeling good about Jennifer, feeling good about being together, dividing the travail and multiplying the triumph. Without that the act was followed by depression. He knew because after Marie's death the feeling had disappeared. The sensation was as intense, sometimes sharper than ever, but the feeling was locked away where it couldn't be hurt. And after sex he had felt deflated and alone.

He had gotten too close to Marie, had held her too dear and her death had almost destroyed him. He had curled in upon himself trying to cover his wound. Unwittingly he had insulated himself from Jennifer so as never to be that vulnerable again. He knew that now. He had shunned Jennifer because he was afraid of losing her the way he had lost Marie.

Marie was a quiet child. He taught her to fish and sometimes they sat for hours, nothing passing between them but an occasional smile. She laughed so quickly and happily that his heart melted. She needed to be held and reassured. She was not as forward or as daring as some because she feared disappointing him. Sometimes she was ten and sometimes she was fifteen—thirteen was not an age but an average—but she was his child, his flesh, and he couldn't let her go.

Sherrill took another drink hoping he could get drunk

enough to cry. He had not been able to cry, fearing he would be swept away in grief, lost forever in sorrow. He tried to cry, willing the sobs to come. "Marie, Marie." As he cried Marie appeared in the doorway. He was so startled he stopped crying, but it was wrong. He knew it was wrong. "Marie."

He wanted to go to her but he was afraid if he got up she would see the girl on the pad beside him. "You can't come here. Not this place."

"You called me. Daddy, you called me."

"Not here, Marie. You can't come here." He cried, more bitterly than before, hiding his eyes behind his hand.

"Can I come here, Daddy?"

He opened his eyes to see Marie in a field. It was the field near the stream where they fished, the field where they had played hide-and-seek. Marie ran barefoot through the oleanders. "They're poisonous, Marie. Oleanders are poisonous. If you lick your feet, you'll die."

Marie laughed. "It's okay to be here with you, isn't it, Daddy?"

"You're dead, Marie," he tried to explain. "We can't play anymore."

Marie turned her face so he could not see her tears and she went away. "God," he moaned, clinging to Jennifer who was sleeping beside him. "God, I want her back." He felt a small arm encircle his neck and felt a warm face on his shoulder, so close he could smell the warm ginger and sage of her. "Marie, you can't come here."

"I can go anywhere you go, Daddy."

"Aren't you happy where you are?"

"Yes."

"Why do you keep coming back?"

"You call me, Daddy."

"You have to go back." He tried to remove her arm from his neck but she clung to him tightly, pressing her body against his. "You have to go back, Marie." He tried to push her away but she caught at his belt. One hand went inside his trousers. He felt her mouth on his.

"Dammit." Sherrill struggled off the pad and rose to his feet to escape the Vietnamese girl. "Jesus." He shuddered at what had almost happened. She could have given him a disease. "They've got diseases we've never even heard of," he had heard a doctor telling troops. "You'll carry your dick home in a jar."

He was so angry with the girl he wanted to strike her but saw she was a child. He was so astonished he looked again, unwilling to believe what his eyes told him—the outlines of ribs, the tiny buds of her breasts, the hairless body. God damn Harry was prostituting a child. The idea sickened him. Sherrill knew if he had touched that child, if he had harmed her he would kill Harry.

He picked up the dress and threw it at her. "Didi," he said, waving her on the other side of the partition.

"You fay," she said.

"No biet."

"You fay shree dollah. You boom boom. You fay."

"Didi. Get over there," he said with such vehemence that she picked up the dress and moved to the other side of the partition. Three dollars. She was driven to this extremity for three dollars. He reached in his pocket, took out the money and dropped it behind the partition, but he could not escape. He was bound to her until it was light.

She was a child and a prostitute. God, what kind of a country was this? He knew. The Communists had killed her mother and father, or they were VC, or the government had arrested them as political prisoners. She was the sole support of those in the hovel. Her sex was her only commercial value and she wasn't even pretty. The makeup and padded bra made her look less a child but not sexy. He wondered why Harry dressed her like—suddenly he knew. Harry sold her to be debased, abused.

Someone should kill Harry, but that wouldn't save the girl and those she had to support. How then was he going to save them? He had not intended to get so involved in their lives, to know this much of misery but now that he knew he couldn't walk away without trying to help.

He could take the girl with him when he went home but he couldn't take them all and what would happen to her family? The other children were too young to be pimps, prostitutes or pickpockets. That would leave the old mamasan to beg and dig through garbage cans. He went to sleep thinking of ways to help them and fell into a dream of roaches. Hundreds of them. His knit shirt was sticky with them. He tried to wake up but could feel them crawling on him and was afraid to move. Carefully he turned back the cover, waking Jennifer. He slipped off the bed, and treading on roaches, hearing them crunch beneath his feet, he turned on the bathroom light. By the light he could see the bed covered with roaches. Jennifer screamed, staring at the floor. He turned to look. Marie was lying naked on the floor. Roaches emerged from between her legs. "What did you do to her?" Jennifer screamed.

He moaned. The moan became a groan, a howl, a high-pitched shriek that filled the room. Children clutched at him, pressing their tiny bodies to his. "No, no," he said, trying to push them away, afraid of touching them. Then the earth leaped beneath him with an ear-splitting roar. The impact stunned him. For a moment he could not think. Again there was the low, guttural moan that became a shriek and the earth erupted, part of the house collapsed, the lantern crashed to the floor. His face and lungs filled with dust.

Whimpering children clung to him, burrowed beneath him. He was acutely aware of the tiny bodies pressed to him, their circular mouths stuck to him like eels. They screamed and wailed in their fear. "It's all right, it's all right," he said, although he knew they did not understand. "It's all right." In the distance he could hear sirens and sometimes screams but there were no more rockets. Still he spoke to the children, his skin gone dead to their touch, talking to them until they were asleep.

Maybe he could move in—if he could stand to live here. A week's room at the Caravelle would feed them for a year. If he bought some furniture—No, he would have to find a different place, one with privacy so he could lock his door. Running water. He could deposit his camera, watch and most of his money at the hotel. He could lock his clothes in his bag, but he'd have to have a mirror, a bed, an electric fan. . .

At first light, the girl moved the sleeping children and put back the curtain. "I don't know how much English you can understand but I want to help you," he said. "I'll try to find a place where we can all stay together and I'll feed you. And I'll protect you so you don't have to do what you're doing. And I'll never let Harry come to you again."

"You boom boom," she said. "Shree dollah."

"Listen, you don't have to do that. I'll help you find a way."

"You cheap charlie. You fay shree dollah."

He tried to leave but she clung to him. He pushed her away, and gave her money. Discovering the head band Si had pushed into his pocket, he gave her that also. He passed out money to the children who reached up to him with little bird-beak hands. The old woman lay face down in the corner, partially covered by the collapsed wall. She was dead. He backed out of the shack. The girl and children followed him. He pushed them back inside, threw coins on the floor and ran, trying to escape.

He walked through what seemed to be an enormous trash heap, some of it discarded from the houses, some of it washed up by the river, all of it wet and stinking. He picked his way along a muddy path. Children climbed over the piles of rotting garbage searching for food. He wished he had never come here, never seen such depravity, never known there were people who lived so desperately.

A short distance away was a hole where a rocket had landed. Rags, tarpaulin, twisted sheets of metal littered the streets. Vietnamese threaded their way through the debris without a glance but Sherrill stopped to watch old women propping up a house that had been blown down but not obliterated. Other houses, though standing, had been holed by shrapnel and splattered with mud and bits of cloth. The smell of earth fouled by centuries of habitation mingled with the odor of drying blood. Flies buzzed. Sherrill saw a matted, bloody thing that he thought was a rocket-blasted rat but might have been the scalp of a small child.

He was trying to find his way back to the hotel when he heard a car stop and saw that it was the network sedan. The television crew looked like they had been cast for television. Short, thick chested Rick Belk with a dramatic mane of curly blond hair; a tall, muscular, crew-cut soundman who looked like he should be wearing storm trooper boots; and a little Japanese cameraman with slicked-down hair. "Hop in," Belk said.

Gratefully, Sherrill climbed into the car. He wanted a bath; he wanted to wash his hair, his mouth. He wanted to forget the nightmare that would be a part of him forever. His skin was crawling inside his clothes.

"If you've got a girl in this part of town your balls are bigger than your brain," Belk said.

He was disgusted by the thought of the girls, the women of this country who would be used, abused and abandoned. "How far is it to the Caravelle?" Back to clean sheets, air-conditioned rooms, people who clothed their desperation with decorum. The car was not going to the Caravelle but to Tan Son Nhut. They were after a story on the troops who were searching for the VC who had fired rockets into the city.

"I don't have my field gear," Sherrill said. He didn't have his camera, field uniform or boots.

"We'll take care of you," Belk said. "Brotherhood of the

press."

Belk found him a belt and canteen and when he got in the helicopter a soldier gave him a helmet and flak jacket. Norela Cook was in the helicopter. She did not acknowledge him.

Sherrill followed the troops along jungle trails although the small cloud of a headache that had threatened that morning had turned into a thunderstorm by noon. He was wearing sponge-soled shoes and his feet were raw and blistered. In the early afternoon he announced he was going back on the next chopper.

He waited at a little clearing being hacked out of the jungle by a handful of soldiers who were to unload the helicopters as they came in. Rick Belk was talking into the camera about fleet Viet Cong, heavy-footed soldiers, no nearer the end than yesterday. A grenade landed behind him.

Luckily it was a dud because everyone stared at it until the shooting started. A man behind Belk was hit before Sherrill could get to the ground. Dirt and debris kicked up by the bullets stung his face. Behind him someone yelled, "I'm hit, I'm hit." Nobody seemed to be shooting back. "Shoot goddammit, shoot goddammit," he screamed.

He could see the TV cameraman filming as the VC moved in. They were going to be overrun. He looked at the soldier beside him. "Shoot goddammit," he screamed. The soldier had the eyes of a child, wide with wonder. Sherrill looked into the eyes and saw there was no one there.

Sherrill reached for the man's rifle and pulled the trigger. It fired. He fired again and again, over the dead soldier, at first without raising his head, without aiming, trying to keep the enemy back. When the rifle stopped firing he fumbled trying to reload, then dropped it and crawled to a rifle lying on the ground a few feet away. He fired at everything that moved. When the rifle stopped firing he reloaded, successfully this time. He heard more shooting behind him and saw Charlie pulling out. "They're getting away," he yelled. He jumped up to chase them, firing as he ran. Then someone was tugging at the rifle. "It's okay, it's all over," the soldier said, pulling the rifle from his hands.

"They're getting away," he yelled.

"Let the choppers chase them," the soldier said.

"They killed that man. We can't let them get away."

"What are you going to do, chase them into Cambodia?"

"I'll chase them all the way to Hanoi," Sherrill said. "We can't let them get away."

"Do you think we ought to bomb them?"

"Hell yes, bomb them."

"Do you think we ought to bomb Hanoi?"

"Bomb them all the way to Hanoi."

"How many did you kill?"

Sherrill looked at the questioner without comprehension. It wasn't the soldier; it was Norela Cook. He was surrounded by reporters, crowding in, asking questions. Where were the soldiers?

"There are three dead gooks and some blood trails." It was a soldier and he was speaking into a radio. "Which way did they go?" he asked Sherrill. Sherrill pointed. "Headed west, across the blue line," the soldier said into the radio then looked at Sherrill again. "How many? How many did you see?"

See? He saw movement out of the corner of his eyes. He saw movement in the grass, the trees. Everywhere he looked he saw movement. There were. . .He saw. . .He didn't see. . . a face in the bushes, a young fresh face that looked somewhat like that of Harry's. . .the girl. A sandaled foot that quivered.

"Were there a dozen? Two dozen? How many did you see?"

"One."

"How many do you think you killed?"

"Maybe a dozen," the soldier said into the radio. "We have a patrol in the area. They'll put out air panels and pop red smoke."

"Damn good shooting. Where'd you learn to shoot a rifle?"

"I'm from Texas. I grew up with guns."

"Aren't you a noncombatant?"

"They were going to overrun us. Somebody had to do something."

"Do you think correspondents should take part in the fighting?"

"Should the press take sides?"

"Should the media support the military?"

"Do you feel more comfortable with the military or the media?"

"The military is more reliable."

"Do you think the others were cowards for not fighting back?"

"The fucking gooks were going to kill us. The fucking reporters were hiding in the fucking grass not doing a fucking thing except taking fucking pictures. Somebody had to do something. Somebody had to stop them." He realized he was screaming.

"Would you kill the VC if you could find them?"

"I'd find them."

"Why are you here?"

"We're here to save these people."

"You kill them to save them?"

"You have to kill some to save the others. You have to kill—" He was babbling. "This is war. You have to kill the enemy to save—" His legs were trembling so he could not stand and he collapsed on the ground. He tried to light a cigarette but failed. Belk lighted it for him.

"You'd chase them into Cambodia?" Belk asked.

Sherrill was confused. Where had all the soldiers come from? Which questions had been asked by the military and which by the media and what had he said? He looked down and saw his civilian shoes. "I'd have to get my boots first," he said, trying to smile.

"Would you like to have a rifle?"

He did not feel safe; the jungle was still there. "Damn straight."

It took him several minutes to understand that a work party had been coming to pick up supplies when they heard the first shots and had arrived at the LZ on a dead run, driving off the VC. It took him a long time to understand because he was stupid with shock. The LZ was littered with equipment, clothing, bodies. He counted the bodies. Four. He counted them again. Four; three of them Vietnamese. There seemed to be so many more.

He was amazed that men were walking around, that Belk was talking into the microphone while the camera filmed the dead and wounded. He sat on the ground, his muscles quivering. He listened to others explain how he had saved their lives. He was the only one who didn't know what had happened.

He couldn't speak. All the way back to Saigon he couldn't speak although Norela tried to start a conversation and the network crew and photographers talked about what they might have on film. When they got back to the safety of the city Sherrill wanted but he didn't want. He itched, not his skin but his insides. He did not want to be alone and he did not want to be with anyone.

"Come to my room," Belk said when they got back to the hotel. Norela was already there. Belk splashed bourbon into glasses. Norela toasted Sherrill. "To our hero," she said. "God damn, Sherrill, you were great. You saved our ass." Sherrill drank without speaking, fighting the bourbon and himself. Norela stood up. "I've got a story to write," she said. "'Give him boots and a rifle and he'll march into Cambodia.' Corny, but effective."

When she left, Belk filled the glasses again and Sherrill settled a little in his chair. He realized his teeth were chattering. "To women, life's greatest distraction," Belk said.

Sherrill drank steadily, listening to Belk toast the women he had known. Liz, Becky, Valerie, Mary Ellen. "To Tracy Trimble, the tension reliever." Belk had gotten to names that Sherrill recognized as belonging to women who made soap and aspirin commercials. "She was like a telephone. Always going off at the wrong time."

Belk was enjoying his role as connoisseur of flesh. Or was it gourmand? Sherrill wondered if Belk enjoyed any of those women the way he enjoyed their bodies; that was why it was called trifling, because it trivialized love. Belk didn't want to feel as much as Sherrill had felt with Jennifer and Marie. He didn't want to know that much. Love was a diversion.

Belk hoisted his glass again and surveyed it with one eye closed. "To Belinda, the blonde bitch I may still be married to." He sighed. "The most expensive piece of ass I ever had was free. If you don't pay to get in, you pay to get out."

Rick's attitude was too similar to Harry's to suit Sherrill. "Why do you do it? Why do you make love to someone you don't love?"

"How else can you say who you are? This is me, somebody to be reckoned with. Somebody who can make you cry, make you beg, make you pregnant." Belk babbled on. "To war," Belk said. "Life's greatest distraction."

"Change the subject," Sherrill said. He admired Belk's courage and that of his crew. He was astonished that they could film and Belk could comment on the shooting even as it raged around them. He had not yet considered the incident, had not put it together and he didn't want to talk about it.

"To television, life's greatest distraction. Because it brings us women and war, not the real bloody thing, but a bite-sized semblance."

"There wasn't any wire around the bakery in Chu Lai," Sherrill said.

"It was kids watching a ball game between some grunts but it was the picture I needed. It made the right statement."

Fiction was changing the facts to tell the truth; that's what he told his students. "I thought that was fiction," he said.

"We have to keep their noses to the screen. We have to woo the viewer and we have to do it with pictures."

Woo the viewer? He had thought the relationship between television producers and viewers was like that between the citizens and the government, based on mutual contempt. "But you're sending pictures to people who haven't been trained to see. It's like sending Michelangelo's David to someone who never heard of the Bible. It wouldn't look religious; it might even look pornographic."

"No one has to be trained to look at pictures," Belk said.

"Of course they do. Some people can't distinguish between the Venus de Milo and a magazine centerfold. They can't differentiate between Ho Chi Minh and Mahatma Gandhi. Hell, some of them can't tell the news from the ads. They not only think there's wire around the bakery, they not only think what they saw was the real picture, they think it was the whole picture."

Belk refilled their glasses. "It was the true picture," he said.

"What are you going to show them after Vietnam? They're going to be hooked on violence. Gratuitous violence where we can thrill and cheer without pain or guilt."

"Peace don't photograph," Belk said. "Happiness I leave to the wedding photographers. If people want blood, we give them blood. I've shot some pretty sick stuff but the people determine the news they get and television hath made voyeurs of us all."

"I thought news was what people needed to know, not what people wanted to know."

"That may be true but it won't sell soap, celebrities or politicians. It won't tell people how to be glamorous, popular, or how to be mothers or lovers. What tells you how you're supposed to look, to act, who you are supposed to be? Not who tells you, but what. We decide what's real, what's good, what's true. You're an agnostic, Sherrill."

"Doesn't it bother you that Lincoln couldn't be a politician,

Kafka couldn't be a celebrity, Jesus couldn't be a star?"

"No one has to study by firelight any more. And television has told that story better and to more people than Lincoln ever did."

Lives had become so banal, purposes so ignoble that it was necessary to trivialize heroes in order to understand them. "Didn't Lincoln give us more than a story?"

"What?" Belk asked.

"Don't we need Lincoln to help us understand who we are and what we can be? Don't we need Abraham, and Moses, and—and Tolstoy? Not just their stories but who they were? Aren't we creating a movie view of how to act? Dignity is Henry Fonda in *The Grapes of Wrath*, courage is Robert Taylor on Bataan, patriotism is Jimmy Stewart going to Washington. There are noble things in each of us, monstrous things, that we don't dream we're capable of because we don't have any insight into ourselves. All we have are good guys who never fear or doubt and who don't need Greek mythology, or the Bible or Shakespeare to tell them who they are."

Sherrill told Belk about his second book, about a cowboy who shot his wife acting in accordance with reality as it had been presented to him.

"It was true if he believed it," Belk said.

"He has to believe it, even when he knows it's not true, because not to believe is to admit that he is evil or insane. Don't you understand? What we have to fear is illusion. The politician or entertainer who convinces us that everything is great, that lies are truth, that we're the only moral people, and that everything that opposes us is evil."

"Television has done a damn good job of showing what a horrible, evil thing this war is."

"Then why do people watch? Do they like horrible, evil things or have you turned war into entertainment?" The real evil was believing that everything could be shown in pictures and understood by emotion. They didn't show what happened to men's minds, what happened to women and children far from the fighting. "You don't show the children."

"War is entertainment. Don't you go to the movies? Don't you watch TV? Don't you fucking read books? Entertainment, diversion is where it's at. Life is so fucking empty that everybody wants to escape and they pay millions to be distracted. We're in the hottest business going."

"There's a difference between using the war to inform, for moral instruction, than in using war to titillate. That's as obscene as using sex to titillate."

"I'm not a fucking preacher or professor; I'm a newsman. Information doesn't sell soap. Titillation does and you can use it to sell anything."

"Even more sex and violence?"

"Anything." Belk shook his head with disgust. "How long are you going to play the country-bumpkin bit? No one is going to accept you like that after they see the footage I got. You're going to look like a phony."

"You really think I'm going to be on television?"

"The play we get depends on what else happened. If the President hit someone with a golf ball—Norela's doing your story, the wire services covered it so the network will have to give you some time."

"I talked to that guy in the delta. He didn't want me to do a story on him because it could get him killed, but he talked to you."

"No offense, Sherrill, but what could you offer him? I said, 'If you died tomorrow, how do you want to be remembered?' He said, 'Someone at peace with the world.' I made him somebody to millions of people. That's what I'm telling you. Get your face right because tomorrow you're going to be a whole different person, the hero of hairy-armed America."

"Hero?" He had always wanted to be a hero to Jennifer. He had envied laborers, like ancient hunters, going home at the end of the day with money in their hand, money for food and maybe trinkets for the wife and children. His check went directly to the bank and after classes he went home to his office where he worked on a book until dinner. Even the publication of his books had been no more than a pocket on the fabric of a life without style or show.

"Better than a hero, a celebrity, because when you're a celebrity they love you for who you are. 'Chase them into Cambodia, bomb Hanoi.' If the cameras hadn't been there that little skirmish wouldn't even be reported but it's going to make headlines. It's even bigger because you're not a soldier and you're wearing those funny looking shoes. You caught the glare and you had your lines ready."

"I didn't say chase them into Cambodia and bomb Hanoi."

"I got it on film. 'Give you boots and a rifle.' That'll stick in their minds. But you dug yourself a deep groove when you called the reporters cowards and said the military was more reliable."

When did he say that? Reporters cowards? Military more reliable? "I was talking about combat; the military was safer to be with."

"What the world is going to hear is that the military is more reliable than the media. Hey, the reporters understand; you got your gig, they got theirs. A lot of people will agree with you and those are the ones who'll love you. A lot of people will disagree and those are the ones who'll hate you but as long as the spotlight is on you everything you do will be interesting. You better hope you don't have anything to hide because nothing is as interesting to the media as a media celebrity."

Thank God he hadn't touched that girl, but if he had she wouldn't have known it was abuse; it was her lot in life.

"I don't have anything to hide. Unless it was something else I said."

"You struck your pose and REAL is going to love it. But you've got to get rid of 'brave but naive.'"

He had been scared but he had also felt relief. There had

been a giant boil inside him and it had erupted, leaving him weak but clean.

"You are courageous because of your convictions. Give you boots and a rifle and you'll chase them into Cambodia. You'll kill them to save them. 'Hot damn, I'm Sherrill O'Connell and I have no fear or doubts.' It'll fly."

"I have doubts."

"Not any more. It's not the face I would have picked but it's the one you got. Get it on straight and decide what you're going to do with it."

Sherrill came from a time and place where character was formed by the sun and wind, by season and circumstance, not by images on a screen. "I'm not going to do anything with it. It's not me."

"It's going to be you, the only you anyone knows. You can go almost anyplace you want to go, even the network maybe, but you can't go back."

Sherrill thought it funny that Belk's idea of the top was the network. He knew he shouldn't listen. "I want to be myself."

"You can be yourself when you're by yourself. I've been a celebrity and I've been nobody. Celebrity is better but you can't go back to who you were when you didn't have an image and nobody cared about your opinion. You're a celebrity because you're here and you're kicking ass. Get three or four stories that confirm your image, the kind of stories your readers want, and you can go home. But the attention span of America is short. Once you walk out of the scene you're out of their mind."

If he was going to be in the news, if he had their attention he had to do something useful with it. Maybe he could help this country. Maybe if people listened to him he could do something for the children. Get the attention of his readers by writing what they wanted, then direct their attention to the plight of the women, the children, the crippled veterans. He could rewrite the earlier stories, make them appealing to

REAL, and to Si and his friends. Make the heroes bigger and simpler. He could write the story of the shootout at the LZ, and the Support story in Da Nang, the job the men there were doing hauling supplies. "They want me to do a story on Support in Da Nang but I don't know how much of a story there is."

"Dammit, Sherrill, don't you get it? You're the story. People will read what you ate for breakfast, about the wet dream you had last night. You can sell a hundred stories. People will listen as long as they hear what they want to hear—how you kicked Charlie's ass."

Like other professors he was familiar with adopting moral postures in the classroom, accustomed to taking stances. He could do it for REAL. That's what Stone had been telling him. He was aware that he had dropped his glass but didn't bother picking it up.

"We're talking Big, talk show Big."

Talk shows, and he didn't have a book in print. "Do you think I could get my books back in print?"

"You can sell toothpaste. You can run for office. The spotlight's on ye, me boy. You can sell anything, but you can't be dull and you can't change your mind. You were pretty outrageous out there and you're going to have to keep on being outrageous. You can't start looking tentative or confused. You can't be shy. You've got the magic for the moment so everybody's going to be shooting at you, but that's okay because it keeps you in the limelight. Just hold your pose, damn the torpedoes, and you'll be okay."

Yesterday he had been defeated. REAL had rejected his stories. Harry Tompkins had involved him in a world he didn't want to know. He had almost been killed, and then something good, something unbelievably good had happened. He might go home to talk shows, to books in print. For a moment Sherrill caught a glimpse of himself as one of those whom the world applauded.

Quang Tri

They called themselves "The Wild Bunch" and that was what they had painted on the side of their truck, but they looked more like neighborhood punks, the kind that hung around pool halls and terrorized Boy Scouts and the fathers of teenage girls. They were uneducated, undisciplined, unclean. Worse than unclean, they seemed to glory in their torn and greasy fatigues, longer than regulation hair and grimy faces.

Two of them were in uniform because they had chosen the Army over jail. None was smart enough to be a conscientious objector or enterprising enough to go to Canada. None had rejected the Establishment because they had never been established. That, like college deferment, was for those who wore rags as a fad and pretended to be disfranchised.

They were numbered among those who fought for their country; patriots who defied authority, defaced whatever was of value to others and despised whatever was foreign to their miasmic mentality; soldiers who made their peers not only anti-war but anti-military. The Army, pacifists said, had made them animals.

Sherrill did not like them, not even the young black lieutenant who had been the only one to greet him when he climbed over the bullet-scarred armor plating into the back of the guntruck. It was a regular deuce-and-a-half fitted with armor-plated sides and armed with two M60 machine guns, two 50-caliber machine guns and an M79 grenade launcher. The crew did not even look at him but sprawled on the floor amid cartridges, ammo links, empty beer cans and half empty cans of C-rations, the contents spoiling in the warm afternoon drizzle. They had spent the morning escorting empty trucks from Phu Bai to Da Nang and were waiting for the trucks to be loaded for the return trip.

"You'll have to excuse our appearance," the black lieutenant said. He was religious, devoted to his mother, and wanted to be an aerospace engineer. He had joined the Army to help with their fleet of airplanes, but the Army did not need black engineers. They needed small, cheerful black lieutenants and placed him on the guntruck with the churlish white crew.

"We lost our driver yesterday," the lieutenant said as though that explained everything. The driver had been killed in an ambush in the Hai Van pass and his blood stained the windshield, stuck to the steering wheel, ran in dust lined ribbons across the seat, hung in blackening beads from the panel, and dried in a puddle on the floor. The crew had not bothered to clean up after him, choosing instead to mount the second 50 caliber machine gun. They believed in fifties the way they had once believed in sex, Harleys, and rock and roll.

"Nobody fucks with me when I got a fifty," rasped Dillman. Large and dark with thick eyebrows and a knife-scarred face, Dillman looked like what he was, member of a motorcycle gang who had chosen the Army over charges of rape and sodomy. In yesterday's ambush he had burned out the barrel on an M60. Today he had the rear fifty and a bad look in his eye. He did not want to be fucked with.

It had seemed an easy story to write that morning in the major's air-conditioned office in Da Nang. Setting up a chart against the wall of the hootch, the major, who had the bulbous head and the grave manner of a political science professor, had talked of the fight that was never reported, the battle of Support Command against the elements—the war with mud, dust, primitive roads, floods, and unrelenting heat.

"Why isn't it reported?"

"Not glamorous enough," the major said, frowning a little in genial disapproval that Sherrill's question interrupted his practiced lecture. "Just men doing their jobs."

That was the story Sherrill was after and he jotted notes as the major flipped through his chart calling off the numbers from memory—75 tons of meat, 29,000 dozen eggs, 34,000 gallons of milk, 30 tons of bread, 610 tons of ice for the food and milk and to keep the scout dogs cool, 510,000 pounds of laundry, and a classified amount of POL, ammo, and equipment.

"The men of Support Command drive a half million miles a month over the worst roads in the world and because of them the men at the fire bases have one hot meal every day. That's our mandate. One hot meal every day. And all the ammunition they need," he added, tapping a sign on the wall behind his desk. "A soldier can live years without sex, days without food, hours without water, but not one minute without ammunition," the sign read.

It had sounded heroic to Sherrill, even noble, toiling up and down the hills through heat and ambush, carrying the hope and promise of the free world to desperate, embattled men. He felt a little noble for writing about them and their trip up a stretch of highway the French had called "The Street Without Joy." He had already chosen his title. "With the Wild Bunch Up the Street Without Joy."

That had been at Support Command. At the Convoy Assembly Area was the dirty, scarred truck, the surly crew, and a sign that read, "If You Can't Truck It, Fuck It." What was the Army doing to him? REAL had no black readers, black advertisers or, Sherrill suspected, black employees. They were not interested in black officers. They wanted blue collar heroes, not this fucked up crew.

The convoy pulled out of the assembly area—twenty trucks and tankers and two bobtails. "Once we get into the Hai Van we can't stop," said the lieutenant who had radio contact with the trucks, and—when the gods of war smiled—with artillery and air support. "Going up, the bobtails are at the rear and if a truck gets overheated or has trouble pulling the grade a bobtail gets in behind and pushes. Going down, the bobtails are in front so if a truck burns out its brakes a bobtail can get in front and slow it down. On that road if you miss a curve you're in the shit."

After a short ride the convoy stopped at Red Beach to see if all trucks were operating properly. Mamasans swarmed over the trucks selling soft drinks, beer and souvenirs. Dillman put his thick hand in the face of a young girl and shoved her off the truck. "Charlie's early warning system," he called her. "She wanted to see how many guns we were carrying. The others are finding out what the trucks are hauling."

The drivers reported they were ready, although one of them wanted a bobtail behind him from the start, and the convoy pulled on to QL 1 and rumbled through the world's stinkingest garbage dump at the end of the Nam O bridge. Deadpan picked up the half-empty C-ration cans and threw them at the children who prowled the dump. Sherrill wondered if Deadpan acted out of contempt or compassion but Deadpan's face expressed nothing. It was a skill he had mastered.

"Fuck," said Dillman as he looked up at the mist-shrouded pass. "No air cover today. You can't see thirty meters in that shit."

"Nothing personal," Deadpan said. Deadpan had learned

to distinguish between affront and misfortune.

Machlin looked up, his sun-damaged face seeking light like a radar disk. He examined his face with his fingers, scratching at blackheads. Stubby chewed what remained of the nails on short stubby fingers that looked chewed on as well.

"That's the pucker factor," the lieutenant said cheerfully. "Only one road north from Da Nang and that's through the Hai Van. Six and a half miles up, six and a half miles down. They say it takes an hour and a half under the best conditions. I've never seen the best conditions."

The trucks whined past an old stone fort, surrounded by a second generation of concrete pillboxes, surrounded by a third generation of sandbagged bunkers that guarded the entrance to the pass with redundant inertia.

Behind the laboring trucks that belched and farted their way up the steep grade was a long line of motorcycles, cars, buses, and lightly loaded trucks. Until traffic from the opposite direction forced it over, the guntruck straddled the highway to keep civilian traffic out of the convoy.

"Scooter slime," Dillman snarled at a Vietnamese who was maneuvering his Honda bike behind the truck. "Pedal pussy." Dillman believed in Harleys. Hondas were for social workers and other queers.

When the cyclist tried to whip around the truck, the lieutenant tapped him on the head with a stick to dissuade him. "Nobody gets in the convoy today," he said.

Whenever shooting started, the civilians abandoned their vehicles leaving a roadblock of cars, buses, and cycles scattered over the highway. The convoy had to keep moving or be chopped to pieces. The guntruck's mission was to rush to the spot of the ambush and draw enemy fire to allow the trucks to escape. Abandoned vehicles were as dangerous as mines on the narrow, clif-edged road.

In yesterday's ambush, in addition to suppressing enemy fire the guntruck had to push abandoned cars off the road to clear a path for the transport trucks. "Our driver is exposed up there—no armor plating," the lieutenant said. "When the shooting starts, he's got to get us in position and get under the truck. Yesterday he couldn't because he had to clear the road for the convoy. If I had kept the traffic out of the convoy he might still be alive."

The lieutenant's fine, handsome face turned hard for a moment. "He'd been with us a long time." He swallowed with difficulty, looked at O'Connell and the cheerful face returned. "Ain't nothing but milk been down my throat since yesterday; that's all I can swallow."

A Citroen sped past the guntruck and the lieutenant radioed the trucks ahead to run it off the road. A fat American civilian in a Hawaiian shirt and a government Ford repeatedly tried to pass the guntruck until Dillman jerked the bolt handle on the rear fifty, cocking and loading it, and took aim at the front of the car. The car skidded to a stop, the driver throwing up a hand.

Despite the tension in the truck, Sherrill was taken with the beauty of the highway, with splashes of ocean occasionally visible from a sharp curve, rocks jutting through the dripping green foliage, waterfalls splashing through rocky gorges, Buddhist shrines, rain soaked ARVN watchtowers, bullet-scarred rocks from God knew what war, and above them clouds shrouding the mountain tops.

"They got the train," Stubby said with a whoop as though it were a personal triumph. Far below, between the second and third tunnels, boxcars lay torn and tangled by a mine. Despite the distance, Sherrill could imagine the pain and panic of those trapped and crushed in the wreckage. "They blow it up once a week," Stubby said, puffing out his fat cheeks.

Stubby was short and thick, almost gnomelike with a mouth scarred by a harelip operation. Sherrill believed he was below Army standards for stature and I.Q. He was equally repulsed by Stubby's appearance and his delight in destruction.

"Test fire your guns," the lieutenant said as the convoy began to disappear in the mist. "Let Charlie know what we got for him." The two fifties responded with an ear-splitting burst. "This is where we got hit yesterday," he said when the shooting stopped. Sherrill was the only one who looked at the gouged-up road.

There was gunfire ahead of them and the driver pulled the truck around the convoy, racing up the road, slamming on his brakes when the road disappeared in the mist, finding it again, racing, braking, cutting sharply, whipping around trucks and buses that appeared suddenly out of the mist. Sherrill was thrown from side to side but the men hung onto the guns and suddenly both fifties cut loose, followed by the M60s, and the lieutenant firing the grenade launcher into the misty hillside.

The firing went on and on, the noise of the guns isolating Sherrill from every sensation except sound, as though no one could bleed or die until the noise stopped. The last truck of the convoy passed, the guntruck began moving again, and the guns stopped. Sherrill's ears rang. He could smell the bitter stench of cordite and taste the sourness of his mouth.

"There ain't no losers here," Stubby said, blowing out his cheeks.

"They were too high to see us," the lieutenant said. "They were firing at the sound, hoping to get lucky. They got quotas; at the end of the month they'll shoot at anything."

"Fucking amateurs," Dillman snarled, his face contorted with rage at the thought of being killed by a random bullet.

"Nothing personal," Deadpan said.

Through the mist emerged the stark, ghostly outline of an ARVN firebase that marked the summit, and the heavy rumble of the trucks turned to the high-pitched scream of geared-down transmissions as they began their way down from the pass. "We're through the worst of it," Lt. Wright said. "When we hit the Lang Co bridge we're home free."

"Where's your camera?" asked Machlin, the sun worshiper.

His face was as dry and pitted as an attic football, and his hair that had been bleached by sun, surf, and lemon juice, was now dirty and matted. Two narks had talked him into enlisting. It had taken them almost six hours. Machlin wasn't quick but he was stubborn.

Machlin had been shot at for the first time in yesterday's ambush and had hugged the floor behind the armor plating. Today he was prepared and he had gotten his first shot at the enemy. Tomorrow he planned to have his own fifty. "You should have gotten a picture of me smoking Charlie."

The camera, still encased, hung from Sherrill's neck. He took the camera when he went to the field but he usually took pictures as an afterthought. The camera forced him to decide what he wanted to say before he wrote the story. He wanted his senses to be the film, to record the sights, sounds, smells, so that he could develop them in the darkroom of his mind—washing, fixing, reducing, enlarging those images to life. He took out the camera and snapped pictures of the truck, the crew, the highway, and put it back in the case, out of the way.

"Hey, I wasn't even scared," Machlin said. "Was you scared?" he asked Stubby.

"I never go through the Hai Van that my asshole don't chew the seat out of my drawers," Stubby said.

Number Two truck reported that its brakes were overheating and asked for a bobtail. Because of the clouds, the bobtails had not overtaken the convoy. Number Two truck was overtaking Number One and pulling the whole string down the pass. "Slow it down, slow it down," the lieutenant yelled at the drivers.

The bobtail trying to overtake Number Two truck missed a curve and overturned. "Is he over the cliff," the lieutenant yelled into the radio. "Is the road clear?" The guntruck pulled around the convoy, forced a Renault off the road and raced to the accident.

The bobtail was on its side, steam escaping from the

radiator. The front wheels dangled off the cliff, but the road was clear. The driver lay on his back beside the truck with a bad case of the shakes. The lieutenant yelled him into the cab, then the guntruck took off in pursuit of runaway Number Two.

Twice more the lieutenant warned the drivers the convoy was going too fast. When the guntruck swung around the last curve across the inlet from An Cu and rolled out onto the flatlands, they saw Number Two truck a hundred yards off the road, buried to the top of its wheels in a rice paddy. The driver sat atop the Sea-Land van waving peace signs with both hands.

REAL would like that bit of heroism. The driver had chosen to risk his life rather than race out of control through the village that spilled carts, dogs, pigs, bicycles and children onto the narrow highway. His decision failed to win the approval of the guncrew.

"I'd have run through the fucking middle of the ville," Dillman said.

"They'll strip the truck, steal the cargo and engine, and we'll have to pay for damage to the rice paddy," Deadpan said.

"Damn straight. We come over here to save their country and have to buy it a pig at a time," Machlin said.

"Makes my butt want to dip snuff," said Stubby.

The truck turned onto the Lang Co bridge and, except for Dillman, the gunners collapsed on the floor. The black lieutenant smiled cheerfully. "Ours not to give a fuck," he said. "Ours but to dodge and duck."

Sherrill smelled Phu Bai before he saw it. It was the single characteristic of Phu Bai—the stench of burning shit, collected in oil and set afire. Sherrill reached for his notebook, struck with the metaphor of the fires burning day and night like some existentialist gehenna.

At Phu Bai the gunners waited in the rain to be released to their area at Gia Le. Instead they were ordered to stand by an ammo truck that had broken down outside Camp Eagle and been left by the rest of the convoy. The driver was hiding in a cemetery beside the road, cradling an M16. He made no effort to mask his relief at their arrival. He and Little Man crawled under the truck to see if they could get it moving, eager to get behind the wire at Phu Bai before dark.

There was a village a short distance away and the ground rose all around them. It was not a good place to wait. Dillman held his gun on the village, Deadpan watched a ravine that ran close to the road, and Machlin and Stubby covered the high ground on either side. While they waited they talked of love.

"This chick is always trying to get me to marry her," Machlin said. "I kept saying, wait until you start showing. She had a miscarriage every month and came running to me that she'd lost our baby because it made her nervous not to be married. Now she writes she's going to marry some asshole and give him my baby unless I write her that I definitely am going to marry her. I told the bitch to wait until she started showing."

"I was hit by a car, beat with a chain, cut in the face, stabbed in the gut, drowning in my own blood," Dillman said, "And my old lady is squatting over me and saying, 'Speak to me, you bastard. Tell me you love me and I'll call an ambulance.' I hit her in the fucking face."

"When she told me she was pregnant, I kicked her ass out," Deadpan said. "'That's your problem,' I said. 'If you're that forgetful then hit the road, bitch.' She cut her fucking wrists to prove she wasn't careless, so I married her."

"The reason I don't like to go in women's rest rooms is because you have to sit down," Stubby said. He sometimes slipped into women's rooms to masturbate to the sound of urination, but preferred lying in bed and listening to the voice of the woman who gave the time and temperature, timing his orgasm for the words, "the temperature is. . ." Stubby had never had a woman, but Little Man had promised to get him laid on R&R.

"What about you, lieutenant?" Stubby asked, puffing out his cheeks to make himself childlike and inoffensive. "Do you have a girl?"

"I plan to screw around until I finish my education."

"What do you need an education for? You plan to be a preacher?" Dillman asked.

"Something like that."

Black plus education equaled preacher. It was something they could understand.

The hills were getting dark; the truck wasn't ready to roll, and the good moment was past. They fidgeted around the guns. "How about you?" Stubby asked Sherrill.

Sherrill took out pictures of Jennifer and Marie and dutifully passed them around. The men took a quick look and said, "Nice. . .Cute kid. . .What kind of car is that?"

"How old is she?" Stubby asked, taking one last look at Marie.

Sherrill did not want to discuss Marie with anyone on the truck. "Thirteen," he said. She would always be thirteen.

"Too young for me," Stubby chuckled, bobbing his head up and down.

They lapsed into silence again as a light rain began to fall. Little Man climbed into the back of the truck with something in his hand and sat down to work on it. None of the gunners turned to look, but to Sherrill's inexperienced eyes it looked like he was wiring something. "We're going to be here all fucking night," Dillman said.

"If it can be fixed Little Man can fix it," the lieutenant assured the crew about their new driver.

Sherrill wasn't reassured. Little Man looked more like something found in an alley than a garage. His narrow eyes were red and puffy with mucous in the corners. His pimpled face appeared not to have been washed within memory, and thin, white, old woman hairs shone on his chin.

While he worked, Little Man, who had scarcely met the

gunners, put their minds to rest. He had skipped his high school shop class to attend a rock concert. For three days he lay on the ground accepting the sun, rain, music, girls, boys and drugs that came to him. A job also came to him, wiring and repairing speakers, amplifiers and lighting equipment, and carrying bags for a band looking for a break.

The job was a dream. He was fed, loved, beaten, robbed, drugged, raped, arrested. He woke up in a van, culvert, jail, girl, hospital. He had hepatitis, gonorrhea, anemia, depression, and a draft notice. The draft notice was a surprise.

It wasn't that he was opposed to the war, he explained to the draft board, that was another world, man. They not only didn't hear him, they didn't see him. He was fucking invisible. The Army did see him. They saw him as a truck driver.

When it got too dark for Little Man's experienced fingers, Lt. Wright held a light for him, trying to mask it with his body. It was another hour before they got the ammo truck running. With the guntruck in the lead, they started for Camp Eagle only to run into a barbed wire barricade across the road. "Move the fucking wire," the lieutenant yelled at the ARVN bunker guarding the road. No one came out. "Drive through it," he ordered. The men kept their guns on the bunker until the ammo truck was clear and then they barreled down the road, driving through the next barricade without slowing down.

"Hey, our protector's back," a beefy, red-faced officer said as the lieutenant led Sherrill into his hootch. The reference was not to the lieutenant's assignment on the guntruck but to his color. Some black troops were hostile to white officers. "I tell everybody there's a brother living in this hootch. They won't frag it as long as he's here. If they transfer him, I'm going over the wire," the beefy officer said to Sherrill.

Lt. Wright pointed out a cot with a stained mattress and an oily blanket. Sherrill took off his boots and flak jacket, and lay down in his clothes. They were wet but they were cleaner than the bed. He read a sign tacked on the wall. "In the event of a heavy weapons attack on this compound, bend over and kiss your ass goodbye."

"They found a grenade pin wired to their door with a note that said, 'This time I got the grenade, you got the pin; next time I get the pin,'" the beefy officer was saying.

"Some fucking reporter wrote there was nothing the Army could do because they can't trace a grenade," said a thin, gloomy man with big glasses and ears. He looked like the kind of man who looked over his shoulder and pissed on his feet. "I can't believe a man would write that even if it's true. You goddamn reporters are declaring open season on lifers and officers."

"This reporter is with me," the lieutenant said. "Don't lay nothing on him."

"Hell, he ain't no brother, he's white like me."

"You ain't white, you gray like a rat. Now get your rat ass out of my face."

The two white officers left and the lieutenant brought over a bottle of Wild Turkey, poured some in a cup and handed it to Sherrill. The lieutenant drank his in milk. Now that he was free of the truck he seemed to lapse into black dialect. "Those men in the truck, they scared. They so scared they ready to shoot each other. That's why I walk light, because they just dumb. But I ain't taking no shit off no officer. They s'posed to be my equal."

Sherrill sipped the whiskey and felt the day's tension drain out of him. "Help yourself to the bottle. I got to write my fiancee," he said, pointing at the portrait of a black woman with big eyes and resolute mouth. "I don't say nothing to the men because I don't want them jacking off with her picture in their mind."

Wright walked away leaving Sherrill to think of Stubby looking at the picture of Marie. The idea troubled him. He thought of giving Cassady a child, or stepchild, the daughter of one of those who died, an older Marie discovering her sexuality and her helplessness to prevent boys from writing things about her on restroom walls, of visualizing her in disgusting, often violent fantasies, of using her name and image in their self indulgence. How could he explain to her that it was all right?

"Boys are flesh, girls are blood," I told her. "Someday those looks and thoughts will seem charming and together you and some boy will grow a heart and that heart will make you flesh and blood." She didn't understand and her eyes, still shadowed by hurt, were also bewildered.

He turned his thoughts to the story he was after. He hoped Belk was right, that he was the story. Except for the driver who ran his truck into a paddy to avoid hitting someone in the ville all he had was a long ride in the rain; okay for National Geographic maybe but not for REAL. Belk had also told him to ride big convoys on main roads where they could get air cover fast and to stay until someone was killed. When he looked up he saw that Lt. Wright was watching him.

"Gonna ride tomorrow?"

"I'll ride for a while." Sherrill had an unpleasant picture of himself riding up and down the Hai Van waiting for someone to die.

The lieutenant had seen it too. "I don't wish you no bad luck but I hope you got to ride longer than I do."

Sherrill stumbled over the rain-sodden ground, tripping over piss tubes and stepping in puddles of water, following the lieutenant to the guntruck. It was raining and the darkness was accentuated by the distant rim of floodlights around the perimeter. The crew sprawled in the back of the truck, wet and miserable in the rain. They had not showered, or been to bed, or eaten, but they had mounted a third fifty on the truck.

"Where's Dillman?" Lt. Wright asked.

"He ain't going," Deadpan said.

Wright dropped lightly to the ground and Sherrill climbed out of the truck and followed him to Dillman's hootch. The hootch was crowded with bunks, dirty clothes, muddy military gear, and shiny stereos. It smelled like early morning in an all-night movie.

"Time to go," the lieutenant said to Dillman who was lying in an upper bunk.

Dillman was facing the wall. "I ain't going," he said.

"This reporter and I are going," the lieutenant said to warn Dillman that his action was subject to interpretation by the press. "What are your bike buddies going to think if they read you were afraid to go?"

"I'm short."

"We're going to the DMZ; we need a good man on the gun."

"I'm too short to go to the DMZ."

"Your buddies are depending on you. Don't that mean nothing to you?"

"Fuck 'em, I ain't going."

"I'm asking one last trip."

"You're too late. I already made my last trip."

"You're asking for a courtmartial, soldier."

"What are you going to do, send me to Vietnam?"

"I'm ordering you on that truck."

Dillman rolled over. He had a .45 in his hand and it was pointed at the lieutenant's head. "I ain't going," he said.

"Go get in the truck," Wright said to Sherrill without taking his eyes off Dillman.

No one seemed surprised or curious when Sherrill climbed back in the truck by himself. "I hope he comes," Stubby said. "I feel safer with him on the gun."

"What are they going to offer him, a medal?" Deadpan asked. "When I'm that short I'm going to hide until time to get on the bird."

"If he ain't going, I ain't going," said Stubby.

"Me neither," said Machlin. "Did you look at the armor plating? A hundred and forty rounds hit the truck in the ambush and most of it was around Dillman's gun. I ain't going with no new guy."

They fell silent when they heard footsteps in the mud. Dillman and the lieutenant climbed into the truck. Dillman lay down with his face to the steel wall. The lieutenant sat cross legged on the floor and explained their job. Firebase Alpha was in need of ammunition and repair for one of its guns. Air supply was ruled out because of cloud cover. The last two convoys had been unable to reach the firebase, the first because the trucks had bogged down on the steep, muddy road. The second had turned back when the lead guntruck had hit a mine and the rear guntruck had been hit by an RPG. Only the firebase's guns and the arrival of Cobra gunships had saved the convoy from destruction. It had taken two hours to turn the trucks around on the muddy, narrow road. A new convoy was being formed in Quang Tri, the trucks lightly loaded and escorted by four guntrucks. The Wild Bunch, the fourth guntruck, would join the convoy at Dong Ha.

"I been to Alpha," Little Man said. "I was hauling eight-inch shells and just as I got to the crest of this hill the wheels started to spin, and she went over backwards. The shells flattened the cab, and when I come to I heard this officer saying, 'Forget the driver; it'd take a mighty little man to get out of there alive.'"

While the guntruck raced up QL 1 over the River of Perfumes at Hue, past the old blockhouse on the Song Bo, the sand marshes at Phong Dien and Hai Lang, and around Quang Tri, Stubby talked about the third fifty. "Machlin deserved it more. He's a better shot."

"You been here longer," Machlin said. "You got to respect yourself. How you gonna show?"

"How can I respect myself; I volunteered for this shit," Stubby said, his head bobbing as he chuckled. "Everybody thought I was a fuck up but I thought I could come over here and prove different."

"Have you?" Sherrill asked.

"When we was ambushed I stood up as long as anybody. These are the best men I've ever known and I stood up as long as they did."

Deadpan talked about going home on R&R. "Everything was just like I left it. Cigarettes and change on the dresser. My good pair of trousers over a chair. Bitch is slow getting around to things."

Machlin talked about childhood memories. "That was my first birthday. Dad put me on his shoulders and let me ride his surfboard. I got my first board when I was six and paddled it out and turned around to smile and a wave swamped me."

"How can you remember all that shit?" Stubby asked.

"My momma took home movies of everything. My first birthday, my first step, my first dance. I don't have any memories, I got home movies of everything. When I think back all I see is movies."

Dillman said nothing but lay facing the armor plating. When Sherrill got the chance he asked Wright how he convinced Dillman to go. "I told him we were going to Alpha." Sherrill looked at him without comprehension. "They got their shit wired at Alpha."

"You offered him drugs?"

"I didn't offer him nothing except a chance to get killed. I told him where we're going, that's all."

"Don't you think there's a better way to lead these men?"

"You think I should have appealed to his patriotism? He was drafted because his patriotic fellow citizens wanted him off the street. You think he wants to give his life for his country? His idea of a hero is a biker who uses chicks like you use rubbers, takes shit off no one, especially cops and do-gooders like yourself, and dreams of ripping off the system.

"Maybe I should have asked him to do it for his family. He

stabbed his father, broke his mother's jaw and molested his sister. Where do you think you are, Harvard? Boys from Harvard don't die for their country. Boys from Harvard get rich for their country. If he wants to stay high from the time we get back to Phu Bai until they shovel him on the Freedom Bird, that's his lookout."

"Don't you care what happens to him when he gets home?"

"Man, I am thinking about today. I need his white ass to cover my black ass. And so do you and so does every man in this convoy. They give me shit like him to do a job with and if I don't do it right they send my ass home in a body bag. Do you think anybody would cry? My mama would cry. My woman would cry. My country would say, one less dude on welfare and all them pacifists would say, serves him right, over there killing poor, down-trodden people. This is the fucking Nam. I don't have the luxury to worry about him when he gets home. I'll leave that to the folks that sent him here."

The convoy was lined up along the road outside of Dong Ha, just north of the Song Do Dieu. An armored car with THE ASSASSIN painted on its side was to lead the way. In the rear was a half-track mounting fifties and a recoilless rifle. THE COPULATION CULMINATION was lettered on the hood. Three quarters of the way back was a guntruck marked LI'L SURE SHOT.

A black captain standing in the turret of the armored car waved THE WILD BUNCH into its slot. "Lieutenant, in the event of a breakdown behind you, your truck will be rearguard of the lead element," the captain said. He was a big, deep throated man with a bald head and a full moustache. "There will be no turning back and no stopping without direct orders from me. Disabled trucks will be left on the road. We are the lifeline for those men up there. They are counting on us and we will get through."

Sherrill thought it was a rousing speech but the gunners

had either heard it before or did not hear it at all. Sherrill noticed that they were all standing by their guns, even Dillman, but the convoy waited. Then roaring and clanking, an ARVN armored column of tanks and APCs rumbled across the road and into the hills. The lieutenant thought they were a diversionary action to draw the VC off the road.

"They know a fight's coming and they're getting out of the way," Deadpan said. "If they wanted to help us, they'd send those tanks up the road ahead of us."

"Hey, you got another one of those?" Machlin asked as Dillman lighted a cigarette.

"I ain't giving nothing away as long as I'm breathing," Dillman said. "When I'm dead you can have them."

The convoy rolled smoothly along the highway and turned off on a muddy track. Immediately the trucks began to wallow. For the next hour no one spoke except to mutter "Jesus" in reverence, amazement, or disgust as the heavy trucks strained up the steep grades, slithered around curves and went sliding, careening, at the limits of control, down the retrograde.

"Jesus God," Deadpan said as the truck ahead, loaded with black powder, almost turned over slipping into the water-filled crater that marked the spot where the last convoy had ended. Belching and roaring the truck slowly righted itself before losing momentum and sliding backwards. Little Man backed the guntruck out of the way until the driver got the powder truck under control and continued forward, coaxing the slipping, spinning wheels up the grade.

"We're making two miles an hour," Lt. Wright said. "Still got eight miles to go; four more hours."

The trucks ahead reported they had been fired on and the guntruck hurried to cover them. "There it is," the lieutenant yelled as they came around a curve. Dillman and Deadpan took turns firing at a spot just below the crest of a brush-studded hill. Sherrill could see nothing but puffs of dust and the glow of tracers, but the two gunners took turns firing at the area until Li'l Sure Shot came into sight.

"Mark it for them and let's go," the lieutenant yelled and Deadpan fired one long, final burst. For the next hour the guntruck slowly overtook the transport trucks to regain its position in the convoy. There were explosions ahead and heavy firing. "They hit the front of the convoy," the lieutenant said. "Automatic weapons and RPGs. One truck knocked out. About forty NVA. Estimate eight killed. They think Charlie is hauling ass."

It took the guntruck half an hour to reach the site of the attack. The damaged truck was skewed half off the road, its cargo scattered, the chassis warped as though a giant fist had hit it, doubling it on itself, twisting the front end off the ground. The engine cover had been blown off, the windshield smashed, the radiator riddled. The headlights dangled from cords like eyeballs from empty sockets.

Beside the truck lay the driver. Something had torn away half his skull, so that his brains oozed into the mud; his shoulder had been torn away and his arm lay twisted and bleeding across his back. There were other bodies, enemy bodies, shockingly close to the road. When Sherrill remembered his camera it was too late.

Above, Sherrill could see the scarred hill that offered sanctuary behind its wire, bunkers, big guns. He sighed in relief when they rolled through the wire gate that was guarded on one side by a tank and on the other by THE ASSASSIN. He expected some kind of reception, cheers of greeting, flag waving; they had gotten through. The men at the firebase seemed oblivious to their deliverance. The only ones in sight were in the gun pits, beginning a desultory fire at some distant target.

"Get those machine guns on the perimeter," the captain yelled. "We're too good a target for Charlie to pass up."

Little Man backed the truck into position along the wire. The firebase was uglier and drearier than Sherrill had imagined; squat, sandbagged bunkers huddling in the red mud behind a thicket of barbed wire, elongated gun barrels poking out of stark holes in the ground. Sherrill took a note for his book—Cassady coming ashore in Korea, expecting to be greeted as a deliverer and finding instead angry officers, officious clerks, confusing orders, and an indifferent populace.

He was too jittery to write more and the guncrew seemed as uneasy as he. Getting the trucks in and unloaded was taking too long. "Let's get the fuck out of here," Dillman said.

"Damn straight," Deadpan said. They looked ready to start shooting each other.

"Hey, we got it light," the lieutenant said cheerfully. "The halftrack is still out there."

The radio brought the news that the halftrack was under attack, one gunner dead, and The Wild Bunch was ordered to its support. The captain stopped them at the perimeter gate and they waited, not knowing for what, having no control over going or staying, unable to abandon hope, not knowing what to hope for. Waiting at the gate was worse than waiting on the perimeter. "Why don't they send the fucking tank?" Machlin asked.

"Charlie skyed," the captain said, "but standby, they may be hit again."

Sherrill lighted a cigarette and knew when he inhaled that he was chain smoking. Then he saw the bobtail dragging the smashed truck, and behind it the halftrack. Across the hood of THE COPULATION CULMINATION lay the dead truck driver, his blood cooking over the hot engine. Over the armor plating and into the cab hung the dead gunner.

Dutifully Sherrill got out his camera to record the halftrack as it clawed through the mud, the gunners crouching over their guns. Seeing him the men began mugging and striking poses, smiling, waving guns or peace signs, leaving the dead men cruelly exposed.

"Fucking vulture," Dillman said.

"You queer for corpses?" Machlin asked.

"Nothing personal," Deadpan said. "We die, they buy, you fly."

"Listen up," the captain yelled. "We're not going back to Quang Tri until the trucks are unloaded, so let's move it. We're a fucking big target up here. That's North Vietnam you're looking at and they've got enough guns and rockets to turn this hill into a hole."

The gunners and drivers joined the men of the firebase in unloading the trucks; the artillerymen stacking the supplies where they needed them, the men from the convoy dumping materials on the ground in their frenzy to get the trucks cleared.

Sherrill asked a man called "Tex" where he was from only to learn he was not from Texas. "His mama named him Spade for some movie cowboy," a friend explained. "But every time I yelled, 'Hey, Spade,' about ten blacks turned and gave me that dead motherfucker look, so I call him Tex."

One of the drivers recognized a friend at the firebase. "Hey, Dizzy," he yelled. "It's me, Bugs."

"I ain't Dizzy."

"Bugs, from Washington High. Don't you remember?"

"Bugs is back in the world. Bugs sleeps in a bed. Bugs went to college; he don't have to worry about no draft. Bugs is a fucking honky."

"Dizzy."

"I ain't Dizzy and you ain't Bugs. Bugs got a car and a girl, and they go to football games and shit. They laughing at us. They saying they gonna get all the girls and all the jobs so when we get back we can shine their white ass."

"Dizzy, I enlisted."

"My name is Mossul El Saad, motherfucker. Call me Dizzy again and you cacadow."

As soon as the trucks were cleared, the drivers went to the

mess bunker to eat the roast beef and mashed potatoes they had brought from Quang Tri. The Wild Bunch was the last to be released. Sherrill quietly joined them. They lined up in a cloud of warm humidity as suffocating as dust. It enveloped Sherrill, clung to him, saturated his clothing, beaded his face, but when he sucked it into his lungs it gave no life.

A huge black soldier looked at Sherrill in open contempt, then slung a dollop of mashed potatoes at his serving tray. The potatoes remained glued to the spoon. With a sneer, he took one thick black finger and raked the potatoes into Sherrill's tray.

The next man slapped roast beef half on, half off the tray, spattering him with grease. Sherrill looked at Dillman, but Dillman did not even look at the man serving him. "More," he snarled, as though it were his last meal, and received another helping of potatoes and contempt.

The black captain stepped on a table and called for silence. "I just want to say to all of you—those in Support and those on the hill—that we lost two good men getting you a hot meal and ammunition. They were our friends and they died doing their job. I want to assure the men of this firebase that Support will continue to do its job. We intend to see that you get everything you need to protect your lives and accomplish your mission. Charlie can't frighten you off this hill and he can't frighten us off that road. Keep up the good work."

Sherrill thought it was a moving speech but no one else had stopped eating. The captain was scarcely outside when a white sergeant yelled, "Eat this shit and get the fuck out of this bunker. A direct hit would kill everybody in here." He received the same attention as the captain.

When they walked out of the bunker Deadpan was the first to notice. "Some of the trucks are gone," he said.

Lt. Wright confirmed it. Two trucks needed work before they could make the return trip, two trucks were not yet unloaded and the maintenance van would have to stay behind until the gun was repaired. The Wild Bunch had been left behind to escort them off the hill the next day. "Nothing I could do," the lieutenant said and walked quickly away.

The Wild Bunch screamed obscenities. They swore to kill the captain. Deadpan stood, hands in pockets, trying to decide if it were personal. Machlin beat Stubby on the chest and arms. Dillman kicked apart a crate of C-rations and stomped the contents into the ground. Their anger amused some black gunners. Angered even more, The Wild Bunch responded with racial insults. The lieutenant appeared from nowhere and imposed himself between them.

Sherrill left to explore the firebase. There was a network of trenches, squat bunkers sinking into the mud, and rows and tangles of barbed wire laced with trip flares, claymores, mines, and scraps of tattered cloth marking the spot where an enemy had died.

Craters ringed the firebase, most of them fresh and half-filled with water. Beyond the wire in all directions were ridges and misty mountain tops. To Sherrill they had a beauty that concealed their terror.

"Incoming," someone yelled and Sherrill ran to the closest bunker, slipped around the blast screen in front of the opening, and dived head first into another screen inside. There was an explosion, followed by two more, and Sherrill crawled around the screen and into the blackness.

"Move and you're a dead motherfucker," a voice said.

"Bao chi," Sherrill said. "REAL Magazine."

There was a silence. "You a reporter? Don't move," the man said, striking a match and lighting a candle.

Sherrill regretted the light once he had it. An M16 was pointed at his face and less than two feet away lay a huge coiled snake. A large, middle-aged man came from behind a waist-high wall of sandbags and talking gently, slipped both arms around the snake and picked it up. "Python," he said. "Sixteen feet. He ain't full grown yet but he scares the shit out of people.

Keeps the rats out too."

There was a whistling, shrieking, and an explosion close enough to shake dirt out of the sandbags and fill the inside of the bunker with choking dust. "They usually come in threes. Better get over here." For the first time Sherrill noticed the man wore six stripes.

Sherrill slid around the inside barrier of sandbags as two more rockets landed. "Stay down," the sergeant said. There was a rustling outside the bunker, followed by the thump of something on the floor, then a grenade exploded between the outside and inside sandbags.

The concussion was tremendous and for a moment Sherrill could hear nothing, could scarcely breathe because of the dust and smoke. "Missed me, fuck head," the sergeant yelled. "I'd rather die than let them draftee shits know they got me scared. They roll a grenade in every time we have incoming. One time they pushed in a claymore but I cut the wire. They can't figure out what kind of defenses I got in here and they're afraid to come in and look because of the snake."

Sherrill had been so frightened by the rockets and the grenade that he had forgotten about the snake in the darkness with him. When the sergeant found the candle and relighted it, Sherrill saw there were cartons of C-rations, cans of water, and a trench behind the line of sandbags. At one end of the trench was a hole used as a toilet.

"Eighteen days and a wakeup," the sergeant said. "They'll have to take me off this hill three or four days before I DEROS. Hell, I could last a month if I had to. They won't get me. I don't know what I'll do about Mopey. I can't take him with me and if I leave him here they'll kill him. They hate the snake."

"Why are they trying to kill you?"

"They don't like the way I give orders, like they're slaves and have to do what I tell them. They want to be asked to do things. I give orders to everybody the same way and I take orders from anybody that's got more stripes than I got. I don't know no other way to be."

The sergeant looked forlorn. The darkness, the dampness, the fetid air was suffocating Sherrill. The snake began sliding off the sergeant's shoulders, muscling its way between Sherrill's legs and gliding into the trench. For sixteen feet. "The shelling seems to have stopped," he said. He could feel the snake moving in the bottom of the trench. "I better go."

"Do what you want but the shelling never stops and it's still light out there. Some people will shoot at anything that moves around this bunker."

As if in prophecy the shrieking began again and Sherrill ducked, afraid to drop into the trench with the snake. "Some things are given to you, some you have to learn. That one is going to miss," the sergeant said as a corner of the bunker caved in with a tremendous impact and a flash of light.

Sherrill wondered if his eyes were open or shut, if the flash had been in his eyes or only his brain, if he were buried alive or suffocating in dust. He couldn't think, couldn't move. His ears rang, his head throbbed as though someone had hit him in the nose. He tasted blood in his mouth, felt something moving beneath him. He thought it might be his arms or legs twisted beneath him and moving involuntarily. It was the snake.

". . .disposable bazooka. A LAAW. I got perforated steel plates between the sandbags, like they use for landing strips. It'll stop a grenade but I don't know if PSP will stop a LAAW."

"Die, motherfucker," someone yelled.

"I'm still here, capon cadet. Come and get me."

Sherrill had a bad moment waiting for another LAAW to demolish the rest of the bunker. Staying was worse than leaving. Better to die in the open. He tried to get up but couldn't find his hands or feet.

"Everybody up here is a little crazy," the sergeant explained. "You can't take normal, healthy men at their sexual prime, put them on a hill for six or seven months with nothing to do and not have trouble. The guy next to you snores or licks his fingers. It gets to eating on you, only you're afraid to say anything because everybody up here is edgy and armed. So you grit your teeth and take it until something snaps."

Sherrill's senses slowly returned. The ringing in his ears became a dull roar, the throbbing in his head an echo. Bloody mud bubbled from his nose. He tried to get up but everywhere he put his hands was on a snake.

". . .went around whistling until he ran into a rifle barrel and knocked out his front teeth. Another guy got to reading his Bible. Every time you looked at him he was reading his Bible—eating, taking a crap, brushing his fucking teeth. If you spoke to him he read you a scripture. One night somebody wrapped the Bible around a grenade and threw it in the wire. He grabbed a '16 and was going to waste every atheist up here. You never saw so many foxhole conversions. I found a Bible and I went out reading the Psalms as loud as I could. I traded him the Bible for the rifle. I don't know whose Bible it was but nobody asked for it back. And not one officer said, 'thank you, sergeant,' or 'good job, sarge.' They won't back me up. They had rather pretend everything is okay."

Sherrill found the top edge of the trench and trying not to excite the snake, slowly pulled himself up.

". . .if we've had a real attack or if the whole hill just blows up and starts shooting at once. We let off a lot of pressure, make a lot of noise. Breaks the monotony. Sometimes we take casualties. Mostly lifers; mostly grenades. Sometimes we find dead Charlies in the wire."

Sherrill pulled himself up until he was on the edge of the trench, his feet on the opposite edge, the snake in the darkness beneath him. "I hope you starve to death, you fucking lifer," someone screamed.

"Come and get me, taffy ass." The sergeant's words were drowned in the blast of a grenade.

Sherrill waited to be certain a second grenade did not follow, waited for some instinct, some intuition to tell him it was a good time to move. He was bunching up to spring when the sergeant grabbed his collar.

"I always knew I might die in this uniform and I thought it would be an honor." The sergeant shook Sherrill gently by the collar. "I don't want my wife and little girl to know my men are trying to kill me. You copy that? My little girl thinks I'm a hero and nobody is going to tell her I was killed by the uniform I serve. If you write that, I'll waste you. I don't care how far or how long I have to look."

With that he gave Sherrill a shove and with the assist Sherrill sprang across the bunker and ducked into the darkness. He was running full speed when he fell into a hole. He lay in the mud for a minute catching his breath, laughing with relief at being alive and in the open.

A flare popped beyond the wire and he looked over the edge of the hole trying to orient himself. There were bunkers everywhere; he didn't know where the guntruck should be. He saw something move. The flare went out and there was nothing but darkness and green spots. He hugged the mud, frozen with fear.

A mortar tube popped, followed by a rustling, then another flare ignited over the wire in a different part of the perimeter, throwing different shadows. There was something moving. A flag. Outside one of the bunkers a Confederate flag slowly moved in the slight breeze.

When the flare died, Sherrill took a deep breath and forced himself to move. He had taken a half dozen steps when he saw a body, the blood still oozing, guts crawling on the ground. He forced himself to walk toward the body. It was sandbags, torn open by a shell, spilling clods that turned into mud. A tatter of plastic glistened like a dying eye.

He tried to regain control of his imagination. When he looked again he saw a barbecue grill, golf club, bean bag chair.

He forced himself to touch the grill. It was hot and he could see live coals beneath a layer of ash. Beside it was a tub of ice. He ran his fingers over the golf club. He dipped his fingers into the icy water and brought up a can of beer. Someone had been having a backyard barbecue. He huddled in the mud clutching the beanbag chair, no longer certain of his senses.

The guttural moan was like a reprieve and he ran for the nearest bunker and dived into it as a section of the perimeter exploded, mixing mud and wire with shrapnel. When he allowed himself to breathe, to think, he heard others talking.

"Hey man, how does your mind feel?"

"It swims, man. It fucking swims. Like flies in the sea."

"Wow, man."

"No shit."

"Hey man, it's like wow, man. I mean it's fucking all, man. It's just totally fucking wow. A total reference, you dig? I mean, I got total. . .it's. . .it just fucking is."

"Yeah, man, yeah."

"I see Jesus."

"Wow."

"I see France."

"Oh man."

"I see Charlie's underpants."

There was a high-pitched cry that turned out to be giggling, and then one of the men started shooting at the sandbagged roof. Sherrill flattened himself and crawled outside, around the bunker, crawling through mud, slime, something that smelled like rotting oranges.

Seeing the guntruck in the light of a flare was like seeing the Statue of Liberty, the Golden Gate Bridge. If he could just cross that open stretch of ground and crawl under the guntruck he would be safe. He was almost there when the whole top of the hill seemed to explode. He jumped into the nearest bunker in a storm of smoke and steel.

"Find another hole, we're full."

"You're on my fucking foot."

"Shut the fuck up, I'm trying to sleep."

Sherrill collapsed on the damp floor in relief. He had found The Wild Bunch.

The earth convulsed. Sherrill covered his head with his hands and gave himself up to the shuddering roar, hoping only to endure. There were explosions within explosions. The earth seemed to dance beneath him, to coil and rebound and pound him until he could scarcely hang on to it.

When he thought he had reached the limits of his endurance there was a resounding shock and concussion that snapped his jaws together and left him limp. "Satchel charge," Dillman yelled as small arms fire broke out close by. Sherrill tried to get out of the way as the others tripped, shoved, and fell out of the bunker. Lt. Wright was already in the truck. "Sappers in the wire," he yelled.

The machine guns were firing when Sherrill climbed into the truck. He covered his ears with his hands and ducked low, trying to see what was going on. Flares, gunflashes, streams of tracers, blossoms of white phosphorous. The tank that had been guarding the gate rumbled behind them, moving to another position. The truck shook under the pounding of the heavy machine guns.

Sherrill crouched behind the armor plating, in the way but not as frightened as when alone. Little Man maneuvered the truck over the torn ground, around craters and bunkers, into position for the guns to cover a hole that had been blasted in the wire. Something struck the truck. Machlin recoiled, the gun swung around and Sherrill grabbed the barrel, searing his hand. He fell to the floor of the truck and curled around his wound, shutting out the noise, the danger, absorbed in the stinging pain. It sounded as though the firebase was being overrun, the machine guns in continuous firing. Absorbed in his pain, he did not care. He wanted them to notice his suffering.

The shooting stopped suddenly as if by mutual agreement. Sherrill began to hear other noises—shuffling, sobbing, moaning, cries for a medic, friend, God. Sound was muffled as though through water. Machlin dropped heavily to the floor of the truck, barely missing his puffing hand. "Jesus," Machlin said.

"Everybody okay?" the lieutenant asked.

"I burned my hand," Sherrill said with mingled embarrassment and relief. He looked up at them, grateful for their concern.

"How the fuck did you do that?" Wright asked, like he was addressing a willful and careless child. With disgust he examined the blisters rising on Sherrill's palm. "Somebody's got to take this reporter to the aid station," he said. There were no volunteers. "Machlin."

"I got to check the head space on this gun. Charlie may be back."

"Dillman."

"I ain't going."

"Fuck it, I'll go," Deadpan said.

Sherrill had to be helped out of the truck because of his useless hand. "Thanks," he said when he was on the ground, but when he looked up there was no one there. "It's been good knowing you guys," he said. No one answered. "Good luck to you."

Deadpan insisted on leading him by the sleeve of his jacket over the torn ground littered with broken bunkers and tangled wire. Smoke clung to the ground and stung his nostrils. He noticed another smell. The cooks had been preparing breakfast in the mess bunker, ignoring the fight.

At the aid station an annoyed sergeant took his name and zap number. When he turned to say goodbye, Deadpan was gone. A medic sprayed his hand, wrapped it in gauze and left him to wait for daylight and a medevac with the other wounded, most of them dopey with morphine and shock. They mumbled and groaned. One of them thrashed about on the cot he was tied to while an orderly cursed and wrestled with him. One man babbled, "in the wire, in the wire." Another said, "Wow, man, a total reference."

Sherrill avoided looking at the dead enemy. He hoped someone would ask what had happened to him. He lay awake listening to the roaring in his ears.

Morning was filled with fog, mist, cloud, rain. Sherrill thought the medevac would not come, but it found the hill and Sherrill was lifted aboard with the more seriously wounded. No one from the guntruck came to see him off.

The doctor was irritated at having to spend his morning treating enlisted men. He was young, incisive and he believed their wounds were caused by carelessness and stupidity. He also believed he should receive combat pay. "I see more dead and wounded than any ten grunts," he said as he hacked the dead skin off Sherrill's hand. Although in a war zone, the doctor had more amenities and physical comforts than half his countrymen in their own homes. Having voiced his complaint to Sherrill he lost interest in him. "Here, clean this up," he said to a nurse as though Sherrill's hand was a mess and the nurse was a chamber maid.

"Abandon all pretense ye who enter here," the nurse mocked, but her touch was gentle. She had soft dark hair, soft brown eyes. He wondered if she were beautiful or if it had been that long since he had seen a Caucasian woman. "You're the guy who saved everyone's life at LZ O'Connell."

"I'm a reporter," he said.

"It's just an adventure with you, isn't it? Running around, shooting at people, getting hurt, posing for pictures."

"It's not an adventure," he snapped. "I'm trying. . ." What was he trying to do? It had seemed so clear when he left home. "I'm trying to help."

After the nurse had finished with his hand, he was met by

a press officer who brought him a clean set of fatigues, a blanket and a towel, and took him to the transient barracks—a metal roofed, sandbagged hootch with two rows of five cots each. The hootch was empty, the mattresses folded neatly on the beds. The press officer was a slight, young lieutenant who fingered the fresh moustache that augmented his pale face. "Da Nang called yesterday to tell us that you were doing a story on Support and asked us to assist you in any way. Will you be wanting a flight to Saigon?"

The only way he wanted to see Saigon again was from the runway at Tan Son Nhut. "I'll be working here for a while. And I want to see the general." He had been shot at, he had maybe killed someone, he had come closer than he had imagined possible to indecency with a child, he had been accused of adventurism by a nurse, and he didn't like the stories the Army was giving him. Being here had subjected him to those things and he was by god going to get the kind of stories REAL wanted.

"I don't know if the general. . ."

"You tell the fucking general I want to see him."

"Yes sir." The lieutenant almost saluted. "I called Saigon and asked them to send a roundup of stories about you."

"About me?"

"About the firefight at LZ O'Connell. With luck they'll be on the afternoon plane. They're also forwarding your mail. This is all I have at the moment on last night's action," the lieutenant said. He handed Sherrill the morning MAC-V release with a brief summary of the fight at the firebase. "In Quang Tri Province—During the night U.S. forces northwest of Dong Ha came under mortar, rocket and ground attack. The enemy force was repulsed with minor material damage to facilities. Result: friendly (US) eight wounded. Enemy: eight KIA by body count."

The lieutenant left. There were no sheets and no pillows, but with his good hand, Sherrill unrolled a mattress and stretched out. "Minor material damage. Eight WIA." The words were empty. How could they convey what he had experienced in four lines or forty? When he closed his eyes he saw a steep muddy road that twisted and turned, with dread around every curve. He was awakened by the lieutenant standing at the foot of the cot.

"Here are the stories," the lieutenant said, fingering his unaccustomed moustache. "After you've read them, come over to the O club and I'll buy you a drink. The general will try to see you tomorrow."

"Any mail?"

"No sir, not on this plane."

Sherrill nodded, still groggy from having slept most of the day. He looked at the copied pages. There was a straightforward wire service report that mentioned the presence of Belk's television crew and illustrated the surprise attack by emphasizing that "one of the reporters, Sherrill O'Connell of REAL magazine, was wearing civilian shoes."

A sidebar story said that when rescue came, O'Connell was the only one firing. "I had to take the rifle away from him," a soldier was reported as saying. "He was still trying to kill gooks." "At least one dead Viet Cong was in front of O'Connell's position. Both rescuers and survivors credit O'Connell with saving the small force. They quickly dubbed the tiny landing zone 'LZ O'Connell.'"

He read the story again, wondering how the story would have been handled if he had been wearing field clothes like the others.

There was a photograph of him sitting on the ground, his helmeted head bowed between his shoes. "Newsman ponders civilian shoes," the cutline said. Sherrill did not know when the picture was taken but he knew how he had felt—devoid of feeling, empty of thought, spent beyond words to tell. Another story had the same photograph with the cutline, "Give him boots and he'll chase VC into Cambodia."

There was what purported to be an interview that Harry Tompkins had sent to several papers including the one in Sherrill's home town. Harry described Sherrill sitting in a Tu Do bar, still shaken from the firefight at the LZ, and pieced together an interview from remembered conversations.

"O'Connell is tall, lanky, with pale blue eyes beneath a receding hair line. If you forget the grass-stained Jungle Jim suit that he imagines to be the uniform for war correspondents and his now famous Thom McAn shoes you may be able to imagine the Texas cowboy he claims to have been." Sherrill did not own a safari suit or Thom McAn shoes. He had been a Texas cowboy but nothing like the image those words brought to mind. "He's a long way from the bunkhouse now, and his back slapping, death-daring rowdiness is appreciated only by the military and jingoistic REAL magazine."

Tompkins called Jennifer "Janine," credited Sherrill with having written only one book and wrote that Sherrill had quit teaching to write "How I Zapped the Cong" stories for REAL and to research a novel about a man with a death wish who went to Vietnam and became a hero instead. Sherrill hoped Harry's misrepresentation would discredit Harry and his story in the eyes of those who knew him but as a writer he knew both the power and the weakness of the printed word. He feared that some who knew better would believe Harry's fabrication, or believe both the truth and the fabrication. As for those who did not know him, the false portrait would be all they would ever know of him.

Sherrill was quoted as being fed up with students "whining over their misfortunes of stupid parents, fertile girlfriends and unfair grades." He had told Harry that his biggest surprise in Vietnam was the ability of teenage soldiers to perform difficult, even hazardous duties under adverse conditions. He was familiar with students who wrote, "God, how could you let me go to bed with that bastard" in their journals, missed classes because they overslept and exams because they had hangovers. It had been an incidental remark, not an opinion he would have made in public.

"O'Connell admits to no plans for researching his book other than getting shot at, yet denies he is attempting to act out the life of his fictional hero. There is no point in asking what LZ O'Connell was really like and whether he enjoyed killing a Commie; we'll have to wait for the novel for that. What we can ask is whether O'Connell is in Vietnam to research a book or to publicize himself."

The entire paragraph was nothing but a shoddy device to cover up the fact that there had been no interview. Sherrill wished he had punched Tompkins when he had the chance. He wasn't acting out the life of his fictional hero but the reverse, as any novelist would know. His fictional hero was acting out his life, or at least his questions about life.

Si Hardeman wrote of the dangers and rigors he had faced in order to bring accuracy and authenticity to his novel about "a dove who finds love even in war-torn Vietnam. . .We had talked of danger, Sherrill O'Connell and I," he wrote. "Neither of us had realized it was so close." Hardeman deliberately created the impression he too had been there.

Si described buying presents for their daughters before "being heli-choppered into combat. I suggested one of the colorful, hand-made headbands for O'Connell's hippie daughter who is not entirely sympathetic to her father's adventures in Vietnam. In one of her letters she wrote, 'Daddy, please come home soon. And please don't hurt the children.'"

Sherrill was filled with rage. To use him was one thing, but to use Marie, to use his dead daughter. Of course it was his own stupid fault for lying about Marie in the first place.

Si's second column, a description of the exotic night life of Saigon, contained the line, "We sampled the fleshpots of Tu Do, Sherrill O'Connell and I. How are they going to get O'Connell back on the campus now that he's seen Nhanh Le?" Nhanh Le, a combination of North and South Vietnamese words for fast, was used by some Saigon types to mean "fast life," but many readers would think it a bordello or a woman's name.

He knew Jennifer would be pained by the mention of Marie. She would be angry that he had discussed Marie with someone like Si and confused that he had not told Si that Marie was dead. She would be puzzled by the reference to Nhanh Le.

Norela Cook's column appeared to be written for Hollywood with the dashing hero saving the daring heroine, only this misguided hero rescued a heroine (herself) who had intended capture by the courageous enemy to write their side of the story. Norela quoted him as advocating invading Cambodia and bombing Hanoi, and wrote that he had aligned himself with the military in its war against the "subversive" press. However, she paid tribute to his courage and sincerity.

Sherrill wondered if Lindly and his other colleagues would believe that he had saved the LZ. He feared they would think him an attention seeking opportunist. Except Jennifer. Jennifer would never believe he had done something foolhardy or crass.

Sherrill lay back on the cot and tried to sort out his feelings. He was amazed that he had received so much attention. No one had ever listened to him before but everyone heard what he had babbled at the LZ. Belk had it on film. MAC-V summarized the incident in one line; the media had given it coverage only because some of them were there and nothing else had happened that day. His impulsive actions and thoughtless exclamations represented him in a way his lectures and books never would.

How had it happened? Stupidly he had let Harry involve him in the misery of a family, but he had done what he could for them before escaping and thank God he had not touched the girl. At the LZ he had fought out of fear and, he confessed, nameless rage. Whatever he said had been under the duress of the moment; surely that would be considered. With The Wild Bunch he had done his job as a reporter and had burned his hand by accident. He had done nothing to be ashamed of. He had not sought publicity, but now, as Belk said, he had to use what he had to get what he wanted.

The first thing was to write the LZ story and of The Wild Bunch. After that he should rewrite the earlier stories that REAL had rejected. Maybe Stone would take them after the publicity, particularly if he centered the story around himself. With one or two new stories, he might get enough attention to get his books back in print, maybe enough to get on a talk show. That should guarantee a contract for the next book.

He wanted to be recognized for his books rather than the other way around and he was dismayed with the inaccuracy of what had been written, but he liked being important enough to be noticed. He felt bigger and smaller at the same time. Outside was this bigger-than-life performer but inside he had lost something of himself, some depth, some sanctity. Something about his civilian clothes, his shoes, had captured their imagination. He was distressed that attention was something he could not earn but must be bestowed, like talent, like beauty, like fame, but he had it and he had to use it until it vanished as capriciously as it had come. Then he could go back to the world, back to being himself.

The Army had furnished him with a desk and typewriter but the typewriter was useless because of his burned hand. He would have to write longhand and get someone to type it for him. He spent the first couple of hours trying to explain why Vietnam was not the way it looked in pictures—men shooting, women crying, children screaming, hootches burning—because the moment, the event was personal, narrow, circumscribed. He hadn't seen guns, helicopters, fire. That was some other war. He had seen dirt kicked up, blood spraying, eyes dying, a hand clutching nothing, a fresh young face behind a bush that exploded, branches and leaves blowing into the air, a sandaled foot quivering. There had not been one LZ shootout but eight, ten, however many men had been there. They were all different. None of them looked like the evening news.

He wrestled with the almost irresistible urge to cover his private terrors from curious eyes. He struggled with a story that had no beginning, no end, no middle but was all moment. By morning all he had were impressions.

"I was never at LZ O'Connell," he wrote. "At least not the one you may have read about or seen on television. LZ O'Connell does not exist on any map, it is not a place or a time. LZ O'Connell is a memory—green, hot, sudden, alien.

"Hot with the sweltering humidity that smothered me in my own juices. I wiped water from my face while my mouth turned to powder. Green like no green I've seen before. Shade upon shade, layer upon layer of green. The sky, where it could be seen, was green. The water was green, the uniforms green. What was not green was red—the water, the leaves, the uniforms, first with dust, later with blood.

"Sudden like death is sudden. Death that leaves you numb, breathless, incurious, certain only that the world is not the same. Alien the way a bullet is alien, a wound, a photograph of yourself as a happy child. Extrinsic, inconsonant, discrepant. It can never be part of your life, yet you can never be free of it.

"It did not happen the way you imagine it. It did not happen the way I remember it. Memory does not spill like blood. Does not smell like dust and sweat. Does not taste like fear. Does not feel heavy, hot, sticky, wet. Does not sound like animals squealing, panting in fear, groaning, crying in anguish. Memory is a reluctant messenger, slowly revealing things, speeding over some, skirting others. Sometimes I think it did not happen at all, an impression that stands without reference. Yet four men have ceased to be."

As directly as he could, he told what he thought had happened. Caught in the violence and terror of the moment, he had picked up a rifle and had fired into the bush to save himself. In his excitement he had not wanted the attackers to escape. He wrote nothing of pursuing them into Cambodia or chasing them back to Hanoi. He ended the story with a tribute to the men who had been killed or wounded fighting beside him.

He liked to put a story aside for several days before rewriting it but there was no time for that. He would have to rewrite it while it was being typed. It depressed him to read what he had written. He had not captured the moment at all. He had written a calm, reasonable and dispassionate account of chaos, insanity, bedlam.

He could ask for a clerk-typist but he was sensitive about weighing nuances and mouthing words for their texture and coloration in the presence of some thick-fingered soldier. He would have to type it himself. He went to the hospital and found the nurse who had treated his hand. "I need something for my hand," he said. "I have to type a story."

"I can't do anything for your hand but I can type," she said.

She came to his hootch and typed, waiting patiently when he wavered for long minutes between one word and another, retyping pages without complaint when he felt compelled to redo them for minor alterations. When he finished he had no idea if the story was good or even coherent. He felt he had chopped huge blocks of words out of himself and hastily pasted them together without time to heal. He felt raw and wounded.

"It's beautiful," the nurse said. He looked at her, wanting to believe her but afraid to. "You're so different in your writing than you are in person, so much more sensitive and kind. You shouldn't be afraid to let people see it."

"People see what they want to see."

"Stop looking so determined to save the world," she said. "I wasn't going to like you until I saw how lonely and unhappy you are. I thought you were another one of those people who has never done anything and wants to be admired for it. I gave up magazines because ninety percent of the content is information I don't want to know about people I can't stand. I think if Hitler were alive he would be the most celebrated person in the world. Magazine covers, talk shows. He would be repentant, admit that he went too far but his intention was honorable; he was just poorly advised. He would tour the colleges and Hollywood would make a movie showing him holding hands with Eva Braun and saying, 'Where did I go wrong?'"

Sherrill laughed with her and they exchanged stories of how those who tried to discover new worlds, new cures, new ways of thinking and seeing and hearing were ignored while magazines honored those who trivialized emotion, ambition and suffering, and television spent millions of dollars declaring that the most important thing that had happened in the world was the discovery of a new and improved soap.

Sherrill thanked her for her help. "I enjoyed it," she said. "It makes me feel that I'm a part of something, not just patching up people so they can die somewhere else."

"I'll buy you dinner."

"There's no place to go. Besides, when was the last time you got a good night's sleep?"

Sherrill was too tired to remember. He closed his eyes and was instantly asleep. He was awakened by his throbbing hand. He had rolled over on it. When he sat up, he saw the nurse was there, smelling faintly of freshly ironed linen. He decided she was pretty. Dark hair, dark eyes, dark complexion that was earthy but not coarse.

"I brought you something to eat," she said. "You may forget someone who stops you from bleeding to death but you never forget someone who feeds you."

"You're right," he said. "Everyone remembers their mother."

It was several days before he saw the general. An officious major with a fat face, bulging eyes and the flush of high blood pressure, smoothed down Sherrill's hair, adjusted his clothes, knocked on a door and opened it. "Sherrill O'Connell, sir, " he said.

Sherrill started into the room when the general froze him with a glance. The general was a big man, the kind of big man who smoked a big cigar that he pointed like a pistol, who carried his size like an additional star, who intended to be in charge of the interview. "Sit down," he said, pointing the cigar "Glad to see a reporter from REAL. Damn fine magazine. You may not know it but I'm a stockholder in REAL because REAL has writers like you."

Writers like Sherrill were America's only defense against the deception industry that was trying to get the U.S. to desert Vietnam. The military had been given a mission to bear any burden, meet any hardship, support any friend, oppose any enemy in the name of liberty, but the politicians thought they could kill Diem, interfere in the politics of the country, send boys and PXs over here and then say we were just kidding.

"The real war is the one you are fighting back home. We can win this war; we just have to stay the course. We have to give the Vietnamese time to find a leader they like and trust and will follow."

"Do they have anyone like that?"

"We'll find one for them. The main thing is to get the media behind us. What would have happened if the press had turned on their military after Bataan and Corregidor? They're trying to convince the American public that this is an immoral war."

"I thought all war was immoral."

"It is. Like cancer. You have to go in there and clean it out. You were right on target—chase them all the way to Hanoi."

"I'm not sure about chasing them to Hanoi."

"That's the fast way. The slow way is letting them hide out in their sanctuaries until we can lure them out and kill them. That exposes our men to unnecessary risks. I can show you camps on the border. . ."

"General, I was at a firebase on the DMZ and some of those men are trying to kill their sergeant."

The general shook his head. "Too many boys are hiding out in college, coddled by the very people who are supposed to be teaching history, values, things like that. The ones we get know they're here because they don't have the money for college, lawyers or Canada. Naturally they're unhappy that they're separated from their friends and loved ones and risk death and injury while the rich kids are having the time of their lives. They don't have anyone to take it out on but us and the pinko press treats them like heroes if they turn on their superiors. But fraggings are greatly exaggerated."

"I talked to him. I was in his bunker when it was attacked."

The general made a note. "I hope you got a hell of a story for REAL. I consider Fred Stone a personal friend."

"Frankly, they weren't the kind of heroes REAL is looking for."

"You want heroes, I'll get you heroes. And I'll show you how the politicians and pinko reporters make it possible for Charlie to hide in sanctuaries beneath our very noses." The general stood, shook hands with Sherrill and the interview was over.

His mail caught up with him bringing two letters from Jennifer. "I am miserable without you and I don't know who I am any more. I was taught to believe that being a wife and mother was everything I wanted. It was wonderful but it wasn't everything I wanted. Now it isn't even respectable and I am just another woman looking for a job."

His heart sank at that. Jennifer had worked so he could go to graduate school, worked so they could make a down payment on a house, worked until Marie was born. She had talked of working again when Marie was older but this was different. She had to get a job because he had not written a story that REAL would accept. That had changed. Didn't she know that because television was at the LZ everything had changed?

"I've changed, Sherrill, and I hope you like what you see, but either way there's no going back."

He didn't want her changing, not now when he wasn't around to see her change, to change with her. As if reading his thoughts, Jennifer wrote, "You want to change everything but you don't want anything to change." It was true he expected her to live in passive voice while he was gone but that was because there were problems at home, problems he hadn't been able to deal with before he left. They had reached the point where when Jennifer wanted to be alone she said, "I'm going to bed." He could face those problems now. He was changing too because by accident he had been made temporarily important and he wanted to solve the old problems before facing the new ones. There was something very solid in their marriage; he had always known that and time and distance proved him correct. He loved and desired her more than ever.

"Al is helping me find a job." Sherrill wondered what kind of job Lindly could find for her and when she began calling him Al.

"I hope you are having a good time," she wrote. He read the sentence again trying to hear the inflection, to imagine the expression on her face. Jennifer thought a man surrounded by his wife and children was happy, a man away from his wife was having a good time. That couldn't be what she meant unless she was referring to Si Hardeman's story about Nhanh Le. He thought the inaccuracies would cause her to dismiss the column with its reference to exotic girls. However, Jennifer had at the same time believed she couldn't trust anything Al Lindly said, and believed without question Lindly's statement that Sherrill's students fell in love with him.

The second letter appeared to be answers to questions he did not remember asking and raised more questions than it answered. "Yes, your mother is coming." When? For how long? Was she moving in as she had suggested to Sherrill? "The house is fine for now." Was she referring to the mortgage or to the paint? And how long would it be okay? "I got the pictures okay." What pictures? He hadn't sent any pictures. Had REAL sent pictures? "Dorothy is back home." Had Dorothy, Jennifer's sister, been to visit Jennifer? Had Dorothy been injured in the accident of an earlier letter?

"One morning I overslept and got dressed so fast I put on my dress without taking off my pajamas. I knew something was wrong when people stared at me." Sherrill read it again. Was she late for work? Late for a job interview? Was this at the grocery store? Was this the accident?

He looked at the postmarks but could not read the dates. The letters seemed to be written by two different women, neither of whom was the wife he left at the airport. It troubled him that Jennifer was getting vague in his mind. Her letters explaining everything were still floating around the country and he didn't know what to do with the pieces of information he had because he didn't know what the completed picture was supposed to look like.

There was a letter from his mother-in-law. His mother was cautious; his mother-in-law rash and outspoken. She too was a widow but rather than worrying about being a burden, she insisted on it. She had devoted herself to her children and she demanded the same. Usually she feigned illness—in the beginning it had been physical but as she became more sophisticated it was often anxiety or depression—pretended helplessness, and let them coddle her and arrange her affairs, with a lot of infighting about what should be done. By the time they returned to their homes they all hated her and were angry with each other but she loved it.

"Jennifer went home yesterday," his mother-in-law wrote. She had taken the wrong medicine in the wrong dosage. She was in the hospital for two days and Jennifer had stayed a week to clean her house, fill out the insurance forms and help until she could manage on her own. Sherrill had not yet received Jennifer's letter mentioning the visit but the visit must have taken place before she got a job.

His mother-in-law was going to visit Dorothy. Nothing made her happier than to be needed by her children. She thrived on family problems, listening to anyone, child, in-law, grandchild, giving sympathy and advice and doing house work and keeping children to pay for the privilege.

When Marie died, she had descended to take them to her bosom until everything was all right but Jennifer could not be comforted by becoming a child. She had to keep busy so she and her mother competed to see who would answer the telephone, greet visitors, introduce relatives to friends. When Jennifer would not accept her mother's comfort, she received her mother's abuse. "I've never seen a mother who cared so little for her child." When she had reduced Jennifer to tears, of rage more than grief, she declared it was time for everyone to leave them alone so their lives could return to normal, and led the exodus, pushing everyone before her.

"Why are you in Vietnam? I thought you had finished your book," she wrote, as though writing books was more like dying than dish washing. "If you expect a family, you'd better get yourself home."

The letter was three weeks old. He read the sentence again. Did she mean if he wanted to have a family he'd better get home and make babies? Or was she saying that if he didn't come home soon his marriage would be over? If so, why did she say "family" when she meant Jennifer?

Lindly's letter began, "No one questions your courage, not after that civil rights march we made." Sherrill, Lindly and a handful of other whites had marched with nonviolent blacks. When night approached, Lindly called a cab to take them back to the campus where they were applauded by faculty and students for their courage. He had asked Lindly if they shouldn't have stayed with the black marchers. "It's not safe,"

Lindly replied. The next day he and Lindly were pictured and quoted on the front page of the newspaper that failed to mention a single black marcher or to indicate the number who had been hospitalized with injuries received after the whites had withdrawn. "What they can't understand is your support of a racist war. The Vietnamese wouldn't know what to do with democracy if they had it. Communism is their only hope. Look what it's done for China, from a backward, starving mass into the twentieth century. You had better be damn careful about what you write.

"Jennifer is lonely and misses you more than she is admitting in her letters." It sounded as though Jennifer were writing more letters than he was getting. It also sounded as though Lindly knew what Jennifer was writing. Lindly had always been presumptuous.

There were two letters from REAL. The first was a form letter requesting a biographical sketch and a photograph so they might better promote his story. To "establish credibility" the letter recommended that he pose with leading participants and authentic backgrounds. He dropped the letter in the trash.

The other letter was written by Fred Stone. Stone had seen Belk's film of the incident at the LZ, was delighted at the publicity and was waiting for the story. "Keep yourself in the center of the story. The reader wants to know how you feel; act out his fantasies. He wants to know the kind of man you are; drop tidbits of information about your life as a college professor and a Texas cowboy. You are beginning to develop an image. We can help you shape it but you have to give us more to work with. The Thom McAn shoes gave you name recognition but it's too collegiate for extended use. Choose something consistent with your image, a rifle, grenade, and use it every chance you get. You have their attention now, they know who you are, so rub their noses in it."

He had been the center of the LZ story because he didn't

know what it was like to anyone else, but he was not going to be the center of The Wild Bunch story, and he was not going to drop bits of personal information like some rural Si Hardeman or macho Norela Cook. Stone wanted him to spend a few hours of a soldier's year and then make a breast-baring display of his courage and his anguish over the death and disfigurement of his provisional buddies. It was neither fiction nor journalism but war as talk show.

"Our next guest is Mr. Sherrill O'Connell who has been in Vietnam and is going to tell us what it's like."

"It's hot, steamy jungle, and bomb cratered countryside. Bullets tatter the air and stitch the bamboo wall behind which I crouch."

"I suppose you've seen a lot of men die."

"Yes, and I'd just like to say that I am sorry to see anyone die, no matter what color his skin. As a novelist I am more sensitive than common folk and I feel anguish deep inside, tears run down my face. You can never know the pain it costs me. But if it means killing every Communist in Asia to maintain the American Way of Life, then I say, kill them all."

APPLAUSE

"I think most Americans feel the same way. I know I do. And we'll be right back with more about suffering and dying in Vietnam after these words from our sponsor."

APPLAUSE

Sherrill wished he wrote for a magazine that was more interested in ideas than in ads. He had thought the only thing that mattered was the kind of story he wrote and the kind of reader who read it. Now he knew the magazine determined the kind of story and who read it. REAL wanted male fantasies and he would be their reporter, if need be their actor but he would not be their clown.

For several days he worked on the story of The Wild Bunch trying to decide which picture he wanted to draw. Well-fed young men driving expensive machines carrying sophisticated goods over a trash dump where the very old and very young scrambled for scraps of survival? Faith in firepower driving men to place larger and heavier guns on the truck, qualifying them for increasingly difficult and dangerous tasks? The black officer used like a vaccine to immunize a hootch against his kind? The illusion of safety represented by more sandbags, better barbed wire? Ordinary men on a mountain top trapped inside the wire with ancient crimes, isolated from each other by primeval misunderstandings, driven mad by antique fears? None of those pictures was acceptable to REAL.

This wasn't REAL's kind of war. These men might act as heroically as their fathers had done at Tarawa or Bastogne but no one was going to see it that way because it had already been decided that these men weren't fighting Evil, they were killing innocent peasants.

He wanted to portray The Wild Bunch as loyal and dutiful, doing their job without passion or conviction but doing it because it was their's to do. Where did the story begin? Almost a year earlier for Dillman and to leave that out would be to paint him a coward. Being assigned to the guncrew for the lieutenant and to understate the reasons would distort his portrait. The trip through the Hai Van was where it began for Sherrill but it was routine for the crew. The convoy to the firebase was the only part that had been reported and while he might be able to make it gallant to the folks back home to those who were there it was one more job.

He decided to write the story with all the chaos, lack of focus and tedium of the trip, but he couldn't use Lt. Wright as the hero because the only blacks mentioned in REAL were criminals and athletes who dated white women. He couldn't use Dillman because REAL wouldn't use the story if he mentioned drugs and it would probably get Lt. Wright courtmartialed.

The dead men in the convoy made the trip reportable but they also raised questions: What did they die for? and was it worth it? He had to write it so their lives did not seem a waste and he had to make their deaths significant to people who had been spectators at the slaying of a president and his assassin, and who every evening had the rubber-sheeted bodies of the dead and the cries of the wounded with their evening meal.

He worked on the story every day and when she was off-duty Kelty typed and retyped it. She had an intimate knowledge of men, and when he strayed toward the sentimental or the sensational, she set him straight.

The lieutenant brought him a roundup of stories about the firebase. "Sherrill O'Connell, novelist and adventurer, burned his hand on an overheated machine gun defending the besieged post," said one story. Sherrill feared he would be thought the source of that self-publicizing lie. He doubted that those who knew him would picture him in such Hollywood poses and those who knew anything of war or machine guns would hold him in contempt as a liar and shameless publicity seeker.

Rod Reaves wrote that Sherrill posed as a fighter but hung around Saigon "looking like a head wound wouldn't stop him and writing stories of his heroism, a subject interesting only to himself. On one of his rare excursions into the field, O'Connell was shot at and promptly claimed credit for the enemy dead." Reaves reported that at the firebase Sherrill had accidentally burned his hand while ducking for cover and had jumped into a medevac helicopter displacing the more seriously wounded.

The other stories about the firebase described desperate convoys fighting their way foot by bloody foot up perilous roads and deadly hillsides where even the elements opposed the American presence in Vietnam, to the tortured garrison where terror stalked the muddy, embattled men who had no mission, no goal but to survive. There were photographs taken from a helicopter. "The Agony of Alpha," the cutlines screamed. "U.S. soldiers Scramble for Safety." "Here Charlie Decides Who Lives and Who Dies."

The stories conveyed more terror than he had seen, yet caught none of the tedium that was more deadly than the enemy outside the wire. There was no mention of the Confederate flag, the iced beer, the sergeant hiding from his men, drugged soldiers turned on by the fireworks.

He feared how his story would look to readers who were certain they already knew what Alpha was like, who had read about it, seen the pictures and drawn conclusions. When Kelty came he was sitting on the floor of the hootch with the pages strewn around him. "I can't write the story; I don't know what it was like."

"You were there," she reminded him.

"It's already been decided what it was like. I can't contradict that." It was preposterous, yet convincing. "No one is going to believe what I write when they already think they know."

"Who do you want to believe it?"

He wanted The Wild Bunch to believe it, and he wanted the world to accept it, and Jennifer to admire him for it.

Sometimes Kelty brought food and liquor and they had a picnic in the hootch. Because there was no place else to sit, they sat on a bunk and leaned back on a rolled-up mattress. While he ate, she told him about herself. She was from a small town in the Midwest, and the day she was sixteen and was elected sweetheart of the football team, her mother had told her she had been born out of wedlock. "For a little while it had been the happiest day of my life," she said.

"My father, the only father I've ever known, with tears in his eyes begged her not to tell me. 'It's not her fault,' he said. 'She has to be told,' my mother said. Every time something good happened to me she reminded me I was illegitimate. I thought she hated me for being popular but she was afraid I would get in trouble and end up like her, married to some kind man she couldn't respect because he didn't mistreat her. That's why I became a nurse, to prove to them they were okay. Do you understand?"

He understood. She was one of those women no one took to dinner and everyone took to bed.

Sometimes he told her about his book, working out his ideas as he talked. "Everyone is from the same town except that he's from a farm outside the town so he doesn't know the personal things their families want him to tell. 'Did he say he forgave me?' 'Did he mention my daughter?' 'Did he say what I should do about his mother?' He begins to develop a mythology about the men: the brother who forgave his sister with his dying breath. The husband who accepted his wife's child as his own. The son whose last words send his mother to a nursing home. The father whose last request is that his daughter take piano lessons."

Sherrill admitted that most of it was based on his own background as a farmboy, rising early to milk the cows and feed the horses before riding the bus twelve miles to school. After school he had more chores before supper and homework.

It was a lonely life but not without pleasure. He liked being outdoors, he liked herding cattle, he liked sitting with his father, usually in the dark, listening to the radio when the chores and home work were done. He liked working alone. When he was driving the tractor or riding out to check the cattle, he dreamed. His father told him what to do and left him to do it. His mother, glad of the company, talked.

Sherrill talked of his father, a short man, shorter than his wife, a little stout, smelling of sweat—not an unpleasant smell, but the smell that came from fresh air and hard work. "He was quiet, quick, never idle, but I think he was a dreamer too. I don't know what he dreamed, but we used to stand with our arms on the top rail of the corral and look across the land. We didn't talk and both of us were seeing something no one else could see, something bigger than the farm. One time Mother stood with us without saying something needed fixing or what a lovely sunset it was. That's my favorite memory. Then he died."

At school the other students seemed embarrassed for him and the adults treated him with self-conscious respect. He was both a student and outside the school—not one of them because he did not share the bond of games, parties, class plays, yet given a certain deference because he had experiences they knew nothing about.

"That's why you want Cassady to be an outsider," Kelty said, excited at the discovery.

He told her about the class reunion he had gone to some years later, mainly to be part of something he had missed. He listened to questions: Do you remember the time? Remember the game? Remember the girl? After repeated failures to remember, someone had asked, "Are you sure you went to the same school we did?" The question was asked in jest, but Sherrill was not certain of the answer.

"I'm going to have Cassady invited to a battalion reunion. He doesn't want to go because everyone he knows is dead, but the town expects him to go and the unit expects him to come because he is one of their heroes. They say, 'Remember that hill, or town, or battle?' He doesn't remember because he was never in the hills, or towns, or battles. Just that one trip down the road. One guy says, 'I don't think you were ever in Korea.' Another says, 'Are you kidding? He knows more about Korea than anybody.' Cassady knows that both statements are equally true, and equally false."

She snuggled against him. "How did you become a writer?" she asked.

He had taken a night class at a nearby junior college. His professor told him he wrote well, a small compliment, but enough to make him discontent to spend the rest of his life on the farm. He wasn't sure what he wanted, not daring to believe he could write, but he was so restless he was steeling himself to leave his mother and his father's farm when she said, "You aren't happy here. I think it's time to sell."

His mother was proud, self-reliant, but she had been tempted by the false security of a home-bound son. They agreed that she would buy a house in town and open a gift shop and he would be given enough money for college. From that day his course had been set as a writer. Because he believed his talent ordinary, he required of himself an extraordinary devotion to writing. His only lapses had been Jennifer and Marie.

Since Marie's death he had been unable to talk about her to anyone, not even Jennifer. Especially Jennifer. But Kelty listened without trying to share his pain or to add her own.

He told Kelty about the Marie who never stood out in crowds of children the way he thought she should. The Marie who learned to ride her bicycle but couldn't stop and yelled for him to come and get her off, yet had the perseverance to win the city bike rodeo. She pinned the blue ribbon on her wall but when her teacher asked her to wear it to school for the other children to see, she lost it. He found it twice, once in a drawer. When he found it in the trash he put it in the box in his office with her first tooth, her report cards and every picture she had drawn.

He told her about the two days he and Jennifer had spent outside the intensive care ward waiting for some word from a doctor who would not answer their questions but peddled wizard machines that he had a financial interest in and consultants who were his partners. Neither Sherrill nor Jennifer ever saw the wizard machines or met the consultants but were willing victims of extortion, eager to buy any mirage. A chaplain was sent to tell them of Marie's death; the doctor was unavailable.

"A child is a blood-letting," he said. "And the wound never heals."

"Oh Sherrill," Kelty said. He was trembling with repressed rage and grief and she held him like a child, his head on her shoulder, her head against his cheek. At first he thought the tears running between their cheeks were hers. When he realized they were his he felt only surprise.

"It's all right," she said, stroking his face, kissing him, not passionately but softly on the forehead, the eyes, the lips. She covered him with her body. When his hands found her breasts she groaned.

"I'm sorry," he said, sitting up.

"It's all right."

"I'm married."

"I know," she said. For a while neither of them spoke, both thinking of words that became dead ends.

When it came to sex, Sherrill was orthodox Methodist. He had never needed or wanted anyone but Jennifer. What he felt for Kelty was lust and he would be taking advantage of her no matter what she thought.

"What's she like?" Kelty asked.

"She's a mother," he said. That's how she saw herself. She loved him, but sometimes he thought she loved being a mother more. "She's a good wife." He didn't like talking about Jennifer; it seemed a betrayal.

After that there was a restraint between them and they avoided touching or looking directly at each other. Discreetly, he watched her as he worked. She was so intent on what she did and when she read something she liked, she smiled. Yet in her smile was a hint of mockery that he took words so seriously in a world filled with fear and misery.

"I can't type if you look at me like that," she said.

"I'm sorry," he said.

"Stop saying you're sorry."

When he wrote Jennifer it was mostly about his book. "I have been unable to create the confusion of shells exploding, guns firing, men screaming, noise that more than sound is heat, pressure, pain. I need that sound to effect the stunning silence that follows when the guns stop; moans, sobs, the burning of truck tires, the dripping of fluids from men and machines, the crunch of footsteps on the road, the thump of bayonets stabbing through cloth and flesh, grating against bone. I have to create such violence and confusion that Cassady doesn't know what happened. Because he survived, he thinks perhaps he was a coward, but the military, the press, the folks back home tell him he is a hero.

"The town builds a monument bearing the names of those who died and they ask him to pose for it so that it will bear his face but not his name. I want to know if he can maintain his view of himself and what happened against prevailing opinion. Is there an 'accepted' truth that pretends to be reality, that poses as truth, against which truth cannot prevail?"

He didn't tell Jennifer he had written a scene where Cassady was taken to a hospital. His wounds were slight but he was in shock and could not stop shaking. His teeth chattered. A nurse tried to calm him, stroking his arms, bathing his face. He clung to her, pulling her close, burying his face in her breasts. He didn't tell Jennifer because he tore up the pages. It sounded like something Si Hardeman would write.

"I love seeing the way your mind works," Kelty said one day as she again retyped pages of The Wild Bunch story.

"I don't know what I would do without your help."

"Don't get carried away because I'm going to ask a favor. It's not for me, honest, it's for my folks. But if you could write a story about me to say that they're okay, that they don't have to be ashamed of me or themselves or anything they've done."

He explained that REAL did not publish stories about women, at least not her kind of woman. "I wish I could repay you."

"All day I give love," she said. "No one calls it that because it's unprofessional but that's what it is. Those men need it. They're scared. They're afraid they're going to die or lose their manhood or be so scarred not even their mothers can look at them. They hang on to me, with their hands if they have any, with their eyes if they don't. Sherrill, I'm loved out. All day I've been nurse, maid, mother, wet dream. I just want to be a woman. I want someone to look at me the way you look at me. I want someone to share with me the way you do. You don't say 'shut your mouth and open your legs.' Men say that, maybe not aloud but they say it."

He desperately wanted her and what he felt was close to love. Already, they teetered between less-than-marriage-and-more-than-friendship. To let the relationship go further would mean both less-than-marriage and less-than-friendship. In marriage, sex was a place setting; in an affair it was the centerpiece.

He thought of how urgent and pointed sex was before the act, and afterwards—not pointless, never pointless—but blunted, diffuse. Afterwards would be regret. Jennifer would never know but he would carry Kelty in his mind, something that would always be between them whether Jennifer knew or not.

He and Jennifer had reached the stage in their lives where the fires were banked and raged only when fanned by anxiety and grief, but the heat was real and in the dark nights of his life Jennifer was the fire, she was the light he wanted.

"I love my wife," he said.

"I'm not trying to take you from your wife. I just want you to love me for a little while."

He thought loving her a little while as unlikely as being dead a little while. "Does it bother you that I've known other men?" she asked. It did, not because he thought less of her or because he feared others might be better lovers but because he would be no different than other men. He and Jennifer had never known anyone else. It was the homage they paid their union. By making it special they made themselves special.

"I think I'm in love with you, Sherrill," she said.

It was his worst fear because he had her scent in his nostrils and in his dark heart he dreamed of running away with her to Bangkok. She would be a nurse, he would be a writer and the war could look after itself.

She took his free hand and ran his fingers across her lips. "Know what that is?" she asked. "The thighs of the soul."

"Thighs of the soul?" he asked, mocking her.

"Don't laugh," she said, biting and kissing his finger at the same time. She ran his fingers down her throat. "And this is the bridge to bliss." She raised his hand to her lips again and gently caught it in her teeth as a warning not to laugh. Then she led his hand over the bridge and between the two mounds. She had unbuttoned her blouse and she wore no bra. "You climb the peak and you go around and around, and it gets higher and higher, until you are at the very tip." For a while his fingers traced the tip, then she led him across the valley and up the other peak, around and around until he reached the top.

"Then you slide down the valley, down to the pool of deception. You can go around and around but you can't go deep. Then across the meadow, and through the high grass, and slide into the lake, and there, there is the little boy in the boat, and it rocks back and forth, and when you make a wave it goes up and down and up and down and down into the deep. . . "

He could feel himself sliding under, losing control. "Kelty," he said, catching her hand with his. "I can't."

For a while they lay side by side without speaking. "What do you want, Sherrill? I know, someone to type for you. Jesus, I never wanted to be a man but I get so tired of having to charm snakes. It's such a damn nuisance to always have to check your hose and lock your door and be sure not to provoke some male into rape, battery, adultery or getting you pregnant. If you would just pick up your own damn socks, do your own fucking typing."

He didn't know if he could explain, even to himself. He had promised always and forever and that also meant never. "I'm so far from home. Sometimes I feel like I'm so far from myself. I don't want to go home not knowing who I am."

"All that grandstanding playing Dix Deveraux for the cameras and you want to go home the way you were? Get real, Sherrill. You don't know who you are now."

"I don't know any more what I'm capable of doing."

"The same things as the rest of us. You're capable of killing your own mother, raping your own daughter, betraying your own interests."

But he was also capable of being cast among the stars, of realizing his fondest dreams. He tried to explain. The LZ had been an accident but the cameras were there and for the first time in his life he had attention. He wanted to focus that attention on his books, to get them back into print and to get a contract for the one he was working on. "It's the best thing I've ever written."

She stared at the roof of the hootch, slowly shaking her head from side to side. "You can't form life in your body so you run around pretending everything you do is some kind of creation. It isn't, Sherrill. It's just a book."

"If I'm willing to make any sacrifice, pay any price, go anywhere, maybe I can write something so true, so beautiful that people all over the world will recognize it."

"You're building a mighty big monument to yourself. Be sure it isn't your tombstone."

It wasn't a tombstone, it was a book. And in his mind it was grand.

One night Sherrill was awakened by someone sitting on the bunk next to his. "Let's have one last drink together," the man said. In the dim light cast by the perimeter lights he saw that it was the sergeant who had been hiding from his own men. "I'm going back to the world." The sergeant handed him the bottle. Sherrill took a drink although his stomach was uncertain. The whiskey stayed down.

The sergeant took a long pull at the bottle and passed it to Sherrill, who emulated him. "They had a farewell party for me, gave me a plaque." That wasn't the way Sherrill remembered the place. He held the plaque and stared at the sergeant, trying to relate this man to the man hiding in a bunker, to the story he was writing.

"They were trying to kill you."

The sergeant brushed the idea aside with a wave of his hand. "Don't mean nothing."

Sherrill took another pull at the bottle. "Was there a ground attack while I was there or was that just everybody blowing off steam?"

"There it is," the sergeant said. "But how you gonna show?" He poked Sherrill on the knee. "You remember that snake? I killed him and we ate him." The sergeant took another pull at the bottle and handed it to Sherrill. He looked older than Sherrill remembered. His face was slack and sweat and whisky dripped from his chin. "They sneaked a whore in for me. Now before they let me go home the doctors have to be sure I don't take nothing home with me. And shit, I don't even know if I got screwed."

"Do you think they brought the whore in to give you a disease?"

"I love those guys," the sergeant said.

"I'm trying to write a story about that place and I don't know how."

The sergeant took a long time considering, then leaned across the space between their bunks and stabbed Sherrill with a finger. "Vietnam is not real. Korea was real. Korea had the same gooks, same damn rice paddies, same damn hills but Korea was real. And colder than hell.

"That's why I stayed in the Army. The Army is real. It don't matter if you're poor or Catholic or what shit. There is reveille. There is inspection. Real by God life and death. But this shit—that's why they have all you press fuckers over here. Hell, sometimes there's more reporters at a battle than VC but you bastards still can't tell what's going on here because it don't mean nothing."

They both took a drink. "That's why I hate these fucking gooks. Because not even war is real any more. You wanna know why this war is not real? Because in this fucking war you have to take a God damn blood test to find out if you've been fucked."

The sergeant walked into the darkness, leaving Sherrill to wonder what story the sergeant would tell when he was back in the world. To wonder if the story he wrote for REAL would be different if he waited until he got home to write it. Back in the world he was part of a different way of thinking, a different way of seeing things. This wasn't Harvard. This was the fucking Nam.

He decided to take the sergeant, the snake and his exploration of the firebase out of the story. That also eliminated the drugs, the barbecue pit and the iced beer. It made a neater story.

"You've got a message," the lieutenant said, taking Sherrill to what appeared to be a communications center. The officious major with the fat face and bulging eyes waved him over and handed him a headset. Sherrill was frightened that something had happened to Jennifer. "After you've made your transmission say 'over,'" the major said.

"Hello," he said.

"Over," corrected the major.

"Hello, over," he said, feeling foolish.

"The LZ story was great. We had to make very few changes."

His reeling brain told him it was the voice of Fred Stone but magazines did not contact their writers through military channels. "What's wrong?" he asked, steeling himself. At the major's prompting, he added, "over." He had been so surprised by the voice he had not heard what Stone had said.

"We cut your poetry and went directly to the action. It'll be on the stands next week."

They had accepted a story. By God.

"Everybody wants to read about you. Tell us how you burned your hand mowing down gooks. We can finish the story here."

"That's not what happened."

"It doesn't matter what happened. What people think happened is what happened. Get us that story. People are begging for it."

There it is, he thought. Either you were visible or invisible and right now he had the glare and they wanted the story. "I'm working on it, but I've got to have some money. Send it to my wife."

"We gave you an advance for three stories."

"They're coming, but my wife's got to have some money."

"Okay, but write that story today. Put it in the hands of someone who is flying home. Have them call me collect when they get to California. Send lots of photos. Send a picture of you wearing your Thom McAn shoes."

In the field he wore a uniform. He had left his shoes, along with his other civilian clothing, at the Press Center in Da Nang.

"And with your hand bandaged."

"My hand's not bandaged."

"Get someone to bandage it and get a picture. Today. Out."

Sherrill took off the headset and handed it to the major. Jennifer was all right and they were going to send her money.

He took a deep breath. They would read anything he wrote. All because some photographer had taken a picture of him in his Thom Mc—civilian shoes. He felt like a presidential candidate, not knowing what the public would think important, what they would forgive and what would capture their imagination.

In his story of The Wild Bunch he hadn't mentioned burning his hand. He hadn't mentioned himself as being present. But Fred Stone was right. What the reader thought had happened was what had happened. It was no more possible to change the way they perceived the event than to change the seating arrangement at The Last Supper.

He was going to have to write the story again with himself at the center and begin when he joined the guntruck. It wasn't the real story but it was what REAL wanted, what the public knew, and he believed The Wild Bunch would accept it as what they expected of the press.

"I need someone to take a picture of me," Sherrill said to the major. "I need some civilian shoes. And a bandage." He was compromising himself but he would make something good come of it.

The story was not difficult to write once he had assumed the persona that had been created for him as adventurous, chase-them-to-Hanoi Sherrill O'Connell. His emotions and feelings were the story—his pride as the men and machines battled their way through the worst the enemy and elements could throw at them, his contempt for the cowardly foe that dared not confront American firepower, his anguish over the loss of his buddies, his regret at having to leave because he had burned his hand on a hot machine gun. He did not say it was an accident; people believed they knew what happened, let them think it. He did not write no one from the guntruck said goodbye.

The story was easy to write and confirmed what people

thought they knew but it reduced the men to stereotypes. Dillman: tough biker who was even tougher behind a fifty than behind a Harley. Maclin: laid-back, sun-loving surfer until the action started. Stubby: clown and crew mascot. Little Man: fearless driver who had miraculously survived the destruction of a previous truck. "Even a little man can chase Charlie." It turned his heroism into a lame joke but REAL would like it.

Making identifiable heroes of the crew made Lt. Wright a problem. In the pages of REAL the black officer's love for his mother, his piety, his ambition to be an aerospace engineer would be read as caricature, and since he couldn't be Superhero in REAL how was he going to command heroes? By skinning and grinning, the way blacks had always controlled surly whites in literature and film.

He examined the photographs he was sending with the story. There were the two dead men, naked before his camera. If some photographer had invaded Marie's privacy, assaulted the dignity of her death he believed he would have killed him. Yet he had dutifully shot photographs of the terrible wounds of two young men who had mothers, fathers, girlfriends. He tore up the photographs although they, more than anything he had written, represented reality.

The other photographs said what his story said. Dillman glowering over his fifty. Machlin striking Hollywood poses. Stubby puffing his cheeks like a demented child. Little Man barely visible over the steering wheel of the truck. Lt. Wright grinning from ear to ear. Himself wearing borrowed shoes and make-believe bandage. He had ridiculed Belk's filmed reports as "picture postcards" but what he was sending REAL was no closer to reality than a travel brochure was to a vacation.

He gave the story and photographs to the lieutenant to put on the next plane to Da Nang and the world. No sooner had the plane left than he was overcome with shame. He didn't care what they believed back home, the story was not true and he didn't want his name on it.

"I have to see the general," he said to the major, whose eyes bulged even more in his florid face. "The story I sent contained some things that might be seen in a negative way. I need the general to have someone pick up the story in Da Nang and return it to me."

"I'll tell him but right now I have to get you down to the pad. The general has a story for you, just what you were looking for."

"I have to stop that story before it leaves Da Nang."

"You do this story for the general and the general will bring the whole airplane back."

"What story is it?" Sherrill asked getting into the jeep.

"Whatever story you told the general you wanted."

The helicopter landed at a buttoned-down combat base that looked as though it were expecting an attack. Sherrill saw Rick Belk and his crew and thought they had come to photograph him but they were waiting for a flight to a remote outpost. Belk seemed happy to see Sherrill and told him of the footage he had shot at LZ O'Connell. The network had cut the first part of the film showing the dud grenade landing behind Belk because it lacked reality but had left intact the sequence showing Sherrill pointing at the Viet Cong he had killed.

Sherrill did not believe he had pointed at a body; he had tried to avoid looking at the bodies. Yet the camera said he had done it and millions of people believed it. He wondered what Jennifer and his colleagues at the school thought. Did they believe he had claimed a dead body as a trophy?

"Fucking war. If I don't come up with a story fast, I'm through," Belk complained. He had spent days and bribed officials to get a story on the disappearance of American rice before it reached the farmers to whom it was intended. The network complained that the film lacked drama and was too hard to understand. He had missed one story because the battery pack had failed in the rain, another because after spending three days in a swamp carrying a 25-pound sound camera, tape recorders, amplifiers and battery packs the fight took place after dark and all they got on film was gun flashes.

They had traveled halfway across Vietnam on anything that moved to reach a hamlet that had been attacked and burned by the Viet Cong. Belk had gotten footage of the ruined village, dead civilians, stunned survivors, an interview with one old man who had fought with the Viet Minh.

The story was not aired because on the same day the President hit someone with a golf ball. Filmed interviews with the President, the man who had been hit with the ball, a golf pro who explained why the President had sliced the ball and witty remarks by a news commentator on what this would do to the President's image as a straight-shooter left no time for a story about eighty-eight dead Vietnamese.

"I've got the face, I've got the voice for a network anchorman. All I need is one big story, but if that camp falls tonight I'm in deep shit."

The next morning they were told that all flights to the camp had been canceled because of conditions there. Sherrill was relieved; Belk exploded. "I've got to get in there," he screamed. "You're wrecking my career. If that camp is overrun I've got to be there."

Belk's repeated demands to be taken to the outpost brought the colonel. He was thin, his hair close cropped over a bullet-shaped head, his leathery skin stretched tight over high cheek bones. He looked at the television team as though they were so many Viet Cong. "I'm trying to fight a war," he said. He sounded like he needed to clear his throat. He turned his clear blue eyes on Sherrill. "You the guy the general sent?"

Belk and the others looked at him with suspicion. "I'm Sherrill O'Connell from REAL magazine."

"The general told me me to get you in there so I'm going to fly you in there myself."

"How bad is it?" Sherrill wasn't a coward and he didn't want to look like one in front of the others but he saw no reason why he couldn't write the story where he was.

"We're going too," Belk said.

"Too risky," the colonel said.

"I'm not going by myself," Sherrill said.

The colonel turned to stare at the television crew. "I can't guarantee I can get you out. All available space will be needed for the wounded."

Belk and his crew stared back at the colonel. Sherrill knew that they would not back down; he hoped the colonel would cancel the flight.

"I'll get you in there and I'll try to get a helicopter in at dusk to get you out," the colonel said. "I advise you to get your asses on it."

Belk was elated. "I owe you a favor," he told Sherrill. "We couldn't get in there without you."

Sherrill turned away so Belk could not see the fear in his eyes.

Mountain peaks poked through the low cloud cover. The difficulty of finding the strip and landing seemed to improve the colonel's disposition. He assured them the cloud cover was good because the helicopter couldn't be seen by enemy gunners until they were almost on the ground.

The colonel corkscrewed the helicopter through a wispy opening in the clouds, skidded around a mountain peak, for a moment got caught between the clouds and a mountain ridge, seemed to guess where the cloud-shrouded ridge ended, plunged out of the clouds into a valley, and followed a stream through a narrow pass.

Sherrill caught a glimpse of a raw, red slash in the mountain greenery, zigzag trenches and the long houses of a Montagnard village. Then they were over the wire and trenches of the besieged compound. With the helicopter hovering and shells falling around them, they spilled out of the chopper and fell into the nearest trench. The helicopter nosed forward, picked up airspeed, lifted up through streams of tracers and disappeared into the clouds.

They ran to the closest bunker. Inside they found two photographers taking pictures of Montagnard irregulars squatting on their heels in the mud. Heavy rains had crumbled the log-and earth-covered bunker and water was standing inside.

Sherrill recognized the two photographers. One of them was a bearded, fox-faced man of thirty who was known for his photographs of nude women who looked like soft boys. He was in Vietnam to change his image from cheesecake photographer to photojournalist. The other man was older than Sherrill, bald-headed, and famous for his photographs that made his subjects look lonely although surrounded by the paraphernalia of their success—a writer in the midst of his books, an actor surrounded by clippings and awards, a mother mobbed by her children, a President surrounded by advisors.

"What's happening?" Belk asked. "Are we under attack?" The photographers shrugged. They had persuaded two helicopter pilots on a "doughnut dolly" run to drop them off at the outpost. The pilots, bored with routine flights, had landed with the girls waving from the doors, dropped off the photographers and flown away without a shot being fired at them.

From the crowded bunker the view was more depressing than from the air. They were in a valley ringed by thick wooded hills that disappeared into the mist. For defense there were mud-filled trenches, log-covered bunkers half buried in mud, and barbed wire—strung, rolled, woven, twisted, row after row so that everything Sherrill looked at was underlined, framed with barbed wire.

The command post was flooded. The entrance had collapsed so that they had to climb over and under the logs that had once been the roof and sides. Inside was an over-aged, sharp-faced captain with hair that grew almost to his bushy eyebrows and a chin that pointed up, giving him a tough, pinched, no humor look.

There was a story that when the captain's chin had been sliced open by shrapnel, the captain had sewn up the wound himself, looking in the mirror. Sherrill believed it; the captain would not have permitted anyone else such an amateurish job. The generator was going and so was the stereo and refrigerator.

The captain was sitting on a table, eating a can of C-rations, answering radios and he was not happy to see the press. He got them cold beers and turned off the stereo. "We play rock until an hour before sundown, religious until dark, military marches through the night," he said.

"Are we under attack?" Belk asked.

"We have been under attack for four days." He accented "we" to exclude them.

"Why are you fighting in this place?" Belk asked, as the cameraman panned the muddy outpost encircled by mist-shrouded hills.

"This is where I am."

"Does this place have a name?"

"We call it Tombstone, the camp too tough to die."

"Why aren't your men properly dug in?"

The captain hung his head and sighed as though explaining to the class simpleton. "Nothing but steel-reinforced concrete will stop what they have in those hills. We don't have steel, we don't have concrete, we don't have the time or the manpower, and if we did I would not build a static defense that Charlie would just slip around. And if I did, you would ask, why aren't these men in trenches where they can fight and move and protect the village?"

"Why is the aid station so close to the air strip when the air strip is the center of enemy shelling?"

"The aid station is near the air strip so the wounded can be evacuated. If it weren't, you would ask, why do the wounded have to be carried in the open to the airstrip?"

"If you died tonight, how would you like to be remembered?"

"As a good soldier who punched out a reporter."

Belk needed more drama on film than thirty seconds of the captain eating. Would the captain inspire his troops, shoot at the enemy or something? The captain would not. "I'm willing to die for my country, I'm willing for you to use my death for profit and entertainment but I will not be your puppet and I will not clown for the evening news." The captain tossed the empty ration can in the corner. "Thank you, gentlemen, but I have work to do. I hope you enjoy your stay."

Belk and his crew went in search of more dramatic material. Sherrill had no impulse to leave the illusory security of the bunker. "What are you waiting for?" the captain growled.

"To get out of here."

The captain almost smiled. He studied maps, wrote reports, talked on the radio, listened to men who came to the bunker and sent them out again.

"This place is the cork in the bottle, right?" Sherrill asked.

The captain almost smiled again. "This border is a sieve. Charlie can cross it any place he wants to. He'll lose some men but he can do it. There are two wars being fought here. One is a real war and the other is the bullshit war. Every time we meet Charlie we kick his ass. The only kind of war Charlie can win is bullshit and you guys are his storm troopers. Giap needs more bullshit and he'll sacrifice any number of men to take this place and you guys will call it a victory."

"I don't get it."

"We're the cheese to draw Charlie into the trap where we can napalm him off the hills and chase him with B-52s."

Sherrill didn't like being in the center of the trap. "What if the airplanes can't get through?"

"We'll be overrun."

"You think this place can be overrun?"

"Any place can be overrun if you're willing to pay the price."

The captain looked out at the mist-shrouded hills. "We're outnumbered and outgunned. If we can't get Spooky gunships through that cloud cover we'll be overrun tonight."

Sherrill was almost paralyzed with dread. The forces of North Vietnam could come pouring out of the hills. Cloud cover or enemy gunners could prevent a helicopter from rescuing him. "What happens then?"

The captain let the question hang in the air for a moment. "If we're overrun, we'll blow the ammo bunker. That'll cause enough confusion for us to break contact and assemble at the mortar pit. We'll break out toward the river and stay together as a fighting unit as long as possible. Artillery will plaster this place and B52s will bomb the escape routes back to Laos."

Sherrill stared at the captain as though he were talking to a madman. "That's the plan?"

"The plan is to kill so many of them that they will wake up to the fact that their strategy isn't working."

"What about our strategy?" Sherrill asked, but the captain picked up his rifle and left the bunker.

Sherrill sat with the radio operator, listening to the flat, bored voices, heartened by the knowledge that someone, somewhere knew what was happening to him.

As hours passed dread was slowly replaced by boredom. He should at least interview some of the men. He might capture their immortal last words. "I regret that I have but one life. . ." The idea sickened him. He ought to get their names and home towns anyway. He crawled though the logs and outside the bunker and looked at the open ground he would have to cross, exposed to every gun on the Laotian border. Fuck it, he'd get the names from the Army.

The hours dragged. Belk and his crew returned. "Great stuff. Some of those guys were sending their last letter home. If this place is overrun, this story will get me an anchor. Geez, I'll have to get my hair cut. This is okay for out in the field but it's not serious enough for an anchor. I need something distinguished but not professorial. I've got to start studying styles in the magazines. Shorter but maybe fluffed up. What do you think, Sherrill? What are the movie stars wearing?"

"Who gives a shit what an anchorman's hair looks like? He's just reading the news to people who are too lazy to read it themselves."

"An anchor sells the news," Belk said, dropping into his on-camera voice. "He has to have authority, he has to have credibility because he tells America what to believe. The anchorman is the closest thing America has to a. . .uh. . .a high priest, a guru."

"Have you ever listened to television news? An anchor isn't a priest, he's a parrot. He doesn't need a mirror; he is a mirror to tell us how trivial our lives, our concerns, our deaths. . ." Sherrill didn't know why he was angry but he was incoherent with rage.

Belk was surprised at Sherrill's vehemence. "It's not much of a story for you is it? By the time your story hits REAL this place will be completely forgotten. Reading a dying man's last words isn't very dramatic if you've already heard them from the man himself and already forgotten he died."

"Shut the fuck up, Rick."

"A lot of guys wouldn't have come here for a Pulitzer and you came just so I could get in. I owe you one, tiger."

If Rick was trying to mollify him it was working. He liked television owing him a favor. "Just mention my books," he said, trying to make it sound like a joke. Rick seemed to think it was.

When the captain returned to the bunker he reported the situation. "We've had no serious casualties today so I canceled the dust-off. Too risky. I guess you're going to be with us a while." He seemed pleased.

They squatted in the dim bunker with mud dripping from the roof, listening to the muffled explosions outside, watching the mist-shrouded hills hiding hundreds of North Vietnamese that were waiting for darkness. Sherrill could feel dread dissolving his bones. He was afraid to believe the captain, afraid not to believe him. His stomach was eating itself as the moments of daylight ticked away.

"The Army knows we're here," the fox-faced photographer said. "If we are killed it'll be a black eye for the military." The captain seemed unperturbed.

Sherrill considered telling the captain that the general had sent him there so he could write their story but he couldn't write it if he was dead. He didn't think the captain cared whether the story was written or not.

Someone climbed through the tangle of logs at the entrance to the bunker. "It's raining. Can't nobody can get in through that," he said.

"Nobody but Charlie," the captain said.

The newcomer nodded. He was short, stocky and round-faced; perhaps Samoan, although he lacked the accent. He lay down on the table and closed his eyes.

Sherrill felt something like relief. At least there was an end to uncertainty. There would be no agonizing wait to see if the helicopter made it through the mist and gunfire, no desperate dash through the shelling to get aboard, no helpless terror as the target of every gun within range while the leaden chopper struggled back into the air. Now that he knew what was required, Sherrill began preparing himself to die. It was the alternating hope and despair that he could not endure.

The radio sputtered to life. ". . .ple Fox inbound. Request sit rep."

The captain picked up the radio-telephone. "Light rain, light mortars. No wounded. Repeat, no wounded. Do not advise sit down."

"Roger that. How many pas?"

Sherrill's newfound resolve drained away as the captain counted passengers. Someone would have to stay behind; Sherrill was sure of it.

"Six pas plus television equipment," the captain replied.

By God, he was not going to stay behind if the cameras left. He placed his camera on the table, hoping the others would take the hint.

"That's tight." The radio buzzed while Sherrill tried not to heed the impulse swelling in him to claw his way aboard the helicopter at any cost.

"Have pas at the pad," the radio sputtered. "ETA five minutes. We'll give it one shot. No—repeat—no go around."

Sherrill wanted to run for the strip but the captain was going to send the Samoan with them to get them to the right place. He had been dozing on the table and he sat up, stretched, put on his helmet, yawned, picked up his rifle and stopped to listen to the radio.

"Best approach?"

"Approach over river from southeast."

"Roger. I copy."

Sherrill thought they were going to leave but the stocky man stopped, blocking the way through the logs. "When we get out there, follow me but keep a proper interval. Crowds attract attention. Move quickly but deliberately. Keep a hole in sight at all times. Is that understood?" He paused until Sherrill was ready to kick him through the logs. "Let's go."

Although Sherrill had promised himself that he would not crowd, he kept running into the back of one of the photographers who repeatedly stopped in spite of the thickening gloom to take pictures of those left behind. "Onward Christian Soldiers," was playing over the loudspeaker.

They passed a soldier with tears running down his face as he looked across the wire. The photographers stopped to take pictures. ". . .marching as to warrrr. . ." The loudspeaker ground to silence as the generator went dead.

They crouched in a trench and listened as the helicopter passed to the north of them drawing fire, then pulled up in the clouds. Was that the one attempt they said they would make?

Bastards didn't even try. Shells landed around the strip driving them deeper into the trench. Sherrill swelled with hate. He hated the captain, he hated the helicopter pilots, he hated everyone lying in the mud with him. He could not bear the uncertainty. If he had a weapon he would shoot at the helicopter himself so he would no longer be tantalized by hope.

"He's coming back," the Samoan said.

Sherrill did not look up. He could not bear seeing the helicopter so close, yet unable to land. "Go, go, go," the Samoan screamed. The others were out of the trench and running. Although he was the last to get started, Sherrill quickly passed the Japanese carrying the sound camera and battery pack.

The helicopter was moving down the runway towards them trailing streams of tracers. One of the photographers jumped on a skid and turned to take one last picture but was jerked inside by the door gunner. Belk jumped for the door and Sherrill boosted him inside and was dragged in himself, skinning his shins.

A bullet came through the windscreen and died in the armor plating beside the pilot. Sherrill grabbed the sound camera, and the Japanese cameraman was hauled aboard. The helicopter skidded sideways when a shell landed nearby, sending the reporters sprawling on the floor as a bullet passed through both sides with a double thunk.

The helicopter had picked up speed but was not lifting off because Montagnards had grabbed the skids. The photographer who loved isolation and the Japanese cameraman took pictures as the door gunners kicked the soldiers loose. Sherrill saw holes appearing in the sides of the helicopter and tried to claw himself into the metal floor and then they were enveloped in the clouds.

Because of damage to the helicopter they landed at a remote mountaintop ARVN post that didn't look any safer than the place they had left. Sherrill was almost overcome by the stench. The ARVN, coming to the relief of the outpost, had collided with the NVA. The bodies of the dead were being brought in and placed in long concrete buildings left by the French.

The Americans sat outside in the cool, thin mist, smoking cigarettes although it didn't seem safe to Sherrill. Belk came out of the command bunker where he had been trying to get transportation to Saigon, at least for his film. He had a story if he could get it to the network fast enough. The two photographers, also anxious to file their film, questioned Belk with their eyes.

"Fucking ARVN. Something about needing all their helicopters to pick up their wounded and resupply their troops."

"Who gave them the fucking helicopters? Who trained their fucking pilots?" the fox-faced photographer asked.

"Did you tell them you'd make them famous?" Sherrill asked Belk. "And ask them if they died tonight how they wanted to be remembered?"

"Hell yes, I even offered them a bribe. Fucking ARVN don't even speak English. I don't know how much they understood."

The others cursed their fate at having their coup turned to crap by the stupidity of the ARVN and the inefficiency of the military in general. The elation of having survived had left Sherrill and he did not have the possibility of a triumph or the anxiety of a failure to sustain him. He collapsed on the ground.

Occasionally the wind brought the sound of guns but Sherrill didn't know whether it was from Tombstone or the ARVN battle. It got cold so they went into the bunker. The Vietnamese politely made room for them and offered them tea that had been boiled several hours before. In return, Sherrill offered cigarettes.

"Please," one of the Vietnamese said to Sherrill, pointing at an old, sad-faced ARVN machine gunner. "This man sergeant.

Very brave. Fought Viet Minh. Fighting fift' years."

Sherrill looked at the other Americans. "Fifteen?" he asked them. They weren't listening.

"You take picture."

Sherrill turned to the photographers. "This guys an ARVN hero. Do you want to take his picture?"

"Fuck him," said the fox-faced man.

"Ask him where the fuck our helicopter is," said the other.

"Big battle," the Vietnamese said. "Many wounded. Helicopters busy."

"Tell him we have some important film here," the other said as though Sherrill were an interpreter. "Boo coo important," he yelled at the Vietnamese. "Boo coo important photographer," he said, pointing at his companion and himself. "Boo coo important television man," he said, patting Belk on the shoulder. "Jesus, don't any of you guys speak English?"

Sherrill didn't have a flash for his camera. The Vietnamese, aware of the problem, arranged lanterns around the man but it was hopeless. "You going to write a story about him?" Belk asked.

"REAL wouldn't use a story about an ARVN if he won the war by himself."

"There it is," Rick said.

Sherrill sat down beside the sergeant who didn't look big enough to carry a machine gun. He wished he could talk to him; he tried to think what the man dreamed of, what kept him going. If he was disabled he could go to Saigon and beg outside the Majestic Hotel. If he survived maybe some day he could go back to the nothing he had left.

There was a lot of activity on the radio and sometimes out of the Vietnamese they could pick out messages from Tombstone—situation reports and requests for illumination and supporting fire. Spooky could not get through the clouds.

Sherrill hung on to the thin, impersonal radio voice as though it were a heartbeat, knowing that when it stopped it would signal the death of the outpost. About midnight a calm but deeper voice stated, "Be advised that Charlie is inside the wire. Request fifteen minute delay for orderly withdrawal then blow this place off the map. Out and 'All the Way, Airborne.'"

There was nothing to be said or done but they sat smoking and waiting. It was like the hours he had waited while Marie struggled for life, waiting because there was nothing else to do, waiting because it would be a while before life resumed.

At first light a helicopter landed with wounded aboard. The two photographers and the television team crowded on it but Sherrill decided to wait. It wasn't just the anguish and mess in the helicopter. He wanted something more, some confirmation it was over.

Trucks brought fresh loads of bodies. Some were in ARVN uniforms, some in NVA uniforms, some in no uniforms. The stench was inescapable. Still Sherrill waited, smoking steadily to deaden his taste to the pervasive smell.

Late that afternoon the captain, two other Americans and some Montagnards climbed the hill. They had fought their way out of the camp, escaped down the river and had gotten separated from the others in a series of running battles. Having reached safety they fell on the earth, so weary they were oblivious to the smell of death.

"That fucking Griggs. I told him to grab the pop-ups before he blew the ammo bunker. Ortiz forgot where we were going to reassemble and we had to go and find him. Bo wouldn't leave his buddy who was wounded, so they're both dead or captured."

"What is this going to mean?"

The captain looked at him as though he were stupid. "We do what we're supposed to do, Charlie does what he's supposed to do, you guys decide what it means and who should be elected because of it."

Sherrill didn't want to interview the captain while he was

exhausted and confused; he just wanted to know what happened.

"Charlie's dodging bombs back in Laos now. We'll rest up tomorrow, give the men more time to show up, then we'll go back and rebuild."

"Won't the NVA come back?"

"That's the plan."

Sherrill studied the captain's face for signs of irony. There had to be more to it than that. "Is this a good place to fight?"

"If the government had asked where we wanted to fight a war, no one in the military would have picked Vietnam. There are more than three hundred miles of land border that the enemy can cross at any time and we have to wait until they're over here and tag them before they get back over there. It's like Blind Man's Bluff plus they've got King's X and we're it. They drive trucks up to the border and we have to send million-dollar planes to stop them. Bombs aren't as effective as bayonets but they cost more money and the more the military spends the richer civilians get."

This was the story the general thought he wanted. "That seems like a dumb way to fight a war."

"There it is. We didn't pick the place and we don't make the rules, and rule numero uno is: they don't have to fight by the same rules we do. But we can't just walk out on these people. We have to give them a chance to develop leadership."

"How long will that take?"

"Have you been in these villages? They don't have alarm clocks. They don't even have calendars." The captain gestured for a cigarette. Sherrill gave him one and lighted it. The captain took a puff and studied the smoke for a moment. "They know we got rid of Diem because he wouldn't work for us so now they think any leader we let them have is our puppet."

"Are they right?"

"You've seen these people. They don't have TVs, radios, newspapers or magazines. Except for the guerrillas most of them have never been twenty miles from where they were born. They don't know the difference between France and America. Where is this informed electorate we say is necessary for democracy to work? It's going to take a while."

"In the meantime. . ."

"In the meantime we keep killing them until they say 'uncle.'"

"But aren't they also killing us?"

"We," the captain said, excluding Sherrill, "are soldiers. We know we may die but we kill a hell of a lot more of them. They can't sustain those losses forever. Some day they're going to realize they lost a whole generation and quietly go home."

"Do you have that much time?"

"That's up to you guys, isn't it? Tell the American public we have to kill the enemy wherever he is. Tell them No Sanctuary and we'll get this war over with and go home. You can sell soap and cigarettes, why don't you try selling your own country?" The captain got stiffly to his feet and went inside the bunker to sleep.

REAL would buy the story if he emphasized the heroism of the men, how many of the enemy they killed and that they were going back. Stone would love what the captain said about the media selling their country. Should he write that the cheese in the mousetrap was working and that the enemy was at the point of collapse, or should he advocate chasing him out of his sanctuaries? Laos. Cambodia. North Vietnam?

He had been quoted as saying something about chasing the enemy to Hanoi but he had never believed he said it, and if he had he was talking about chasing the enemy home. He had never suggested invading North Vietnam. Besides, everyone understood that he was frightened and confused. He didn't know the media was listening.

Sherrill had never studied military tactics or strategy. He hadn't thought of victory in more concrete terms than saving the people, preserving freedom and going home. The captain was right, it would take a long time to win the war if the enemy could hide in sanctuaries and cross the border at will.

He wondered how his readers would react to "No Sanctuary." REAL would buy it but he didn't want to appear a fanatic who appealed only to REAL. If he couldn't appeal to a wider audience, if he couldn't be heard by Jennifer, and Lindly and his colleagues, then it was pointless. REAL readers already knew what they believed. He had never before considered what his readers wanted, but he had never before been famous. He had attention and he didn't want to squander it on some foolish scheme that not even the military would consider.

Before he advocated attacking the sanctuaries or invading North Vietnam he wanted to know if attrition was working and how seriously "No Sanctuary" was being considered. He needed to talk to men in the military and the media who had been here a long time and knew what was going on. He didn't want to go back to Saigon so that meant Da Nang. He was certain of one thing: he wouldn't have to risk his life to get those answers.

Da Nang

The helicopter returning him to Quang Tri was hit. A bullet struck the belly, spraying the inside with metal fragments. The glasses of one of the door gunners were shattered, his face blossomed from a half-dozen tiny cuts. "Fucking DMZ," he screamed at Sherrill. "I'd extend if they'd let us go over there and clean those bastards out."

The pilots called Quang Tri and the lieutenant met Sherrill at the strip and took him to get his belongings. "Am I glad to see you. The media said you were at Tombstone and no one knew what happened to you."

"I have to call my wife and let her know I'm okay."

The lieutenant looked doubtful. "Can't you get one of the reporters at Da Nang to send it?"

Sherrill nodded. That would be faster than a letter. "Did the general get my story back from Da Nang?"

"He told the major it was all right."

"All right?"

"You sent it with Captain Ramos, right? The general asked

Ramos to read the story to him. He told the major to tell you he understood your concern but that the American people had the right to know the unprofessional side of the military."

Unprofessional? He had eliminated the fragging, the drugs, the prejudice.

"He said he hoped you liked the story he gave you. Are you going to write that we should attack their sanctuaries?"

"Is that what the general wants me to say?"

"That's what everybody says we have to do."

"What do you think we should do?"

"I'm a lieutenant, they don't pay me to think. I don't see why it's okay for them to cross the border and wrong for us but give me eight months and they can do what they like with these people."

"Do you know any of these people?"

"There's an ARVN liaison officer that hangs around but I've never talked to him."

"Doesn't he speak English?"

"Yeah but we got nothing to say."

He went by the hospital to say goodbye to Kelty. Kelty was not in the hospital. Maybe she had been sent to one of the battalion aid stations; maybe she was on one of the airevacs to Da Nang. No one seemed to know. He left a message for her. Now that he was leaving he felt free to tell her how he felt. "Thank you for all you've done. I'm sorry that I was such a fool. I love you."

At the airstrip the lieutenant handed Sherrill his mail and promised to call Saigon and direct the rest of it to Da Nang. Sherrill boarded the C-130 crowded with soldiers, Vietnamese families with their belongings, and slot machines being sent to Da Nang for repair. He opened his mail.

One of the letters was from his agent. Because of the publicity, his publisher might reprint his first two books. He had found an audience and this might be a good time for the books to be reissued. He read the letter again. They had made no promises but finding an audience meant reprints. He wished they saw his work as of value rather than trying to capitalize on accidental publicity but he believed in the books even if they didn't. If it took REAL magazine to get them in print, so be it.

There were three letters from Jennifer. The first letter said she was fine, their mothers were okay, the president of the college said Sherrill seemed to have found what he was looking for in Vietnam. The generality troubled Sherrill. What did "fine" and "okay" mean? What was the president talking about?

The second letter was more puzzling, full of people he didn't know, places he hadn't heard of. She sounded happy, content. Jennifer was a passionate but deliberate person. Accidents did not happen in her kitchen. Friendships were not initiated by others. Meetings were never by coincidence. Her mind was like a zipper, her thoughts in a row. Yet her letter seemed frivolous, even gay.

In her third letter Jennifer wrote, "I hope you are getting my letters. I know how terrible it is not to hear. Don't worry about things here. Everything will work out; it's just so frustrating not to know, to have to face things alone and make decisions without knowing what you want or plan. I am getting so irritable it is unbelievable. I put off going to bed until I am so sleepy I can hardly keep awake. Nights are the worst aren't they? Lying in bed alone. I hope you don't mind but I don't have anyone else to complain to. Somehow just writing to you relieves a great deal of tension but the more I write the more I miss you.

"I am now business manager of a street theater. I do everything—bookkeeping, fund-raising, reporting to the board, hiring and firing when the board says so. I don't agree with a lot of the things they say—they say it's necessary to overstate in order to sensitize—but they're good kids. They have one show where one actor in a false beard, hippie hair and dirty clothes goes into a store and asks to try on suits. Other actors are in the store as customers. The store asks the hippie to leave or refuses to let him try on clothes. The other actors start arguing with the clerks, taking different sides, and soon the real customers get into it. When the manager is called, the 'hippie' gets behind a rack and takes off the beard, long hair and dirty clothes. He has good clothes on underneath, of course, and the manager can't figure out what's going on. The actors say it makes merchants and customers see hippies as real people."

The letters were undated and the postmarks smudged but he believed the second letter was written after she had gotten the job. He didn't know how she got a job with a street theater or why she wanted it—she was embarrassed when mimes selected her for attention—but it made her happy and that made him happy. Jennifer was the star in his darkest night. Across the distance she brought light, and hope and the way home.

He turned to Lindly's letter. Lindly hoped Sherrill knew what he was doing, alienating everyone who cared about him. "Your colleagues are shocked at your attack on the free press." The world heard off-hand remarks he may or may not have babbled when he didn't think anyone was listening. "I am equally disappointed in your idea for the next book. I thought you understood. War has been outmoded. It's old-fashioned. No one wants to read about it, hear about it or think about it. Even more out of date is a hero trying to preserve his solitary view of reality. Individualism, a perversion with which Judeo-Christianity infected the world, is as dead as God. In fact, the individual died with God. If you expect to get published outside fascist magazines like REAL you have to go with the flow. What's going down? Do you really like killing gooks?"

There were fewer and fewer things Sherrill understood but it angered him that Lindly, who had insisted Sherrill could not comprehend *Canterbury Tales* because he had not read it in

Middle English, was convinced he could understand Vietnam by experiencing television news.

The rest of Lindly's letter was news about the college. Lindly was recommending that the school no longer require a standard, middle-class, Anglo-Saxon writing style. "How can we tell a black or brown student that ours is the only correct way of writing English? Who are we to tell students what kind of education they should get?"

Sherrill stared at the letter in bewilderment. No college would permit students to graduate without the ability to write with clarity and precision. It was maddening that Lindly would try to amuse or deceive him. He was beginning to understand why Jennifer had never liked Lindly.

He opened the letter from his mother. Buried beneath the lines about her store, her garden, her health, was a mother's concern for her child, her belief and fear that her son was different from others, her wish and fear that he was not.

The mail that had begun with such warmth and promise left him with frustration. The letters contained not substance but shadows of people he once knew, their gestures wooden, precipitate, driven by unfixed impulse. He tried to recall the way Jennifer looked, that firm but solid line of her profile but could not.

Sherrill was picked up at the Da Nang airfield by a sleek, surly, black Marine jeep driver who ignored the easy equality Sherrill offered him. In a refugee jungle called Dog Patch a small boy darted between tar paper shanties and threw something under the jeep. Both Sherrill and the driver were trying to jump out of the moving jeep when they heard the harmless pop of a fire cracker.

"God damn kid," the driver raged, his black face turned gray. "I've lost two buddies that way. One of them lost a foot when a kid threw a grenade under his jeep. The other got ten years for shooting a kid who was just pretending. That's why

I don't carry a weapon. One day I'd shoot one of those little bastards and they'd put my ass in the brig. I only got four more months of this shit."

Sherrill asked if the driver thought they should attack sanctuaries in Laos and Cambodia. "Say what? I don't know nothing about that shit."

The Press Center was a double row of Quonset huts, plus a press operations shack and open mess on the bank of the Song Han. A paved area between the operations shack and the mess served as basketball court in the daytime and open-air movie on the nights it didn't rain.

Looking like something between a run-down motel and a boys camp, the Press Center was an information and lore enclave in a city swollen with a large air base, military port and support facilities, Navy hospital, and crowded to bursting with refugees. Across the wide, muddy Song Han was the headquarters compound. To the right was the bridge to the Marine base and airfield at Marble Mountain. To the left was the bay of Da Nang and beyond the bay, the blinking red radio towers on Monkey Mountain.

The colonel in charge of the Press Center looked like the ex-basketball player he was—tall, well-built, with the sleek, self-congratulatory look of a psychology professor who did weekend seminars on "Learning to Like Yourself." The colonel liked himself and he liked the press center that was his kingdom.

After the welcoming speech, Sherrill explained that he had been at Tombstone and was trying to write the story. "Should we keep sending men back to those exposed camps or should we close the sanctuaries?"

The colonel leaned over him. "Ninety percent of what happens here will never be reported. Our job," he put his hand on Sherrill's shoulder to include him in the job, "is to see that the ten percent that is reported accurately reflects the whole. If you need anything, let me know. There have been some problems in the past with press relations," the colonel admitted, "but things are getting better." The center had a new cook, a better selection of imported wines and the best movies in Vietnam. "No country has ever spent so much money and manpower accommodating the press. Take care of the press and they'll take care of you. That's my posture. They gave my predecessor hell. He will never make general."

"Thanks, colonel," said a small, pinch-shouldered man with eyebrows that began at his temples and persisted to the bridge of his nose. "The shower is working now."

A young sergeant, in charge of the Vietnamese who operated the mess and bar, introduced him to the habitues who weren't working. The sergeant had a jagged scar across his forehead that puckered one eye. "You want a scar?" he asked. "I know a gook that gives good scars. A guy like you needs a tasteful scar on your forehead or chin to show you risked your life to get a story." Sherrill winced, wondering if the soldier knew he had posed with a bandage over an injury that had healed.

A slender, delicate Vietnamese beauty with a face like a prayer and eyes like a curse worked behind the long narrow bar in a room adjoining the mess. "Pretty," the sergeant said. "But off-limits. Her husband is a National Policeman, her father is in Vietnamese Intelligence. They come in here sometimes looking for the reporter who fathered her child but MAC-V got him out before he ended up in a tiger cage."

"Rosie" was a long-haired, slender-faced, twenty-five-year-old who wore Korean tiger-stripe fatigues with a curiously slack posture as though he was standing and sitting at the same time. Having failed at college, heterosexuality and suicide, he had come to Vietnam to find his drafted lover, had accepted a camera in exchange for a blow job and had become a freelance photographer. "He's damn good if you need a photographer," said the sergeant. "But don't get in the shower with him."

Manfred was a robust German doctor doing a year's service at a civilian hospital. Manfred was a surgeon but the hospital had no equipment for him to work with. When he could stand the suffering no longer he came to the center and got drunk. "Don't ask him to sing."

Major Groff was an oversized, fat-lipped psychologist who ran a Psychological Warfare Operation, the kind of man who laughed at children and took doctors seriously. "He tries to undermine Viet Cong morale by dropping giant condoms that make them feel inadequate."

Roger was a college student getting information for a research paper. "Whatever information he gets goes to a group in Berkeley that airmails it to Hanoi."

Bird, who used only his last name, was a bearded, long-haired, over-age hippie correspondent for several underground newspapers. "Part of a drug smuggling ring but we haven't been able to catch him."

The beetled-browed man Sherrill had seen earlier was a wire service reporter. Sherrill introduced himself. "There were reports that I was at Tombstone when it was overrun. Could you report that I'm okay?"

"We heard some correspondents may have been at the camp. No names were mentioned but there was a rumor around the Press Center that you or Rod Reaves parachuted in to save the place."

"Fuck you," Sherrill said.

Sherrill walked into his hootch that contained a shower, commode, ten cots, a large wooden cabinet crammed with helmets, flak jackets, packs, cameras, ruined film, dirty shorts and socks, a gas mask and a civilian suitcase. There was a small bookcase containing some battered mystery and western paperbacks, a history of Vietnam in mint condition, and a few nudie magazines with most of the pictures torn out.

A photographer in camouflage jacket and jockey shorts sat on one of the bunks examining his photographs. "You

O'Connell?" the photographer asked, taking pictures before handing Sherrill an engraved card rather than introducing himself.

Sherrill picked up a photograph of a dead Vietnamese family sprawled in a ditch.

"Sold that six times. A photograph has one subject. The subject of that one is atrocity, a popular subject."

"Who did it?"

"In a left-wing publication it's a U.S. atrocity; in a right-wing publication it's a VC atrocity. Photographs don't have political views."

"What about photographers?"

"I have a fee."

Also on the bunk were photographs of a legless Vietnamese boy with oversized eyes, wrapped in an American flag and sitting in a doorway, sitting in rubble, sleeping on the ground under a cross, peering through barbed wire. Sherrill had seen the pictures decorating calendars, posters, leaflets, tee shirts, album covers and dust jackets of poetry books.

"I got to get another kid. A girl, I think. With Negroid features."

"What about the boy without legs?" Sherrill asked.

"A face has only got so many pictures in it. Besides, he saw a photo of himself and that changed the way he looked."

"What will happen to him?" Back in the world he would try to find a career in movies and television but this was a tough country for a boy without legs.

"I taught him to speak English. That's his meal ticket."

A legless boy who could speak English could be a spy, a pusher, a pimp. The thought brought memories of Harry Tompkins and a girl in Saigon. "How do you sleep?" Sherrill asked.

"First come, first served," the photographer said, misunderstanding the question. "Put your boots under a cot and it's yours." He pointed out the bunks that had been previously claimed and went back to examining his work looking for new poses.

Sherrill stayed at the press center, sitting in the open mess, drinking coffee and working on his story about the fall of Tombstone. From Da Nang, what had seemed arrogance, "We call it Tombstone, the camp too tough to die," seemed gallows humor. What had seemed bravado, "I fight here because this is where I am," was a straightforward answer that neither he nor Belk understood. It wasn't a good place to fight but he was a soldier and rather than complain about it, he fought as best he could where he was.

The hard part was deciding what the fall of the camp meant. He could call the story, "The Camp Too Tough to Die," and emphasize the enemy body count and that the camp was being rebuilt. That would persuade REAL readers that the plan was working but didn't do much for the captain and his men. He could call the story, "A Dumb Place to Die," and convince REAL and its readers that giving the enemy sanctuaries from which to attack at will foolishly endangered the lives of valiant men. That's what the captain wanted but if they attacked the sanctuaries, did the NVA move them? Necessitating more attacks across the border? Combat bases in Laos?

At night he stood in the small bar at the end of the mess and listened to the others.

"You want us to lose the war," said Major Groff, whose hair follicles had migrated to his ears.

"We just want the war to end," one of the reporters said. "As long as we're winning, it'll continue. If we lose, it'll end."

"What about these people?"

"Who gives a shit? Nobody cared about them before we came over here, nobody will care after we leave."

"You are fucking up people's minds," the major said. "I got a kid in college who doesn't know where he is. Half the time he thinks he's in the Supreme Court interpreting the laws for the country and the other half he thinks he's in a concentration camp being persecuted for his religious beliefs. He's a Presbyterian for God's sake. 'You're in college,' I tell him. 'They got a right to make you go to class.' You guys are distorting reality. You aren't reporters, you're fucking referees. You call the game the way you see it, only they don't have to play by the same rules. We got a right to attack our enemies anywhere they are as long as we got the power to do it."

"The reality is the war isn't for Vietnam, it's for the folks back home, their votes and their bucks," said a thick man with a bushy moustache over a mouth that was always in motion as though kissing itself. Sherrill recognized him as a political columnist on a two-week tour. "The battle is over public office and public opinion. Are we going to continue FDR's, Truman's, Eisenhower's world cop role or are we going to take care of problems back home? That's what the war is about."

Sherrill glanced at the television set above the bar. The sound was off but images flashed what he presumed was news. If so, the only thing that had happened that day was wars, race riots, accidents and sports.

"It goes deeper than that," said a history professor turned reporter. "Is American policy, both foreign and domestic, going to be based on moral principles or business principles? Are we here because it's right or because it's good for business?"

"Bullshit," said the man with the kissing mouth. "What American war was ever fought for moral principles? Was the Boston tea party over morals or money?"

"The Civil War was for moral principles."

"Bullshit. If the North wanted to free the slaves why didn't the government buy them and set them free? That would have been a hell of a lot cheaper than the war but it would have made the South even richer."

"The government didn't buy the slaves because it's immoral to buy and sell people. That's why it was a war over moral principles."

"If Robert E. Lee had had a sanctuary at his back we'd still be fighting the Civil War," said a reporter for a southern newspaper.

"If Lee had been as smart as Giap he would have turned his army into guerrillas," said the columnist with the kissing mouth.

"It wouldn't have worked because Yankee carpetbaggers came down and colonized the South, the same way we whipped the Indians by giving their land to farmers," said the southerner.

"The settlers weren't enough," Sherrill said. "To win a war of attribution you have to shut down the enemy's movement and destroy his commissary. The Army forced the Indians into reservations and exterminated the buffalo. No one is willing to do that to the VC."

"The media is the free marketplace of ideas," intoned the historian reporter. "We lay out our goods and the public buys its reality."

On the television screen was the spectacular smash of three racing cars, or perhaps the crash of the same car from three angles.

"It isn't exactly free," Sherrill said. "Some ideas are packaged with millions of dollars worth of music, movie stars and politicians. Others can't even afford paper to be written on."

"And all ideas aren't represented," said kissing mouth.

"The fall of Tombstone was all over the news," Sherrill said. "At the same time there was a major battle with the ARVN driving the NVA back into Laos but no one was there to cover it."

"It doesn't mean anything back in the world," said the columnist. "It doesn't show American will or American might or American decadence or a failed foreign policy. What are you going to do with it? There are a limited number of ways of reporting the news."

"And the metaphors have been decided," said kissing

mouth. "There won't be any Alamos in Vietnam. There can be Dien Bien Phus."

"What about Bataan and 'I shall return,'" said the major giving a power salute.

"That fucker ran when it got hot and didn't come back until his troops had secured the beach," said the southerner.

"The Alamo wasn't the Alamo until it was The Alamo," Sherrill said. "If there hadn't been San Jacinto—"

"The media is not here to argue strategy or review tactics," said the wire-service reporter. "Vietnam is like any other story. We are here to report the facts and very few reporters are here long enough or have the background information to understand what the facts are."

"Fuck the facts. News is the unusual, the extraordinary."

"It's not just the unusual, it's the off-beat about the unusual," said a man Sherrill recognized as a columnist who wrote human interest stories with pathos, irony, and a knowing smile at human folly, who twice a week met someone whose dream had failed. "The fact is thirteen-year-old girls have babies. It's not news. A thirteen-year-old girl having triplets? Maybe. A thirteen-year-old white girl having black triplets? That's news."

"Yeah, like that story about that LZ that was blown clear out of sight because some reporter shot back," the major said. "He did what thousands of soldiers do every day and he's a fucking hero."

Some of them looked at Sherrill. "I didn't make it that big."

"You weren't exactly shy," said the columnist. "'I shot gooks, I kicked Charlie's ass, I wanted to chase them to Hanoi and if the cowardly media had backed me up I would have.'"

"I really don't think I said that."

"Jesus, even the press is misquoted," the major said.

"You wrote it."

"I wrote that?"

"You want to see it?"

"Damn straight." The columnist left to get the magazine and the others waited for Sherrill to say something. He was relieved when the colonel announced that the movie was starting and the drinks and conversation were put aside in search of a new diversion. The columnist returned with his story and joined the others at the movie.

His name jumped from the page. "GUNFIGHT AT LZ O'CONNELL, written by the man who saved the outnumbered American forces." Below the bold title was the picture of him pointing, except that rather than pointing at a dead VC he was pointing the way to Cambodia. As he scanned the text he saw what Stone meant about cutting the "poetry" out of the story. "I, I, I," screamed at him from the page. "I came, I saw, I killed."

"LZ O'Connell is not exactly the kind of place I'd have chosen to have named for me. No one is likely to ever picnic there or live there for long. But it's the kind of place where men die in this heroic effort to save this tiny, rice rich country and these helpless people." He hadn't written "heroic" effort or "helpless" people. Vietnam was compared to a woman who was repeatedly attacked and killed in full view of students, liberals and the left wing press who did nothing to assist her but harassed the police who tried to apprehend her killer. He hadn't written that.

It wasn't his story. Not exactly. The words were his, most of them, although adjectives had been changed or added to embellish the prose. The tone of the story was not. He had tried to understate the story to give it gravity. Men had died here; stand in silence. Meditate. This story screamed. It was a celebration of his courage, his machismo, his killing of the enemy, his desire to pursue them across the border and kill more. Now he knew what the columnist meant. He had blown the incident out of proportion. But he hadn't. He hadn't intended it.

With the story was a sidebar about him, without a byline but probably written by Fred Stone. He was described as the successful author of two books—the descriptions were taken straight from the dust jackets—and a distinguished professor at a select private college who had grown up in a rural "America not afraid to be proud of itself." Fed up with pinko professors, draft-dodging hippie students and limp-wristed liberal journalists he had left his successful career to find and write the truth about Vietnam. Unlike journalists who got their news in Saigon, he had courageously ventured into the field and when attacked had fought back while the other correspondents cowered under his protection.

Jesus, didn't Stone realize how many enemies he was creating for him? He hoped Belk was right, that they had their bag; they'd let him have his. But Belk had also said he had set himself apart; he was all alone up on a cloud and everybody was going to be shooting at him. He was surprised they would speak to him.

He was equally surprised that those who knew him, who had read his books, like Jennifer and Lindly and his colleagues at the school, couldn't recognize that it wasn't him, that he wouldn't write something like that. Maybe he was exaggerating, hypersensitive because it was his story and it wasn't as arrogant and boastful as he thought. After all, the other reporters had been friendly. He tried to remember what he had written in "The Wild Bunch" story. More heroics. He wished he had gotten that story back but it was too late now.

He looked at the television screen as it scanned what seemed to be a stadium full of people. Men and women in costumes, masks, painted faces and dyed hair were waving signs and banners, gesturing like madmen and jeering, or maybe singing. A protest? They seemed too jubilant for that. Political rally?

The camera turned and he saw that it was a football game. The referees signaled no catch. The scene was run again and again, from different angles, in slow motion, in stop action.

The receiver caught the ball, came down in the end zone but it was not a touchdown and nothing could make it a touchdown. That's what the referees said.

"Did you see that?" Sherrill asked no one.

"It's a game, man," said the over aged hippie. His head was nodding and he seemed to have sunk inside himself. "Make us think it means something. It don't cluster, you know? You got to open your head to the antic. All those little pictures. They don't fuse, man; it's fission. It's chain reaction. It's where it's at. Trying to pretend it has a point drives people crazy."

Sherrill disliked arguing whether life had meaning; however, he could see that easy, facile visions of patterns and purpose could drive people insane. Maybe that's what insanity was—the ability to see meaning in everything.

"You sideburns chap my ass." Sideburn was Bird's contemptuous expression for those not brave enough for long-hair rebellion or crew-cut conformity. Although his eyes were angry, his voice was gentle, even warm, and he was too chubby, too amorphous to be threatening. Sherrill had trouble remembering his name because Bird was inappropriate unless he thought of a short, plump robin.

"War is shit, man, and you write about it like it was a traffic accident. Killed, injured, charged with negligence. This is no accident, this is murder. When some pig orders the burning of women and children, you call him Mr. President, you call him General, you call him fucking Sir. You've sanitized the news until it's nothing but numbers. Your castrated words can't describe what is happening."

Bird, with his long hair and Indian headband, reminded Sherrill of Lindly who appropriated the speech and clothing of whatever minority was currently approved but Sherrill could not ignore what Bird said. "Village searched for weapons" carried none of the anguish of families wailing the desecration of their home. "Detained and questioned" conveyed none of the fear and confusion of men pissing away their ideals.

"Civilian casualties" suggested none of the horror of a mother and father setting themselves afire trying to claw sticky flames from their screaming children.

His sanitized and castrated words conveyed none of the numbing shock and violence, the madness at the LZ. His account of The Wild Bunch was no closer to the truth of their tense and chaotic life than the "foot by bloody foot up perilous roads and deadly hillsides" versions.

His thoughts were interrupted by an explosion that jarred the building. Bird explained that it was the Vietnamese river patrol dropping grenades in the river to kill any VC frogmen trying to blow up the bridge. "First time I heard that I jumped in the bunker out there and some reporter was fucking one of the Vietnamese waitresses."

Sherrill was troubled by his thoughts but unwilling to abandon them. He created a world and characters out of what he was and what he believed, and his imagination and experience. That was fiction. He had thought nonfiction was the opposite—writing about people and a world not of his making. But the LZ story was more fictitious than Cassady who had survived an imaginary ambush. Yet, those who read the LZ story believed he was the O'Connell of that story. One's experiences shaped one's life and how others perceived those experiences also shaped one's life and the lens of attention distorted until only the distortion was real.

"You writing about the Vietnam in Berkeley or the Vietnam in Washington?"

Sherrill looked up to see Bird watching him through eyes slitted by puffy eyelids. Sherrill wondered if Bird was wired. "What's the difference?"

"About a million lives."

"Do you think all war is evil or just this one?"

"Evil is a word, man. Evil don't mean shit. I see you writing, writing. Writing sucks. Writing says it means something and it don't."

"Do you think we ought to let the North Vietnamese take over this country?"

"I think we ought to take over our own country. Man, we moved in but we ain't unpacked."

Bird was nodding slightly; Sherrill decided he was wired. "Aren't you going to the movie?" he asked.

"America's contribution to world culture. Tarzan and the Lone Ranger. No England without Errol Flynn." Thought seemed to escape Bird and he sat staring into his lap. "We are overdosing on illusion. You're our magic lantern. Mirror, mirror on the wall. America standing tall. Bigger than anybody. Better than God. Camelot, hot damn." Sherrill thought Bird had gone to sleep, but he slipped from his stool. "I'm not going to let you infect me with insanity. I get wired to get my head straight. Peace," he said in parting.

Sherrill looked at the screen and saw a referee signal that a fumble was not a fumble. He turned his back to the screen. Sherrill couldn't decide whether or not he liked Bird but he admired his courage. It wasn't easy to proclaim a separate reality. Sherrill wasn't sure he could do it. He feared if he were color blind, capable of seeing only shades of gray where others detected reds and brilliant blues, that eventually he would convince himself that he saw colors too. Was that the reason for drugs? Did Bird wire himself so he could see the clarity that others saw or to fortify himself against a mad world?

He walked outside. The movie being shown against the side of the open mess seemed to be about a psychopath who killed women. The screen showed scenes of violence, close up, slow motion, repetitive violence, the camera making love to the violence. Sherrill turned away. What kind of mind could invent such violence, write it, enact it, finance it, view it, glory in it?

He walked behind the mess and stood where the river flowed past the press center, watching sampans floating by and an occasional helicopter flapping over the city. In the early darkness of the evening he could see the outlines of houses and a church spire across the river. He pondered what Bird had said about him. He was the magic lantern, the mirror. What did that mean? A sentry on the bridge fired two rapid bursts at something in the water and the tracers tumbled over the river and sailed lazily into the night.

He wrote "Tombstone: The Camp Too Tough To Die." The vulnerability of the captain and his men was the responsibility of the generals and politicians, not his. He painted the enemy as cunning, cowardly, waiting in their sanctuary for darkness and rain to cover their sneak attack. He emphasized the captain's courage, the price the enemy had paid for what the media was calling a success and that the camp was being rebuilt. "The plan is to bleed Charlie and at Tombstone he bled. He wasn't pursued because that's the way things are done here. When Charlie steps across the border he's the same as a civilian."

Since Stone wanted more personal information, he wrote of the time he had discovered a fire in a neighbor's wheatfield. It was not yet out of control and he could have put it out but because it was a neighbor's field he first told his neighbor of the fire. The fire swept over his field and another neighbor's before it could be brought under control. If the reader wanted to interpret the story as saying it was easier to stop Charlie in Laos than in Vietnam, let him. That's as far as Sherrill could go.

He studied his photographs: ruined bunkers, mud-filled trenches, mist-covered hills, the captain eating C-rations and looking bored. They did not illustrate the story he wrote but he sent them anyway.

After mailing the story, he wrote Jennifer, telling her REAL had changed his story and asking her not to read any more stories about him. "There is a lot of competition for the news here and things get blown out of proportion. Believe me, I am not engaging in heroics and I am not going in the field again, I can promise you that. The streets of Da Nang are safer than the streets of San Antonio and I am staying right here and writing the stories. I am also working on the new book." He told her of his plans for the book as a way of preserving them. In the humidity of Vietnam paper disintegrated although he carried it in a plastic bag.

"Tom Cassady is trying to hold a solitary and unacceptable view of what happened to his unit in Korea. The Army can't admit it was a massacre; the town can't accept that its citizen-soldiers had died squealing and screaming like animals. He falls in love with the widow of one of the men and believes he can tell her the truth. She insists that her husband was as brave as Tom had been.

"His mother's belief that her son is special gains credence when he is the only survivor. Her belief turns to dismay as she realizes what being special costs him as the town turns him into something that is not her son, something that not even her mother's heart can touch. He is the model for the monument. At the unveiling of the statue, his mother begs the town to give her son back to her. The town cannot let him go; he is the only thing the rest of the world knows about them. They are made in his image. If they let him go back to who he was before the statue, before the medals and photographs and ambush, he is nothing and they are a lie. His mother decides not to begrudge her son his world. Or, maybe, in her secret heart she wishes he were like everyone else. Or, that he had died like everyone else, leaving her memory of him certain."

He studied the page wondering why he had written "certain." Because if Cassady had died she would remember the tiny promise she had held in her arms, the way he remembered Marie. She would remember the boy who clung to her on his first day of school. The man who clung to her before boarding the train that would take him, that would take all of them to Korea and death. And the memories would be intact, unbroken, certain.

But the memory had been broken. Something had happened to him in Korea that neither she nor anyone else could understand. And on the other side of that break had emerged a man who was flesh of her flesh, bone of her bone, and as separate from her as grapes from wine.

A Vietnamese journalist, named Bui, came to the press center. The others ignored him because they considered him an outsider, there because of the cheap food and drinks. Sherrill, because he believed he too was an outsider, befriended him. REAL wouldn't do a story on the ARVN but Sherrill believed Bui might give him valuable information.

Bui had studied in France and the United States, had twice been wounded while covering ARVN battles and had been imprisoned by the government in Saigon. "Why did Saigon put you in prison?" Sherrill asked.

"In America journalists write like of people and live like of officials. In Vietnam journalists write like of officials and live like of peasants." Bui smiled. Sherrill nodded without understanding.

"What do you think of the American fighting man?" Sherrill asked, hoping to get a pithy quote.

"VC fight in swamp, Americans drain swamp. VC fight in jungle, Americans plow jungle. VC fight in mountains, Americans blow up mountains. VC fight Americans. What do Americans fight?"

Sherrill put down his pen. All he was going to get was oriental inscrutability. "What do you think Americans fight?"

"Vietnam." Bui smiled. Sherrill refused to nod. "All of it. They fight the land, they fight the city, they fight the people, they fight the rain, they fight. . ." Bui searched for words. . . "they fight the air." Sherrill did not nod. "I show you," Bui said in exasperation.

Bui took Sherrill to the black market that sprawled over several blocks, much of it roofed with a bandit's collection of tarpaulin, sides from ammo crates, sheets of corrugated steel, panels from airplanes and helicopters, and floored with PSP and the plastic foam used to encase bombs. Rats and thumb-sized roaches scurried over the goods, pursued by hungry children.

"Put your money in your hand, your hand in your pocket, and I will protect your watch," Bui said. They made their way through U.S. uniforms, weapons from both NATO and Iron Curtain countries, signal flares, smoke grenades, television sets, stereos, air conditioners, cameras, blue jeans, crates of rations, cigarettes, liquor—the riches with which American had invaded Southeast Asia.

Sherrill was besieged by a horde of dirty children trying to pick roaches off his legs. Bui put both hands around Sherrill's watch; Sherrill put both hands around his money. A sore-eyed girl ran past, triumphantly carrying by the tail a rat that was still twitching. "See," Bui said. "America in Vietnam."

Back at the Press Center, Sherrill probed Bui. "You're saying that instead of fighting the enemy, America is trying to overpower the whole culture?"

"Imperialism, no?"

"No. We don't want Vietnam." Sherrill wondered how many times that had to be said.

"I show you. Television, rock and roll, hippie clothes."

"You're saying instead of bringing America over here, we should become more Vietnamese and fight the enemy instead of the country?"

"You fight the air."

"Okay, given that, how do you think the war is going?"

"America very rich country, has very much money. Vietnam very old country, has very much time."

After Bui left Sherrill was joined by Gunnery Sergeant Shivers. "I spent the day with a Vietnamese who spoke Engish and I didn't understand one word he said," Sherrill said.

The gunny shrugged. "C'est la vie, c'est la guerre and say no more."

Gunny Shivers looked like a man who had been torn apart and put back with a welding torch. His hands and arms were twisted, his face slightly askew, one eye higher than the other. It gave him a fierce and comic look.

He had come to Vietnam as a reconnaissance scout. Wounded on a patrol he had been attached to a SPIE rig, a heavy nylon rope dropped through the jungle canopy by helicopter. The chopper was hit and skidded sideways, dragging Shivers through trees and breaking most of his bones. He was taken to a hospital in Da Nang but it was a day of heavy casualties and the doctors were only seeing those with reasonable chances of recovery. Shivers had stopped one of the doctors. "Doc, ain't you going to do anything for me?"

The doctor shook his head. "You're seventy percent dead."

"But I'm still alive ain't I? Don't you have to do something for me if I'm still alive?"

The doctor grudgingly admitted that regulations required that Shivers be attended to. "If you're still alive when I've taken care of these other men," he said.

Sherrill studied the gunny's fierce, misaligned eyes wondering how much of the story was bullshit. It was easy enough to believe he had been left for dead.

After recovering from his injuries, the gunny almost accepted a medical discharge. "On the way to Pennsylvania I had a coincidence." He ran into the man who had saved his life in Korea. "He had stayed on the ridge throwing grenades so the others could carry me out. When a patrol picked him up he had frost bite so bad he had to crawl but he was bringing his rifle with him. That man had balls."

In Pennsylvania his rescuer was afraid to have a drink with Shivers because his wife might get mad. He was afraid to go for a walk because children made fun of the way he wobbled on his damaged feet. "I don't know what it is about civilian life that makes a man a coward. One morning you wake up with your grandfather's toe nails and it's all over."

The gunny returned to Vietnam but was not physically fit for reconnaissance. While in the field with an infantry company, the gunny had been talking down a resupply helicopter trying to land in darkness in rough terrain. The gunny was standing on a little mound watching the blinking red light of a helicopter in front of him unaware that he was talking to the helicopter landing behind him. The rotor from the helicopter behind struck him in the head knocking him unconscious. His helmet saved his life. After that everyone was afraid of him. "I acted the same as before but everybody was looking at me different. Hell, in my family there's only been one suicide and no retarded children."

The doctors declared Shivers unfit for combat duty and the Marines assigned him to the Public Affairs Office. Since then he had gotten to the action only by bringing some often unsuspecting or unwilling newsman with him. "A gung-ho guy like you has got to do some stories on the Marines. We've got an operation coming up soon."

"No, thanks," Sherrill said.

"How'd you like to visit a ville? We have Marine squads living with the Vietnamese, teaching them how to defend themselves, helping them build schools, pagodas or whatever. They play with the kids, vaccinate and treat them when they're sick. Groups from back in the world send pigs and seeds to help them improve their stock and improve their diet by growing cabbage and things."

Marines raising pigs and cabbage? He could imagine how Stone would react to that. "Not my kind of story."

"Those guys are doing a great job but I can't get anyone to do a story about them." Sherrill thought he knew why; no fragging, drugs, corruption, prostitution, villages destroyed, babies burned, women raped. No headlines. No hook. No focus. He was going to pass too; he wanted to stay in the mainstream with the big story. "Anyway, I wanted to give you this."

It was a column by Norela Cook saying that Sherrill, "the closest thing the media has to a Dix Deveraux," had demanded that he be taken to Tombstone despite the risk and was the last to leave.

There was a photograph of him with a soldier in a fighting hole. In the panic of running to the airstrip, he had jumped into a hole when a shell landed nearby. But he hadn't been encouraging the soldier as the cutline stated; the soldier had been helping him climb out of the hole. One of the photographers had taken the picture of him and Rick Belk had given Norela the story. That meant Belk had repaid the favor he believed he owed him. Sherrill preferred choosing his own favor.

He saw the gunny was amused that he had studied his photograph so intently. "I wrote a story on the captain," he said in explanation.

"His family will appreciate that." Sherrill looked at him sharply. "The captain and two 'yards were killed on a patrol. The Army has abandoned Tombstone."

Tombstone abandoned? The captain had been betrayed. He had been betrayed. After the gunny left he remained at the table unable to raise his head. He hardly knew the captain; why did he feel so bad? Had he too betrayed the captain? Ridiculous; his story hadn't even been published. But it had been written and his intentions were to make the captain and the plan look as good as possible with REAL's guidelines in mind. Was there anything more he could have done to help? He had admired the captain and his men and he was determined not to let himself off the hook if he could have helped them but he could think of nothing.

His thoughts turned to his story. What did it look like now? Perhaps before it hadn't been wholly true but now it was entirely a lie. There was no time to rewrite the story and he lacked the heart for it. "The enemy is entrenched in sanctuaries across the border," he wrote Stone. "Tombstone is too vulnerable. The captain has been killed and the camp abandoned. Please kill the story. I know no way to write it now."

Gunny Shivers came back to take Sherrill through the Marines' mine and boobytrap school at China Beach. "It's like the real thing except you can't get hurt." That's what Sherrill was looking for.

He went through the school accompanied by a Marine platoon that for half an hour thrashed and blundered along jungle trails and through a ville. Sherrill had backed away from a Viet Cong flag only to hit a trip wire behind him. He had detected a thin wire along a tree branch and while avoiding it had fallen into an animal trap with rubber spikes instead of pungee sticks. He had brushed against a tree and brought an oil drum, shredded so that jagged edges pointed in all directions, crashing within a foot of his head, and the irritating voice of the instructor, "You are dead, you are fucking dead."

After they had killed and maimed themselves innumerable times, they sat on the sand while the instructor smiled a tight little smile that said he knew something they didn't. The instructor was a sergeant in his early twenties but as he showed his deadly wares Sherrill could see that he had no nails on his twisted fingers and scars ran up his arms, his neck, and the side of his face.

"Nothing is what it appears to be," he said, holding up a ballpoint pen that blew off your fingers, a camera that blew up in your face, a rock that slivered your testicles, a bicycle pump that took off your knees. "Traumatic amputation," the sergeant screamed, showing rows of mindless machines and demonstrating an infinite variety of ways to conceal them.

"There is no safe place to put your foot, no safe place to hide your ass. The dream of safety is a boobytrap. Get rid of it.

When you get in an area that is mined there is no easy way out. That's a boobytrap. There is no one who can come and get you out. That's another boobytrap. Face those things here and now so you don't panic later. If you are lucky you will see a boobytrap. If you are unlucky you will hear it. A little click. If you're real lucky, that's the last thing you'll ever hear."

Sherrill could feel the men fidgeting around him. He could feel his genitals crawl. "There was a platoon that got into an area like you were in only it was real. Everything they touched blew up. The wounded thrashing on the ground set off mines, the corpsmen trying to reach the wounded set off mines, the mines set off mines. The lieutenant called helicopters to lift them out. The rotor wash shook grenades out of the bushes; the choppers dropped ropes and everything the ropes hit blew up. The lieutenant grabbed a rope and got dragged over a mine that blew off both his legs. He bled to death before they could winch him aboard."

The sergeant's hairless, nail-less hands played with one of the little clicking machines. "I called off the choppers and said, 'Get out your bayonets, we're digging our way out.' We felt a path out and then we went back and carried out our dead and wounded. The five of us that still had arms and legs."

The sergeant tossed the mine into their midst. Sherrill fell over one man and was tripped over by another as they all sought safety. "Welcome to Vietnam," the sergeant said, picking up the mine made of hard rubber.

On the way back to Da Nang they drew sniper fire from the sacred marble mountain that overlooked the Marine base. "I thought you said it was safe," Sherrill screamed.

"Viet Cong have been in those caves for years," the gunny said. "But we're not permitted to clean them out because we might damage the shrines."

"What? They have sanctuaries inside the country?"

"There it is. C'est la vie, c'est la guerre and say no more."

"How come they can shoot at us but we can't shoot back?"

The gunny shrugged. "You can wash a plate but you can't wash a sandwich."

Norela's story and the photograph of him at Tombstone meant that Stone would not kill the story. Sherrill knew he had better rewrite it. He needed a picture that would tell readers how to see it but the reporters were right—it wasn't the Alamo. Dien Bien Phu had been over-worked and wasn't acceptable to Stone anyway. Sherrill believed the men at Tombstone had been as brave as men had ever been but he couldn't portray them as Greek heroes defending civilization against the barbarians. The world had decided otherwise.

The only way to write the story was to again make himself the center of it and describe what it was like flying into Tombstone, being there, flying out. He didn't like writing it that way but he had been there, he had risked his life. He would emphasize the heroism of the soldiers and to deflect jealousy he would describe the daring of the photographers and the television crew. He wouldn't say the plan worked but would emphasize the body count and add a sidebar that the captain had returned, had been killed and the camp abandoned. He would call it "Brave Men, Brave Mission."

He sat in the open mess drinking coffee and working on the story. Bird came in and sat down heavily across the booth from him. "Is it a story if nobody reads it?" Bird asked.

If he couldn't write it so that REAL liked it it wasn't a story but he did not want to get in a conversation, particularly not with Bird. He continued writing, hoping Bird would take the hint.

"Never judge a war by its popularity," Bird said. "War is not cereal." Sherrill looked at him to see if he were already stoned, if he had intended "serial." "Nothing as immoral as popular war." Bird's chin came to a rest on his chest. He seemed to be asleep.

Bird spoke without raising his head or opening his eyes.

"Japanese bastards bayoneted children, raped women, tortured prisoners. First one I ever saw was beaten in broad daylight on Main Street. He begged people to call a cop, call an ambulance. My mother dragged me away. 'I hope they kill every one of them slant-eyed bastards,' she said. Making hate a virtue is the worst vice."

Bird was right. No matter how appealing it was to REAL, fanning hatred, glorifying death brought no honor to the men at Tombstone. Their purpose had to justify the killing.

"Brass hasn't found a way to look successful," Bird said. "How you gonna show? Al Capone bigger hero than Dorothea Dix. Had pizzazz."

The strategy had to be bigger than cheese in a trap.

"New car every year. Better job. Younger wife. Gooks don't have a scorecard, don't have to look successful."

As usual Sherrill wasn't exactly sure what Bird was saying but he seemed to say that courage, honor, integrity didn't count, that it didn't matter how the game was played. The only thing that mattered was the scoreboard. Victory by fraud was just as sweet. Sherrill couldn't accept that. If that were true in war, how long would it be before it was true in sports, business, politics? "I know the grunts mock honor and integrity but when the shooting starts they live and die by those codes," he said. "If they didn't, there wouldn't be a man here who wasn't looking for a place to hide."

"We're fixers," Bird said. "Not a damn thing in this country we can fix. Same river floods same land every year. We send doctors, nurses in the bush, vaccinate whole villes. Charlie comes in, burns the hootches, kills the people. Every dead son of a bitch is immune to small pox."

Bird dozed. Sherrill scratched out "Brave Mission."

The next time Shivers came to the center, Sherrill asked him about the abandonment of Tombstone. "Too exposed," the gunny said.

"Why were they put there if they can't seal the border?"

"Monitor infiltration. Who? How many? Where were they headed?"

The gunny took Sherrill up the hill to the Reconnaissance Battalion where Marines jogged, did pushups or practiced point and fire shooting. A recon team told Sherrill of their surveillance of NVA units as they moved into the mountains, filtered down into the lowlands for rice and infiltrated the villages. "We know where their staging bases are in Laos. They rest there, resupply and when it's to their advantage, cross the border and kill the men we have out there. Then we have to go find them so the grunts can run them out."

The team gave Sherrill a taste of recon by smearing his face with camouflage paint and loading him with a scout's gear. Bush cover to camouflage his head and keep off the sun. Gloves to camouflage and protect his hands; any break in the skin meant infection. No helmet or flak jacket, too heavy. No skivvies, caused rash. Three extra pairs of socks, change at every opportunity. Poncho and liner for bed. Seven canteens of water. Rappelling line for skinning down cliffs, with snaps for hooking onto ladder or nylon SPIE rig if there was no helicopter sit down.

Rifle, twenty-five magazines of ammo, eight grenades and a claymore. C-rats—one meat and one fruit every day for energy. The rest, freeze-dried long rats for easy to carry. Two battle dressings in right trouser pocket. One canteen of water, one long rat in other pocket. Mirror and compass in jacket pocket. If forced to didi, drop pack. Food, water, bandages, compass and mirror in pockets. Head east and flash with mirror anything that flew over.

The gunny took photographs of Sherrill posing with the team. On the way back to the center Shivers revealed that the Marines were planning an operation to clear the NVA out of the villes and lowlands and drive them back into the hills. "I'm after a different story," Sherrill said.

At the press center Sherrill had a letter from Jennifer and one from his mother. His mother's letter was cautious pages of Monday through Friday that revealed nothing of who she was. She had been what her husband wanted, what her son needed, slow to discover herself, even slower to let him know her as a person rather than Mother.

They loved each other and after his father's death had spent their lives together; he hiding his vices from her, she hiding her needs from him. In time he came to see her through Jennifer's eyes—a pretty woman in a determined sort of way, her hair well done, her clothes well chosen, her posture erect. She loved Jennifer like a daughter but it was one of her friends who revealed that she suffered vaginal bleeding but feared going to a doctor.

Even after Sherrill confronted his mother, it was the friend who revealed that it wasn't cancer she feared but that confirmation of cancer would rob her of her hard won independence. Despite the insurance premiums she had paid for years the doctors would take her home, her store, her retirement and leave her a shell in a nursing home.

After hours of struggling between his conscience and her wishes, Sherrill had taken her to a doctor. It proved not to be cancer but their relief was mitigated by his overstepping established boundaries. After that every call or letter had a paragraph about the state of her health, written to reassure not to inform.

"Gordon Baxter called the other day," she wrote without explanation. Gordon Baxter had introduced himself one day when Sherrill was a student. "I guess your mama told you about me." She had not. "I been seeing your mama," Gordon had said. He looked like a farmer or rancher, dressed in boots, khaki pants with wide belt, khaki shirt, holding a straw hat in his sunburned hands. He was awkward, embarrassed, a little apologetic, like a man who was returning a crate of eggs and wanted his money back.

Gordon Baxter held his head up but did not look Sherrill in the eye out of consideration for Sherrill's feelings. Sherrill stared over Gordon's shoulder. "I want to marry your mama but she won't unless you say it's okay. I told her I was going to ask you."

"Okay," Sherrill said stupidly. They had talked for a while without saying anything. "If she wants to get married I think it's fine," Sherrill said without enthusiasm. He wanted to thump Gordon in the chest and add "Dad" to the sentence but couldn't.

"I've got a good name, people will vouch for that. And your mama is a fine woman. A man couldn't ask for a better woman."

Gordon seemed to be waiting for something and after he had waited long enough he left. Sherrill wanted to shout after him, "Hey, you old son of a bitch, I'll buy you a beer," but he couldn't. When he mentioned to his mother that Gordon had come to see him she had said nothing but she too seemed to be waiting for something. "He seemed like a nice man," he added, and when she said nothing he dropped the conversation.

She didn't marry Gordon, as far as he knew never saw him again and never said what had happened. He always feared that he had not approved enough and wondered why Gordon had called his mother after all this time. And why his mother had mentioned it. Was she still waiting for something he didn't know to give?

As if in recompense, the next paragraph referred to his father. When she spoke of his father, which wasn't often, it was to reproach Sherrill. "Your father always drove fast," meant slow down.

In the letter she wrote that one of her friends wanted her to drive to Alaska. "Your father wanted to sell the farm and move to Alaska. I told him that was okay for a bachelor." Sherrill stared at the letter in disbelief. His father had wanted to sell the farm? He had been taught that the farm was his birthright, his heritage. Every day of his adult life he had shouldered guilt because he was an ungrateful child who had forced his mother into selling his father's farm, who had betrayed his father's wishes. But his father too had wanted something different.

"Going to Alaska would mean closing the store, at least for a few weeks and I don't want to do that. The happiest days in my life have been spent in that store. I wanted to sell the farm the day of your father's funeral but I was afraid you would never forgive me."

Sherrill looked at the words in disbelief. All those years he had thought his mother had disapproved of him because he had sold the farm. All those years he had sought her forgiveness, her approval and he had it without knowing it? They had sat in the same house both pretending they wanted to be farmers, both feeling guilty for something that both wanted to do? How could two people be so close and know so little of each other?

Jennifer wrote, "Sometimes I am afraid your stories will be a success and that they will want you to stay as long as the war lasts, that you will take chances that you don't have to take. I am trying to reconcile myself to it. If you were here now I could reconcile myself to anything. Lin said that every man dreams of living the kind of life you do and that he didn't know anyone who could do as much with the opportunity as you."

When had Lindly said that? Sherrill looked at the envelope but as usual the damp had turned everything to smudge. "See, Lindly can be nice. He said, 'We've lost him, you know. He's seen too much.' He has read something about you but pretends he can't remember where he read it. It must be awfully bad. Please come home, Sherrill. Soon."

Sherrill wrote the story of Tombstone again, this time stating that the plan wasn't working. They killed a lot of the enemy but didn't stop infiltration and the cost in American lives wasn't worth it. Unable to attack the sanctuaries in Laos, the Army had closed the camp. This time he called it, "Goodbye to Tombstone."

After he had mailed the corrected version of the story, he wrote a synopsis of the new book and sent it to his agent hoping to capitalize on the publicity he had received. Then he wrote a story about the booby-trap school calling it "The Last Klick." Grunts called the walk to the Freedom Bird that took them home "the last klick" and he wanted the irony of the title to emphasize the difference between walking to the plane and being carried. Stone didn't like such literary devices and it wasn't the kind of story REAL wanted but Sherrill hoped the attention he had gotten and the earlier death-defying stories would make it acceptable.

Then he worked on "Swift, Silent, Deadly," about the men who tracked Charlie's infiltration and called down fire and bombs on him. He colored the story with the details he had gotten from the team—hunting, hiding, heat, the feel of camouflage paint, the weight of the pack, ass-kicking mountains, snakes, entangling vines, dark jungle filled with shifting shadows and sliding eyes, the night filled with uncertain sounds. He wanted to create the illusion that the reader was there.

One day everyone at the Press Center was invited to a beer and steak party at China Beach but he was in no mood for pranking and talking. He wanted to stay at the center, write his stories and go home. The bar and mess were open but empty. He found a sulky Vietnamese waitress and cajoled her into bringing him food and coffee. The girl pouted in a corner, pulling at her long black hair, refusing to look at him until he rapped his coffee cup on the table. He worked until time for the mess to close and took a drink back to his deserted hootch.

The door of the hootch opened and he looked up to see the waitress. She produced a pad and pencil. "Who is your name?"

she asked. "You write me." Sherrill wrote down his name not sure whether she wanted his autograph or his name for a complaint to the colonel.

"You write me letter," she said, handing him a dirty business card with the name and address of a photographer. "He gib me baby. You ask he don't write. I boom boom. He don't gib money. Baby sick."

She was pretty in a high-cheeked, sullen-mouthed way and he could believe the photographer had convinced himself he loved her, but he could not understand how the man could go back to his safe, comfortable life leaving this girl solely responsible for his child. He would have felt more obligation to a stray dog.

"Dear Neal," he wrote to the name on the card. Maybe he couldn't do anything for Harry's—those children in Saigon but he could do something for this woman and her baby. "The baby you gave me is very sick. If I do not get a letter from you soon with some money for your baby I will be forced to ask the generous reporters here for the money to bring the baby to you. Your loving. . ." He turned to the girl. "What's your name?"

"Poo see."

Sherrill looked at her doubtfully. "Susie?"

"He say me Poo See."

Sherrill added that to the letter, then added a note of his own. "P.S. If this woman does not receive immediate and satisfactory assistance, I am going to write your employer and apprise him of the situation." He signed his name and addressed the envelope. He didn't want the woman hanging around him but he didn't want a sick baby on his conscience either; he put ten dollars with the envelope and handed it to her. She removed her shirt. She was smaller than he had realized, her shoulders thin but nicely rounded, her arms firm and smooth, her stomach flat. He looked away.

"No," he said. He wondered how he could tell her that he

wanted to help her and her child, that he cared. "Poo see," he said. He didn't even know her name. "Most men aren't unfeeling toward women and children." He hadn't been able to explain to the children in Saigon but maybe this woman would understand. She sat down beside him and pulled her pajamas over her feet, her brown legs flashing at the corners of his eyes.

"No," he said. "It doesn't have to be like this. We can be equals."

"You wear," she said, handing him a condom.

Jesus, why him? He had never been irresistible to women before. Then he came to Vietnam where there were about a million guys for every good-looking woman and the women were all over him. He could feel her bare breasts against his back. She seemed to be breathing with her hips. "I want to help you, not use you. I don't know how."

"You wear," she said, pushing the condom between his legs. He was so horny he almost ejaculated. "Get out," he yelled. "Didi."

"You number ten lover," she said. "You cheap charlie. You poo see."

Sullenly she put on her clothes and left, taking the envelope and money with her. Sherrill did not feel virtuous; he felt depressed. She had not seen him as a person and had reduced his charity to a commercial transaction. Everyone needed help sometime, but he didn't know how to help these people. No one wanted to hurt them, to take advantage of their misery, yet everyone did.

When the others returned from the party he pretended sleep. They stumbled around grousing about the party. "If the colonel couldn't get nurses he should have brought the Vietnamese waitresses," one of them said. "I didn't expect to get laid but I did think there would be some women there. Hell, we might as well be in the bush."

"Watch out for the waitresses," said another. He explained

that one of the waitresses wrote to newsmen who had gone home, telling them they had fathered her child and asking for money. "Chances are they screwed someone and they don't remember the name and they'd rather send money than take a chance on her contacting their families or employer. She's got a boobytrap in her garden."

"I thought all women did," said the first.

Sherrill was angered at their cynicism, their sophomoric worldy wisdom. He had been stupid to give the waitress his name but what could he have done? He couldn't have refused to help her. Not if he believed her story and it was easy enough to believe. Once again he had betrayed himself. A real booby. To avoid one trap was to step in another. To grab a souvenir was to destroy oneself, to stay on the trail was to die by the trail, to turn away was to fall into a pit. The words of the instructor rang in his head. "There is no one to come and get you out. A little click. If you're lucky that's the last thing you'll ever hear. You are dead. You are fucking dead."

Sherrill took his mail to his hootch to read until the bar opened. Several of the letters were from people he didn't know and he read those first. Fan letters, he had never gotten fan letters before, applauding him for standing up for America and supporting the troops.

There was a letter from Fred Stone saying that the Tombstone story was too good to kill. Stone would make the necessary revisions. Sherrill smiled; he had beaten Stone to the punch.

He read Jennifer's letters hungrily, trying to catch sight of the woman he loved. He read the letters slowly trying to hold her for a moment in his mind, to draw warmth from her words.

"Goodnight my love, and tonight you are my love because I heard from you today and I read your letter again in bed, and I am going to sleep with it beside me and dream of you and your taste and your smell and your hands and lips and the way you feel inside me. I realize I never touched you enough. I wish I could touch you now and feel you grow big inside me."

Jennifer was becoming less inhibited about sex. She was trying to seduce him. He smiled at what that might mean when he got home.

"You probably get tired of all these letters but I like writing to you as it makes you seem closer. I hope you are okay. I don't watch the television news any more since I thought I saw you."

She hadn't seen him, of course, but he liked the implication. He was "newsworthy," someone who might appear in the papers or on the screen and the expectation gave birth to the reality. As long as he was expected to be in the news he would be in the news. He opened another letter.

"I have been so busy I haven't had time to think and that's a relief. When I think, I think of you and I start missing you and then I get angry because you are in Vietnam and don't have to be. Or I think of that awful book where everybody dies. Where everything is a lie." What awful book? What was she reading?

"It's all falling apart, all we've dreamed of, worked for, held between us. I thought when Marie died that was the worst thing that could happen to me. When you left, I thought, no this is worse, having a dead child and a husband in limbo. I don't know if you're dead, I don't know if you've left me, I don't know if you're ever coming back. I write you, I curse you a while, cry a while, I swear I'll never like you again and end up wishing you were here because I love you so. I can't believe I may never see you again, that you can just walk away from all we had and never look back. Don't you ever cry? Don't you ever think of Marie? Don't you remember the way you used to ride her on your knee to see her laugh? Don't you ever think you could give up the rest of your life and whatever promise it has just to laugh together the way we did then? Come home. We can start over. We can work out any problems we have."

He was surprised by the tone of the letter. He thought it must be an early one, written soon after he left home. Still, the tone disturbed him.

He opened another letter. Jennifer's street company had crashed The Locker Room, a raunchy private club of the sleazier, more rapacious politicos, lawyers, bankers, contractors and businessmen. The only women permitted in the club were waitresses who wore topless costumes. Two of the actresses got jobs in the club to help with the disruption. A third actress tried to enter the club saying she wanted to join. The management barred her way, the two actresses inside argued that women were allowed inside but not as equals. The police were called, the actresses quit and two more waitresses quit with them. Another waitress was fired.

"Some of the board members thought it was degrading to the women to work there but it was Lin's idea and he's chairman." It didn't seem fair to Sherrill that waitresses quit or were fired because of actresses who were only pretending, but he knew how Jennifer got her job. Lindly had gotten it for her. When had she started calling him "Lin?"

"I think I am over the worst of missing you. I have to admit that sometimes it has been dreadful but I'm glad I decided not to sit around waiting on you but to make a life for myself. I can see now that I leaned too much on you and I am sorry. Maybe that's why you had to leave. When you come back you will find a woman who can take care of herself. Maybe you won't like her and I will be sorry for that but that's the way it has to be. Sometimes I am frightened by how quickly things are changing."

The letter was disturbingly similar to the way Jennifer made the bed after they had made love, putting away the wild liberty of passion and organizing herself for the next act.

Jennifer liked completion. She liked everything nailed, battened, dogged down. "Closure," Lindly and real estate salesmen called it. Once he had found her in Marie's room, dumping Marie's things into boxes to be given away; cleaning up, letting go so she could begin to heal.

It wasn't that he wanted to keep the room forever as though Marie would return. He wanted time to heal a little, to prepare himself to sit alone in her room and go through her things one by one in a kind of telling. In their anguish they could not say what they felt. He had screamed, "You're denying her, trying to forget she ever lived." She screamed, "She isn't coming back. She's dead. I'm not going to make up her bed every day."

He stared at the familiar, circumspect handwriting, feeling severed, cut adrift. He depended on Jennifer for balance, for his point of reference. She had been as consistent as the Five O'Clock Follies, the six o'clock news, the middle of the road. Now, when he wanted information what he got were feelings to which he had responded only to be jerked back and forth until he no longer knew what she meant. Which of her attitudes were passing and which were set?

If he could talk to her for five minutes, if he could just hold her, all her questions would be resolved and all of his. He could call her but such calls were difficult to arrange, allowed no privacy and would mean taking the slot reserved for some poor grunt who might not get another chance. There had been no telephone on the farm and he had no confidence in his ability to communicate over one. He was quickly bored, his attention wandered and he never believed anything he was told over the telephone.

He went to talk to the colonel. The colonel wasn't in but the sergeant was and Sherrill explained why he needed to call home. "I don't know what's going on."

"If you got something to tell her, I'm coming home, I'm not coming home, something like that, call. If you want to straighten something out, forget it. My wife was mad for two months because I hadn't thanked her for the birthday present that I still haven't gotten. I called once because I thought she was going to commit suicide. She was depressed, she couldn't sleep, she couldn't eat. I broke my ass trying to get a call through and she didn't know what I was talking about.

"Realize what's going on. She probably writes you every day. One day her mother calls, she's happy. Next day, she's got the cramps, she's blue. Next day the washing machine breaks, she's mad. She doesn't tell you all that because she doesn't want you to worry. Then you get the letters a bunch at a time and she's mad, she's happy, she's blue and you think she's losing her mind. If you call and tell her that she's going to think you're losing yours."

On the way back to his hootch he saw the sulky waitress and he got his camera. Major Groff said many Vietnamese believed when you took their picture you captured their spirit. Interrogators took pictures and did things with them to mess with the suspect's minds. Sherrill took a picture of the waitress.

She stopped in mid-stride and turned to look at him, her sulky eyes gone wide. "If you shitcan, maybe I die," she said.

"If you mail that letter I wrote or write to my wife, I shitcan your picture," he said. That was one boobytrap he had escaped.

He went back to his hootch and read Jennifer's letters again, trying to separate momentary irritations and emotional responses from developing attitudes. He read them again, looking for the Jennifer he knew, the Jennifer who saw herself as clearly as she saw him, and admitted him as the only inconstant in her life. It disturbed him that she was going ahead with her life. Of course he knew she must make decisions, plans, but he didn't want her going too far.

He wrote her. "I have been hard at work and have sent REAL several stories. I intend to stay in the Press Center and get the others I need. It isn't necessary for me to go into the field again so you needn't worry. I am not taking any chances or doing anything dangerous. My only fear is failing you, seeing disappointment and disapproval in your eyes. I am afraid because you are not beside me and I don't know how you are. You are the occasion of my fears and the origin of my courage."

He threw the page away and began again, telling her that he was doing well, writing regularly and would not go into the field again. "The book is going well. And it looks like they may reprint the first two books. I know it has been difficult but it looks like we are about to make it. I believe in Vietnam I am going to find the big breakthrough I have been looking for.

"I know it hasn't been easy for you. I know that I did not pick a good time to leave. I know that I have wronged you. Jennifer, no matter what our crimes, we created one faultless thing. Marie. She is ours forever, and the cord she birthed can be cut only by our forgetting. She cannot change or grow, but she can live, can smile, can bless us with elemental pee as long as we hold her memory between us."

When she was in kindergarten, Marie had come home singing "elemental pee." When Jennifer asked where she had heard it, Marie said her teacher had taught her. "Abcdefg-hijk-elemental pee." Sherrill knew Jennifer would laugh at his mention of it.

Sherrill felt better. Writing had brought Jennifer close again, close enough to feel. She felt real. He arranged her letters so that he could read last the one that began, "Goodnight, my love."

Someone came in the hootch and Sherrill looked up to see Rick Belk. "You are past tense," Belk raged. "I told you, you have to be interesting. I gave you your chance and you didn't exploit it."

"What are you talking about?"

"I'm talking about that fucking Tombstone. I risked my ass to get that story and the network didn't use it because some sophomore raised a VC flag and chained himself to the flagpole so campus security couldn't get it down. I needed that story. Don't you understand, my life is on the line. I got real competition. Either I win or I'm dead. I told you, you have to be outrageous. You're getting tame. You're starting to sound like everyone else. I sold that LZ story for you and you didn't do anything with it."

"What did you want me to do, get killed?"

"I asked for this shit because I thought being here would guarantee big stories and I get upstaged by a college sophomore. Brien, the asshole who wants my job, gives some kid a fucking flag and it's not even a VC flag. And the network doesn't give a shit because no one knew the difference. I picked the wrong horse."

"What do you mean wrong horse?"

"Don't play the virgin with me. I made you, Sherrill. No one ever heard of you until I put you on the screen. You were nobody and I made you somebody, and you volunteered."

"What am I supposed to do, kiss your ass?"

"You're supposed to be somebody people want to hear about. You're supposed to say something or write something that grabs their attention or makes them mad or some damn thing. They said my story had no bite. I couldn't get any spark out of the captain and you sat around scratching your ass. You didn't even go back to Saigon to be interviewed."

"I waited for the survivors to come in. I interviewed them."

"The story was the fall of Tombstone, the camp too tough to die. It died, I died, my story died because you didn't know what the fuck the story was."

"How do you know what's news and what isn't?"

"You don't until it's news and sometimes it isn't until you make it news. But if the competition covers it, you better cover it too. Nobody reported on the survivors of Tombstone."

"They went back. The captain—"

"I don't give a shit and neither does anyone else. It's not news. That story has been told a thousand times. Everybody went after that kid with the VC flag. . .what was supposed to be the VC flag."

"And the other guy who wants to be anchor gave it to him?"

"Everybody wants to be anchor; he's the guy I have to beat

and he gave the kid the flag and the handcuffs and he got the story."

"That doesn't seem honest."

"It was the biggest story that day. I'll end up doing weather in Dubuque." Rick sat down on a bunk and put his head in his hands.

"Did you come here for sympathy or to chew my ass?"

"I'm here for the same reason you are, to cover the Marine operation. And I got to have a big story. One with bite."

"I'm not going."

"You have to go. You're Sherrill O'Connell."

"I can get all the stories I need right here."

"Who's going to believe you?"

"A lot of people write stories from Da Nang, Saigon. Hell, some people write them from Hong Kong."

"Not you. You packaged yourself as the gung-ho guy who has to see it for himself. That's the image you wanted. You're going to look like a phony who was playing hero to get publicity. You can't weasel out now."

"I'm not weaseling out. I just don't see any reason to go."

"Jesus, after all I've done for you. You better get your ass out there and you better have something catchy to say or you're dead."

"These other guys don't have to be in their stories."

"They're reporters. You're a celebrity. They write stories, you are the story. They didn't say they were Sherrill O'Connell. They didn't say they wanted to kill gooks all the way to Hanoi."

"I didn't say that," Sherrill yelled as Belk walked out the door.

He picked up Jennifer's letters and tried to read them again but he couldn't concentrate. He was a celebrity and he was past tense. He was a hero and he was a phony. It was like playing with binoculars when he was a kid. Look through one end and things were big and close. Look through the other end and they were way off and too small to care about. Now the LZ was big, now it was small. Now he was important, now insignificant and it had nothing to do with who he was or what he did.

He put the letters away and went to the bar for a drink. Belk was standing at the bar; Sherrill went to the other end. "Look who's here," said a man wearing jungle fatigues and love beads with a pendant made of a bullet-pierced child's skull. Rod Reaves. "Swashbuckling Sherrill O' Connell, more swash than buckle." Sherrill nodded and ordered a drink.

"Hear you were at Tombstone," Reaves said. "How long were you there?"

"Too long."

"You didied on the first chopper out," Reaves said. It was an accusation.

"Damn straight," Sherrill said.

"You ran out on those guys." In a manner of speaking, yes. He wasn't a soldier; what was he supposed to do? "You turned yellow. You jumped on the skids of a chopper that came for the wounded." His voice was getting loud and shrill. The others in the bar were watching.

"No, I didn't," Sherrill said calmly.

"Don't lie to me, I've got a picture." Reaves slapped on the bar a clipping from some newspaper that showed him hanging on to the side of the helicopter while the door gunner fired over his head. He had just shoved Belk inside and was trying to scramble in himself but the cutline said, "Americans flee doomed camp." The impression wasn't exactly true but how did you argue with a photograph? People believed what they thought they saw

"I was there, where were you?" Sherrill asked.

"I was at a forces camp for four years. I've been wounded twice and have killed eleven Cong." Sherrill turned his attention to his drink. "Where are my pictures? You fly in, get your picture taken and get your ass out. Where the fuck do you get off being a hero? Who did you ever kill?"

Sherrill didn't want to get into a stupid argument over who was the bravest or who had killed the most men, not in front of soldiers like Gunny Shivers who had fought actual battles or newsmen like Rick Belk who had risked their lives to get a story. He saw with regret that he had the attention of everyone in the bar. He tried to break the tension with humor. "Talk to Rick here, he'll take your picture."

"Don't patronize me, powder puff. The Marines are planning a big operation and I'm going along. Only I'm not going along to have my picture taken. I'm going for a story and I'm going to carry my own pack and cover my own ass. Now where is your taffy ass going to be?"

Sherrill wasn't a soldier; he didn't have the training or the time to spend weeks in the drudgery and terror of the field. He looked at Rick for help. Belk had been at Tombstone. He knew what happened.

"That's why we're here," Rick said.

"Grow some balls, you pussy," Reaves said.

"I'll go anywhere you go," Sherrill said.

"Don't bother to pack his p.j.'s. He'll be back before dark," Reaves said and stalked from the bar.

Sherrill ordered another drink and waited for the attention to shift to something else. Rick moved down the bar to him. "You should have punched him while you had everyone's attention," Rick said. "You don't have the instinct."

"What's the matter with him?" Sherrill asked.

"What did you expect?" Belk said. "You could write your whole life, hell, you could win the Nobel Prize and not get the attention you got for wearing those silly shoes. You're not even a journalist and you come over here, shoot somebody and you're famous. That guy's been here for years, he's seen more combat than both of us and he's lucky if he can get ink. I put you on everybody's screen but you didn't get there by hard work. You didn't get there by doing something no one else could do. It could have as easily been him. It probably should have been him. You got it too easy, Sherrill, and now you got to prove you're who you say you are."

He wasn't the one who said he was who everyone thought he was. But no matter. "I'm going on the fucking operation."

"You almost committed status suicide. Celebrities are two-dimensional. You can't start showing depth, contradictions and a different side of your face. You got to stick to your image. But wear a scarf or something distinctive so you stand out. Why do you think Reaves wears that bone around his neck? You're creative. You can think of something."

Instead of committing status suicide he was going to risk his life. He ordered another drink.

"I've got a problem and I need your help," Belk said. "You see anything funny about the way I'm holding my head?"

"No."

"Look at my mouth. Do you see anything funny about the way I move my mouth?" Sherrill thought not. "I sent this great footage of a Riverine operation and all they had to say was that I was holding my head funny and doing something strange with my mouth. One producer thought I was chewing gum on camera. I don't even chew gum."

"I don't see anything wrong."

"I'm in deep shit, Sherrill. I got to get a big story and I got to hold my head straight and not do something funny with my mouth. You got to help me, Sherrill."

Sherrill promised he would.

The Arizona

A cloud of red dust hung over the combat base that seemed to consist of nothing but roads, wire, trenches and bunkers around a short landing strip of perforated steel plates. The Seaknight disgorged reporters and photographers to the waiting Gunny Shivers. "Dead Marines are good for business," the gunny said. "You never lose money when Marines die."

Shivers assigned the newsmen to Marine escorts who led them up a hill to the Command Center. "I got something special for you," Shivers said, leading Sherrill to a Huey flying resupply.

"Why me?"

"You're not a quitter."

Despite his apprehension, Sherrill was pleased with the compliment. He and the gunny got off when the helicopter landed on a hole-infested hill. Lt. Stolkalcyk made no pretense of being happy to see them. He was older and rougher than Sherrill expected second lieutenants to be, a mustang who had risen through the ranks and been commissioned because the

Marines needed lieutenants. When they no longer needed him as an officer he would go back to the ranks. He knew that and while he carried the responsibilities of an officer easily enough, he had never bothered to take up the bearing.

Stolkalcyk handed Sherrill a battle dressing. "Carry it in your right trouser pocket so if you get hit the corpsman will know where to find it." He picked up a rifle and bandoleer of ammunition and handed them to Sherrill. "If you go with me you'll have to carry your own weapon and cover your own ass." Then he handed Sherrill a poncho. "Pick out any bed you like," he said, gesturing at the muddy holes. "We leave at midnight."

"God hates a coward," the gunny said, wrapping himself in his poncho and liner and lying down beside a hole. "And He is not real fond of queers and reporters."

Sherrill knew he needed to rest but it was too early and too hot to sleep. He sat on the side of the hill. The lieutenant joined him.

"Some of these men haven't been shot at before," Stolkalcyk said. "They're scared because they don't know how they'll react."

Sherrill didn't know how he would react either. That was his fear—discovering something in himself he could never forgive. "Do you know how you'll react?" he asked.

"Absolutely."

Sherrill dismissed the statement as bravado but as they talked he understood where the certainty came from. Oscar Mike Stolkalcyk had been altar boy and boy scout, average student and average athlete. In class he never raised his hand but he got his work in on time. A light but dogged linebacker, he never made a spectacular play or missed a practice. A slow but determined distance runner, he never won but always finished.

The coach had encouraged him to run sprints and dashes to build his speed. One spring, Oscar Mike stumbled coming off the blocks and trying to catch himself had stepped on his hand, the spikes lacerating his palm. Despite the pain and bleeding he had finished the race, had finished all the races in which he was entered, although his hand throbbed and his pumping arms slung blood from the sweat band he had wrapped his hand with. "You stepped on it, you bandage it," the coach said to show his displeasure. Oscar Mike had not been encouraged to expect approval or admiration.

It was inevitable that he join the Marines, advance through the ranks, marry the home town girl who accidentally got pregnant and become a lieutenant when the Marines needed one.

The enlisted years had served him well. He could do the job of any man in his platoon from machine gunner to radioman and do it better. He had a reputation with his superiors for following orders, getting things done the way he was told and shaving every day even in the field. His men criticized him for being methodical and relentless and respected him for his willingness to go anywhere and do anything they did. "We got an understanding," he said. "If I can't do it, they don't have to."

Sherrill lay down on his poncho. He was beginning sleep when someone whispered, "Second Platoon is Oscar Mike." Oscar Mike was the phonetic abbreviation for "on the move." Sherrill suspected the lieutenant was secretly pleased that they used his name for reveille.

Sherrill took his rifle and bandoleer and the loaded pack the gunny had brought him. It was drizzling and men stood in the blackness cursing and grumbling under their breath. Sherrill leaned on his rifle, the weight of his pack already hurting his shoulders. "A lot of people are going to die today that ain't never died before," the gunny said. Sherrill ignored him.

They walked off the hill. Word was passed to keep the interval because of mines. All Sherrill could do about the mines was think about them and when he thought about them his testicles tried to crawl into his stomach. They marched for what seemed hours into misty darkness, stopping occasionally for everyone to drop to the ground and face out. Sherrill's mind was busy writing his own death. He reached out and the gunny shook off his hand.

The column plunged into the stream and began wading along the channel. The stream was cold, the bottom slick. They followed the channel, then fanned out and lay down as though expecting an attack. They got up and began walking again.

It was comforting not to know what was going on. They walked into heavy brush. Sherrill could see nothing but he could feel the wet brush in his face and water falling from the branches onto his back. They lay down. Sherrill could hear footsteps of others passing behind him.

The gunny caught his arm and they pushed through dripping trees, floundered into deep mud that became cold water then mud again, then a hedgerow they could not get through. The gunny tapped him on the helmet and he slithered through the mud, following the gunny's boots, conscious of the ripping sounds of thorns and branches on his helmet and clothing. The gunny pushed him down until his head was almost in the mud. Not more than twenty meters away was the dark mass of a ville.

The silence erupted with automatic rifle fire to his left. He could see nothing but gunflashes and tracers. He hugged the ground. Bullets splashed into the water and zipped through the trees around him. There was the shock and concussion of grenades and the skittering of shrapnel through the trees.

The firing stopped. There was a single shot, silence, then the firing broke out again with more grenading. "They're coming out of that treeline," someone yelled and firing broke out around Sherrill although he could see no one. Leaves and small branches dropped around him.

Shivers tugged at his sleeve and with the others he ran across the paddy and fell into a ditch in the ville. He could see the outlines of the hootches and figures running in the darkness but he did not know who they were. More shouting, screams, a baby crying.

They moved around hootches, along a footpath, across a garden. There was running, shouting around him. He lay down under a banana tree. Someone screamed in front of him, writhing, thrashing in agony. A bullet smacked the soft pulp of the banana tree.

He crawled through something that smelled like cabbage, pushing through bushes that were wet and sticky, his senses reeling from the smell of fresh blood, of feces, the feel of something slick against his hand. He buried his face in the blood-smelling ground, exhausted, drained, unable to move. He could hear others around him. "We're Oscar Mike." He got up and followed the shadowy figures.

Daylight came imperceptibly through thick gray clouds. The trees slowly separated themselves from the darkness. He was crouched in head-high bushes under dripping trees. In front of him a field was enveloped in mist, vanishing into gray, and beyond was the hint of a small woods. They were going to cross the clearing because someone thought the enemy was in the woods.

The lieutenant stood up and waved his arms. Around him gray, ghost-like figures stood. Sherrill stepped into the soft mud of the rice paddy. He tried to think of a way out, certain he could not make it across the clearing. He saw glitter in the gray, mist-shrouded woods and splashes in the water before he heard the shots and he was running, awkwardly, half-stumbling in the sucking mud, and around him there rose a shout, not of fear or anger, but of joy. They were closing in on the kill.

Sherrill floundered through the water, afraid of being left behind. He tried to get out of the exposed paddy and into the trees but there was an impenetrable wall of trees, thorns, vines and brush growing to the water's edge. The trails into the woods were covered by automatic weapons fire. Around him

Marines were hacking at the brush with Ka-bars. The gunny disappeared into the trees and Sherrill followed his boots into the green tunnel. A few feet away someone screamed. "God, I'm hit. God, I'm hit."

Morning kept pushing back the gray but distant objects were still lost in the mist. A few feet to one side was a partially destroyed bunker. Sherrill slid into the bunker, squatted in the bottom. Blood, urine, even the smell of their bodies remained. He stayed in the hole.

"Charlie didied," the lieutenant said. "We're going to sweep the woods, look for rice and weapons caches."

A medevac was dropping into the clearing to pick up wounded Marines and dead Viet Cong were being stacked at the edge of the paddy for his inspection. In the woods, weapons and rice were being blown up. Sherrill didn't care. He sat beside a tree. The lieutenant sat down beside him and lighted some C-4 to heat water. The gunny came down the trail brushing rice from his helmet and shoulders. "Either I been to a Chinese restaurant or I just got married," he said. He sat beside Sherrill and offered him a cigarette. The lieutenant handed him a canteen cup of coffee.

Sherrill leaned back against the tree, took a sip of coffee and inhaled deeply on the cigarette. Happier than he had ever been. No words he had written, no honors received, matched the glory of that moment. Nor sex, nor love, nor anything. Not even the dripping of water down his back spoiled his joy. He had survived the night.

The sun broke through low gray clouds and for the first time he saw the kind of country they were in—a valley of rice fields, intersected by paddy dikes, bordered by hedgerows that ran into ravines and small, dense woods. Rising out of the valley were low rock-strewn, brush-lined hills. Beyond the hills the mountains loomed through the mist like a specter, like a promise, like a mood painting by a demented psychologist.

Sherrill followed Shivers down a trail through shoulder high grass, through thick bamboo. He floundered through a marsh. Sinking into the sod, rusting beneath the stranglehold of vines, creepers and roots, was the hulk of an ancient-tracked vehicle—French or Japanese.

Many of the Marines laden with packs, grenades, signal flares and ammunition plowed through the sucking mud with cameras swinging from their necks. They took pictures of each other at war. "This is me shooting at Charlie. This is me eating in a VC ville. This is my buddy after he stepped on a boobytrap."

"Why are you taking pictures?" he asked a skinny-faced kid whose ears stuck out like flags.

"When I get back in the world I ain't going to believe this."

The rain came like a clap of thunder, curtains of rain that exploded into the water of the paddy. He could see nothing, hear nothing; the line stopped. The men on either side of him stood frozen waiting for their sight and hearing to return.

He was grateful for the rain. His uniform, his hands, his face were filthy with mud, blood, rotted debris, bits of feces. He wondered how he could be almost totally immersed in water and burning with thirst. When he took off his helmet and opened his upturned mouth the rain tasted like mud. Not even the rain was clean.

Hidden beneath trees were scattered hootches, some of them with masonry walls and tile roofs. Old women and young children squatted in front of the hootches. They smiled, their eyes fixed on nothing. "You know how to tell Vietnamese apart?" the gunny asked. "Count their teeth. None of them have the same number of teeth."

Around the hootches were paths through the grass and bamboo, markings left by the base plate of a mortar, ruts left by the wheels of a mounted machine gun, bits of bone and flesh and trails of blood.

In front of one of the houses a shattered American helmet lay rusting on the ground. A dead child lay in a garden. An old woman sat in front of a hootch holding a naked baby. The woman's pajamas were stained by the baby's diarrhea. A corpsman administered pills. He was a big dark Chicano with sad eyes and sad moustache that all slanted downward. His name was Solis, but everyone called him Solace, even those who knew better. "Nothing big," he said. "Kid's going to die anyway." Sherrill looked in the doorway. There was a pool of blood in one corner and a single sandal.

On a footpath just beyond the ville, Sherrill saw the enemy. He was young, with short irregular teeth and dark uneven hair falling over his forehead. Thick body fluid drained from a hole in his back. His comrades had taken his rifle and left him a grenade but he was unable to use it. He lay on the ground surrounded by knee-high grass, shrunken, quivering, trying to shrink away from the pain, from Sherrill's camera, shrinking into himself, gathering his life into him until it glittered for a moment from one eye and then was gone.

"We did a J.O.B. on him," the gunny said, stripping off the pack and handing it to the lieutenant.

In the pack was a cloth bag of brown rice, a plastic bag of long-grain American rice, coarse tobacco twisted in a banana leaf, a paper of pills, a hemp hammock, a U.S. Army manual, a Ronson lighter and what Stolkalcyk believed was an herb used for toothache but Shivers said was a dried testicle from a victim. Charlie was a war criminal or maybe he was cutting his wisdom teeth.

Every day Sherrill's pack found a new way to hurt, his boots found a new place to rub. Solace gave him repellent that kept the mosquitoes off his neck and drove them to his eyelids, lips, the inside of his nostrils. His feet shriveled and turned fish-belly white. He picked at the soft flesh that crumbled in his hand. "That's like chewing your lip when you've had novacaine," the gunny said. "It may not hurt now but it remembers."

Blue sky, water buffalo, appalling green beauty. Everywhere there was death. In the tree line, on the paddy dike, in the mountains, in the dark water among the rice shoots was death. They lay in stinking water trying to keep the wounded from drowning and called for air strikes. They charged treelines with feet stuck in mud. They loaded the dead and wounded into helicopters and humped on, with nothing to look forward to but the resupply helicopters before dusk.

The helicopters drew mortar barrages. The barrages caused casualties that brought medevacs that caused additional barrages and more casualties and more medevacs, until too exhausted to think, too miserable to sleep, Sherrill lay half buried in the mud in a dream filled with explosions, cries of pain, calls for corpsmen, the wap wap wap of helicopters. He waited for dawn. They moved out at first light with nothing to look forward to but dusk.

"Being in the Marines is like being in love," said Shivers. "It's not real unless you're miserable."

They were pinned down in a ville. Sherrill crawled into a hootch, its straw side offering the illusion of shelter. A dead woman lay in a corner. Beside her sat a baby girl, too dazed to cry. The straw exploded around her and Sherrill pulled her down and covered her head with his flak jacket. When Stolkalcyk called a medevac for the wounded civilians, Sherrill took the baby, her eyes big with fright, her head swiveling like an owl. The door gunner waved him away.

"Her mother's dead. Take her to an orphanage. I'll pay for it."

"Where did you get the kid?" Shivers asked.

"Her mother's dead. There's no one to take care of her."

"She's got a father," Shivers said. "Who do you think was shooting at us?"

"Come on, man," said a scholarly-looking Marine who

seemed too fragile for this world, who had a festoon of Viet Cong ears around his neck. "Get real."

Sherrill sat down on the packed earth. The child held tightly to his neck, her head turning, her eyes unable to encompass what they beheld. She was no more dazed than Sherrill who was trying to grasp a man who shot into his own ville. He, or those with him, had killed his wife and almost killed his child. Out there was one man prepared to lose two generations for what he believed. If there were many like him, killing them until they decided the price was too high wasn't going to work.

The gunny gently pulled the girl from his neck and put her beside the well. She sat where she had been placed, her head turning, not even Sherrill recognizable in her new world.

"The children," Sherrill said. "What's going to happen to the children?"

"You'll never forget them," Shivers said. "But you can't think about them now. C'est la vie, c'est la guerre and say no more."

The rain slanted through the trees, huge drops that fell with a hiss and exploded on his helmet like a shot. He was falling behind again, the gap in the line ahead of him growing larger. "Pick it up," Shivers said.

"Okay," he said, as he had said before but he couldn't catch up. He walked blindly, not wanting to know how much farther he had to go, how far he was falling behind. He realized the column had stopped, the men were fanning out, another paddy to be crossed.

He looked at the foul expanse of mud and water. He could not make it. He hoped for a bullet, a ti-ti wound so he could lie down with only his nose above the water and wait for a medevac.

"Move out," Stolkalcyk screamed. "Move out."

"Second Platoon is Oscar Mike," they yelled without humor.

He hugged the ground in a wooded ravine as a tree exploded. A Marine clawed himself along the ground, his ruined head turned under, like some giant lizard trying to bury itself in the ground. "Corpsman," Sherrill screamed, trying to hold the man down.

"He's dead," Solace said.

"He's still breathing." The man's muscles jerked in spasms, his hands and feet pushing his torn head along the ground. Sherrill couldn't hold him.

"Ain't no way."

"He's still moving."

Solace put a hand on Sherrill's shoulder. "He may move around for a while but he's dead. There it is."

Solace gathered himself and keeping his head low, moved up the ravine and into the trees. Sherrill tried to cradle the Marine in his lap while the wounded man crawled up the air. Sherrill thought he would never die.

They discovered fresh, unmarked graves. They followed blood trails into a grove of trees. Dead, moss-covered trunks covered the ground and the light shifted vaguely about like the light at the bottom of a pool. The wind blew through the tops of the groaning trees and the leaves and branches creaked and rattled. Sherrill knew it was an evil place. Silently they set up an ambush.

He watched the darkness come alive with sound and motion. There was shooting in the distance, flares, mortars. Someone yelled a long way off, a machine gun rattled.

He felt their presence before he saw them; they were everywhere. One of them seemed to be staring at Sherrill. Sherrill was afraid to blink his eyes. He could feel a sound, a groan of fear or helplessness, growing in his stomach, rising to his chest, his throat, and the night blew up around him. Claymores, grenades, rifles, machine guns. The jungle appeared and reappeared in flashes of light. A man jumped in front of him, fell, got up, fell, got up again, this time so close that tracers from the machine gun set his clothes afire.

Someone pulled at this arm and Sherrill looked into the gunny's face. "We got to get out of here." There was a thud in front of them, then another, and both of them tried to crawl under a log as the grenades went off. The gunny jerked him to his feet and they ran into the darkness, branches whipping his face, roots and vines tugging at his boots.

Sherrill stumbled, fell, bounced up, hoping to run forever. The gunny pulled him down. The others crawled in one or two at a time. One man came in supporting another who sobbed softly, "My arm, my arm," before throwing up. "Give him more morphine," the gunny said.

"If I do we'll have to carry him," Solace said.

They beat off an attack. Crawled, stopped to listen while the wounded man heaved, gasped, heaved again. The bullets found them again. They threw grenades, ran, fell to the ground, tried to quiet the wounded man. A man got lost and they crawled around until they found him.

Behind them a fierce battle was taking place, artillery shells drowning out the sound of small arms fire. Helicopters came blasting the woods with rockets and flashing a spotlight on the trees. They lay in a close circle and beat off three attacks. At dawn a helicopter picked up the wounded and they began moving again.

A resupply helicopter brought mail and a Navy chaplain. The chaplain was wearing a camouflage uniform to identify with them but his face was smooth with reason, his eyes steady with certitude, his lips had not forgotten how to smile. He looked like a citizen of a country they had abandoned and could remember only in dreams. Relieved for a moment from the postures of War they resembled lonely, frightened teen-agers posing in men's uniforms. The chaplain moved among them talking of girl friends, mothers, loyalties, trying to bridge the gap between system and chaos, to demonstrate that his world was the real one.

"You religious?" Sherrill asked the gunny.

"I never liked a religious man as well as I liked his money."

The same impulse that drove Sherrill to write had earlier driven him to consider being a minister. The desire to seek, to know, to tell. To know what life meant and truth and being human. Then he learned that a minister was supposed to have the answer before he began the search, the answer had to agree with the answer in the back of the book, and not everything that was known could be told. He was still devout and found comfort in the chaplain, although it wasn't anything he said. It was the voice from home reading the familiar forgotten words.

Sherrill was surprised to discover he had mail. He lighted a cigarette and sat on the edge of his hole to read his mail before darkness brought mortars or sniper fire. There was fan mail from clubs and organizations applauding him for backing the fighting men, killing the enemy, supporting the bombing of Hanoi, the invasion of Cambodia. . .

There was a letter from his agent. His publisher was not interested in the new book; war was not popular now, particularly the Korean war. He balled the letter in his fist. Didn't they read his synopsis? The book was about a man who had a unique experience and was trying to hold on to the reality, the truth of that experience that no one else could accept. The book only began in Korea.

He opened another letter. Jennifer had burned her bra at one of the street company shows. "It was fun until television cameras showed up and then it got wild. Three of the spectators were arrested for showing their breasts to the cameras. Two of the actors were arrested because of the fire, public nuisance or something like that.

"I went out with a bunch of the kids after the performance.

It's the first time I've gotten to know them. They're good kids, very sincere and so brave. They wanted to know all about me. They think it strange that I'm married to you. They see you as some really evil person. They only know what they've read and I tried to tell them what you're like but I could tell they didn't believe me. I don't associate that person I read about with you and then someone brings your name up and reality comes crashing in. Who are you, Sherrill? Do you know who you are any more? Has this evil side always been there without me knowing it? Without you knowing it? I try to believe that all those stories are wrong, that you're not that way. What I can't understand is why you want all that publicity. Why you need it so. Why you make everything so big.

"One of the girls said I must be very confused. Lin came in then and said or very independent. I guess I am, or at least I'm getting that way. Lin told them that you were stubborn but fearless, that he had seen you hold an unpopular opinion at faculty meetings even when it annoyed the administration. He also said he didn't blame you for exploiting the news even though your speech did look like you were running for public hero.

"Lin came by to talk about the next show, 'What if They Gave a War and No One Came.' Everyone looked at me. They wanted me to say something but I didn't. I didn't want to seem disloyal but I don't understand."

Understand what? he raged. He had not made a speech at the LZ; he had forgotten the press was there. He didn't think anyone outside that small circle would hear what happened or care. He didn't create LZ O'Connell or the overblown heroism that was attributed to him. But once he had been described that way, everything he did—burning his hand, flying into Tombstone was seen as super patriotic heroics.

Jennifer's other letter was about the company's effort to save the whales. Whales? The tone of the letter was cool, informational. He preferred the angry Jennifer to this detached woman who was willing to share his quarters but little else. Who had more passion toward people she had never seen, causes he had never heard of.

Lindly wrote that Jennifer had asked him to send Sherrill her love and to tell him she was mellow. Sherrill did not believe Jennifer said "mellow." The college had selected a rock musician to receive an honorary doctorate. The school had received national publicity when, instead of the usual speech, the candidate sang his top twenties hit that praised drugs and advocated violence against parents and other symbols of authority. One magazine credited the school with being among the first to recognize rock music's contribution to the American economy and the singer gave a thousand dollars to the school to fund the study of popular culture.

The school's featured guest lecturer had been a poet who had held students and faculty spellbound by scribbling poems and then burning them unread to protest literary criticism. The students were so enthralled that he had been invited back the following semester. Sherrill knew if he had been there he would have held an unpopular opinion.

Student protests had forced a congressman to cancel a speech and the faculty and administration had agreed that no one holding an opinion unpopular with the students would be invited to the campus.

Lindly was disappointed that Sherrill had become an apologist for the national policy of genocide. "You are too ambitious," he wrote. "I have learned to be laid back, to go with the flow. You need to go for a walk in the country, sit under the trees and feel the peaceful vibes of the people. Fighting for peace is like fucking for virginity."

Even for Lindly that simplistic slogan was too cute. What if they gave a war and no one came? What if there was a disease and no one caught it? If there was hunger and no one had it? Why couldn't Lindly face reality? Here are two choices, consider them, then choose but keep mindless slogans and witless cliches and simplistic dream-thinking out of it. The over-simplification disturbed him more than the message. Or maybe that was the message.

The gunny came over and sat beside him. "Mail from home?"

"I don't understand what's going on."

Shivers put an arm over Sherrill's shoulders. "The old gunny is going to tell you all you have to understand. When a little girl cries, the tears fall on her tits and make her soft. When a little boy cries the tears fall on his nuts and make him hard. C'est la vie, c'est la guerre and say no more."

He wrote a letter to Jennifer. "I can be what you want me to be. I can catch up to your ideas." Could he? he wondered. What if they gave a war? Fighting for peace? He didn't believe anything would ever seem simple again. He gave the letter to the chaplain to mail.

He sat on the ground, waiting for darkness. "Here's a story with your name in it," someone said, handing him a magazine with an article about Dix Deveraux, "America's favorite hero," promoting his new movie. Dix revealed he had traveled to Dallas to study the way cowboys stood. "That's the difference between a star and an actor," he said. "An actor is willing to take chances."

Dix was going to star in Si Hardeman's yet to be released novel about a man who went to Vietnam and became a hero. "A real hero, not like that Sean O'Connell. When he understands he is fighting peace-loving peasants, he walks into the jungle to atone for his crimes. He meets a guerrilla— Anna Anger is dyeing her hair for the role—and they fall in love. The ending is so exquisitely beautiful, so right, so true that I can't reveal it. You'll have to read the book. When I heard about this book I knew I had to do it because it has such content. It demonstrates that if people would lay down their arms, there would be peace all over the world."

What if they gave a war and no peace-loving peasants came? Sherrill thought. What if they gave news and more was required of heroes than notoriety? What if they made a movie and content wasn't synonymous with pap?

A mine was triggered by the fourth man in the column. He disappeared in a shuddering cloud of smoke, dirt, and steel. "Freeze," Stolkalcyk yelled, "freeze," while smoke and dust hung in the air. "Doc up, doc up. Keep your eyes open. They'll hit us while we're not moving."

Solace made his way up the column, causing a little flurry of concern when he came close to another man, trying to step in the footprints of those before him, past a steel helmet that hung from a nearby tree, a flak jacket that lay on the trail, to the wounded man who lay in a tangled green, white and red heap. "You're okay, you're going to be okay," he was saying.

"Jesus, it's not as bad as I thought it would be," the wounded man said, and tried to cough. Even among the young he looked conspicuously young. He had tried to grow a moustache but had barely grown a nose. His screwed-up face more resembled a baby about to cry than a man in pain. His tousled blond hair still defied his mother's efforts to tame it. "I knew it would hurt but it's not so bad."

Solace looked at the lieutenant, looked down the trail at the other men, his eyes squinted, his lower lip pushed up tight, making his eyes and moustache even sadder. It was a quick glance, quick as pain, quick as love, but it told them what they needed to know. Fucked up. He went expertly, efficiently to work.

"Emergency medevac," the lieutenant said into the radio.

"You got the best corpsman in the world. You're looking at him," Solace said. "You just hang on. You just keep looking at him. Keep breathing now. We're going to get you out of here. You're almost home."

"It's not bad is it?" the wounded man said, still trying to

cough. "It don't hardly even hurt. I can stand it."

"Keep breathing. Easy in and out. Keep your eyes open. Look at me. You want to remember your corpsman. He's going to get you out of here. You're on your way home. A free man. Keep your eyes open. Look at me."

There were other sounds. The radioman talking to the medevac, moans and little sobbing sounds that frightened men make, muttered curses, mumbled prayers. Sherrill was too close. He could see torn entrails, could smell hot blood, excrement.

"What's that?" the wounded man screamed, his blond hair jerking from the ground, catching sight of his intestines fouled with dirt and bits of leaves. "Oh God. Oh God, help me. God. Noooo."

"You're not going to die," Solace said, trying to get himself between the man and his wounds. "Look at me. Come on, man, look at me. Don't close them eyes. Look at me."

The wounded man's head rolled to one side. His eyes recoiled from a world he could not bear to see.

"It's just dirt, man. We'll get that off. It don't mean nothing. Look at me, you son of a bitch. Get a grip, you bastard. You fucking bastard. Don't you die. God damn you, it's just dirt. Lots of guys look worse. Open them eyes you son of a bitch. You—" Slowly Solace's hands fell to his side. He raised his head and looked at the lieutenant. Sweat and tears dripped from his moustache; his arms were wet with blood to his elbows. "He quit. I could have saved him. I could have. The bastard just quit."

The lieutenant turned to the radioman. "Change it to permanent routine." He patted Solace on the back. "You did the best you could." He turned to look at his platoon, cowering beside the trail. "Keep your eyes open. Now move out. We'll carry him until we find a sit down LZ."

The morning was gray and filled with mist. Fog rose from

the ground and hung in the low places, enveloping them as they moved silently through the trees, listening to the dripping of water. No insects buzzed, no birds sang. Trees, rocks loomed out of the mist, the uncertain light filled with uncertain things. The Marines stopped often, mouths open, eyes darting, nostrils sniffing with animal concentration.

The sun did not cut through the mist but turned it opalescent. They walked in and out of clouds in a film maker's dream of hell. Arcane and miscreated objects appeared and disappeared as if at will. They reached high ground and saw the tops of trees rising out of the mist as though they were shrubs. They floundered through a bog. They swam through light drizzle, their passage marked by rhythmic breath and liquid sound in a skin diver's nightmare. Sherrill followed without thought or will, his mind flitting from light to shade, swept with waves like fever.

They climbed over bomb craters and shattered trees. Bits of cloth and strips of flesh hung from branches. They lay under trees that dripped gore while a half-crazed survivor wandered about, softly reciting what might have been his comrades' names, a song, a prayer. He was young, giddy with fear. A slight, scholarly-looking Marine who seemed too fragile for this world, rose from the ground and with an embrace, killed him with a Ka-Bar, the forlorn boy curling into the knife like a child curling into his mother's arms, like a woman curling into her lover's embrace. The Marine held up a dripping ear to signal his success; his comrades flashed silent smiles. Afterdeath dripped from above.

They ran. Helmets bouncing, rifles waving, packs flopping, they ran. They had bumped into the VC and the enemy was running for the hills. The platoon was going to cut them off. "How far?" Sherrill panted as he ran.

They ran headlong at the edge of control, the lieutenant and NCOs screaming them into a formation. "How much longer?" Sherrill asked, his breath coming in great sobs, his pulse beating in his brain, his tortured veins threatening to hemorrhage. He drank water until his stomach distended. Shivers carried his pack. He and other stragglers were pushed, prodded, cursed. He ran on legs that were numb, that had gone from live pain to dead pain. His muscles cramped. His Achilles burned like a live wire, his raw feet glowed. He tried to escape his mind until only the throbbing, cramping, burning remained.

They caught the enemy and there was a fierce fight. Sherrill collapsed under a tree, seeking shade as much as shelter. The sudden cessation of movement made the throbbing in his brain worse. His head felt swollen with blood; he wanted to empty his canteen over his face but he had no water. They ran again. "Think of the people back home," the lieutenant yelled. "Thoughts of those who love you will sustain you."

Sherrill thought of Jennifer waiting for him at the end of the race. He held that picture until the anguished cries of his body became too loud. He gave himself to the pain, thinking of nothing but the pain, hypnotized by it, wallowing in it. In his mind there was room for nothing else.

They cut the enemy off, pinned them against the river and stopped to prepare the final assault. They had nothing left but the will to kill. Their eyes were bright, their minds, their bodies focused to a single point. Sherrill avoided getting in their way or brushing against them. "What are we waiting for?" they snarled.

The waiting so intensified their rage that Sherrill thought that was its purpose until a helicopter landed. "Thanks, asshole. Tell Charlie where we are," one Marine screamed with such vehemence that Sherrill feared he would start shooting at the helicopter. When Rick Belk and his television crew got out of the chopper, the Marines screamed and waved their rifles. Sherrill feared for their safety but the Japanese cameraman put it on film.

When the camera was ready the assault through the trees began. Heavy firing broke out off to the left but the platoon encountered light resistance, and the pace quickened as they feared the enemy was escaping. Faster and faster they moved, firing into the trees, into the bush, into every hiding place. Suddenly they were at the river.

The enemy was in the river, some wounded, some dead, some pretending to be dead. It made no difference. The Marines, denied the battle they had tried to earn, vented their rage by shooting at everything. The water erupted in bloody foam.

In less than a minute it was over. Heavy firing continued to their left where the major battle was taking place. OV-10s came to rocket and strafe. The platoon took up positions to block escape across the river. "We zapped them," they complimented each other. "We blew their shit away." Sherrill dipped water from the river and poured it on his head before filling his canteen.

He went to look for Belk. Belk was speaking into the microphone, providing the commentary for the film the crew had taken. ". . .sad day for the Marine Corps. An even sadder one for America."

Sherrill didn't understand. "We outran them," he said.

Belk looked at his cameraman who shrugged his shoulder. "Bunch of guys. Waving their rifles, running through trees, shooting at the river."

"I told you to wear something distinctive," Belk said. "I don't know whether I got you or not. You may have faded right into all those other guys. Okay, let's get a shot of Sherrill saying something."

The camera turned on him. "We outran them," he said.

"Hold it," Belk said. "Sherrill, we can't interview all these guys. Imagine that you are their spokesman. Tell us what happened."

"And hold the rifle up so we can see it," the cameraman

said. Belk adjusted the rifle so that it looked like Sherrill expected an attack.

"Charlie ran for the river," he tried again. "We beat him to it and blew him away. Nobody got across that river."

"Okay, try it again, but this time put an edge to it. Call them 'people' instead of Charlie."

"People?"

"And point at the river. We got good footage on the river."

After several more tries, Belk turned to his crew. "We're the only reporters here," he said. "Except Sherrill. Does this story have enough bite to get on the screen? Is there enough content to get some time? I want at least fifty seconds." They nodded. "Let's get back to Da Nang."

"I may need a ride," Sherrill said. He went to talk to Stolkalcyk. He disliked being a quitter but he didn't know how much more he could take and the mountains were going to be even tougher. "I know I've been holding you up and it'll be worse across the river," he told the lieutenant. "Maybe I better go back to Da Nang," he said.

"We won't cross the river," Stolkalcyk said. "We'll pivot here and sweep back through the lowlands."

"How do you know?"

"That's what we always do?"

"You've done this before?"

"This is my third time. They never learn."

"Who never learns." Behind him he heard the helicopter lift off and watched as it flew away.

"No one ever learns. We kick Charlie's ass and run him into the mountains. Next operation we kick his ass in the mountains and run him into Laos. We move to another section of lowlands and run him into the mountains. Then we go back to the mountains and then we come back here and start all over. I'll fight for these people. I'll stay as long as it takes, but I hate these operations because all we do is tear up the country and kill people. We don't save anything. We don't keep anything and every time we go through those ville we turn more people into Viet Cong."

"Then why do we do it?"

"MAC-V loves it. They can't think little or slow."

"Are we winning?"

"We kick their ass. We run them into Laos."

"How will we know when we've won?"

"I'm a lieutenant. I don't define victory."

Sherrill went in search of the gunny. "Are we beating the gooks?" he demanded.

"We're not fighting the gooks," Shivers said. "We're testing our tactics and weapons for fighting Russia. They don't work very well here but nobody cares because they're not intended for here."

"There has to be some kind of strategy."

"We have money, bombs, tanks, airplanes. What do we need with strategy?"

"You mean it's all a waste?"

"I told you about the CAPs but you weren't interested. You wanted airplanes and helicopters and napalm and pretty pictures. When we get back to Da Nang I'll take you to see the CAPs."

"The next time I see a rice paddy is going to be on the way home. "C'est la vie, c'est la guerre and say no more."

Going back was exactly like going out—following trails, attacking through paddies, setting ambushes in trees, sitting in holes waiting for mortars to drop. The terror and fatigue of the night blended into the weariness and fright of the day. It was the same except that going out he had only thought he was tired. Now he was exhausted beyond thought, beyond the ability to rest.

Every night he dreamed of taking a medevac or resupply helicopter back to Da Nang and listened to the imagined taunts of the Marines when he left, of the press corps, of Rod

Reaves, when they learned he had quit while the operation continued. Every morning he determined to walk every flesh-eating klick.

He was going to tell Stone that the war wasn't working and he had to be able to tell Stone, and anyone else, that he knew what he was talking about because he had been there every brain-numbing minute. Not like Belk who flew in, took a few feet of film and flew back to the showers, cold drinks and soft beds in Da Nang where he could talk about edge and content.

What if Stone wouldn't listen? What if REAL wouldn't print the story? Belk said it was news if the competition covered it. If others quoted him REAL would have to run it. He would get Belk to put him on the screen. Belk made him spokesman for the others at the river, he would be their spokesman again, and he would say that no matter how honorable or necessary the war, the strategy was doomed to failure; he had seen it with his own eyes and somebody had better do something damn quick.

In the beginning he had kept meticulous notes. Now misery deadened his thoughts, shutting out awareness of the growing, rotting, sprouting, dying profusion that made movement difficult and seeing impossible. His eyes swam in seas of green. His mind recoiled, refusing to see.

He cursed the rain and when the sun popped through to beat down on his helmet and turn the paddies into silver shards that exploded in his head, he cursed it too. Lying in the stinking water trying to keep the wounded from drowning he longed for the dikes; running under fire, his feet slipping, skidding in the heavy mud of the dikes he prayed for the treelines; in the breathless, grasping, tangling, boobytrapped treelines he dreamed of the hills; climbing the steep, slippery, gut-wrenching hills, he wished for the villes. They were fired at from the villes and forbidden to fire into them, and everything in the ville was boobytrapped—the straw mats, the clay pots, the bamboo baskets, the smiling faces. No one had seen anything. The entire country conspired to prove that whatever his present misery, the next moment would be worse.

Rage enabled him to shrug into the filthy pack and rise to his feet. Rage was the only passion left, the strength that pushed him through the sucking mud and up the back-breaking hills. As he walked he dreamed of a recoilless rifle. First the trees, then the dikes, the villes, hootches, pigs, chickens, ducks, water bulls, people—blast them not just to death but to oblivion. Fuck the story and fuck Belk, he just wanted to go home. One more klick, he said. One more klick.

When he reached the wire of the combat base he dropped his pack and rifle and kept walking. The last klick, he told himself. He walked until he reached the other side of the perimeter and attempted to flag down anything headed for Da Nang. A Korean Marine truck stopped and he rode to Da Nang on crates of grenades. In Da Nang he flagged down a jeep and paid the driver five dollars to take him to the Press Center.

Hordes of rat-like children roved the streets, prowled trash cans, waited at intersections to snatch a watch or cap from unwary Americans. The driver whipped around and between them. Children played some game with a rubber thong. Traffic slowed as the game crowded into the road and the children swarmed over and under the cars and trucks stealing gas caps, mirrors, canvas straps, windshield wipers, anything removable. Half a dozen children ran behind the jeep trying to tear off the radio antenna and the spare tire that was chained to the chassis. Unable to outrun them because of the traffic, the driver fishtailed the jeep to keep them off. Three climbed on the back of the jeep. "Get them off," he yelled.

Sherrill swung his arm to drive them back. One of the boys grabbed at his watch. Sherrill twisted out of his seat, grabbed the child and threw him from the jeep. The other boys tugged at his clothes, his camera. He shoved them off the jeep also and turned looking for more.

"Right on," a driver yelled. "Teach the little shits."

"Kill the motherfuckers," yelled another.

Sherrill checked his belongings. He still had his watch and camera, the ballpoint pens were gone.

"Lose anything?" the driver asked.

One of the boys limped away holding his arm. Another sat on the ground holding an ankle that was broken or sprained. He raised a tiny fist in the air.

"Just the war."

He walked past the ancient Vietnamese who guarded the gate to the Press Center and headed for the bar. He knew no one in the bar and the clean and shaven reporters were repelled by his smell and the grimy, stained jungle fatigues. He didn't care; he hated everyone who was clean and content. He ordered two double bourbons and drank them straight.

"Are you a correspondent or a Marine?" asked a neat, well-fed reporter who had the kiss of sweet reason upon his brow.

Sherrill wanted to bury his fists in the man's face. "What the fuck is it to you?" The reporter quietly left. The others turned away. That was fine with him.

When he woke up the next day he didn't know how he had gotten to bed but he had at least passed through the shower. Although not entirely clean he had had some contact with water. His hair was wet, he had an unexplained knot on his head and he was sore all over. He walked stiffly to the shower to wash away the hurt and put on clean clothes. He left his film at the photo lab and went to the press operations shack. The colonel was surprised to see him. "I thought you were back in the world," he said. "Some mail came for you and I had it sent to your home."

The thing that had kept him going was his mail and they had sent it home. "I was on a Marine operation," Sherrill snarled at such stupidity. He was going to complain to MAC-V, to REAL; here was someone else who was never going to make general.

"We thought you went home after that incident at the river. I'll notify MAC-V you're still here."

"If you don't mind," Sherrill said, icily polite. "I'd also like the reports on the operation." He went outside and stood looking at the river. Jennifer's letters had been returned. It could be weeks before he got any mail. His hands itched for the feel of the M16, the heft of a grenade. If no one else fragged that son of a bitch he'd do it himself.

"Hey man, you are going to die of terminal rage." Bird loomed before him. "Don't tell me, man, you're homicidal. You want to waste everyone in this whole fucking place."

"Fucking colonel sent my mail home."

"The mail is always screwed up," Bird said. "The more you move around the more screwed up it is."

Fucking Bird never left the Press Center and thought he knew everything going on. Sherrill took a deep breath and went to the mess for steak and eggs. While he waited he read the MAC-V reports—KIA, WIA, MIA. Others might quibble over whether the numbers were accurate, he knew they were false no matter how correct they might be. Bodies were so eye-attracting and memory-searing that twelve dead men under green dripping trees looked like Gettysburg. Numbers told nothing of the eyes of the villagers, the eyes of the dead, the eyes of those who awakened to one more wet and bleeding morning.

The words signified nothing of what he had experienced. It was not just some other operation; it was some other war in some other world. He wished his photographs were ready. They would tell him what he had seen.

He took the rain-and-sweat stained notebook out of the plastic bag he had used to keep it dry. While he ate he flipped through the pages searching for clarification. "Boys riding water buffalo," he read. "Old man stooped over in rice paddy trying to catch finger-long fish in cone-shaped bamboo trap."

"Vietnam is a beautiful country. There is something primeval about the land, something haunting, as though before we were born, in some primitive earlier existence, this was our home."

When had he written that? The words seemed as false to him as the MAC-V press releases. He flipped through the notebook looking for his keen observations. He turned the pages looking for something that clarified, evoked, captured what the operation had been like.

A vision of steak and eggs had kept him going over a lot of miles but his body wasn't interested in the reality. His jaw tired of chewing, his throat closed. He smoked cigarettes and drank coffee.

He heard others talking about the operation. He turned and saw the neat, reasonable reporter he had insulted the night before and others who had been in the bar. How had they gotten back, gotten clean so fast? Why hadn't he seen them in the field? The reasonable man talked about his interview with a colonel who pretended the operation was a success. Another had discovered a subtle change in Viet Cong tactics. Another had criticized the heavy-footed Marines. Bravo Company maneuvered well but First Platoon, Charlie Company had run into log bunkers and been pinned down and the Third Herd had lost radio contact and was slow to react.

Sherrill was amazed at how little he had understood. He had no picture at all. One sniper shooting at him, one boobytrap in his path had more significance than the ambush of a company, the strategy of the Viet Cong. He had thought living the story would permit him to write it better but the closer he got to the truth the farther he was from the picture. He would have known more if he had stayed in Da Nang, collected the MAC-V reports and interviewed the colonel and a couple of privates.

He joined them although he saw the same look they had given him last night. "They sent my mail home," he said, a plea for sympathy.

"It happens," said the reasonable reporter. "By the time your mail gets to Cu Chi you're in Chu Lai so someone stamps it 'Not here' and sends it to Saigon and some clerk sends it home. It's happened to me twice."

"Better hope your girlfriend didn't write you because they'll send the letter to your wife," said another.

"They thought I'd gone home," Sherrill said.

"Everybody thought you'd gone home."

"I was on the same operation as you guys."

They nodded, sharing glances, knowing something he didn't know. "The operation has been over for weeks."

"It ended yesterday."

"As far as news it ended at the river," said the reasonable man. "After that it was a repetition of killed, wounded, weapons captured."

"You were at the river," one of them said.

"Right."

Again they shared glances, something in their eyes reminding him of the eyes of the peasants in the villes. "A lot of people were looking for you after Belk's piece hit the screen back home."

The binoculars had flipped; he was big again. He didn't feel big. He felt expended. Would Jennifer think he was running for public hero?

"A lot of people thought you ran out on the others after the river, that you were hiding someplace back home."

"Hiding from what?"

"Man, you guys wigged out."

"Who?"

"You and that platoon you were with, pushing people into the river and using them for target practice."

"What are you talking about?"

"Didn't you see an atrocity?"

"I didn't see anything that wasn't an atrocity."

"Rick Belk got it on film. You killed women and children."

"He can't have it on film because it didn't happen." Something in their eyes kept him from laughing at the absurdity.

"The rest of the world believes it was an atrocity and that you were in the middle of it. After what you've written it wasn't hard to believe."

An explosion jarred the hootch and he was on the floor when he realized it was the Vietnamese patrol boat blowing up the river. He also knew how he got the bump on his head; there was the vague memory of trying to dive into a foxhole sometime in the drunken night. Their eyes were like cameras, recording his action. "I was with the operation too long," he said as he took his seat. Wrong thing to say. "I got in the habit of ducking when there was an explosion."

"Are you saying there was no atrocity?" The mental note-taking was over; they were writing now.

"I didn't see an atrocity and I didn't take part in one." As he spoke he saw headlines, "O'Connell denies part in war crime."

"So you're contradicting your previous statement that everything was an atrocity.

"That was. . .Before I say any more I want to talk to Belk."

"We'll be ready when you have a statement to make."

"Want to read about yourself?" one of them called after him. When he turned, the man produced two copies of REAL. "Keep it, we've read it."

Belk was somewhere after a story. Sherrill walked to the Cham Museum on the corner to read in privacy. How could anyone believe he had taken part in an atrocity? How could it have happened without his knowing it? He had the trained, honed conscience of a writer. What had he written in REAL that would permit anyone to believe he committed an atrocity? Like the young Marine who had died of shock after seeing his dirt-smeared guts, he had to know the size of the wound.

The Wild Bunch story wasn't too bad. There were photographs of the guncrew pretending to be fighting and of himself pretending to be wounded but few would know. There was a graphic photograph of the dead men on the halftrack; he had torn up his photographs out of respect for those men and REAL had gotten their picture from the Army. REAL had added, "written by the kind of man pinko professors and campus cowards fear the most, an intellectual not afraid to fight for freedom." That wouldn't help him any back on the campus.

The end of the story, taken from the rejected "The Feelings of the Dead," had the Wild Bunch coming to say goodbye as he was medevaced to Quang Tri. "Six men stood at attention, their eyes and mouths tightly closed against the dust, their uniforms flapping in the gale. I returned the salute with my painful, bandaged hand. I wish I could have done more." They had taken a platoon's pathetic salute to a dead comrade and turned it into self-congratulation. It made him look like an egotistical self-appointed messiah but not a war criminal.

REAL had called the second story "Tombstone: The Camp Too Tough To Die" gambling that readers wouldn't know Tombstone had been abandoned or wouldn't care. There were photographs of him with a rifle suggesting he had defended the camp although they were not taken there. The story had been spliced out of the two versions he had sent, including the "I flew, I saw" version but leaving out the death of the captain, the abandonment of the camp, the cost in human lives.

There were many references to "the captain and I." "We are going to keep Tombstone open. No fucking gook is going to tell me we're not number one," he was quoted as saying. There was no mention of Belk and the photographers so that it sounded as though he were the only reporter brave enough to go. The wheatfield fire remained but in the context the metaphor was Communism spreading over the world while Congress and the left-wing media shrugged because it was in someone else's field.

"Swift, Silent, Deadly," carried a photograph of him, in full paint and battle gear, with a recon team. The text left the distinct impression that he had been with the reconnaissance team checking NVA infiltration.

The stories weren't too bad if the reader saw them before the atro—before he heard there was an atrocity. But if anyone believed he had committed an atrocity there was nothing in those stories to dissuade him. He had faith in American's sense of justice; they wouldn't believe there was an atrocity until they saw it with their own eyes and Belk couldn't show it because it didn't happen. Jennifer wouldn't believe it, Lindly and his colleagues wouldn't believe it if Belk showed him committing an atrocity with his bare hands. That made him feel better even though the reporters had believed it easily enough. That was because they were after a story, he told himself. An atrocity was a big story.

When Belk returned, Sherrill went to his hootch. "I thought you had gone home," Belk greeted him.

"Did you say there was an atrocity?" Belk tried to remember the stories he had done, what he had said. "At the river?"

"Hey, that got big play back in the world. Almost ninety seconds on the network. I told you, you got to be outrageous. I hand it to you, you got balls. I couldn't have done it."

"Done what?"

"Shot women and children in the river."

"I didn't shoot women and children in the river."

"Everybody thinks so."

"Not anyone who was there."

"I was there."

"You were there fifteen, twenty minutes at the most. I spent weeks with those guys. I know them. That makes me the authority doesn't it?"

"You were with them too long. You became one of them, thinking like they did, seeing things the way they did. That's why some people think you're a hero and the rest think you're a criminal. Admit it, Sherrill, when I showed up at the river you guys were itching to kill somebody and you didn't care who. Hell, I was afraid you were going to kill me."

"I wanted to kill you. We had broken our ass cutting Charlie off and then had to wait for you set up the camera. And you said it was an atrocity."

"It was the only story there was."

"We outran them, we cut them off, we kicked their ass."

"Not on film you didn't."

"Rick, you filmed one-thousandth, one-millionth—"

"We can't film the whole war, we film a sample."

"It's not a scientific sample, Rick. You show up at a wedding, take a picture of the bride picking up a knife and say it's domestic violence. Whatever slice you take is the highlight—"

"If they run it."

"If they run it it's a representative slice of the war. If not the story of the war, at the very least it's that day's story of the war."

"We don't make that claim," Belk said.

"You say, 'This is the world's news today.'"

"Look, Sherrill, I'm sorry if I talked you into this. When I said you should be outrageous, I meant—"

"Goddammit, Rick, everything that happens is not done for you and your fucking camera."

"Okay, okay, just relax. People are already bored with the atrocity. They're angry about something else now so just let it lie."

"It wasn't an atrocity. I am not a war criminal."

"Jesus, Sherrill, people applaud every time you shoot somebody. What do you want, adoration? Say they were Commies and needed killing. Say you were defending freedom, America. Say it was war and there are no atrocities in war. Don't say you didn't know what was happening and don't say you shot women and children because you were scared."

"Weren't you scared?"

"I didn't tell everybody I was Mr. America, the brave and the free. You scared the shit out of people in the bar last night. No shit, you're scary when you go into your tough guy act. One man told me he thought you were going to waste everybody here. I thought LZ O'Connell was a fluke but after I saw you at the river I was convinced."

"I'm not like that."

"You? The only guy with guts enough to fly into Tombstone."

"I didn't write I was the only one."

"The story has your name on it."

"Do they run your stories the way you send them?"

"I'm not there to edit them so they cut footage; they sometimes frame the question, the context a little differently. The story they run may be just part of the story I shot."

"That's what happened to my stories."

"Maybe so, but why did you spend weeks in the bush if you don't like killing people?"

"I had to find out. I had to know. Rick, I learned something out there. The strategy isn't working."

"That's kind of lame isn't it? Almost everybody in the media has been saying that for months. Your friends back on the campus are saying this is an illegal war, that the generals and politicians and maybe some of the soldiers are war criminals. And after careful consideration by zapping a few gooks you've decided the strategy is a mistake?"

"I'm not saying the war is evil or that the men who fight it are criminals. I'm saying the strategy is wrong."

"Some people like you and some people hate you but even those who hate you have a kind of grudging admiration because you've got courage and you've got certitude. Lose those and it's down the tube."

He went behind the mess and sat on the boat that was used to ferry newsmen to the compound across the river. It wasn't an atrocity because it couldn't have been. He couldn't have witnessed, participated in an atrocity without recognizing it. He tried to recall what had happened. It seemed so far away, not just in time but in space, vestige of some other existence, and he, shadow of someone he vaguely remembered but never really knew. He looked at the rain- and sweat- stained notebook that was his touchstone of the past. "Outran VC today. Belk at the finish." That was his only note for what the media, the world, had decided was most important event of the weeks-long operation.

Mist blotted out the city, the bridge, the winking red towers on Monkey Mountain. He buried his face in his hands. He had always believed in his own decency. Had he changed the way others believed he had? No.

He smoked, staring into the mist, listening to the whisper and lap of the river as it slid past on its way to the sea. He had taken the wrong road and every step took him farther from what he was and into what he did not want to be. A sampan glided silently along the river. It did not look real; not the river, nor the sampan, nor the blinking red lights on Monkey Mountain, nor the flare that blossomed over Marble Mountain.

Hearing someone behind him he turned to see Stolkalcyk who looked different. "Thank God you're here," Stolkalcyk said. "I was afraid you had run out on us." Sherrill realized what was different about the lieutenant. Without his helmet, flak jacket, rifle and platoon he looked shrunken and uncertain. "Was it an atrocity?"

"Did you see an atrocity?"

"They said it was."

"You were there," Sherrill insisted. "Did you see an atrocity?"

"No."

"There it is."

"The brain reacts by habit and sees what you expect to see.

If you're looking for Charlie, you see Charlie."

"Who have you been talking to?"

"Everybody. Investigating officers. Doctors. Psychologists. They're fucking with my mind."

Sherrill felt the earth shift beneath him. "Have you talked to your men?"

"The only thing they remembered was the camera. They all wanted to be seen by the folks back home. Jesus, I thought that was one of the biggest moments of my life. I wrote my wife, 'They can't call me a plodder any more.' But the film is—it's cold. You can see something. Hell, I don't know, the film is fuzzy. But watching it made me sick. They showed it over and over. 'Is that an atrocity, lieutenant?' Over and over." Stolkalcyk scratched at the jungle sores on his hands.

"I don't care what the film says," Sherrill said. "I was there. I know what happened. Just stick to what you remember. You've been through worse than this."

"This is the worst thing I've ever been through. Not to know what I did, what kind of person I am. No matter what, I always knew that."

Stolkalcyk took a deep breath and blew out his lips. "I think they're waiting to see if it blows over. If it does, they'll say I lost control of the platoon. I'll be returned to the ranks and honorably discharged when my enlistment is up. If some reporter or politician takes an interest and makes an issue, it could be brig time and dishonorable discharge."

The Vietnamese patrol boat came down the river dropping grenades and they waited for it to pass.

"Death before dishonor. I used to pray that I would die before I disgraced myself or the Corps. I don't mind going back to the ranks, that's where I belong. I never liked being an officer but I liked being a Marine. That's what hurts, going out like that. Slipping out the back door. Saying I was incompetent so they don't prove I was something worse."

If the incident were seen from the magnifying end of the

looking glass, Stolkalcyk would be publicly dishonored; if seen through the minifying end he would be privately disgraced. Sherrill wondered if the same were in store for him. Neither had control over the looking glass. "We made decisions in the heat of the moment based on the information we had," Sherrill said, remembering the errors in the Tombstone story.

"If I decided to kill every fucking gook in The Arizona and you wrote it was the right decision we wouldn't get as much attention as a rock singer who misses a concert because his piles act up," Stolkalcyk said. "That's how much our decisions are worth. They give more space to a fucking sanitary napkin." He got in the jeep and drove away in a shower of gravel.

Sherrill tried to recall the incident, to relive it in his mind. He remembered the sounds. Heavy firing off to the left. The beating of helicopter blades. He didn't remember seeing the helicopters or hearing their rockets but he remembered the beating of the blades echoing through the woods. And the rustle and snap of heavy men running through trees. A thin, faint smell that he associated with fear. A man fell in front of him and he had instinctively ducked but the man had only tripped.

Firing broke out and he saw, or thought he saw, movement through the trees. No faces or uniforms, movement, tracers flashing, trees shaking, limbs falling. The river. Shooting at the river. The water frothing. He never saw a face. It wasn't until after it was over, after he had talked to Belk, after he lay beside a hole and tried to sleep that it occurred to him he might have killed someone. It was an indifferent thought.

The next morning he picked up his photographs. If he had taken pictures at the river he couldn't tell which they were. There were battle scenes that did not look like battle scenes, smoke that looked like clouds, clouds that looked like napalm and peasants who appeared to be posing for the camera.

There was a photograph of a Marine forcing a frightened

child to open a metal can. The Marines believed the villagers knew what was mined, but to force civilians to test suspected boobytraps was a violation of the Geneva Convention. Sherrill tore up the photograph and then destroyed the negative. He had not protested forcing the child to open a suspicious can. How then was he certain there had been no atrocity?

He carefully maintained the appearance of normalcy, pretending to work although his thoughts had turned to water. He did not say that he had shot at the enemy. Instead, he wrote of the heat, the mist-shrouded mountains, dark jungle filled with shifting shadows and sliding eyes, circling fog, night filled with uncertain sounds, day filled with unknown terrors, trees that dripped afterdeath. A lost boy who had died as easily as a lamb, curling into the blade as though returning to his mother's womb. In the evenings Sherrill stood in the bar with the others, listening and laughing politely, careful not to draw attention.

His mail was forwarded from Saigon. There were fan letters applauding him for killing women and children in the name of democracy and a hate letter from a pacifist who prayed every day for his death. He scarcely glanced at them before carefully destroying them so the other reporters could not read them.

Fred Stone wrote, "You kicked over an ant hill at the river. The Commie-lovers are coming out from under rocks and bleating like the sheep they are. Get me that story fast and give me the details. I want to know about every Red you killed."

Jennifer wrote, "Sherrill, what is happening to you? I don't know who you are any more. The terrible things they say about you. The telephone has been ringing off the wall. People throw garbage at the house. I can't step out the door without people screaming at me, without reporters following me, taking my picture. Reporters are camped on the porch. Television cameras came out to interview you. They said you had left Vietnam. They didn't believe me when I said you weren't here. Where are you? I can't take much more of this, Sherrill."

He wrote to Jennifer. "I am still here. After the river everyone else went back to Saigon or Da Nang and they lost track of me. There was no atrocity. I am sorry that you are having such difficulty because of stories about me, most of which are not true. The military is working to prove there was no atrocity. I can't leave right now because of that and other reasons I will explain later but I love you, I miss you more than I dreamed possible and I hope to see you very soon. You're going to like the Sherrill O'Connell who comes home to you," he wrote, believing she loved the Sherrill O'Connell he had always been.

He sat on his bunk and tried to think. He had to do something to help Jennifer. He couldn't go home without looking like he was deserting Stolkalcyk and the others, looking like he was guilty and trying to escape. He couldn't go home without bringing more cameras, more insults to Jennifer. Fucking Stone didn't care what the anthill did to Jennifer.

Belk said he was someone people wanted to know about. He had to give them something new to think about. Something positive.

One day he saw the film that Belk's crew had shot. He watched the film with three balding Marine officers who had eyes sharp as glass. There was no sound, only the images of angry men waving rifles, running through woods, shooting at the river. He was recognizable, at least to himself, in most of the footage. Rick Belk talked into the camera, Lt. Stolkalcyk faced the camera but did not look at it, his eyes darting from side to side, flitting suspiciously across the screen.

Then there was Sherrill, his face drawn, his eyes enormous, holding the rifle as though he had taken the camera prisoner, pointing at the river. The film had been spliced so that the camera, following his pointing arm, zoomed in on a snag in the river surrounded by the spray kicked up by bullets. The screen turned white; the film was over.

What had he said? They had outrun Charlie? That's where we beat him to the river?

"Did you see an atrocity?" one of the officers asked.

Sherrill had his speech ready. "I am a trained observer. I have written two novels, I have published nonfiction stories regarding—"

"I've talking about the film. Did you see an atrocity on the film?"

"How could it be on the film if it didn't happen? It couldn't have happened without me seeing it. I am a trained observer. In addition to my two novels, I have written articles on military—"

"Let's look at the film again."

Sherrill sat through the brief showing again, having eyes only for himself. He looked exhausted yet excited. Wild. Not mad.

"Does that look like a child to you?" one of the officers asked. He indicated, in a corner of the film, a snag with a vine or other debris streaming after it, bullets spattering the water around it.

"No."

On the next showing he looked for the fleeting shadow in the corner. "A little girl with her hair streaming in the water?" the officer asked. He could make it look like a girl if he wanted to see a girl. He could imagine her screaming while bullets whipped the water around her. "What is the purpose of these questions?"

"We're going to talk to everyone who was there then write a report for the general. The general will study it then send it to Saigon. That may be the end of it or MAC-V may send it to Washington. We just want the report to be as comprehensive as possible."

"Did you say a lot of people died in the river?" one asked

him.

People? "No."

"You didn't say, 'People ran for the river. We beat them there and blew them away?'"

That fucking Belk had asked him to say 'people' and point at the river. "Is that what I say on film?"

"We're asking you."

"People is an indefinite noun that may refer to men, women or both."

"We're not accusing you of anything, Mr. O'Connell. We are preparing a military report of a military operation. Would you say that Lt. Stolkalcyk had command of his men at all times?"

He had prepared that answer too. "Lt. Stolkalcyk is an exceptionally trained and disciplined Marine. He demands the same quality of his men."

"Did Lt. Stolkalcyk leave stragglers on the forced march to the river?"

"I was the only straggler. I am not a well-trained and disciplined Marine. As you can see on the film I was at the river."

"Then you regard the film as accurate."

"It's a film." What had he said to Belk? "It is a random, minute slice of a long operation. It's even a random, minute slice of what happened at the river because a camera doesn't have peripheral vision. It only sees what the cameraman wants it to see and it doesn't always see that."

"Does the film fairly represent the way you remember the firefight at the river?" They watched him, every motion, every nuance.

It didn't look like what he remembered. Despite its lack of definition the film was more specific, more vivid than his memory. He wondered if from that moment he would remember what he had experienced or what he had seen on film. Like Machlin who had home movies instead of memories.

"It's not what happened," he said.

It was a few days later before he saw Shivers. "You going to run out on us?" Shivers asked.

Sherrill didn't answer directly; he wanted to go home. "They've about finished their report."

"You don't know the military. They won't finish it until the general pushes for it. The general will study it until MAC-V asks for it. MAC-V will hold it until the Pentagon or the White House or Congress or the press demands it. This can go on for months."

Sherrill's heart fell at that. "I can't stay here for months."

"Then get them off our backs."

"I did the best I could."

"Make some new news so they forget about this. Ride with one of the pilots when they bomb North Vietnam."

"There is no reason for me going into the field again. I have seen everything I need to see, I know everything I need to know."

"The lieutenant needs you."

"I told them everything I know. They say there were children."

"Almost every guy with us was a teenager."

"That sounds different."

"Back home if a sixteen-year-old goes after an eighteen-year-old with a hatchet, are they going to tell the eighteen-year-old not to defend himself? If your wife starts shooting at you are they going to tell you not to shoot back? Who makes up these rules?"

"Someone who's never been out there."

"There it is. War ain't kind. I only been in two but I bet they're all the same. C'est la vie, c'est la guerre—"

"Say no more."

More fan letters and hate mail came but he no longer

opened envelopes unless he recognized the return address. Fred Stone wrote, crying for his story of "pushing gooks into the river and zapping them." His mother wrote a long letter describing her daily activities, what she had for lunch, the sales at the store, what she wore to church, who she saw. Between the lines was her fear that he was becoming someone she did not know. With her description of the sameness of small town life she tried to call him back to a world where reason and mercy were as common and as welcome as rain.

Lindly wrote that students had taken over the president's office and had removed Sherrill's personnel file. He did not know what they had done with it. His name had been torn off his office and the door covered with graffiti. As a kindness Lindly did not report what the graffiti said.

"I know I shouldn't write," Jennifer wrote, "because I am so angry. The man who had this job before I did was paid almost twice as much for fewer duties. When I asked for a raise the board said I didn't need the money because you were making a fortune writing for fascists. They talked about cutting my pay because I can't go on location any more. I think they would have fired me if it hadn't been for Lin.

"The company bought surplus army clothes, dressed the men as soldiers and grabbed women and children (actors) off the street and out of stores, forced them into an alley and 'shot' them to show what is happening in Vietnam. That was the plan. Then photographers and reporters saw me and asked where you were, what you had told me about the atrocity. They asked awful things. They asked questions about Marie, if you had ever been treated for mental disorders, if you had beaten me or Marie, if you were on drugs, if you were a anti-social person. That's why I can't go with the company any more. You completely disrupted the show.

"I suppose I should also tell you this. Someone broke into the house. I called Lin and he came over and said there was no sign of forced entry but I know someone has gone through our things. Some of our photographs are missing and I think some of your papers and manuscripts also. I know I shouldn't be causing you more worry but I am so angry that you have brought this on yourself, that you have brought it on me. I am so confused. I am just beginning to realize how I have been a sex object to you and I resent it. I resent all those years that I was used."

Sherrill put the letter down, careful to show no reaction because others were watching, but stunned. How had he used her? How was she a sex object? When he thought of sex he thought of her, did that make her a sex object? When she thought of sex didn't she think of him?

He could scarcely believe what he had read. How could students take over an office and remove files? Where were the police? Why would anyone remove photographs and papers from his home? He was furious that people were causing Jennifer such problems when he was not there to help her, but to go home would be to desert Stolkalcyk and Shivers and to bring more cameras, more attention to Jennifer. He had to do something for Jennifer. He had to deflect the anger misdirected at her.

"Daddy. Daddy." He ran blindly through the trees, the branches whipping his face and lashing his arms. Marie was in the river. The river was carrying her away and he could not reach her. "Daddy. Daddy." He tore a limb from a tree and held it out to her but it wasn't a limb it was a rifle and bullets spurted from it and erupted around her face only it wasn't Marie it was Harry's girl and she was screaming "Ai ee. Ai ee." He was awakened by his own screams. He sat up in bed and lighted a cigarette, aware that he had awakened the others in the hootch, that in the darkness their eyes read his story.

The next time Belk was at the center, Sherrill went to see him. "I saw your film, Rick, but there was no sound. I don't know what you said."

"That was a lot of stories ago. I don't listen to what I'm saying, I'd become self-conscious. Nobody listens. What's on film, that's what counts. If it's not on film it didn't happen."

"What you say might convince someone it happened." Belk shrugged. "You must have said it was an atrocity because it didn't look like one."

"People have forgotten what I said. Most of them have forgotten what they saw."

"I haven't forgotten. My wife hasn't forgotten. My colleagues back at the school haven't forgotten, and the other guys here are waiting for me to say the wrong thing."

"Whatever I said was the story we had on film."

"What did you see?"

"A bunch of guys killing people at the river."

"Did you see a face at the river? Did you actually see a woman or child at the river, dead or alive?"

"If it wasn't on the film when it got to New York they wouldn't have shown it."

"But you didn't actually see a woman or child?"

"That's who was in the river. Everybody knew they were there."

"We had been fighting the NVA. Then some unit flushed the VC and we cut them off at the river."

"The story on film was an atrocity. It's what everyone expected, what everyone believes. The platoon you were with did not have a casualty at the river. Think about that."

"You're willing to hang people, to destroy lives on that evidence?"

"Dammit, Sherrill, get real. It doesn't matter what happened, what matters is perception and the perception is there were women and children there and you were shooting."

He hadn't intended to beg. "My wife is getting anonymous calls. They throw garbage at the house. She can't go out the door for the cameras."

"What do you want me to do, run the film backwards? Do you think the network would put me on the screen saying it was a mistake? It's not news. Who would believe it? They already know what they think."

"Put me on the screen. I want to say that the strategy isn't working but there was no atrocity."

"Maybe if you were with a patrol in Cambodia or Laos—"

"Do it here."

"I couldn't get you fifteen seconds—"

"It's a little more complicated than fifteen seconds."

"Not on television it isn't. People have heard what you have to say."

"Not all of it."

"They think they have. If you haven't said it in fifteen seconds they aren't going to hear it. This is the age of the jingle and it's got to have rock and roll. You are identified with a cause, a way of thinking. They have already heard it. I don't get committed to any way of thinking. Today I show this view, tomorrow that view. That way the viewer doesn't think he already knows what I'm saying."

"I'm saying something new, something different. I'm saying the strategy is all wrong."

"I'll telling you, Sherrill. Say that you're changed your mind and they will fucking tear you apart."

"I'm begging, Rick. For my wife's sake. Whatever they do to me, they have no right to take it out on her."

"Maybe if you say the war is immoral, that you were brainwashed. You took part in an atrocity but it was because you were lied to by others."

"It's not true."

"It's the only truth they'll believe. Tell them you were paid by REAL to sell the war, lied to by politicians, tricked by the military into taking part in an atrocity. You might come out a bigger hero than ever."

If he lied he would be believed. If he deserted Stolkalcyk

and Shivers he'd be a hero. "I can't do it."

"It'll be tough but if you publicly beat your breast, come up with a catchy phrase for what everybody already believes—it might work."

Sherrill walked to the river, the only place to escape the probing eyes. He had to package himself. If he said the war was evil and the fight at the river an atrocity he was home free. That much seemed certain. Leaving Stolkalcyk and Shivers to face dishonor, prison, the end of their careers. And what happened to the Vietnamese? To the children? If he stayed, supported Stolkalcyk, tried to find a way to help these people, he would be contemptible to his colleagues and admirable to those he did not respect. He could lose Jennifer, maybe his life.

There had to be a middle course. He had to come up with a reasonable, logical statement about what had happened at the river and why the strategy was not working. REAL wouldn't print it and he had been so outspoken, so outrageous that no one else would either. That meant he had to find a sympathetic reporter to tell his story, one who had not already made up his mind, who was working for a publication without a slant. That seemed unlikely.

What he needed was a forum where he and an opponent could rationally argue the war, the strategy, the fight at the river without rancor, hostility or emotional, rabble-rousing rhetoric. That seemed even more unlikely. Where would such a forum exist? Not at the college where unpopular views could no longer be presented. Not on the street where Jennifer's company shouted slogans. Americans had become so accustomed to advertising they could only think in jingles and slogans and Vietnam had no rallying cry—no "Remember the Alamo," no "Save the Union," no "Remember Pearl Harbor." Vietnam could not be reduced to a catchword.

Hearing something, he turned to see Bird shuffling heavily, his arms half raised like a sleep walker. He settled his bulk on the overturned boat and rolled a joint. "Bird, whatever happened to reason?" Sherrill asked.

"Reason is a trap, man. Diplomats reason while people burn. No compromise with death. Reason is the enemy. Reason is a lie."

He walked back to his hootch to find Rod Reaves dropping his pack and boots on a bunk. No one who opposed the war would believe Reaves about the atrocity but if he could persuade Rod to reveal his views on the strategy of the war he could start building his new image, at least with the right. "I stayed with that operation until the end and I didn't even need my pajamas," he said to indicate he harbored no ill will.

"Whoop-tee-do."

"I'm glad I did," Sherrill persisted. "It convinced me of one thing. There is something seriously wrong with the strategy."

"That right?"

"All we're doing is tearing up the countryside, killing people, then pulling back into base camps and going back and doing it again. Sure, we chase Charlie into Laos or Cambodia but he comes right back. We can chase him to Hanoi but is anyone back home going to accept that kind of victory? Is anyone here willing to accept that kind of killing? We have to find a better way."

"You know how you find a chicken in a pot of stew?" Rod asked. "Turn up the heat and see who cheeps."

Sherrill wanted to hit him, knew he should have hit him before, but that was the tough guy image he was trying to shed. He left the hootch.

Sherrill went to the bar, separating himself from the others. Someone spoke his name and he turned to see Norela Cook. "I've been reading about you," she said.

He told her what he had told the others. "The matter is being investigated. When it is completed, I'll have a statement."

"I hear you fought off three Vietnamese who were trying to steal your jeep," Norela said.

Where had she heard that? Every time he hurt somebody he was news. Was she mocking him, knowing they were children? "It wasn't like that."

"Too bad. I'm going to Hue tomorrow to interview the university students who are demonstrating and I need a few tips on crowd control."

"Sorry."

"Hey, our hero is back," Rod Reaves said loudly as he came into the bar. "He's still our hero isn't he? Until he runs for home."

Ears turned at that. "I'm not going home," he said.

"Don't you miss your hippie daughter? I understand there's a gravestone back in Texas with her name on it."

Sherrill felt Norela stiffen beside him as he almost lost control. Rod was baiting him but it wasn't going to work.

"Someone get out a camera and maybe he'll show us his recon act."

Sherrill took a deep breath to control his voice, turned and said, "You wanted me to go on the operation, I went on the operation. I was there every fucking day. I walked every fucking step. Where the fuck were you?"

"I wasn't killing women and children to pad my body count, motherfucker."

Sherrill hit him before he knew he was going to hit him. Suddenly, Rod was at his feet, sprawled on the floor in a widening circle of shoes. Blood trickled from his nose. The room had gone silent but noise pounded in Sherrill's head. There was a dull ache in the fist that was still clenched and poised.

Slowly Sherrill turned and pushed his way out of the bar. He could hear the babble of voices behind him. "Damned bully. . .tough guy. . .throwing his weight around."

"We know he can hit," someone said. "But can he can take

it?"

Sherrill shrugged off the threat but he wanted to get away from the Press Center, away from the prying eyes. But not to the field.

"You knocked my friend down," Norela said. She had followed him outside and her voice was flat, almost harsh except for the humor that curled over the ends of the words and played at the corners of her mouth. "That makes things difficult for me. I'm taking the train to Hue tomorrow. It's off-limits to the military because it's always getting itself blown up and I need a strong silent type to hold my hand if I get killed."

"He'll be all right."

"He's not quite as strong as I had thought," she said. "Are you sure you can't find a story in Hue?"

Students rioting? REAL might go for it if he was acrimonious enough and he wanted to get away from Da Nang but he didn't want to make any more enemies. "What's in Hue?"

"Besides the students and the Citadel? Me. Maybe you don't read the papers. People back home think you're a hero or a murderer. I want to help them make up their mind."

Feminist, leftist Norela Cook had a wide readership and was exactly what he needed. That made him suspicious. "Have you made up your mind?"

"I've made up my mind to do the story."

"You don't need me to do the story."

"True, it would be easier without you. I'd rather be fair."

He knew she could be cruel, clever; he didn't know if she could be fair.

"Rick tells me you're a good man to have around when there's trouble and that you're not as bad as you pretend."

Was Rick trying to make amends for saying there was an atrocity? "Rick has known me for a while. I don't make a good first impression."

"It's six hours to Hue by train. I'll be there at least a week. That should give us time to know each other and I'll hear your story through before I write it."

He had not yet understood the LZ; it would be years before he straightened out what had happened at the river. "Sounds fair."

"I'm not a helpless female. I've probably been on as many battlefields as you. What I need is some muscle on the train and with the students. Rick said you were the type who could watch a woman die without getting all cut up about it. Could you write about my death without saying my hair was a mess and my lipstick was smeared, and without making yourself a God damn hero for watching me die?"

The train had been attacked twice the past week before it cleared the five tunnels through the Hai Van but the train was not as dangerous as Norela Cook. "Probably," he said.

Hue

Norela was waiting at the station when Sherrill arrived in the morning mist. She had been interviewing the harried station master who had held the job since leaving Hanoi in 1954. "He doesn't know if the fucking train is going to run," she said. The train had not run the day before because the Viet Cong had destroyed a bridge.

A patrol train had left earlier carrying ARVN troops to clear ambushes. The train had pushed three flatcars ahead of the engine to explode mines but they had not yet signaled that the track was clear. Sherrill explored a museum of French steam engines riddled with bullet holes, U.S. diesels warped out of shape by mines, rusting Wickham trolleys.

Norela called when the train loaded. The fare was 103 piasters first class, 78 piasters second-class. First and second class had the same hard wooden seats but second class cars were crowded with peasants, pigs, chickens, and Norela said first-class had armor plating.

Sherrill and Norela settled themselves in the rear of the

only first class car. The car was not crowded—a woman with four children, all of whom seemed to be three years old; two little boys in white shirts and khaki shorts; a woman with dime-bright eyes set in a prim face; an ARVN soldier who juggled grenades for their amusement; and a high-cheeked, goateed old man wearing a suit and tie who showed them an official document with the seal cut from it.

In addition to the two passenger cars, the train was hauling military cargo to Phu Bai. The tracks loosely paralleled the highway Sherrill had traveled with The Wild Bunch except that instead of climbing the arduous Hai Van pass, the train passed through five tunnels. The first tunnel caught Sherrill by surprise. Without warning the train plunged into darkness. Norela shrank toward him. She was carrying money and an expensive camera and watch. Sherrill leaned in front of her and raised his hands to protect his face and to grapple with an attacker. The train burst into light and Sherrill was caught in his ridiculous posture by the Vietnamese who smiled at him. Norela squeezed his arm. "Thank you," she said. He wondered if she mocked him.

After a brief stop at Lang Co for women to sell bowls of rice and noodle soup, the train toiled along the marshy rice land between two lakes—the Dam Lap An and the Dam Cau Hai—and beside QL 1, the only road north out of Da Nang. Sherrill watched as the train was overtaken by Hondas, Lambrettas, even bicycles on the highway. Bunkers, pillboxes, antiquated forts guarded new bridges beside the wrecks of old ones.

The trip was now safe enough to be boring, the landscape unremarkable. They lapsed into speech. Norela had been a journalism major in college. She had never been editor of the student paper but she had been president of her sorority and had landed the man who scored highest on the state bar exam. She had forgotten writing in the bliss of being the pretty wife of a handsome attorney who never appeared in court but arranged cocktail parties, hunting trips, weekends at country retreats. He had been pleased when, after the children had started to school, Norela began a society column for the local paper and told her who should be mentioned as attending the governor's party and who should not. Some names were to be avoided because the politicians were not interested in them, some were to be avoided because the law was interested in them.

Norela's mouth was plain, her eyes too small, her nose too thin to be glamorous, the way she was invariably described by the press. There was nothing in her appearance that earned her the attention she received.

"I spent fifteen years trying to figure out what was right. Could I hold his cock without losing my dignity? Could I allow myself an ear-splitting orgasm without losing his respect? Then I found out the son-of-a-bitch was paying whores to lick his dick. I said, I'll do it for free; just love me. It embarrassed him. He got shy and couldn't get it up."

Her life was all front page. Sherrill was on guard, fearing she was revealing intimate details to encourage him to do the same.

"I divorced him, put the kids in boarding school, fucked his friends so he would never be sure why they were smiling at him and when I learned the paper wanted to get rid of the governor I told them, 'I fucked the bastard. I know things about him his wife doesn't know.' They didn't use half what I wrote but it got him out of office and me off the society beat."

Norela was trouble, quick to strike back. He knew she could hit hard.

"I wanted to be a television reporter but my voice is too strident for my image. That's what they said, but I could take voice lessons. The truth is I don't have sex appeal on camera. Rick Belk has the same problem. He's got a great voice and in person he's sexy but it doesn't come across on the screen. He had a great story on an ambush." Fifteen VC had walked into his camera and died on screen. Belk thought he had a Pulitzer but Brien had a report from America's largest bakery asking, "Is bread losing its flavor?"

"At the end he smiles this sexy smile at the camera and says, "If bread has lost its flavor are the nation's bakeries saying, 'let the people eat cake?' Rick was pissed but content is never going to win over style and Rick's style is not sexy enough. I told him to lighten up, flirt with the audience, pretend he's making a soap commercial but he thinks he can't compete on that level, that he has to be profound and informative."

Norela pulled a notebook and scraps of paper out of a large bag. "Thrill-seeking, publicity-mongering adventurer," she read from a scrap. "'O'Connell is not just writing of his stupid adventures and silly heroics, as reprehensible as that is, he is preaching a gospel of race hatred, of intolerance for those who fail to applaud his savagery, his love of pain and death.' Did you know they were writing these things about you?"

"No," he said, trying not to betray his dismay, knowing that careful responses to questions often went unpublished while off-hand remarks that were never intended as answers were prominently quoted.

"O'Connell's jousting with windmills has become one more narcissist demand for attention." He ignored it. She held up another scrap. "'My wild night with Sherrill O'Connell,' written by a young starlet on a USO tour."

"I've never even seen a USO show. Where and when was that supposed to have happened?"

"It's a tabloid story, Sherrill, intentionally vague so it's hard to disprove. This young lady said, 'He screamed when he saw my blood red nails on his chest. He said it reminded him of a child he had killed."

"That is such garbage. I can't believe—"

"This writer says you were a liar from the beginning. That your daughter is dead." He nodded. "That you were a farm boy not a cowboy as you claimed." He shrugged; in the field he rode a tractor, in the pasture he rode a horse. "On one of your rare excursions into the field you claimed credit for the one Viet Cong killed although three American soldiers died beating off the enemy attack."

"I didn't claim credit, I was given credit and the numbers are wrong."

"That you burned your hand ducking for cover." It was as true as what he had written. "That you jumped into a helicopter displacing the seriously wounded and seduced a nurse, taking her from her duties with the sick and wounded."

"No."

"That you wrote that Tombstone was too tough to die after it fell." Should he explain that REAL spliced together two versions of that story or would that make him even less trustworthy?

"Tombstone didn't fall, it was abandoned. I wrote the story before it was abandoned." Partly true.

"That you posed with a Marine reconnaissance team 'looking like a head wound wouldn't stop you' and pretended you had gone on patrol with them."

"I interviewed them and wrote their story. Maybe you've done that."

"I'm not Sherrill O'Connell." She smiled brightly. "That you lied about the atrocity."

"There was no atrocity."

She read from another scrap. "'I didn't see anything that wasn't an atrocity,' O'Connell said, satisfaction and melted cheese dripping from his mouth."

He tried to mask his anger at being characterized as a slob. He wondered if there was any point in trying to explain. "I meant every battle is an atrocity regardless of who is killed."

"When asked about killing people at the river O'Connell said that the 'people' included men as though killing men justified killing women and children," Norela read.

It was hopeless. She had every exit covered with some out-of-context misquote. "All atrocities are not military atrocities.

There are also atrocities of the mind. Everyone thinks corruption is stealing money. The real corruption is what the war is doing to America, the American mind. The belief that everything is good or bad and the pacifists are as simple as the Pentagon. The willingness to believe that the war can be understood without pain and rational thought, that it can be shown on television. The cliches and metaphors come from movies and comic strips, that's the level of thinking. No matter how heroic the effort or painful the sacrifice, the conclusion is strictly comic book mentality. And no one is ashamed. They're not even embarrassed." He knew he had said too much.

"I didn't see any women and children. I didn't see them at the river and I didn't see them in Rick's film." A thought occurred to him. "Where are their bodies? If women and children were killed at the river why has no one produced their bodies?"

"Come off it, Sherrill. They wash a couple of miles downriver and the military is going to say Charlie killed them."

"I didn't see any women or children. It was a freefire zone, Norela. There wasn't a ville within miles. If they were there they were there as soldiers. Do you realize how small a part of the story Rick covered?"

"Do you realize how big a piece of our ass Rick and I leave hanging out every time we do a story? We can't wait until the shooting is over and the verdict is in. You can hang around for days, poke around after it's over, brood over it a few weeks. You can reconstruct history but we have to file a report when no one knows what the hell is going on and we'd better be right most of the time. We take the chances and we make the news."

She was right. They had to say what was on fire, how big the fire was and what it would mean if it got out of control when all they could see was smoke. The thought of having to make those decisions terrified him as it must have terrified Norela and Rick. Maybe that was why, once they had agreed that the house was on fire, it was so difficult to clarify that it had really been the garage. History could be revised but news couldn't. News could only be superseded by other news on the same subject.

It had been a mistake trying to experience the entire operation rather than sampling and reporting. Instead of reporting the fire he had thrown water on it. He couldn't describe the ruined house, the destitute family or whether it was accident or arson. He could only tell how the fire singed his eyebrows and withered his face, how the heavy bucket tore at his hands, the water drenched his trousers and caused his socks to slip wetly into his shoes.

If that were true, wouldn't it also be true that he could tell how it felt to shoot women and children if it had happened? If he couldn't describe it, didn't that mean it hadn't happened? "You know as well as I that when you bring a camera to the scene you change the scene; everybody becomes an actor. At the river everyone was showing off for the camera. They unnecessarily risked their lives but they didn't kill women and children. You have to be pretty stupid to commit an atrocity on television."

"You have to be pretty stupid to risk your life when you could be balling chicks on the campus or getting a head start on a career," Norela said. "And Marines are volunteers."

She was baiting him and he had to be careful. "These people," he chose "people" to suggest that he used it naturally, "volunteered for the job their country asked them to do and they have accepted the misery that goes with it. They are good people and they are trying to save this country but do you realize that no one has defined what victory means? Is it preserving the DMZ? Stopping infiltration? Invading North Vietnam? Maintaining a—"

"Do you realize no one gives a shit about strategy or victory or what happens to this country?"

"They have to care."

"Have you looked at this peninsula? We call it Indochina

because that's what the French called it and we preserve their mentality but it's not three countries, it's four. Cambodia and Laos are rarely news and Thailand isn't news at all, yet the price of rice in one of these countries impacts on all. Why isn't it news? The same reason the ethnic groups aren't news. Hanoi hates them as much as Saigon, which hates them as much as Laos, which hates them as much as Cambodia. But the story is too hard to research, too hard to write and no one would publish it: too hard to read. News has to be in isolated pieces and pictures."

"But the pieces don't mean anything."

"People don't want meaning. What people want is the spectacularly insignificant. Has bread lost its taste? Insignificant because whether it has or hasn't is not going to change the price. But amusing rather than spectacular. A good story but not a big story. Running up a Viet Cong flag on a campus flagpole and defying the police to take it down—spectacular and insignificant. It didn't change anyone's opinion or the course of the war but it's a major story. That's the kind of story Rick hasn't come up with."

"It was staged."

"Of course. Otherwise it would be called 'television accident' because the only news would be what the camera accidentally saw. Do you know the most successful piece I ever wrote? I said that sexual inequality began with the wearing of sanitary napkins. It was silly. No one started wearing a rag because of it and no one stopped but that story has been reprinted in college textbooks. Every time I try to write something important my editors say, write about Tampax."

That was what Stolkalcyk had said but news couldn't be that random, haphazard. "Is that why you wanted me along, so we could discuss news?"

Norela smiled. It was a disarming smile. "I wanted to know if you're a baby-killer. I have to stop at CORDS and set up some interviews. It's down the street from a good hotel on the river. I'll listen to your story at dinner and tomorrow we'll see what the students are doing."

She seemed casual about the student demonstrations that were her purpose for being in Hue but Sherrill was pleased that he had made an initial good impression and he hoped for a sympathetic listener.

In Hue, Norela suggested they share a cyclo. For a cyclo driver, she picked an ancient, bandy-legged man with a bandana tied around his bald head. The man bowed low, sweeping them into the cycle where they sat side by side holding their bags in their laps. Sherrill disliked cyclos; he felt on display—rich American rides on labor of poor oriental. He felt foolish being pedaled through the streets by a man half his size and twice his age. At CORDS Norela got out and Sherrill took their bags to the hotel where he paid the driver an inflationary rate that permitted him some dignity and the driver some insults. At the hotel he had a two-dollar room with a million-dollar view. The ornate furniture was uncomfortable and the tiny closet smelled as though an ARVN had died there.

He met Norela for dinner and they ate in the restaurant atop the hotel. He saw no point in telling again what had happened at the river. Instead, he told her the war was worth winning but that the strategy of killing Viet Cong and NVA soldiers until they decided to quit was not working, that giving the enemy sanctuaries was insane, that fighting in the same villages year after year was counter-productive and that no one could help the Vietnamese until they found capable leadership.

"The only credibility any of us has is with the people who agree with us," Norela said. "If you tell them what you've been saying is wrong, you're going to lose the only readers you have."

"That's why I'm here," he said. He had to trust someone.

"You can explain how my thinking is changing, that I believe in what we are doing here but that we have to change the way we're doing it."

She caught on fast. "You want me to break the story so you can see if it'll fly. If it does, there'll be so many questions REAL will have to let you answer them. If it doesn't fly you can say I misquoted you and that you still want to chase Charlie to Hanoi. It might work but why would I do it?"

"I took a risk on the train. I'm taking a risk talking to you."

"So tell me how you got to be so brave—so flamboyant," she said.

"I'm not like that."

"You have to be. That's the way everyone sees you."

He laughed, not knowing how else to respond. He told her Jennifer didn't see him that way and didn't like him that way.

"What's she like?"

"She's always thought the best of me and she's always had definite opinions, but lately she's been confused."

"Everyone thinks 'fuck' is a dirty word but 'change' is the dirtiest word in the English language," Norela said. "The world played a trick on me and every other woman."

"She seems confused about who I am, who she is."

"Men are doing what they've always done: fucking, fighting and making the rules. You change our job description so we never feel secure. We can't enjoy sex; we have to enjoy sex. We have to have a lot of children; we can't have a lot of children. We can't have a career; we have to have a career. We can't go to school; we have to go to school. What you need us to be this year is who we are. No one ever asks us who we want to be."

Maybe that's what Jennifer meant about being used. She was who and what he needed her to be, but he tried to be what and who she needed. Except for coming to Vietnam. With Marie in her grave and him in Vietnam, Jennifer no longer knew who she was or what he needed. He didn't want to discuss it any more and prepared to leave.

"Nurse Big-tits is also confused about you." He looked at her sharply. "I don't do interviews without research."

He hadn't thought about Kelty for a long time, the Kelty who washed battle-grimed men and longed to soak in hot, perfumed bubbles; whose favorite trees were elms, she said, because the leaves were so easy to clean up. When he had laughed at that, she added, "And in the spring the leaves come out so green and excited." "She is a wonderful person."

"It must have been the white uniform; it couldn't have been her brains. She's the kind of girl who made two A's in high school, one in gym and one behind it. It must have taken guts to screw her after all the others."

"I didn't make love to her."

"She was in love with you," Norela said.

"She was lonely for someone to talk to, someone who didn't need her. There was no romance between us."

"Too old? Too big? Not your type?"

"She wanted me to write a story about her for her parents but I couldn't because of the way REAL would make her look."

"No one worries any more about their good name," Norela said. "I don't care what they say as long as my lipstick is straight in the pictures."

She told him she and Belk had been sharing a bed in Saigon when a story broke. She had dressed, grabbed her camera and notepad and had to wait, "for the son of a bitch to wash and blow dry his hair. He said he could be unprepared but not ungroomed; he could be wrong but he couldn't be speechless. He was right. That's what this is all about. We look good and we tell stories. If they like the way we look and are amused by what we say, then it's money and fame as long as we hold their fancy."

They walked down the stairs together and she followed him to his room. "I want to make love to you," she said.

Sherrill did not believe women fell in love with him at first sight and the waitress at the Press Center had made him doubly suspicious. He feared Norela would do anything for information but he did not want to offend her. "Norela, we're friends. Why don't we leave it at that?"

"You know don't you? Rick told you, that bastard," she said without heat. "You're one of those men who can't get it up unless a woman has tits bigger than her brains." She cried. He was convinced she was drunk.

"Norela, it's not you. You're—a lovely person."

"The only thing about me that everyone knows, and everyone tells."

"What are you talking about?"

"My mastectomy, dammit. Like making love to a skeleton. Being impaled on a ribcage. That's what Rick told you, isn't it?"

"Norela, I didn't know, honest." Two Americans saw her crying and paused to see if she needed assistance. He opened the door and let her into his room. "I'm sorry. I didn't know." He sat down on the hard bench.

"Like making love to a little boy, that's what my husband said. After fifteen years. I always tried to be perfect for him. On our honeymoon the damn toilet wouldn't flush. I ran away. I thought I had rather give him up forever than let him see my shit. For fifteen fucking years he never saw me without makeup."

She was wailing now with big racking sobs and he didn't know what to do. He put his arm around her.

"I think the son of a bitch was relieved when I had a mastectomy. He couldn't be expected to make love to a woman who didn't have tits. No real man could. That's what he told me when he divorced me." She regained control, wiping the tears from her face with the backs of her hands. "I told all his friends I got a divorce because he was homosexual."

God, she was tough. Still, he felt sorry for her. He patted her shoulder.

"Stop treating me like your grandmother."

"Norela, you are one of the best reporters—" He could feel her bristle and dropped that line. "Everyone admires you. And respects you. I don't think people know about your mastectomy. I don't think they care that—"

"I don't want your pity," she screamed.

If it had been her room he would have left but it was his room and he was going to have to get her out without offending her. "You should write about your mastectomy," he said. "Think what it would do for other women."

"How can I be a fucking sex symbol if I write that fucking article?" she asked. "I disgust you don't I? You think you're going to see scars and your dick will shrivel."

She was beginning to disgust him and he didn't want that. "Norela—"

"Have you known many women, Sherrill?"

There it was again, that probing, looking for information. "No. My wife and I have a very special relationship."

"Then why are you in Vietnam?"

Jennifer had never understood but maybe Norela would. He told her about his books, how he tried to write something true while his life had been overflowing with banality in a society whose only hunger was for amusement, whose only ambition was diversion, whose only achievement was to be entertainment for fools. He had sought refuge behind ivy walls only to discover that the college had the same values as the community, that education was another form of commerce. He had thought in Vietnam he would find substance, life and death without Muzak and marketing.

"Everyone thought I was crazy when I started working," Norela said. "They couldn't understand why my life was empty when I had my own car and my own bedroom but after you've had your babies and built your house there's nothing left for a woman but screwing around or being president of the Junior League. I was president of the Junior League. My husband was so pleased he gave me a new car."

"I'm sorry that—"

"Don't pity me, Sherrill."

"I don't pity you, I fear you." It was a lucky shot but it was a bulls-eye.

"Just so we know where we stand." She stood up and without a backward look left the room.

She was gone, no small accomplishment, and now that he knew about her mastectomy she couldn't write anything bad about him. Not that he would reveal her secret. He could imagine what REAL would do with the story. She was symbol of what they hated most, a woman with balls. The revelation that she had no breasts would make her a caricature of "the lesser man."

The next morning as they walked toward the university under tamarind trees along a boulevard beside the River of Perfumes, two Vietnamese on a Honda came up the sidewalk behind them. The driver cut between Sherrill and Norela and the rider grabbed at their cameras. Sherrill threw up his arm to prevent the camera from slipping off his shoulder, hitting the rider. The motorcycle skidded and struck a tree. The two Vietnamese jumped up and ran down the street. "Did they get anything?" Sherrill asked.

"No, you were so quick."

The two "Honda Cowboys" stood watching them from a safe distance, ready to run but reluctant to give up the Honda. Sherrill righted the bike. "Get on," he said.

"Do you know how to drive one of these things?"

"No."

He started the bike and with Norela behind him, they started off in a series of jerks and wobbled down the street. The two men ran. They had gone a short distance when the men disappeared in a convoy idling on the road. Sherrill drove around the trucks and came to an altar in the middle of the road and wobbled to a stop. Anti-American banners in English hung over the street. Soldiers stood around the altar. "What's going on?"

"Students and bonzes have blocked the road," a captain said. "If we touch those altars it'll be an international incident. We're waiting for the police to remove them."

"How long have you been waiting?"

"Couple of hours for them to get an okay from Saigon."

Sherrill walked over to the altar and tugged, moving it a few inches. "Get going," he said to the captain who jumped into his jeep. Sherrill gave a sustained tug and moved the altar a foot. Angry students surrounded him but he continued to tug the altar out of the road. Miraculously, photographers appeared and took photographs.

"American, go home," the students chanted.

"You have to let us by," Sherrill said, slowly inching the altar off the road. He knew the students were hostile but not violent.

"You are desecrating altar," one of the students yelled at him. He looked like the driver of the bike.

"I don't want it to be damaged," he yelled. The convoy slowly passed.

The students stopped chanting to watch the convoy pass, then turned their attention on Sherrill. "You are American imperialist," yelled the bike bandit who appeared to be their leader. With the trucks gone the fire had gone out of the demonstration and the leader attempted to restart it.

"I'm a professor," Sherrill shrugged.

"You turn our leaders into puppets and our women into whores. You make us children."

"You're not a child. You're old enough to be in the ARVN. Why aren't you fighting for your country? Win your people's respect, become their leader and you won't be anybody's puppet."

"You must get out of my country."

"When you become leader we'll get out of your country. And to help you, I souvenir you this bike." The leader wanted his bike back but feared looking like an American puppet. He hesitated too long. Sherrill rolled the bike toward him so that he had to grab the handlebars to prevent the bike from hitting him in the crotch. "I souvenir you," Sherrill said and walked away not looking back.

He led Norela through the students to a small cafe on the river. They were joined by the photographers who took pictures while they drank strong coffee with sweetened condensed milk and checked their personal belongings. They hadn't lost anything. "Where did you guys come from?" Sherrill asked the photographers.

"We expected trouble. Why didn't you hit that guy?"

"I didn't want to start a riot."

"Damn, why not?"

"I'm not your puppet," he said, intending a joke but no one laughed.

After they had finished their coffee, the photographers asked them to pose for backup shots. They rented a bike from a student and had Sherrill and Norela pose sitting on the bike, standing with the bike, singly and together. He watched as they posed Norela. "Lift your head. Turn to the left, that's it. . .look glamorous. . .show some cheesecake. . . more leg. . . give us a chest shot." Sherrill took notes. In his book, the sculptor for the memorial statue was going to pose Cassady looking for some expression, some stance, some attitude that Cassady was unable to give.

Then it was his turn. "Look serious," the photographers said. "Look determined. Show me determination again. No. Okay, let's try indomitable. Can you look indomitable? Um, how about steadfast?"

When the photographers had finished, Norela invited him to the Citadel. The walled, moated, French imitation of a

Chinese Imperial City seemed to most Americans the epitome of Vietnamese culture. It was Vietnam's most attractive illusion but he didn't want to spend a lot of time with Norela, fearful that she would interpret it as romantic interest. He also didn't want to run into students, demonstrations or photographers. He went back to the hotel.

Sherrill was too much a farm boy to be idle. He worked on his book using his experience with the photographers to write the scene of Cassady watching the sculptor turn him into something he was not. He also wrote of Cassady's lover-wife who before making love to Cassady always extracted some bit of information from him, information that he had to invent because she could not bear the truth. As Cassady watched the sculptor turn his image into a hero that was not him, he watched his wife fall in love with a man who wasn't him either.

Writing the book was like trying to juggle fireflies. The ideas escaped before he could commit them to paper or memory and every idea released three others that went flying into the night, now sparking, now dead, blink, black, blink, black, and him in pursuit trying to contain one while capturing the other three.

Sometimes to keep REAL at bay, he worked on a story about the Marine operation. Also, if during the course of the investigation they subpoenaed his story he would need to show them something to retain credibility. He couldn't have the public believing he had destroyed the manuscript to hide an atrocity. He wasn't sure he had a story. He had routine, he had violence but he had no climax. He had intended no more than a sentence or two on the incident at the river but that was before it was news. What was believed to have happened at the river was the only thing most people, even most reporters, knew about the operation, the only established fact. Not to mention it would destroy the credibility of the story.

What was he going to say about it? He did not want a moment that had gone unnoticed at the time to dominate the story. What he remembered was frustration and rage that exploded at the river. He had O.D.ed on rage. He had not seen women or children, or soldiers or even flesh and blood. He also knew that if he had it would have made no difference.

He needed a dramatic climax to get the focus off the river but the story had no climax. That was the truth he had suffered all those days in the bush to authenticate—there were no big moments. There were no moments at all. No minutes, hours, climaxes. There were three hundred and sixty-five seamless days that floated in a void with reference to nothing else on this earth. He would have to invent a telling moment.

None of the photographs showed Stolkalcyk the way Sherrill wanted to present him in the story. There was a picture of him sitting in the mud, his rifle between his legs, his helmet on one knee, a map in the other. Depending on how it was captioned, he would look pensive, defeated, bewildered or confused.

The best picture he had was of the lieutenant standing, feet braced, chin lifted, rifle in hand. In the background was a cloud that looked like smoke, in the foreground the legs of a man who was resting but appeared dead. Stolkalcyk was watching the supply helicopter land but if the reader was not told that, Oscar Mike would look indomitable. Sherrill didn't want him to look indomitable; he wanted him to look like a decent man, steadfastly doing his job while his skin erupted in sores, his boots rotted, his uniform turned to filth around his clean shaven face. Stolkalcyk shaved every day.

"Stolkalcyk had finished the race and this time he had been first; he had outrun Charlie, cutting him off at the river. Now he would have to fight his way to his base camp the way he had fought his way to the river, but he and his men would march in clean shaven. 'Get the captain,' he yelled at the radioman. 'Tell him Second Platoon is Oscar Mike.'"

That wouldn't work; it suggested Nazi neatness. ". . .march in knowing they had done the job they had been sent to do." That wouldn't work either; war criminals always did what they were sent to do.

Sometimes he saw Norela at the hotel and they had dinner together; sometimes they went to the MAC-V compound to see the evening movie. One night they saw Dix Devereaux who had become the personification of courage because of his ability to face hundreds of actors dressed as Indians or Japanese soldiers and say, "This is it, men," without his voice quavering. The President had awarded him a medal for service to his country and the public had honored the patriotism that had made him rich and famous for fighting America's foes on film.

Although the audience was composed almost entirely of soldiers there was not a snicker when Dix said, "Fix bayonets, boys, we'll give them a taste of cold steel." Even Sherrill and Norela knew it was phony, not just the soundstage set, the blank ammunition; the emotion was phony, the patriotism phony, the situation not only unreal but ludicrous. Yet no one yelled, Fraud.

After the movie, over a drink Sherrill explained his anger to Norela who pretended not to understand. "It trivializes fear, courage, suffering. It screws up our perceptions of what war is, patriotism, heroism. It makes a mockery of Washington, Robert E. Lee, Audie Murphy."

"It's entertainment."

"That's what I'm saying. We prefer the phony. We are in love with lies that make us feel good. The whole country wants to be entertained. Someday all our heroes, our leaders, our politicians are going to be entertainers. Football players. . .Arthur Godfrey. . .Tab Hunter. . . someone who can be paid to play the fool."

"They won't have that much class," Norela said.

Her pretense of understanding so enraged him that he walked away.

One day at the compound he looked through magazines that had been donated to troops in Vietnam after their covers were removed. He flipped through them to find out what was going on back in the world. There were few words on war, repression or hunger, but stories on diets; a comic who used an obscene word before a White House audience; fanciful creatures seen in the snow, in the woods, in the sky; the crisis of a politician having to decide whether to keep the "good ole boy" image that had made him governor or to change to the slicker, sharper personality that could get him elected to the Senate; and several stories written by persons confessing sexual errors invariably committed with persons better known than the writers. REAL was not as bad as he had thought.

There was a series of photographs called "the greatest artistic achievement of mankind," that had been taken by a machine in outer space. There was the story of a visitor who collapsed at a medical school. The doctors, fearing lawsuits, had run to their offices and locked the doors. A janitor had called an ambulance and had received a gold medal for his bravery. Calling an ambulance was brave?

There was a story about the death of a hero, a minister who had devoted his life to caring for the poor in Appalachia. The photograph accompanying the story was not that of the hero but of Dix Devereaux who had portrayed the hero on the screen, stealing his story and his image.

There was a series of ads—"You may not recognize me but you recognize the car I drive"—with the name and photograph of once famous people. A note at the bottom explained how they had captured the nation's attention: a man who taught a dance step to the president's wife, a nine-year-old boy who had held up a liquor store and become the subject of a movie, a man who ran naked across a football field during a game.

The silliness and self-indulgence of the magazines depressed him. They were no better than REAL. He flipped through another and his name seemed to jump from the page. SHERRILL O'CONNELL ON THE STREET WITHOUT JOY. He could imagine The Wild Bunch sitting in the truck laughing at him. "That makes my butt want to dip snuff." They would recognize the story as a tissue of lies, that he had turned Lt. Wright into a caricature of a black officer. "Nothing personal," he said under his breath.

He had to explain to The Wild Bunch. Phu Bai was only eight or ten miles; he could walk it if he had to. He packed his bag and returned to the compound to catch a ride to the base. It was late when he found the lieutenant sitting in the O club with two black officers. "Hey," Wright said, recognizing him. "Hey, it's the hero." Sherrill was relieved that the lieutenant remembered him but unsure of whether or not he was being mocked. "This is the guy who whupped up on two Honda Cowboys and cleared the road in Hue," Wright said, introducing him.

"How did you know—"

"That Commie fox has been telling that story to everybody. Made Stars and Stripes."

"Sit down, hero, and let me buy you a drink," said a thin, shaved-head lieutenant who masked his angelic face behind dark glasses and a perpetual scowl.

"I'm buying the hero's drink," said a heavy set, thick-lipped captain. His deep voice rumbled in his throat when he spoke. "I was riding a cyclo when two of them fuckers came up on a bike and stole the fucking watch off my arm. Anybody that whups them is a friend of mine."

"My jeep was stopped because of them fucking statues they put in the road," angel face said, the parallel lines in his face going deeper. "This kid asked if I wanted to fuck his sister and held out this Polaroid picture of her and when I reached for it, he grabbed the glasses off my face."

Sherrill laughed, happy to be surrounded by friends. He drank because he was merry.

"It's no wonder they can come through the wire or feel out our trip wires," Wright said. "Hell, they pick pockets for practice."

"I know this medic who delivered a gook baby and when the medic slapped the kid on the butt, the kid stole his wallet," the captain rumbled and they all laughed.

Sherrill was having a good time but he was drinking too much and he hadn't eaten. He struggled to clear his mind because he wanted them to understand why he seemed to be the center of his stories about others. "I didn't want to be a hero," he said.

"If I'd been in your shoes them two cowboys would never need a bike again. If we touched them gooks we'd be in boo coo trouble. We have to take their shit and they ain't even white."

"Check it," rumbled the captain. "But how you gonna show?"

"We do twelve for the man to learn to kill as good as he does, then we get our shit together and we don't tote no more bales for him," said angel face.

"Damn straight," rumbled the captain. "No jive we stay alive."

"The real heroes were The Wild Bunch. I wanted to tell all of you that."

"No skinning, no grinning when we winning."

"I thought we might go to see them," Sherrill said.

"Say what?" said the captain. "See who?"

"The Wild Bunch. I thought we might go see them."

"You don't get no wilder than this bunch," said angel face.

"I ain't on a guntruck no more," Wright said. "I got me a desk job now."

The other officers chuckled. "Now you assigning honkies to the trucks," said the captain.

"Where are they? Dillman? Deadpan?"

"They probably gone home. If not, they still here."

"Stubby? Little Man?"

Wright seemed annoyed by the questions. "I don't know no Little Man."

"He was the driver. Replaced the one who was killed in the Hai Van."

"The driver was a guy we called Dim because he thought the gooks loved us. Used to wave when we went through villages. Remember when them gooks tried to overrun us and he was too dumb to get under the truck? We counted seventeen bodies on the ground and five trying to crawl off. I shot one of them with the blooper. Blew his fucking head off."

"I wasn't with you then. I rode with you on a trip to Alpha."

"Nothing big." He dismissed the subject with a wave of the hand. "I ain't on a guntruck no more."

"I don't feel good about that story I wrote about you."

"If you wrote about us, we're real proud of it. Here, finish your drink."

"You have to understand the kind of magazine REAL is."

"Best damn story I read on Vietnam," the captain said. "Cause I ain't never read one. Glad you came by."

"I didn't want to be the hero of the story. No shit. It was you guys, doing your job. I didn't write that about The Wild Bunch giving me a salute. That was from a story about—"

"Look man, nobody gives a shit. You bit?" Wright said.

"I just didn't want you to think I said those things about you."

"It don't matter what you write about me because when I leave this place, this ain't going to be me anymore. Thanks for coming by."

"The story has to have a hero," Sherrill said, "but he can't be black."

"Hey man," angel face said. "You're a hero. Don't fuck up now."

"That's why I wrote about the way you smelled and gave orders. See, REAL's idea of a black man is bare feet and waterme—"

"Do you get the feeling you're not wanted?" the captain rumbled.

"No, really, you guys are like—"

"Get your white ass away from this table," the captain said. "This is black country."

Wright wouldn't look at Sherrill but the captain's eyes were cold and the lines above angel face's dark glasses were hard. "The Wild Bunch and all that shit, that was another world, man," he said. "You and me ain't on a guntruck now."

Sherrill walked outside. To hell with the lieutenant; he would explain to the others. He spent three days looking for them. He had thought Dillman was back in the world but he had extended and was riding guntrucks through the Mang Yang Pass. Machlin had been medevaced home. Stubby, Deadpan, Little Man were harder to find. "What's his last name?" they asked. "What's the number of his unit?"

It was hopeless. He would never find them, never be able to explain why he was the hero of their story. He also knew he wouldn't like them if he did find them. He only liked them the way he wrote about them.

It was late the next day when he got back to the MAC-V compound in Hue and he went directly to the bar. He saw Norela engaged in an argument with a CIA agent, a short man, with short fingers, short nose and glasses that warped above one eyebrow and below the other. "The stories are all the same," he said. "Waste stories, frag stories, atrocity stories. All you do is change the names and dates."

"That's reassuring," Norela argued. "Amid all the chaos the stories are all the same."

"I missed my chance to be on TV," a captain complained. "I told them the firebase's mission was to give fire support to U.S. and ARVN troops. This dumbass Spec 4 who had been in country two weeks said we were trying to turn mountains into mole hills and they put his ass on TV."

"I just got back from R&R," said a major. "While I was home I got to reading the newspapers and watching TV and Saigon was rubble and VC were running through the streets of Da Nang. I got off the airplane ducking and dodging and everybody thought I was some damn cherry. I said, 'Do we still hold Da Nang?' They thought I was nuts."

"I hear you and another guy had a fight over Norela Cook" a man said to Sherrill. He was one of those neat-is-sissy men. "Is she worth it?"

Sherrill moved to the other end of the bar. "I know you," a pilot said. He reached into his jacket and pulled out a clipping from a paper. "This is a picture of me receiving a medal. You were there."

"That's not the picture of you receiving the medal," Sherrill said. "That's a picture of the rehearsal of you receiving the medal."

"What's the difference?"

What was the difference? One was real and one was sham.

"If you're Sherrill O'Connell they have some mail for you," a colonel said. "They had been holding it in Quang Tri."

Wondering how old it was, he retrieved it and returned to the bar. There was a package and a letter from Jennifer. Inside the package was a pair of panties, a small box of aspirin and a note. "I'm sending these because when you get home I won't be needing either for a long time." It was unlike Jennifer to be that candid about sex. He decided he was going to like the changes in Jennifer.

Her letter began, "I never realized how many things you did. The car has been acting up and I don't know whether to get it fixed or to buy a new one. What do you want me to do?" It was an old letter from the old Jennifer and maybe the package was from the old Jennifer too.

"I met a woman whose husband was shot down over North Vietnam. We had so much to talk about. She hasn't heard a word. She said, 'The terrible thing is, I know that whatever I hear, it will be a relief just to know.' Isn't it strange that sometimes knowing the worst is better than not knowing at all? She has had to start a whole new life without him. We have decided to meet once a week we have so much in common."

He opened the letter from Lindly. Lindly was pleased at Sherrill's success although he was disappointed with Sherrill's right-wing militarism that had so upset the school. He thought the LZ story was the best thing Sherrill had ever written; however, it blew Jennifer's mind.

What blew Jennifer's mind? She knew him better than to believe those were his thoughts. Lindly's determined imprecision infuriated him almost as much as his pretensions of being Professor Hip. How could he think the LZ story was the best thing Sherrill had written? Why had he ever liked Lindly whose progress was confirmed by the things he left behind—four colleges, two Protestant denominations, two wives, three children, and hundreds of ideas and theories that had become unfashionable. He supposed that Lindly was on at least his second mother, having disposed of the first because of inappropriate background.

There was a letter from a woman who had been his student. Neither she nor her husband had read his novels because they could make up their own stories. "Novels are created," he shouted. "It's history that's invented." They had read his articles in REAL and for the first time they knew what the war was like.

"You don't know," he screamed, throwing the letter at the floor. How could anyone believe that fiction was inventing stories? That they could know about Vietnam by reading what were supposed to be the exploits and antics of some reporter? If they believed that—he noticed that others in the room were looking at him.

He ordered another drink and sat at a table. The movie was being shown in an adjacent room and he could see combat footage of men climbing down nets, crouching in the bottom of landing craft. He wondered if anyone ever saw themselves captured in film, forever young and afraid. Forever dead. Some of those men had died, yet their representations went on, climbing down nets, crouching in landing craft.

A flaming airplane fell from the sky, cartwheeled over the water and exploded. He had watched someone die. Someone's final agony had been immortalized on celluloid. Friends, family, children, watched him relive the moment of his death; his eternity the repetition of fifteen seconds of screaming, panic-stricken, flaming hell. They had applauded because the film pretended the airplane belonged to the enemy. On the screen appeared Dix Deveraux giving orders in that real soldier's voice he had learned by going to Ft. Ord and listening to how real soldiers talked.

Sherrill had scoffed at peasants who believed a photograph captured their spirit yet a photographer had stolen a soldier's fear, a pilot's death. The camera had stolen Dix's. . .what? Soul? Not just his soul but his personality, his sexual preference, his personal values and left him a celluloid image honored as America's ideal.

A long-faced colonel joined him. "I need some professional advice," the colonel said. He had anxious eyes and a fringe of hair outlining his red scalp; the kind of man who after he retired would grow a goatee and pretend to be a liberal. "I collect tattoos." He looked at Sherrill with anxious eyes and felt his scalp as though wondering what had happened to his hair. "I have been told I should publish them in a book, that they're worth a lot of money but I don't know how to proceed."

The colonel laid photo albums on the table. "I have them organized—unusual pictures, sentiments, places, combinations."

Sherrill opened an album. Inside were closeups of tattoos—Ann on one buttock, Marie on the other; a cowboy and horse on one buttock, a steer on the other with a lariat looping across the small of the back; twin hula dancers, one on each cheek. "Where did you get these?"

"I'm a surgeon. This album is all butt shots."

Sherrill picked up another album, this one of female figures—nude, dancing, in provocative poses. "These were on dead men?"

"Some were dead or died. Most are alive. Do I have to identify them if I publish the photographs?"

Sherrill looked at another album. Death Before Dishonor. He stared at the photograph, convinced it belonged to the boy he had met at an LZ above the Song Cha Nang. He examined the photograph, studying the shade of the skin, the color of the hair. "Excuse me," the colonel said, turning the page. An entire album of Death Before Dishonor. Sherrill looked at one after another searching for the one he knew. "What happened to this man?" he asked, pointing blindly at a tattoo.

"I don't know. How much money should I ask for."

"All these men were wounded or killed?"

"They were admitted to the hospital. Malaria, snake bite, traffic accident, sunstroke. Most had been wounded or killed. Do I need an agent?"

"This man. . .I knew this man. . .I wrote a story about this man," he said, pointing at a photograph. But the story had never been published. Or, part of it had been but not as this man.

"I know," the colonel said.

"You don't know. I. . .We were like brothers. . ." No, not like brothers. He didn't know his name. He didn't know if he was alive.

"I know," the colonel said.

"You don't know. We shared a death. . .of a. . .a friend. . ." But he hadn't been a friend; no one knew him.

"I know," the colonel said.

"You don't know," Sherrill said. He grabbed the colonel by the collar and shook him. "You don't know, asshole."

"Please," the colonel said.

"Sherrill," Norela said, appearing suddenly at his side. "Come on, Sherrill," she tugged at his sleeve.

"Please," the colonel said.

"What's the matter with you?" Norela asked.

He walked out of the building, blindly down the street. He could hear Norela running after him, calling for him to wait. He didn't slow down.

"What is it?" she said, breathlessly, running beside him. "I feel like I don't know you any more."

Sherrill stopped so she could catch up. "You never knew me. Don't you understand, you never knew me. You knew somebody REAL invented."

"We are all of us invented. How can you be a writer and not know that? You invent people all the time."

He started walking again, not knowing how to answer her. He told her about taking a dying VC's photograph, stealing his spirit, taking his last possession. "I don't do that in writing."

"I've read your stories in REAL."

"Norela, I didn't write those stories. Yes, I wrote them, but they're different. I'm different."

"That's what you expect from REAL. It's not a literary magazine. It's not a news magazine. It's a conceit sheet. Why are you so surprised?"

Why was it so hard to understand? "I want people to know what I think, not trivia that is nobody's business."

"I have never seen such a blushing egotist. You go chasing all over the country, shooting Viet Cong, punching people around, waving the flag and writing about how good it feels and you want people to read about your philosophy of life? Your thoughts on strategy? Get real, Sherrill. Nobody gives a shit what we think. We are not going to be quoted by Bartlett. We are not going to be mentioned in history books. We give readers someone to laugh at, to get mad at, to talk about and on rare occasions someone to admire or love. You've gotten your share so what are you bitching about?"

He didn't want to look at her. "I'm not an actor, I'm a writer."

"It's ink. That's all it is. Right now you're somebody the public is interested in. Hang on to it as long as you can."

Was she stupid or what? He explained that the heroic, patriotic actor they had seen on the screen was the invention of the media. He had become his image so that only the image on the screen was real. "So what?" she said. The question startled him. "Who gives a shit?"

He considered the question insane. Everyone gave a shit. Everyone wanted to know what was real. And everyone was encouraged to write, tell, publish, show, portray, exhibit what was not just false but phony. "The hero in my book believes that he has lost his identity because the town, the press, everyone has forced him to be someone he isn't and now the monument is taking his face."

"It's a book, Sherrill. It doesn't have anything to do with you."

He wondered how anyone could be so stupid; the book was the best, the truest part of him. "Forget it. Forget it, I might as well be talking to myself." He looked back toward the bar. "I'm going to get a drink."

"I have a bottle in my room."

In his agitation he had walked most of the way to the hotel. He followed her to her room. "Where's the bottle?" he asked.

"Haven't you had enough to drink?"

"No and hell no."

She gave him a bottle of scotch and he sat on the floor and drank from the bottle. "Where have you been?" she asked.

"Phu Bai."

"You didn't tell me you were leaving." He ignored her. "Is that where you got those panties hanging out of your pocket?"

"My wife sent them to me. Why do I feel that I have been set up?"

"Success draws a lot of attention but you got the attention that was intended for Rod Reaves. Your fellow ideologues have never trusted you and want Rod to replace you. Rod was supposed to come to Hue, confront the students, open the highway for the military and take your place as right-wing hero, but you punched Rod out."

"Did you write that Rod and I fought over you?"

"Some people wrote that. I said it was a tough guy contest. Jesus, Sherrill, it would have been immodest to say you fought over me and I needed a tough guy for the student story."

"You planned the student protest?"

"We cooperated. They needed the cameras and the banners, we needed to set the time. Rod was to cover it for the right, I for the left."

"How could you and Rod work together?"

"The same way you and I did. You give it your slant, I give it mine. We're trying to create different mentalities as to how the news is viewed but we're in total agreement as to what the news is."

"Are you and Rod lovers?"

"Are you jealous?"

"What do you get out of this?"

"No one takes me seriously because of the things I had to do to get attention. I've got the glare now and I want a Pulitzer. Rod interviewed a lot of VC when he was with the Berets but his readers won't accept him talking to VC when he could kill them. He's giving the interviews to me."

"What was Rod going to do with the students?"

"Talk tough, clear the road. What you did."

"That's what you wanted?"

"We had hoped it would get out of hand, that Rod or the soldiers would start shoving the students around. We thought you'd be perfect and you were but not the way we expected. Don't be angry, Sherrill. It was the best thing that could have happened to you. You proved yourself to people who would have destroyed you if you had been violent or had failed."

"I was intended to be violent?"

"But you weren't. You looked like a hero without killing anyone. I wrote that you took the bike from the bandits but that it was my idea to give it to the leader. I have to be true to my image. I can't be a helpless female rescued by a he-man; no one would believe it."

"That's not what happened."

"It's what everyone believes."

"Why didn't you tell me the confrontation was planned?"

"Because I didn't want you to be the self-conscious prick you're being." He refused to look at her. "You're right, I should have said you were a thrill-seeking, self-righteous bastard. You have to be somebody. Who did you want me to say you were?"

"I am not somebody you invented."

"Damn straight, it was a collaboration."

He wanted to take her thin, white throat between his hands and squeeze until she saw him as something besides what she wanted him to be. "Sherrill, it doesn't matter what people write about you. What matters is how you photograph and we both look terrific." She showed a photograph of him with his arm around her. It was taken when he was leading her through the students, but it didn't look like a mob. Depending on the cutline, it looked they were surrounded by Vietnamese fans or walking through a crowded market.

"Did you write anything about Jennifer?"

"I said she was the kind of woman whose bathing suit was three years old, that you read Jack London to her while she ironed your shirts. Every wife irons her husband's shirts. I said she was a lonely, unhappy child. Everyone was a lonely, unhappy child."

"She is going to think I told you that."

"Sweetheart, I don't write news. I write a light column about my misadventures. I'm sorry to disappoint you but you didn't make front page."

He wanted to strike her, to shake her until she listened to what he was saying. "I didn't want to make the front page. I didn't want to make the gossip page or any page. I want my words, my books to be talked about, not my personal life."

"Do you think I always like being Norela Cook? Don't you think I ever wish I had presented myself another way? A kinder, fuller woman? You wanted to be known. It was a choice you made. You can't whine about it now because you don't like the way people see you. If you want to be a nice little professor with a nice little wife who sends you her panties to hold when you're lonely and you want to write nice little books that a handful of coeds will sigh over then stop bitching because no one wants to read you and no one wants to publish what you write. You can have it your way or you can have it their way but you can't have it both ways."

He took another pull at the bottle seeking clarity. He had wanted to be recognized, to be accepted as a writer so he had come to Vietnam to find. . . He couldn't remember what he had been looking for, couldn't think where he had gone wrong, didn't know when he had lost understanding.

"Sherrill, I didn't write one thing that would damage your image."

"I don't understand the God-like knowledge that you pretend to have."

"It's my job to know."

"You don't know. You can't know. You can think you know. That's the best you can do."

"Everybody knows that."

"They don't know."

"Okay, nobody knows anything. Can you be happy about that?"

He explained that it wasn't the oversimplification or the occasional inaccuracies that was dangerous, or that the media took and gave images and identities that no better represented the bearer than the doctor's tattoos. Without willing or intending they had created an audience that gave cursory, uncritical attention to superficial events and believed they understood their world. He wondered if there had ever been a nation so rich in information, so poor in assimilation and comprehension. They had seen a picture of the moon and believed they knew how to walk there. They had read a book on achieving mental health and thought themselves sane.

"I know," she said.

"You don't know." He tried to describe what the Marine operation was like—the weeks that he had lived and the months the Marines had experienced. "Then Belk comes in, shoots a few minutes of film, a few seconds get on television and everybody thinks they know."

"I understand."

"You don't understand. Rick did not record what happened. He couldn't, even if he had been through the whole thing and had all the film in the world. A camera can't record what people are thinking or feeling. Television requires Belk to tell the viewer what he is seeing. Belk didn't film what happened, he filmed his story about what he thought happened. A picture postcard. 'Greetings from the Nam.' That's all television can do."

"I understand."

"You don't understand. You can't understand. Belk couldn't understand. I can't understand."

"You were there."

Sherrill stopped, took a deep breath. No wonder there were wars; it was easier to kill people that to get them to understand something that was readily apparent. He told her of the time, partly on a dare, that he had run a marathon. He had finished more than two hours behind the winner. He had never believed they had run the same race although that was the way it was reported. Certainly it was not the same experience. Norela said she understood. He said she did not understand.

He reminded her that architects built in distortion because straight lines seemed to the eye to bend. "If it's straight it doesn't look straight. Good fiction curves the line so that it appears true to the eye."

Norela said she understood; journalism was slanted. He wondered if she were deliberately trying to anger him. If so she was succeeding. He told her about the same photograph being used, except that in one of them he was pointing at his victim and in the other he was pointing at Cambodia. Norela said she understood. He fought down the urge to hit her.

He told her how he and Lindly had marched, picketed, posed for pictures and gone home to insured houses and tenured jobs, leaving the blacks to face the terrors of a white-power night. "We didn't know. We could never know."

She put her arms around him. "I'm glad you told me all that," she said. "I understand what you've been through."

He fought the urge to kill her. He was on his feet although he wasn't certain when he had stood up.

"Who are you, Sherrill? I want to know who you really are."

"I'm the person you rode the train with," he said.

"That was a reporter who shoots Viet Cong, keeps three Vietnamese from stealing a jeep, punches out people, chases two muggers on a motorcycle, stands up to mobs and almost throttled a colonel. Who are you now? I want to know who you really are, how you think." He didn't know how to answer. What had he been talking about? "Is this the real you?"

"The real me is in the books I write." He told her he wanted to write a book in which everything that was good in him, that was true and strong would be in the book and that his image would be pressed into the pages.

"I want to be pressed in the book with you," she said, pressing herself against him.

Sherrill wondered what had made him attractive to women— something new, something crazy.

"I liked you from the moment I saw you," she said. "You are

so passionate. When you tried to protect me on the train I knew it would be like this.” She kissed his neck, running her hands down his back and over his hips. She sat down on the bed, pulling him down beside her. “You were so masterful with the students. You were so strong, so brave, just the way I knew you would be. You’re not afraid to hold me are you?”

“Norela—”

She lay down, holding her arms up to him. “I don’t want to beg. Just hold me. Remind me what it’s like to be a woman. Show me who you are.”

He wanted to take her thin white throat between his hands and squeeze the life from her. He put his hands on her face. “Norela,” he said. His hands slipped down her face and his fingers fitted themselves around her neck. He could see the indentation of his fingers in her flesh.

“”I’m not wearing fancy panties. I haven’t shaved my legs,” she said, sliding her clothes down with both hands.

He took her, savagely, not to hurt but to humiliate, to demonstrate his power over her. He demanded, he teased, driving her to the edge of orgasm and then stopping, pinning her tightly while she cursed and tried to writhe under him. He stroked slowly and deeply, increasing the intensity and force until her fingernails dug into his shoulders, then one last stab and quick withdrawal that made her gasp and claw, her blind eye seeking his arrow. He promised and withheld, offered and withdrew, insinuated and took away, hinting fulfillment then frustration, tantalizing her while she struggled to gain possession of him, to absorb him in her heat.

“Now do you understand?” he asked.

“Now,” she said. “Now.”

“Do you believe me?”

“Yes.”

“I am not your invention.”

“Yes.”

“I never intended to hurt anyone.”

"Yes. God, Sherrill, yes."

Her sighs became moans, became groans, became whimpers, became cries. She went rigid, quivered, trembled, convulsed. Frightened by the cries and convulsions, he stopped. She clamped her teeth in his neck, beat him with her hands until he started moving again, stabbing her with a viciousness that forced her jaws apart in a scream that split his ears. He tried to turn his head to escape the pain but she held her lips to his ear until she collapsed. For a moment she didn't move, didn't breathe. He hated himself for what he had done to her. For using his power to humiliate, to manipulate her. He had never been deliberately cruel.

She chuckled. "You were wonderful," she said, holding him close. "Love is sparing nothing."

It hadn't been love. It had been. . .It hadn't been hate. It hadn't been rape because. . . It had been. . .domination. He had wanted to control her, to force her to his will. He had used her. He had made her a sex object.

"You're looking awfully smug," she said.

He didn't feel smug. He felt ashamed. People were angry with him and it wasn't even for the right reason. He didn't understand what was happening to him and he didn't like who he had become. Where had he gone wrong? Accepting the accolades of others as though he deserved or needed them. By surrendering who he was in order to be what they wanted.

"Umm," she sighed luxuriously. "Who did you say you were?"

He had done things he never intended to do. He had become the kind of person he never intended to be. "I don't know who I am any more."

She smiled and kissed him. "That's the way I feel. Like I had just been born and was all sensations and lovely feelings and was everybody and nobody. And as long as you love me like that I don't care who you are. I wrote that you were a decent, honorable man of action who couldn't help getting involved.

That I hate this war as much as anyone but that Sherrill O'Connell would not, could not take part in an atrocity."

He was overwhelmed with shame, and gratitude. "You wrote that?"

"I made a lot of enemies with that column but people are going to see the real Sherrill O'Connell."

"You said there was no atrocity?"

"I said the whole war is an atrocity and that kind of horror happens every day. It wasn't an atrocity in the usual sense of the word. As for you, a hawk, yes, but a brave one."

"God bless you, Norela," he said, fighting back tears. "I'll never be able to repay you for this. I can go home now."

"You can't go home after what I wrote."

"I have to, Norela, and you've made it possible. I am forever—"

"You used me." She sat up on the bed beside him, her face distorted with fury. "Everyone is going to say you used me then discarded me."

"Why would anyone say anything?"

"We have been seen together, photographed together. You're the immovable right, I'm the irresistible left. Reporters kill for that kind of story. Do you think I won a lot of fans by looking like Little Miss Helpless who needed big-strong-hero in order to ride a train? I put my career on the line to write that you weren't a war criminal. Do you know what they'll say about me? That I sold my principles, my integrity for a sweet dick. That's what they always say about women who lose, that she gave up everything because she had to have him. But she was disposable. They're not saying that about me."

"I'm not a war criminal."

"You're a fucking madman having the time of your life shooting women and children, pushing people around and flexing your God damn muscles. You made a fool of me." She was crying.

"I never meant to hurt you."

"You never loved me."

How could she think it had been love? It wasn't even pity. What kind of man did that make him? "Norela, I love my wife. I've always loved her. I never should have left her to come here."

"I don't want to darn your socks and spend my life giving you my rapt attention, I have better things to do. But no one is going to write that you used me to clear your name then walked out on me. I'm not the kind of woman you walk away from. Rick Belk didn't walk out on me or Rod Reaves or Sherrill O'Connell. I decide when it's over."

"This would be a good time."

"Not until I write about the child you deflowered in Saigon."

"That's not true."

"Rod can't write about your pedophilia without offending his right wing readers so he gave the story to me."

"You can't use it without destroying yourself after what you wrote."

"You used me and no one uses Norela Cook and gets away with it."

It was impossible to contend with a person who had no non-negotiables. "Norela, the story isn't true. It can't help you and it can do a great deal of harm to me and to people who love me."

"I hope it hangs you and as for people who love you—there won't be any."

Sherrill went to his room, sat on the bed and smoked. He was dead. A lot of people hated him; they would believe he was a child molester and he was powerless to prevent it. Harry Tompkins sold that story to Rod Reaves who traded it to Norela. Ironically, readers were more likely to believe he was a child molester because she had written he wasn't a war criminal. The first story would make her seem moderate rather than vindictive and there was no one who could help him.

The general. The general was a stockholder in REAL and he had gone to Tombstone for the general. The general owed him. He would tell the general the liberals were trying to do a hatchet job on him and ask for help. If the general could arrange for Harry to be deported or charged with prostitution and drugs that at least would create doubt toward his story. Sherrill could deny it had happened. It wouldn't convince everyone but it was the best he could do.

The next day he rode a guntruck to Quang Tri and walked and hitched rides to headquarters. The general could not see him, the major said. Sherrill said he would wait or come back the next day. The general could not see him while the incident at the river was being investigated. Sherrill reminded the major he had gone to Tombstone as a personal favor to the general. It was out of the major's hands.

"I have to call home," Sherrill said. He had to warn Jennifer before she saw anything that Norela wrote. The telephone-ham radio network that had been set up was booked for weeks. "It's an emergency."

With the general's approval, the major bumped a couple of grunts trying to call home. "It's going to be a couple of hours," the major said.

"I have to call the Marine PAO in Da Nang," Sherrill said, claiming press priority and was able to reach Gunny Shivers. "How are things in Da Nang?" he asked.

"For a while a bunch of reporters tried to tell me there was a child in the film but they couldn't tell me how she got on the film without being in the river and I know damn well she wasn't in the river."

Sherrill breathed a sigh of relief at the gunny's certainty. Last night he might have sneered at the arrogance of anyone who thought they knew or could know the truth but today he was grateful that Gunny Shivers tolerated no doubt. His memory was pure, without nuance, immune to self-deception. There was no way the media or the military could sway the gunny's memory. Then he remembered the gunny's medical record. Unfit for combat duty.

"The whole damn world is killing each other and the reporters want to write about you and Norela screwing each other. A man gets a lot of no's and some scary yes's but she's the scariest yes I've ever seen. A lot of folks thought you were over here helping us kill gooks and then they see pictures of you cozying up to that Commie broad. Makes them think you're on the short end of integrity."

Norela Cook had not only criticized and ridiculed the military, some believed she had given aid and comfort to the enemy. "What pictures?"

"Pictures of you sniffing around that bitch in Hue, riding around on a motorbike. I ought to thank you for getting her to say there wasn't an atrocity but don't forget: today's lover is tomorrow's biographer. You want to hear what she wrote? '. . .a sensitive but flawed novelist seeking in Vietnam the recognition that had eluded him in his books and classes . . . holding steadfastly to his belief that America stands for all that is good, true and beautiful but painfully unaware of what is obvious to others— that his marriage is breaking up, his career as a teacher and novelist at an end, lost in the dizzying vortex of Vietnam that destroys true believers.'"

Norela's story wasn't as complimentary as he had believed. "If that's the worst thing she says about me I'm okay."

"You need some new news—a change in skirt lengths, a new fuck film, a new rock group and nobody will remember what you were famous for."

Shivers was right. America's attention span was short. They would forget about him unless Norela accused him of molesting a child.

The call to Jennifer was further delayed because her

telephone number had been changed. That information sent a chill through him. When he got on the line he heard buzzes, hums, clicks, a distant ringing, strains of music, ghost voices. Jennifer sounded sleepy and he did not recognize her voice. "Where are you? Have you moved? Over."

"What?"

"Where are you? Are you in the house? Over."

"This is Jennifer. Where are you?"

He could hear whispering at the other end of the line. There was a faint strain of music. "Your number has been changed."

"I've been getting terrible calls and I don't know where you are."

"They sent my mail home. I haven't been getting your letters. Are you all right? Over."

"They sent me mail from your Vietnamese wife and that woman you went to Hong Kong with. Lin says no man turns it down and I've tried to understand that you are lonely and in danger but a Vietnamese wife?"

He knew who the "Vietnamese wife" was. His threat hadn't worked and some dumbshit had written a letter for the waitress at the Press Center but who was the other woman? "I don't have a Vietnamese wife. I haven't been to Hong Kong. I swear to you." There was a crash of static so he said it again, because maybe she didn't hear it and he needed a response. "You mustn't believe everything you read."

"I don't know what to believe any more. You told me you weren't going to the front again and then you take part in that atrocity."

"It wasn't an atrocity."

"Whatever it was. Lin said that war was. . .change. . . we. . .remember you. . .were."

Sherrill did not like her use of "we," or references to him in the past tense. "What? I can't hear you. Over."

"He said you had to draw attention. . ." A waterfall of static drowned out her voice and when the hissing and crashing stopped she was still talking. ". . .his idea that you devise. . .wrong image and he wasn't taking the blame for that." The son of a bitch wanted to take all the credit and none of the blame.

"You have to believe me."

"The papers say that you're a liar, that if you would lie about Marie's death you would lie about an atrocity."

"There wasn't an atrocity."

"I can forgive you for using me, for. . .whatever you have done over there, but I can't forgive you for making Marie a part of it."

He had lied about Marie's death to save her from Si Hardeman's gossip, to prevent her from becoming an object, a curiosity. "I can explain. It's so simple if we can just sit down together."

"Then come home and explain."

"I can't, not right now, but soon."

"Is it because you want to be the only survivor? Lin says you always try to live out your books."

He didn't act out his books, his books were the actors that lived his story as any writer would know. "That has nothing. . ."

"Is it because you're with that awful woman that you fought over?"

"I didn't fight over her. I'm not with her. Jennifer, can you please—"

"Is this the worst. Every time I think I have hit bottom things get worse. How much more can I take?"

"There could be another ugly story but it's not true. I promise it's not true. I can explain if you will wait until I get home."

"Lin said he didn't know if you could come back. . ." Her voice swelled then crashed. ". . .campus was angry at you and. . . brought it on yourself. . . could take care of yourself wherever you. . .happiest he had seen you was . . .were in trouble."

"I'm tired of hearing what fucking Lin says."

"You've never talked like that before," she said, her voice smooth as though she were in the next room. "I don't even know you any more. I hardly recognize your pictures. You've become a stranger to me. I'm frightened that when you come home living with you will be like adultery. I just want to give up. I just want. . ."

He knew she was crying. "I'm coming home. I promise, as soon as I can I'm coming home. I love you, Jennifer, please wait. Please."

It was over, the connection gone. He was exhausted. Stunned. He tried to think. She still loved him, he believed that. They had had problems before, angry words, intense arguments, even yelling and cursing each other. All it took was a touch and they were laughing at their childishness and loving each other for it. That's all it took, a look, a touch. Once he was back in the world everything would be okay.

Looming over his optimism was one tiny cloud. Jennifer's anger at the exploitation of Marie. Jennifer had always believed the best about him. Even when he wasn't certain of his own motives, she believed he had acted from his noblest, truest impulses. He could explain and she would understand if she believed in him. She wanted to believe. No matter what Norela wrote, Jennifer would never believe he had molested a child.

Sherrill waited until Kelty got off duty. "I have to talk to you," he said.

"You bastard, I never want to see you again." They walked along the road in front of the hospital, yelling at each other when trucks rumbled past in the evening mist. "I have always fallen for jerks because then I wasn't disappointed when it didn't work out. Then I met you and I thought you were different. I opened myself to you. I told you everything, hoping to drive you away, hoping you were man enough to come back. And you betrayed me to that reporter bitch."

"I thought I was defending you."

"You don't have to defend me to anybody." They waved away a jeep that offered a ride. "Why did you leave that note?"

"Because I was leaving. I couldn't tell you I loved you and stay. I would have tried to make love to you."

"Did you make love to that bitch because you didn't love her?"

"I wanted to humiliate her."

"Jesus, you come crawling back to me." She turned to face him. "When I read your note I wrote asking you to meet me in Hong Kong on my R&R. I had a miserable time. I was afraid to leave the hotel, afraid I'd miss you. My last night I picked up some creep and I hate myself for it and it's all your fault."

Jennifer had read the letter. And he had sworn there wasn't anyone, that he hadn't gone to Hong Kong. "They sent my mail home."

"Oh Jesus, did your wife read my letter? I'm sorry. Tell her you didn't meet me."

"I did but I didn't know about your letter. Now she thinks I lied about that too. Did you mention my note?"

"I said what it meant that you loved me. I. . .you're going to find out anyway. . .I mentioned how close we had been. . .physically. . .and what I was going to do to you in Hong Kong. I was trying to turn you on."

"God, Kelty."

"Fuck. This fucking country turns everything to shit."

"Maybe if you wrote her a letter. Told her we didn't have an affair."

"The thing is some reporter asked about it. I didn't deny it. What good would it do? Norela Cook had already said it happened. I thought you wanted to be a guy who whips all the men and screws all the women. I thought you wouldn't mind if I shared a little of your limelight."

"I didn't tell Norela we had an affair. I came here to apologize for getting you involved at all, for bringing you all that attention."

"I was pissed off at first. I've spent years patching up these guys so they can get shot again and no one says 'thank you.' Then I treat your hand and that makes me important, just because I crossed your path. I was mad for a while and then I started getting letters from people I hadn't heard from in years. What you guys don't understand is that nobody believes the shit you write unless it agrees with what they already think. The people who thought I was a slut still think I'm a slut. People like my dad who thought I was a virgin still think I'm a virgin. Nobody else is even going to remember what was said, just that once someone wrote a story about me."

She was pleased, even grateful that he had caused untrue things to be written about her.

"I'll write your wife and try to patch up things back home," she said.

Would Jennifer believe it? After what she had read in the papers? Or would it look like a cover-up and shatter the last of his credibility? "Don't write."

"Jesus, Sherrill, what do you want?"

What did he want? He wanted to be the person he thought he was in a world that was acceptable to him, a world that valued him for his mind, his spirit, not his entertainment quotient. Maybe he was throwing away the chance to be one of those people loved and celebrated for being amusing. He had come to terms with the dark heart that lusted after glory, that reveled in freedom, that hated job-bound rectitude, that was never satisfied.

He wanted—"I want to go home." Back to Jennifer however she had changed. Back to being a man he knew. He didn't know what he would have to endure when he got home. He only knew that he had faced the Viet Cong, he had endured the mountains and paddies. He could face whatever awaited him back in the world. America's attention span was short; they'd forget him. If Norela accused him of indecency with a child he'd be with Jennifer. The only way to save his marriage was to face Jennifer and tell her the truth. He was running out on Stolkalcyk and the others, perhaps indelibly tainting himself as a war criminal but he had to save his marriage. And he had to get home fast to beat Norela's story.

The World

After a sleepless night in a hootch for transients, Sherrill talked a Herky-jerk into a ride to Da Nang aboard his C130 Hercules. He arrived too late to catch a plane to Saigon. He didn't want to see reporters at the Press Center, didn't want Shivers to know that he was running. He stood in the terminal trying to think what to do.

"You Sherrill O'Connell?" someone asked. "Did you say that the war was unwinnable, that the strategy was all wrong?" That was the message he had been trying to deliver but he didn't want it written in headlines; he wanted to explain it. "Norela Cook wrote that whatever happened at the river changed your views on the war. Would you care to comment?"

Norela could not have gotten the story to her newspaper syndicate and copies of it to Vietnam that fast. "Where did you hear that?"

"She wrote it. She must have left a dozen copies at the Press Center on her way to Saigon. It must be all over Vietnam by now."

"I can't comment until I've read what she wrote."

The reporter produced a mimeographed copy of Norela's story.

"Sherrill O'Connell denies an atrocity and I have presumed him innocent until proven otherwise. Whatever happened at the river, atrocity or not, changed his mind about the war. 'The war isn't winnable,' he said. 'The strategy is all wrong. There is too much destruction, too much killing.' Some believe that he is now denouncing the war to escape the consequences of his alleged war crime. Being suspected of such a crime is enough to change one's views on war, particularly if one supports the war for personal rather than patriotic reasons."

Sherrill realized that he had been gutted but had to admire the skill that wielded the knife. She hadn't even misquoted him but in the context the perception of what he had said was wrong. Cleverly she had turned his supporters against him for being a turncoat, while those who hated his hawkish views could now despise his cowardice in changing his opinion to escape his crimes. But Jennifer could deal with it. It wasn't something new, something worse. He continued to read.

"What will our doughty hero do now? There are reports that he has run home to hide behind the wide skirts of his dutiful wife." Jennifer wouldn't like that but it wasn't a fatal wound. "Others think he remains in Vietnam, although he has lost his stomach for combat, because it is easier to satisfy his proclivity for young girls here than in America where such appetites are considered sick if not criminal."

He had hoped that she would hold that story as a threat. The longer she held it the less of a threat it would be because fewer people would be interested in him or would remember who he was. She must have realized that too. He had hoped to be home before the story was published so he could prepare Jennifer for it. Norela had thrown a rock in the cesspool and the ripples had just begun. A lot of reporters would be after that story.

Sherrill handed the copy back to the reporter. "No comment."

"Are you leaving Vietnam?"

"I. . .No comment at this time." To leave now would be interpreted as guilt but he had to go. As quietly as possible and as quickly. He had to get to Jennifer before the hemorrhage was fatal. He had to convince her that no matter how many lies he had told, how many people he had killed, he had not touched that child.

He learned that a Caribou was flying to Chu Lai and he got aboard claiming press priority. It got him closer to Saigon and away from the reporters in Da Nang. At Chu Lai he found Bird. It was the first time he had known Bird to leave the Press Center. "What are you doing here?"

"Woman with the U.S.O. says she screwed Kennedy."

Sherrill had believed that Bird was part of a drug ring, but Bird had been a legitimate journalist who had spent months investigating a governor's criminal activities and was preparing a detailed account when the governor died. Bird's researched article was replaced by an interview with a woman the governor had known for less than a day but with whom he had spent his last six hours. "It opened my head, man. No one wanted to see the figures on how the son of a bitch had cheated them, they wanted to read how it felt to fuck a dying man."

"So now you're covering U.S.O. shows?"

"It blows my mind you and these other guys trying to make a point like there was one. Trying to make every day bigger and brighter, using up all the words, filling people's heads because there is no Wednesday in America. It's all Friday night or Monday morning because we can't stand littleness and sameness has got to pretend it's different. But it don't work here, man. This is the mundane. You can't explain Vietnam. Vietnam is not new and improved. It don't mean apple pie, in God We Trust, or chicken little. Vietnam fucking is, man. It's the epitome, the summation, the apex, the root and being and mother of nothing. Vietnam is god and god is dead."

"What are you going to do when you get back to the world."

"There ain't no world to go back to," Bird said. "I done been. You can't tell the boys from the girls. You can't tell stroke magazines from news magazines, fuck films from art films. You think it's all been there waiting for you but it hasn't. It's all here. It's all the fucking Nam."

At the 89th Aerial Port at Tan Son Nhut, Sherrill grabbed his bag and headed for the civilian terminal, hitching a ride on the back of a three-wheeled Lambretta. At the terminal he found he had almost four hours to wait but he didn't care; he was on his way home. He collapsed on one of the hard wooden benches and tried to think what he would tell Jennifer.

He knew he had changed but not in any elemental, essential way; no more than she had. The picture he had of her was imperfect, random pages, an unintelligible conversation but Jennifer had changed. She no longer needed him as protector, provider, father of her children. How was he to convince her that she needed him at all?

Nervously, he paced the terminal that was filled with those who had just arrived in Vietnam and were headed toward the undreamed unknown of combat and those who had finished their tours and were turned toward the dreamed unknown of home.

"You must know a lot about the war," one soldier said to another.

"I can't remember what it looked like and I was there yesterday."

A soldier who had learned to judge distance by the days it took to chop through a few meters of jungle declined an invitation to visit a friend when they got back to the world. "That's nine hundred miles."

"It's only three hours by air."

"Yeah, but it's still nine hundred miles."

In a corner a young Vietnamese girl squatted holding a goldfish in a bowl. The airlines would not allow her to take the fish aboard the airplane. Someone said she had been there three days.

Sherrill fidgeted, impatient for the iced drink, imitation veal, dyed peas, synthetic ice cream, air-conditioned comfort of his own pleasure dome taking him back to the world.

He picked up a discarded magazine dedicated to famous Americans. A painter had slashed every painting in a show because no one came to the opening. By morning a crowd had gathered to buy the mutilated paintings that critics were hailing as a new art form. An unknown singer had concluded the national anthem by making obscene gestures with both hands. His photograph appeared in newspapers and on television and his only record made the hit list. A woman television reporter was reporting live from location when one of her earrings fell. Smoothly she caught it, reaffixed it, went on as though nothing had happened and for her grace under fire was being given a shot at network anchor.

"I was up to my ass in the swamp. Half the jungle was below the water, half above it so I was swimming and climbing at the same time. Mosquitoes, leeches, snakes, boots came apart in my hands, uniform dissolved, skin rotted. We had to tie ourselves to trees at night so we didn't go out with the tide. My buddy got a ti-ti wound and drowned before I could dig him out of the mud. I got a letter from my wife and she was pissed because I had forgotten her birthday. I wanted to stick her fucking face in the fucking mud. If she mentions her birthday one time I'll blow her ass away."

Sherrill recognized the rage and wondered if the flight home was enough time to dissipate it. He believed the soldier was one of those likely to ask for another tour in Vietnam after a few unsatisfactory weeks at home. He knew that Jennifer and her understanding was all he needed.

His flight was announced and a line formed to have tickets,

credentials, persons checked. His heart beat like he was riding a helicopter into a hot LZ. No matter what awaited him, he was getting out alive. Not only alive but unmarked.

Two young, smiling Vietnamese stopped him. His passport was not in order. He fought down panic, showed them his airplane ticket, his press credentials, his American money. They smiled. They did not look at him but beyond him, smiling at something he could not see. He had to have an exit visa, they said. "Okay, give me one." He held his wallet in his hand.

Exit visas could only be gotten at Immigration on Vo Tanh, an hour away by taxi. "But the airplane will leave." They smiled, looking beyond him. "I've got a ticket, passport. Money." One of them probed an ear with the long nail of his smallest finger. Dread perched at the back of Sherrill's head. "How long will it take to get an exit visa?" he asked, his voice higher and louder than he intended. Three maybe four days.

He demanded to see the general, the ambassador. He was an American citizen, a member of the press. The other passengers were looking at him. Two MPs said he was creating a disturbance. They were polite but stern.

"My little girl is dying," he said, his voice catching in his throat. He turned to the older MP who might have children of his own. "I have to see her before she dies. It's an emergency. I want to talk to the ambassador." He knew he was yelling but he couldn't help it. He hated them all. Only the fear of never getting home kept him from punching the Nazi son of a bitch.

The two MPs led him to a bench where they sat down, one on either side, and the older one explained that he was not getting on the airplane unless the fucking Vietnamese said he could because it was their fucking country. There was nothing the general or the ambassador could do. They held out hope for a flight the next day if he could get to Immigration before it closed. He suspected it was a ruse to get him out of the terminal but it was his only chance.

Desperate beyond their caring, he retrieved his bag, changed his dollars back to piasters, waved money at a driver, agreed to extortion and promised more to encourage him through the snarl of taxis, military vehicles, Hondas, Vespas and bicycles on Cong Ly.

The blaring horns, squealing brakes and drivers, the near collisions, did not help his churning stomach. He flinched, almost jumping out the door when the cab ran over a hubcap that vaguely resembled a mine. The driver smiled—another American who couldn't tell malice from menace.

Traffic stopped. People ran between cars. Then he saw them— demonstrators chanting and waving banners, monks with shaven heads carrying bowls, riot police trying to contain them, television crews in military clothing filming the event, military police in civilian clothes taking pictures of the leaders, television crews and military police menacing each other by taking pictures. Prostitutes dressed as cheerleaders, go-go dancers, ran shrieking around the fringes.

Sherrill paid the driver and got out of the cab. His one chance of getting to Immigration before it closed was to find a cab on the other side of the riot. Clinging to his bag, Sherrill fought his way through the chanting, shouting mob. Someone caught him by the shoulder and thinking he was being arrested, he reached for his press credentials only to encounter the hand of a pickpocket posing as a student demonstrator. The pickpocket jerked his hand away carrying the wallet with him. To lose his papers now was to lose everything.

Sherrill crashed through a saffron wall of monks, sending them reeling, and tackled the pickpocket as cameras and television crews converged. There was a brief struggle, then Sherrill, much the larger, regained his wallet and got to his feet in time to grab a street urchin-protestor-thief who was trying to carry off the bag Sherrill had dropped while rescuing his wallet.

Sherrill tried to escape the cameras while checking to be sure he was not missing any essential papers. All there.

Camera? Okay. His watch was gone. Fuck it. He didn't look back.

A tailor ran alongside trying to measure him for a coat. He was accosted by a man who wanted to sell him a withered hand as a souvenir. A soldier showed him a French-Indochina coin dated 1954. "It ain't worth nothing but I been offered ten. I'm asking fifteen."

Sherrill found a battered Renault taxi, one door tied with rope. The driver skillfully made his way around the fringes of the demonstration, raced down Vo Tanh, but stopped short of a bunker that guarded the narrow street to Immigration. Sherrill ran, walked, staggered, tripping over the heavy bag, the camera swinging around his neck, down the dirty, pedestrian -clogged street. An open sewer ran along one side and children fished for coins and bits of food.

At Immigration he joined a line of long-suffering Vietnamese civilians although the clock told him there was not enough time. The clerks moved in slow motion, typing with one or two fingers, painstakingly applying mucilage from bottles to the backs of stamps, photographs, certificates, carefully placing them in the appointed spot and waving them dry with maddening languor.

Sherrill hated the clerks. He would cheerfully have wasted the building and its employees. He waited, afraid to leave the line, to take his eyes off his bag, his hand from his camera. His shirt stuck to his back and a bead of perspiration ran down his armpit and across his ribs leaving a trail of fire.

The clerks began clearing their desks despite the lines. Some of the young girls who hoped for America lingered, the other Vietnamese stoically left the building and prepared to sleep in the street until the office opened again. Sherrill humbly, courteously explained that his only child was dying and he must have an exit visa. The clerk left to speak to another clerk. They talked, occasionally turning to look at Sherrill who attempted to look humble, friendly and willing to pay for a favor but afraid to offer a bribe. They left, apparently to speak to a higher authority. Sherrill dared to hope. It took him fifteen minutes to realize they had left the building.

Women came to scrub the floors. Frustrated, outraged, he screamed, hoping to attract the attention of some dedicated bureaucrat still in the building. He called for help in the name of MAC-V, the ambassador, the President of the United States. The women ignored him. Two white-helmeted Vietnamese police appeared behind him. They pretended not to understand although he spoke calmly, slowly, demonstrating that he was neither irrational nor dangerous.

The White Mice eyed him with malevolent suspicion. Their hands rested on their pistols. The women giggled behind their hands. Sherrill took a deep breath. The more he struggled to escape the more entangled he became. He had to avoid arrest. He bowed to the police, smiled, picked up his bag and slowly walked out of the building, aware that they were following, fearful they would drop him with a nightstick before he reached the door. Instead they gave him a shove out the door. He did not turn.

He walked back along the narrow street that was less crowded now, seeing every wire, every can and scrap of metal as a boobytrap although they were virtually unknown in Saigon. He was too close to blow it now. The blood pounded in his temples, his shirt was choking him. He had to transfer his bag from hand to hand to protect it from the Honda Cowboys who whipped past in clouds of dust and exhaust.

Once back on Vo Tanh he flagged a cab and was driven to JUSPAO. It was late but the Marine sentry located a thin, energetic captain who listened to Sherrill's desperation and said he would try to speed up the exit visa. He also brought Sherrill's mail.

Fred Stone wanted more stories. A high school in Oklahoma had made him an honorary graduate, churches in Nebraska thanked him for being on the side of God and

America, a plaintive letter asked him not to sell out the loyal boys who were giving their lives. There was a scroll from Americans for God and Freedom and an award he had never heard of for courageous reporting.

A college had removed his books from their library, students from another school had burned his books at a peace rally, critics had denounced his writing. His first book, "self-serving praise of a white man's courage that was commonplace among Native Americans," was sexist and racist because there were no women in the book and Native Americans were portrayed as hunters and trappers, denying centuries of Native American culture. The critics found his book about a cowboy killing his wife to save her from Indians to be sexist, racist, "a barbarous allegory for the destruction of Vietnam to save it from Communism." Critics who had ignored his books when they were published, now viewed them in the light of who they believed him to be.

There was a petition to the trustees of his college requesting that his tenure be revoked signed by a dozen professors and a hundred or so students. A letter began, "Your name has been in the news lately. Isn't it time you had a press agent to help shape your image?"

His mother had talked to Jennifer and Jennifer was worried because people at his school were angry with him. He could see his mother's fear that there might be something wrong with her creation. When he told her he was going to Vietnam she had smiled in embarrassment as though it were a tasteless joke—like putting on one of her hats. He had a good job, a good wife, what did he want? Writing was somewhere between shooting deer and growing orchids.

The weather had been beautiful, she wrote. It made her want to can and clean the attic. He smiled at those homey yearnings. She hadn't canned in years and had never had an attic. Something about the weather had started her thinking about him. She didn't realize she was crying until Mrs. Harkins came in. "Is your boy all right?" she had asked. "Is he killed?" "I didn't know what to say," she wrote. "I knew something was wrong."

He tried to picture his mother, to believe he had once lived inside that body, that her face had been his most treasured sight, that his well-being had been her greatest need. He wondered what kind of love a mother could have for a forty-year-old son who no longer depended on her. What a strange thing parenthood was. He was certain that he would have needed Marie all her life. Even now he needed the memory of her love. He was going to spend some time with his mother when he got home. How long had it been since they had really talked? He had talked more to the janitor who cleaned his office than he did to his mother.

Lindly admitted that in the past he had been frivolous, without aim or ambition, but now he had found the person who would give him stability. "Don't laugh but I want to be a father." After leaving three children. "She too wants a child, a little boy who looks like me."

Sherrill felt strangled by his knotted entrails. Jennifer had once told him that. She wanted to bear him a son, "a little boy who looks just like you." If Lindly was talking about Jennifer he would kill him. A grenade. As a boobytrap so he would know he had done it to himself. Work the pin loose but not out. Wire it to the armrest inside Lindly's car. Approach Lindly on the faculty parking lot. Lindly would know why he was there, run to his car, jump in, slam the door, the grenade would fall in his lap. Booby. And he would be there to see—

"I said, are you all right?" It was the captain. He seemed to have grown a moustache since Sherrill last saw him. "I talked to MAC-V. They say an exit visa costs seven dollars and fifty cents and takes three to five days. If everything is in order." As he said "order" the captain suppressed a smile and tried to slip his malevolence behind a mask of good cheer. "Is there anything else I can help you with?"

"You haven't helped me with anything yet," Sherrill said to let the captain know he knew what was going on.

At the door the Marine sentry said, "Watch your step." It sounded like a threat.

Outside, the monks and police had gone and the riot had been replaced by the chaos of traffic, beggars, peddlers, armless and legless veterans, prostitutes costumed as Vietnamese virgins, American debutantes; Army clerks costumed as jungle fighters, high school students, hippie tourists.

Sherrill got a room at the Caravelle and discovered they were holding a letter for him. It was from Jennifer. "Since you left I have discovered that I am in love with a wonderful man. We share a beautiful, special relationship from which I derive much consolation and joy. I will feel this way forever. You never knew him because you were never interested in him. All you cared about were characters you invented. You never knew the finest man I've ever know, the one I fell in love with."

He was sick with anger until he read the last line. "The one I will always love. The real Sherrill O'Connell. No matter what happens I will always love, admire and respect that man." Jennifer, who knew him better than anybody, admired him. Why had he never known that?

She realized now that their separation could be therapeutic if they both chose to make it so. After he came home, when things were normal again, they would talk things out. She would wait until then and she would be better about writing. "Be better" sounded exactly like her. "I try to understand what you are going through. I need to talk to you, to be with you. I've been so worried. Is it enough to know that someone cares?"

He had been thinking crazy, but everything was going to be all right. He would be home in three or four days, six or seven at the most. Together they could work out anything; solve any problem. It was obviously an early letter but it convinced him that she loved him. He could convince her he was the person she had admired, the person she had believed him to be.

Find the girl. The answer leapt to his mind. Find the child and get a sworn statement that he did not touch her; that he tried to help her and her family. Take her to the embassy, maybe JUSPAO. Call a press conference and let them question her.

He walked outside and headed down Tu Do towards the river. He wondered if he would recognize her. For all his nightmares about her, he could not remember what she looked like. An old woman tugged at his sleeve. She had a pot of pho balanced on one end of her stick, a charcoal brazier on the other. He bought a bowl of the soup to calm his roiling stomach. It would make him sick but in a couple of days he'd be home; he could take a pill.

The soup was hot and good and he felt his stomach devouring something besides itself. Suddenly he saw her. She was dressed in a pinafore and was carrying a huge red purse. He ran after her. "Wait," he called. He didn't even know her name. "Wait."

She turned and smiled at him. "You buy me one drink," she said. She touched a lollipop to his cheek and removed the stickiness with her tongue.

The teeth were too big, the smile too wide. He moved away from her.

"You cheap charlie," she said. "You buy me one drink."

"Hey, sweetheart, you boom boom?" asked a civilian worker who grabbed her by one hip. He was Sherrill's age, but heavier, in expensive slacks and a Hawaiian shirt.

"Leave her alone," Sherrill said, grabbing the man by the shirt and pushing him into the street.

"What the fuck? She doesn't belong to you," the worker said. "What do you say, baby? A little rock and roll?"

Sherrill walked across the street and pushed his way through the crowd of girls, peering into their faces. There were so many of them and they all looked like children. He would never find the girl. Harry. Harry could tell him where the girl was. He went into a bar, ordered a drink and made his way through the crowded room looking for Harry.

He stood in the rain, floating on the bedlam of auto horns, sirens, whistles, shrieks, cries along Tu Do, trying to decide which way to go. He had been in all the bars down that way. He pushed his way into another, sat on a stool and peered at the faces that floated before him, their hands like butterflies.

He caught a hand that caressed his thigh and tried to find the face that went with it. He could feel his mind slipping. "Didi," he said. He drank for nourishment, trying to fill the hollowness inside him, fighting the void that threatened to swallow him.

He stared at his glass. Hands, his hands, tightly gripped it. He was sitting on a stool and his shoulders ached as though he had been sitting there for a long time. Slowly he raised his head, wondering where he was. He saw an arm beside him with a rolled-up sleeve revealing a tattoo. Death Before Dishonor. "I thought you were dead," he said.

"Damn straight, but how you gonna show?"

"But you're alive."

"Would you believe forty percent alive? Would you believe sixty percent alive and forty percent inactive? Would you believe—"

"What happened to Whitey?"

"Whitey who?"

"The guy with no eyebrows."

"Oh, he died. Lack of stimulation."

"What about Love Child? He had Love Child on his helmet cover and he tried to adopt everyone as a cause."

"Committed himself to death."

The son-of-a-bitch was making fun of him. "What about Kersnowski?"

"He went back to the world."

"He went back in a body bag, asshole. He was fucking dead."

"The world is a fucking body bag. Do you call this living?"

Sherrill studied the man. "Have you ever been on the Song Cha Nang?"

"What the hell is the Song Cha Nang?"

"God damn pogue. You've never been out of Saigon."

"Hell, I've never been out of Tucson."

Tucson? Sherrill looked around him. American soldiers. American music on the juke box. The bartender was small for an Indian but God damn Indians looked like God damn orientals. At a table was a God damn Indian woman in braided hair and a squaw dress. He was back in the world. All he had to do was sober up enough to get back on the airplane. One more stop. He felt something warm and wet in his ear. A girl in a yellow ao dai and black pajamas was licking his ear. "You numbah one lovah," she said.

Sherrill pushed her away and turned to face Death Before Dishonor. "That's not funny, you stupid son-of-a-bitch. I am trying to find someone."

"Why are you looking in here?"

"Because. . .because she's a child. . .a. . .a prostitute."

"Hey, I know her."

"She was a virgin."

"There it is."

If the guy was toying with him again Sherrill was going to break his fucking face. "She lived with her family."

"In a hovel, man. A garbage dump."

"Near the river."

"There it is, that's the one. Place smelled like shit."

"She was. . .I didn't touch her. . .I tried to help her. If I can find her-"

"I know her, man. I can take you right to her."

Sherrill slid off his stool, not daring to believe. It probably wasn't the same child. He followed Death Before Dishonor into the night.

A light mist shrouded the city. Sherrill stood at the corner of a building looking first one way then the other. He wondered where the hell he was. He grabbed for his identification. All there. Money? Gone. Watch? Gone. No, he had lost that earlier. Camera? Maybe he had left it at the hotel with his bag. Airplane ticket? He looked around him in case he had dropped it.

There was blood on the pavement. While he was studying it another drop appeared. And another. He swayed slightly and straightened himself. Mustn't look drunk. The Honda Cowboys would get him for sure. He wiped at his chin and saw blood on his hand. He had been wounded. He pressed himself against the building looking for snipers. He raised a hand to examine his face. His face hurt but the only wound seemed to be in his lip. That lying son-of-a-bitch had mugged him and left him God knew where.

Damn it was quiet. No traffic, no people, no helicopters overhead. He heard the sounds of running footsteps. Jesus, the VC were in the city. Carefully he looked around the building. The street was empty. In the distance a streetlight glowed dimly in the mist.

He did not want to cross the empty street. Taking a deep breath he slipped around the corner of the building and flattened himself on the other side. He could see nothing but he could hear a rustling like the patter of bare feet on the sidewalk. He ran across the street and tried to hide in a doorway while catching his breath. Down the street a jeep drifted across an intersection, its wheels whispering on the wet pavement. Curfew. He was out after curfew. He should have called after the jeep. After a reprimand they would have taken him to the hotel.

How late was it? He looked at his watch but his watch was gone. Water dripped from the doorway onto his head. He decided to walk to the next intersection and look for something familiar. The idea of retracing his steps was repugnant and taking another street was fearful. He might be lost but as long as he stayed on this street he was not confused.

At the next corner was not a neat intersection but a maze of streets running in all directions. To proceed was not only to be lost but to be confused. He searched his pockets for a cigarette. The bastard had stolen his cigarettes. In one pants pocket he found a key, not the hotel key but another key. He held the key to the light to see it better. A car key. Where the hell did he get a car key? He turned it over and looked at the other side. Still a car key. Jesus, he was wearing someone else's pants.

He looked down at his trousers. They looked like his but were looser than they should have been. Staggering a bit, he took them off and held them against the sky. Damn things looked like his. He put them on and sat down on the wet grass to wait for daylight.

Grass. His mind wobbled for a moment. He put down a hand. It was grass all right. Where the fuck was he? He looked around. Something loomed behind and above him. A statue. Beneath the statue was a man sitting on the grass just as he was. In the misty darkness Sherrill could not see him clearly but between his knees was a bottle. Sherrill did not want to admit that he was lost. "What the fuck kind of statue is that?"

"The statue of a hero. You can tell the statue of a hero by its grandeur."

Sherrill nodded. It was one of those things no one had taught him but he had learned anyway. The man offered him a drink. "What is it?" he asked gratefully.

"Black Jack."

"Whooee," Sherrill said in appreciation. He saluted with the bottle and took a drink. "What is grand about it?" he asked, sounding like a child to himself.

"The posture. The posture of the statue of a hero is always

steadfast. The face of the statue of a hero never changes."

By God, the statue was steadfast.

"The eyes of a statue of a hero are always open."

It was true. "He must get a lot of dust and shit in them."

"Yes, but he doesn't close his eyes to avoid the pain. That's why he is a hero. Blinking at life is cowardice."

That was something he had always known but never realized.

"The statue of a hero always looks straight out the front of his eyes. Looking at life from the corners is weakness. Notice how the brow is furrowed with the sorrow of thought, the mouth straight with reason and humor, the chin. . ."

Jesus, the guy sounded like a college professor; he was never going to drop the subject. All he wanted to know was where the fuck were they? "Do you know where we are?"

"This my friend is the world, the fucking rice paddy of life." He took a drink and handed the bottle to Sherrill.

"My little girl is dying. She's dead and she's dying."

"I know, man. We're tight."

"My wife loves me and doesn't know me. I love her and I don't know who she is. I'm afraid I'll never see her again."

"These fucking rice paddies blow your mind."

Sherrill had never been so tight with anyone before, so close to understanding. "I'm going to write a book," he said. "And in it are going to be all the rice paddies of the world."

"Fame. Fortune. Success."

The bastard had already read it.

"Love. Faith. Hope."

"You. Me. Jennifer."

"Truth."

"Fiction."

"Fact."

"Vietnam."

"Swamp. Mountain. Rice paddies."

"But the greatest of these is rice paddies."

When Sherrill awoke it was first light, the rain had stopped and he was alone, the empty bottle beside him. When he saw the Vietnamese moving about he knew the curfew was over. He went to the hotel and had to face the disapproving clerk to get a key.

In his room, Sherrill took off his clothes and checked his pockets, then his bag, looking for his airline ticket. It was in his bag with his camera and traveler's checks. In the bathroom he examined a scrape on his forehead, a bruise on his jaw, a cut on his lip. His hands felt worse than they looked; he had landed some punches himself.

He gently bathed his face and tried to think. No one would believe he didn't molest that child. Not the way he was seen now. Even if he found the girl and she swore he helped her not everyone would believe. Some would always see him as a killer of women, an abuser of children. He could accept that if Jennifer believed in him. He had to be at Immigration when it opened.

He cashed a traveler's check at the desk, bought cigarettes and caught a taxi to Immigration. A line had already formed, made of those who had spent the night in the street but the line moved quickly with none of the surliness of the day before. Within two hours he was before a clerk. He filled out the forms, paid the fee and patiently explained that he had to leave immediately, an emergency. The Vietnamese clerk looked at him with disdain and stamped the visa in his passport.

He left the building quickly, half expecting to be called back and told there was a mistake. He almost ran back to Vo Tanh to catch a taxi. He was going home today.

He took a taxi back to the hotel to get his bag. He would go to Tan Son Nhut and stay until he got on a flight. As he started into the hotel someone called his name. He cringed fearing he had been caught running away.

"I want to return the money I owe you," Blair Scorbic said.

"You saved my life. If there is anything. . .Jesus, what happened to you?"

"Mugged."

"Did they get anything?" Sherrill shrugged. "Let me buy you a cup of coffee. Breakfast. Really, I want to help."

"Help me find Harry Tompkins."

"He's in Laos. That's the word. Drug lord."

"I didn't touch that child."

"I know."

Someone believed him; Sherrill feared he was going to cry. He followed Blair to a quiet Vietnamese restaurant and ordered a bowl of noodle soup. While he ate Blair talked about his stories and the papers that printed them. Good, decent Blair doing the best he could with honest reporting and good writing. No one loved him, no one hated him; he got no respect, no attention. Sherrill envied him.

"You stepped in the shit, Sherrill. The peace freaks are after you for sucking up to Marine killers and the war freaks are after you for sucking up to Hanoi-loving Norela Cook."

"I've got to get out of the country. I was getting my bag."

"You can't do it, Sherrill. It will look like running away."

"I have to save my marriage. You don't know—" He remembered Blair's wife left him and took the children. "Harry's gone and if I can't find the girl there's no way to prove my innocence. And even if I did. . ."

"You're the only proof. I heard those stories. I didn't believe them."

"You know me but most people only know what they've read about me."

"You have to trust the reporters." Sherrill looked at him as though he were insane. "Unless you have your own newspaper or television station you are going to have to stick it out and trust the reporters to be fair and correct the error. It won't be this year."

"It won't be in my lifetime."

"I'll write a story about you, twenty newspapers if they all take it. It's a beginning and it could be picked up by a wire service; they've picked up my stories before. I'll say you believe these people are worth saving but that the way we are doing it is destroying them and their country."

"We believe in bombs and dollars. We don't believe our soldiers can go head to head with Charlie and win these people."

"And you think they can."

"If they can't we've lost more than this war. If our ideas aren't better than their ideas, our form of government, our values. . .If our security is in bombs and dollars we've lost."

"That's good, Sherrill. I'll do my best with it."

"What will it do to you?"

"I'll lose some readers, maybe some papers. If they won't print the story then I'll include parts of it in other stories until I get it told."

Sherrill sagged in his chair. "People don't care about Vietnam. They don't care about ideas. About values. If I didn't molest that girl nobody cares what happens to her. If I did molest her she can be on the front page of every newspaper. Everyone in America will want to know what she thinks of Dix Devereaux and does she like rock music." He felt sick at his stomach. "I'm going home."

"If you do, everything you have done here will come to nothing."

"I haven't done anything here, nothing I'm not ashamed of."

"You saved some people at an LZ. You wrote about a side of the war a lot of people didn't know."

He wished he had done something good, could save something; he couldn't even save himself. "I wrote garbage. I did things I didn't believe I was capable of."

"War is extreme. We've all done things we didn't believe we were capable of—both good and bad things."

He couldn't think of anything good. "You risked your life," Blair said. "You tried. You cared. How will you feel about yourself if you go home?"

He knew the answer to that. One reason for his haste was to get out of the country before he had to face his cowardice, to admit he was running out on the others. He was desperate to get out before anyone knew he was running away.

"Face them. Tell them they're wrong. Show them. Every day. It takes a long time to straighten out something like this."

Sherrill thought of Jennifer. "I don't have that long."

He went to the service center across the street from JUSPAO and waited with servicemen to make a call home. He had wanted to be with Jennifer, to hold her, look in her eyes and make her believe him. He had to do it long distance. "I thought I was coming home today," he said when she was on the line. "You'll never know how much I hoped it, how much it hurts to say I can't, for reasons I'll explain later. I promise I will be there as soon as I can and I will never leave you again."

"Lin says that the students and some of the faculty will try to have you fired for moral turpitude if you come back."

"There was no atrocity."

"I think it's about that little girl."

"I know you are disturbed by some of the things you have read about me. I am not the person you have been reading about."

"All I could think about was your return and then they sent your mail home because you were no longer there. I didn't know where you were or how to reach you. I realized you could be dead or you could be living across town as a whole different person, someone I didn't even know."

"I may not be the person you remember but I am a person who loves you very much." He sounded cold, even to himself.

"I opened your mail to find where you might be and there was a letter from a woman who was meeting you in Hong Kong and a Vietnamese woman who was carrying your baby. After you told me you didn't want any more children—"

"There isn't any Vietnamese woman with a baby."

"Until then I had refused to read any of the awful things written about you. I didn't want to think of you fighting and killing."

"It's lies, Jennifer. A lot of it."

"I think I have always known about that wild, dark side of you but refused to admit it. I thought I could forgive you anything, then reporters called and asked if you had unnatural feelings for Marie, if I thought you had ever molested. . ."

"God, Jennifer, I'm sorry. It never happened. There wasn't any girl. Harry Tompkins owed me some money and—I'll explain it when I get home."

"And the Vietnamese woman with your child?"

"No. I can explain it. It's a scam."

"And the woman in Hong Kong?"

"I never left this country."

"I have her letters," Jennifer screamed. "I know what you told her. And that awful woman reporter?"

He didn't know where to begin. "I will explain it to you. I swear I will tell you exactly what happened."

"Tell me now."

"Norela Cook is trying to hurt me."

"And you didn't go to Hue together?"

"We rode the train together."

"You weren't lovers?"

"I do not and have never loved Norela Cook or anyone else but you. I have to admit something did happen but it wasn't love."

"What was it?"

"It was. . .I used her."

"So she would write a favorable story?"

"No."

"So she would say there was no atrocity?"

Those were questions some reporter had asked her. "No."

"But you said she wanted to hurt you."

"If I could just see you. I can explain all this."

"Explain it now."

"Norela is a very possessive person. She's had a mastectomy—"

"Sherrill."

It was hopeless but he had to try. "She's trying to hurt me because I didn't love her. She has to uphold her image as—"

"I don't believe you. When I heard that you made love to children I thought I must be going crazy. Then I remembered little things I hadn't noticed before, that I hadn't wanted to notice. The way you held Marie."

"Jennifer. Please. I want to be the person I used to be in your eyes."

"The way you took her on walks, fishing. I had refused to see it until you forced me. Now I know that I can never live with you again. And if you ever touched Marie, I will never forgive you as long as I live."

"Jennifer, I am your husband. We shared the same bed, the same child, the same death."

"You always wanted to be different. I guess I've always known that, I didn't know it cost you so much. Maybe you can't be like everyone else but I wish you could be the person you used to be. I don't even know how to remember you any more."

"Jennifer. . ." The connection was broken.

He was so stunned he had to be led away so someone else could use the telephone. He had his airline ticket, his exit visa. Perhaps he could get out today. With good connections he could be home tomorrow. If he went to the house she would have to see him, have to let him in. And the house would be surrounded by reporters. And if she didn't let him in? Didn't let him stay? What would he tell them then? Domestic spat? How would she explain turning him away?

He would forever be stamped with an image imposed by others. He shuddered. He had rather go home a war criminal than a child molester. He needed someone to talk to, but who? He wanted to see his father. More than anyone he wanted to see his father. The father who had little to say but who was there when needed. "Dad." His tongue pronounced the word without his bidding. "Dad, help me."

Once when driving the tractor was still more adventure than chore, he had let a rear wheel slip into a ditch. The tractor teetered, almost overturning. He had stopped the tractor, then frozen, his foot on the clutch, hands gripping the steering wheel for balance rather than control.

Out of nowhere his father appeared. He was aware of the danger, both to the tractor and to Sherrill, but he calmly shouted at Sherrill to cut the power. Fearfully, Sherrill released one hand from the wheel and cut the power. The cessation of noise helped. He felt calmer. His father told him to take the tractor out of gear and slowly dismount on the high side. He did although he could feel the tractor slide a little. His father mounted the tractor. At first his father made the situation worse—the uphill tire had little traction—and almost toppled the tractor. His father kept jockeying until he got traction, then straightened the tractor, got off and waved Sherrill back into the seat. They never talked about it and as far as Sherrill knew, his father never told his mother.

He had forgotten that in the growing sense of his own capability. He had been over his head on the tractor and he was over his head now. He had to do what his father told him to do then: break it down into its parts and take care of them one at a time, and at first the situation might get worse. Something else his father had not told him but had shown him: take the wheel. His father did not run from anything: not danger, hardship, criticism or the disapproval of his wife.

He missed his father, something he could not admit those lonely years he had lived with his mother on the farm. He missed his strength, his courage and endurance. He loved his father and he hadn't properly said goodbye. He had watched his mother cling to his father's body and express her love whether he could hear her or not. Sherrill had hung back, believing that last moment was for the two of them and that he was an intruder. He wished he had thrown himself on the bed with them. He wished he had thrown aside the tubes and machines and held Marie as long as she held life, whether she knew he was there or not. He hadn't properly said goodbye to anyone. Not to his father. Not to Marie. Not to Jen—He hadn't said goodbye to Jennifer. He would be home soon. The Jennifer who had become independent, who had a job and her own life could accept him as the flawed, groping, fool-hearted human he was.

He went to JUSPAO knowing reporters would be there. He had to face them, answer their questions, show himself for what he was. Then he could go home, face whatever he had to face there and win Jennifer back.

He told the reporters he would be back before the Five O'clock Follies and would answer their questions then. He wanted to face all of them at one time to avoid sniping. He went to the Brink for lunch, told his questioners he would be at JUSPAO before the Follies, and ate a light meal. He returned to the Caravelle to shower, shave around his bruises, and put on fresh clothes for the confrontation. He knew he had to be at his best.

He arrived at JUSPAO in time to permit thirty minutes of questions before the Follies; he didn't want it to go on too long. The reporters were waiting and they too had made preparations. As he expected, the first questions concerned pedophilia. "Did you have sexual contact with a minor the age of your dead daughter?"

"No."

Some of the reporters were more concerned with whether the girl was a virgin than whether she was a child as they tried to use her as a metaphor for the rape of Vietnam. He denied any sexual encounter with any female in Saigon. He suggested that if Norela had information she should reveal the information and the source of it, confident that she could not produce Harry Tompkins.

A psychologist had been quoted as saying that Sherrill's denial of his daughter's death was an attempt to escape guilt for his sexual attraction for young girls. "I never denied my daughter's death, but grief is private and I did not wish to share it with Si Hardeman. I take responsibility for the consequent misunderstanding."

The personal records taken from the college revealed that he was under psychiatric care and that the administration had asked him to take a leave of absence. "That is not true."

"You deny that you have ever been under psychiatric care?"

"Categorically."

A reporter passed him a photograph and asked if the girl in the photograph was the alleged child. Although curious to see what kind of girl they had come up with, he refused to take the photograph, recognizing the trick. He did not want to be photographed looking at her picture or to be described as "studying" it. "There was no girl," he repeated.

"What does the other guy look like?"

"Worse. All three of them." It was his image, what did it hurt?

"Vietnamese?"

"Pacifists." They laughed and the session loosened up.

A reporter asked him to comment on a story that he and Norela Cook had a torrid affair until she broke it off because of his pedophilia. "I consider Norela a friend," he said. "Nothing more." A reporter asked if a friend would make false charges. "I have made no charges of any kind against Norela Cook. Perhaps she considers me less than a friend."

How did he account for such stories? He refused to assume the responsibility for explaining such accusations. Could those who disagreed with his political opinions be trying to damage his credibility and reputation? "Perhaps," he said, trying not to appear eager to swallow the bait. No, he could not name any such persons.

There were reports that he had taunted the students in Hue, that he had desecrated altars, taken a motorbike which he refused to return until students allowed a military convoy to pass and that he had roughed up student leaders. He replied that the reports were false, that he and Norela had been walking down the street when two Honda Cowboys tried to grab their cameras and lost their motorbike. Sherrill decided not to identify the student leader as one of the thieves. To do so would incite more student hysteria in Vietnam and America and his only witness was Norela. He didn't trust her and, he believed, in a swearing match between himself and the student-thief, the media would believe the student.

Instead, he said he and Norela used the bike to pursue the thieves and came upon the roadblock. He had moved an altar in order to continue the pursuit and the convoy had passed through. The students had agreed to return the bike to the rightful owner. There were no threats and no violence. Sherrill didn't know the story on film but he believed his version was similar enough not to damage his credibility.

Did he write that Tombstone was too tough to die after the camp had fallen? He pointed out that Tombstone had not fallen but had been abandoned, but no one took note of the correction. He was a little shaken by that but stated that his story was written when Tombstone was being rebuilt. He had believed the Army intended to maintain a presence; he was mistaken. That wasn't exactly true but Sherrill believed that neither he nor anyone else would be able to trace exactly what had happened to his two versions of that story.

Would he comment on Rod Reaves's story that Sherrill claimed a death-defying trip to Tombstone although he was there on a day that was so quiet Red Cross workers passed out doughnuts to the defenders. "We were there on the same day but at different times. Any trip into Tombstone was death-defying whether you were shot at or not."

"There are rumors that you came back to Saigon to see your young sweetheart." No. Why had he come to Saigon? He had walked into that one. He wanted to see friends; he mentioned Blair by name. He also wanted to check on a couple of stories; they were, of course, confidential.

Did he get an exit visa? Were they guessing or did they know? He couldn't afford to take a chance. Yes. Was he leaving Vietnam? "I never intended to stay here forever." There was polite laughter. Did he have airline reservations? No; thank God for that. Was he losing faith in the American effort? He was tired; he wanted to see his family. Was he leaving soon? Soon, but not now. He had almost been lulled into overconfidence, but he had handled it well.

"Did you say that everyone should go home?"

"No."

"Did you say that the war was a mistake, that it was unwinnable?"

"There are no good wars just as there are no good diseases, no good crimes, no good natural disasters. War is a disaster, a disease, a crime, but this one no more than any other. Our intentions are good. We're trying to save these people. But are we saving them or are we tearing up the country, making enemies at home as well as here?"

"You're saying instead of continuing to kill and bomb villages here we should enlarge the war into Laos, Cambodia and North Vietnam?"

"I believe the freedom of South Vietnam can be preserved without enlarging the war into Laos, Cambodia or North Vietnam."

"Perhaps you should share your plan with General Westmoreland." There was general laughter and he could tell he was losing them.

"There has to be a better strategy than attacking the same areas over and over with the resulting loss of lives and property."

"You don't know of a way, you're just saying there should be a way."

He remembered Shivers's appeal for him to do a story about. . .what did he call it? The Marines who were like armed Peace Corps? "There is a program that has been highly successful where Marines live in small villages and grow gardens and—"

"Aw, fuck" he heard them say. "What bullshit." They looked at their watches, signaling that the conference was over. Some left the room.

"Have you seen this program?" someone asked.

"No."

"Then you're just parroting some general." A few more drifted out.

It wasn't even a general, it was a gunnery sergeant. "Come to Da Nang and I'll show you." He hadn't intended that but they were listening. "I'm doing a story about the program and I'm inviting you along."

Some said there were stories in Saigon. Some asked why reporters in Da Nang hadn't written the story if it were so successful. The conference was breaking up. One man asked if this was an indication that he had not lost his appetite for combat as had been reported. Sherrill replied that he had never considered himself a combatant, that he had carried a rifle for self-defense when with small units, and that there was more to reporting a war than writing about death and destruction.

The reporters exchanged knowing looks and the meeting ended with him explaining to two reporters that the program didn't offer headlines or dramatic photographs. After they too left for the Follies, he sat down and tried to assess the damage.

There had not been a single question on the atrocity; no one cared any more. Some of them, perhaps most, realized there was a single unverified story about the child. They would soon realize how overblown it was and that story would die as quickly as the atrocity.

He had defused leaving the country. They were not as interested as he had hoped in his ideas about strategy and none were interested in the program Shivers had touted. That was a plus. They were losing interest in him; his image was slipping. In a few years he would be asked to do commercials: "You don't remember me but once I was famous for killing women and abusing children."

They had forced him back to his walking tall and kicking ass stance and he had committed himself to going into the field again but it wasn't like going into the bush. It wasn't like the misery and danger of an operation and once it was over he was free to go. Overall, he had acquitted himself well. Why had he been so fearful? His silence had created suspicion and allowed the stories to assume the proportions of truth. He believed he had put most of that to rest and he was doing Shivers a favor. He went to a clerk and put through a call to the gunny.

Luckily, Shivers was still at the Public Affairs Office in Da Nang although it was after hours. "What the hell are you doing in Saigon," Shivers responded. "Running out on us?"

"I had to straighten out some stuff here but I'll be back in Da Nang tomorrow. I want to do a story on those guys who live in the villes."

"CAP units?"

"Right. I told some reporters here that it really worked but they didn't seem interested."

"I can have you out there tomorrow night."

"It does work, doesn't it? Tell me it's working."

"War is not efficient. People are sleeping in their homes. They're working their fields. They're eating."

"Tell me about the children."

"They get their shots, they get their vitamins. They play

with the Marines, they play with each other. They go to school."

He went back to his room and wrote Jennifer. "I intend to beat this letter home," he wrote. He also intended his written words to reinforce his spoken ones, double proof that he was telling the truth. Even if she refused to see him, he believed she would read his letter.

"How many times I almost wished I had never come, but no matter how desperately I wanted to be home, I always felt this was where I needed to be. You would be amazed at how many people, even people here, care nothing about the Vietnamese or what happens to them. There is one more thing I must do before I can leave. I think there may be a way to save these people without destroying them."

He told her how he had been tricked into involvement with Harry's girl and her family, how he had needed Kelty and had left to avoid involvement with her, how he had gotten involved with Norela, sparing himself nothing. "I never intended to hurt anyone, not even Norela. I wanted to make her aware of me, of the reality of me, not someone she invented or read about. I am ashamed of that. Sometimes I think that, except for Marie, you are the only person who has seen me.

"I don't know what I've done to make you think that I would or could intentionally harm Marie in any way. The world has warped us beyond repair if we see one another as projected images rather than the flesh and blood we know, if we allow others to show us ogres and monsters rather than imperfect fellow creatures struggling to free ourselves of the mud from which we came.

"I love you, Jennifer. Please believe in me."

Gunny Shivers met him at the airport. "Your favorite Commie is at the Press Center," he warned.

"Norela?"

"For a reporter you don't know much about women reporters. I wouldn't screw a no-tit bitch, but if I was to screw a no-tit bitch it wouldn't be a no-tit bitch reporter. But if I was to screw a no-tit bitch reporter, it wouldn't be a Commie no-tit bitch reporter. But if I was to screw a Commie no-tit—"

"Say no more."

"It looks like the lieutenant is okay. They're going to return him to the ranks and let him stay in. I guess I should thank you for that."

At the Press Center he took a bunk in the hootch he had stayed in before. He didn't know any of the other reporters so he walked across the drive and knocked on the door of the network hootch. Rick Belk opened the door, letting some of the air-conditioned chill escape. "Hey, Sherrill, heard you had a press conference in Saigon. I want to get a statement from you."

Rick positioned him while the Japanese cameraman began setting up the lights and camera. "On camera call me Richard. I like Rick, but the network thinks it's too informal and it's hurting my chances for the top."

"I guess you read Norela's story," Sherrill said.

"That was a smart move, she draws a lot of attention. But I'm the one who made you, don't forget that. Look at you, wearing off-the-shelf fatigues, your hair cut by some soldier. Dammit, Sherrill, you expect everything to be handed to you. At least wear dark glasses, something like Reaves's skull plate." He looked around the hootch for an emblem.

"Lot of new faces around," Sherrill said. "Where's Bird?"

"Went to Chu Lai for a big story and the helicopter was hit on the way back. He and a couple of other guys died. I got some great footage of the burned chopper and an interview with a survivor and the first American on the scene. Great irony: antiwar reporter dying with two soldiers. VC sympathizer killed by the men he wanted to embrace. I played it straight—a journalist dying in the never-ending search for truth."

"Bird was doing a story on some USO trooper who claimed she slept with Kennedy."

"Damn, I wish I had known that, I could have interviewed her. Why do I miss all the big stories? I didn't even get to ask Bird how he wanted to be remembered." He draped a bandoleer of ammo over Sherrill's shoulder. "I'll ask you about being remembered and about the child thing."

How did he want to be remembered? As a man who had the best intentions and hurt a lot of people he didn't want to hurt. "I'd like to be remembered not for what I accomplished but what I attempted."

"Try to say something snappy."

"I want to say something about the way the war is being fought and how no one has defined what victory would be."

"Nobody cares what you think about strategy. Nobody watches talking heads. If I get some good footage of you playing Marine and killing gooks I might can use some of this. If it's a walk in the rain the network won't use it no matter how brilliant or quotable you are or how brave you look." Rick smoothed down Sherrill's hair, adjusted his clothes, redraped the bandoleer of ammo. "Ready?" he asked the cameraman. "Okay, tell us about the girl in Saigon."

"Rick, there was no child in Saigon or any other—"

"Cut. Let's try it again. It's Richard, remember. Richard."

When he went to lunch he saw Norela sitting in a booth. She didn't see him so he watched for a moment deciding what to do. He sat across the table from her. "I didn't expect to see you here," he said.

"Hi, Sherrill. How's the little wife?"

"Fine. I expect to see her in a few days. This is my last story."

"So you haven't lost your taste for battle after all."

"I'll be with pacification teams. They build schools, repair bridges—"

"I know what they do, Sherrill. A dead gook is a pacified

gook."

"Why are you here?"

She studied him, deciding whether to trust him. "A journalist interviewed a dancer who was JFK's mistress. There is a story that she told him about a plot and the CIA shot his helicopter down."

"That's preposterous."

"You still don't know much about news do you?"

"I saw your story about me and some child."

"Disappointing wasn't it? No riots, no lynch mobs, no headlines."

"You tried to hurt me."

"And to help you. I said you were a pedophile but I also wrote that you weren't a war criminal. Let's call it even."

"Even? One was true and one was a lie."

"I don't write the truth, I write news and both stories were news."

"I don't hate you, Norela."

"I don't hate you, Sherrill, I hate everything you stand for. Whatever you can't force you can buy. You have no idea what it's like to spend your life being daddy's little girl. You have to be sweet or daddy will abandon you, but not too sweet or he'll squeeze you too tight. You have to be good or the principal will smack you, but not too good or the boys will knock the books off your desk. You have to bat your eyes at your professor to get a good grade, but keep your distance or you'll get an F for saying no. You have to be attractive so the boss will hire you but not so sexy that he fires you because you won't screw him or because you did and everyone knows."

She patted his hand. "You're no worse than the rest, Sherrill. I could have loved you but I wouldn't have been enough. No woman is when you're trying to conquer the world."

"Norela—"

"I'm here for a story, like everyone else. Treat me like one of the boys." She left without a backward look.

After lunch, a Seaknight helicopter took Sherrill to a remote combat base. Belk's television crew, wire service reporters and a couple of freelancers came also. It was working. However else Sherrill had failed he was doing this for Stolkalcyk and the gunny, putting the spotlight exactly where they wanted it.

Shivers led them to a bunker where they were greeted by a harassed captain who briefed them on his unit's activities. "Last month we treated 653 peasants, medevaced 35 of them for medical care, distributed 365 pounds of food, 146 pounds of clothing, 865 pounds of soap and 1130 school kits. We built a bridge, repaired three culverts, built three bamboo footbridges, repaired and improved a market—"

"How many fraggings have you had?" one of the reporters asked. Others asked how many rapes, how many drug busts.

The captain fought down the impulse to punch someone. "There has never been a fragging in this unit. There have been no charges of rape, misconduct or drugs. Every man in this unit is a double volunteer. He volunteered for the Marines and he volunteered for this program. Of the men in this program eighty percent have been wounded once, twenty-five percent have been wounded twice. One out of seven is killed. Yet, sixty percent of them extend for an additional tour of duty. They believe in these people. They believe in what they are doing. They—"

"Can you tell us what we're doing tomorrow?"

"There's too many of you to keep in one place overnight so we'll divide you among the platoons. The operation will start before dawn."

"What operation?" Sherrill asked but the captain was no longer taking questions. "Did you know there was an operation?" he asked Belk.

"There damn well better be. I called MAC-V and told them

there had better be a story, I wasn't going to waste film on gardening."

"I wanted to show the civic projects these guys are doing. The medical care, the construction projects, the—"

"What did you want me to film, pigs fucking?"

Jesus, a boobytrap and he had walked right into it. Once the cameras got there, it wasn't war any more, it was entertainment.

A jeep took Belk, Sherrill and Shivers down the road where Lieutenant Davis Sikowitz, a chunky, cheerful psychology student turned Marine lieutenant, met them at a new steel girded bridge beside an old bridge of concrete. Two sections of the concrete bridge had been dropped into the river by the VC. "Lieutenant Psycho," he said, with a toothy smile, adjusting his horn-rimmed glasses. "I'm here to study mania, what's your excuse?"

Lieutenant Psycho explained that his three squads, each expanded to platoon size by combining them with Vietnamese Popular Forces, lived in widely scattered villes, linked only by radio and a jeep driver. For support they had a combat base a few miles and several hours away.

"You're scattered kind of thin, aren't you?" Belk asked.

"Mainline North Vietnamese units are in the hills, the VC are in the lowlands. We keep the VC out of the villes and the battalion keeps the NVA in the mountains ."

"Does it work?"

"It works as long as we're in the villes. When we leave to attack the NVA in the hills, the VC moves right back into the villes behind us. I love it," he said. "It's too real."

"Then why the operation?" Sherrill asked.

"For you guys," Psycho laughed. "You're not going to film our cabbage patch or us capturing a couple of VC trying to infiltrate the ville. Every time you guys come out here, MAC-V sends the whole company into the hills killing gooks for the cameras and leaving all these villes open to infiltration. No television coverage, no appropriations. No appropriations, no bullets. No bullets, no promotions. I love it."

"Is that where we're going tomorrow? Into the hills?" Sherrill asked.

"We run this operation every time the press comes. Every man knows what's going to happen and what to do. Hell, I've fought the same fucking battle three fucking times. They never learn."

"Who never learns?"

"Nobody."

Sherrill and Belk were to spend the night with a squad in a ville. Sherrill had been in a hamlet only during the operation and then the enemy had left boobytraps everywhere and routinely shot into the ville and dropped mortars on it. Spending the night in a ville filled him with terror.

Lt. Psycho introduced him to the squad leader, a black Marine called Mother. Mother led him along a footpath into the ville where Mother was greeted by children who sought his attention and held his hands. He bowed to the peasants, called them by name, listened to their needs. They walked past a school that had been ruined by B-40 rockets, through the puddles of a cart-wide path to the deserted market place, an open square of masonry buildings. Every building was marred by bullets and shrapnel. Mother told the children goodbye and they walked along a footpath between hootches, around a well and stopped beside a ruined temple.

Mother introduced Sherrill to the members of the squad who were not on patrol. Taco had only fourteen days to go and if he made it, he'd be the first man in the platoon to ever rotate. "I extended," Mother said. "The others were medevaced or permanent routine."

"It don't mean nothing," Taco yawned. He was thin and lithe as a cat. "I never thought I'd live to see this day, I don't expect to see another one." Taco always walked point.

"You walking point tomorrow?" Mother asked. "You don't have to go. I want this platoon to rotate somebody."

"I don't know if I'll be alive tomorrow," Taco said. "Ask me then."

Dinky at twenty-four was the oldest man in the squad, and had been a sergeant when his platoon had been ambushed, leaving him the only survivor. After that he didn't give orders any more and he didn't take them. "I'm dead," he said. "I'm walking, but I'm dead." Dinky was short for dien ca dow, crazy.

Dinky had been discharged but after a short time at home, he had reenlisted and volunteered for Vietnam. "War makes a man be things he ain't never been before," Mother said. "He needs folks to say what he's been is okay, it's over, he's one of them again. They won't let ole Dinky be Roger Brown again." He put his arm around Dinky who was half a foot shorter and thirty pounds lighter. "Me and Dinky are tight. I don't tell him what to do, but any place I go, Dinky goes, anything I do, Dinky does."

R.D., short for R.D.M.D. or *Reader's Digest* doctor, was the corpsman attached to the squad. In addition to treating the Marines, he treated the peasants. "They got diseases we ain't even heard of, but if it bleeds I can bandage it. All I know is, if I live to be twenty I'll die at home."

"First time I saw the VC I told them, 'lay down your rifles or you cacadow,'" Punk said, the newest member of the squad. "I thought we had to give them a chance to be civilians. They shot up two clips before I got through explaining their options."

Punk had his story together. They all had their stories together, polished, practiced, vying with one another for the attention of the media.

A girl went past. She had a wide smile over a missing tooth. Also missing was one leg. The Marines believed she spied on them; that she had lost her leg setting a mine.

"She's VC," Dinky said, "but you can't shoot her."

"Losing a leg ain't nothing," Taco said. "I had an uncle that had a leg amputated and it didn't bother him none. He didn't do nothing before it was amputated and he didn't do nothing after it was amputated. He was just the same."

"My father was a hero," Punk said. "He died at a parade. Keeled over between *The Stars and Stripes Forever* and *The Sheriff's Mounted Posse*."

Sherrill listened to them competing for Belk's attention, vying for a spot on the evening news. "Is what you're doing working?" he asked.

"What do you mean working?" Mother asked.

"Are you getting anywhere? Is the situation better than last year, better than when you came?"

"Is what you are doing working?" Mother asked.

Sherrill didn't know how to answer the question. Words like peace, and victory and success had become media cliches that had meaning only in the market place. Peace was acquisition, success was money and the only victories were in fashion, detergents and sales. He couldn't think of any way the words had relevance to him.

"I can go to the well and I'll be surrounded by children," Mother said. "Their diet's better than it was last year. They have their shots. They go to school. They sleep in their hootches at night. Suppose Charlie drops a rocket on the school and kills all of them, does that mean it was a waste?"

"War is a waste," Taco said. "Did war free eastern Europe? Did it make England stronger? Did it make America better?"

"Taco has an academic scholarship when he gets back," Mother said. "I got a scholarship too, but mine's for football. Every man in this platoon could be hiding out in college, balling chicks and blowing grass. I would feel ashamed."

"Had you rather spend the rest of your life ashamed or spend it with no legs or maybe no eyes?" Taco asked.

"I don't like to ask that but I'm here. I guess that's my

answer."

"There's guys been hiding out in college so long they're going to have to be college professors," Taco said. "They're going to be teaching the next generation we're nothing but killers." He walked away.

"Taco wants to be a college professor. He'll do it too, but I think he's going to extend first. That's got him torn up. He thinks some of us ought to be teaching future generations what we were doing here, but he's afraid of what will happen to these people after he leaves."

"Do you think everyone in college is hiding out?" Belk asked.

"If this was white people fighting white people a lot of them would be over here. When it's yellow people fighting yellow people they say let the blacks and browns save them, they're not worth white lives. For every white boy in college there's a black or brown over here because he can't afford college, Canada or a lawyer. They can say they're opposed to killing, but they're killing the blacks and browns who go in their place. When a brother dies I blame them more than I do Charlie."

"Don't you think it may be as heroic to oppose an evil war as to fight it?" Belk asked.

"You have to ask them, 'who are they thinking of? Who are they trying to save?' I don't think I'm a hero for being here but I didn't say, 'my hide is too valuable, send somebody not as good as me.' If I don't save one person over here, if I don't make one child happy I can still say I tried. I didn't spend the war trying to save myself."

"But if you could stop the war you could save a lot of black and brown lives."

"You are standing here in my ville telling me these people aren't worth saving? They're not even good enough for black and brown lives? Get out of my face, honky. I can't stop the war no more than I can stop disease but I can stop Charlie from coming in here, taking boys and stealing rice."

After Mother walked away, Belk said, "If the camera had been here I might could have used some of that. I didn't know anybody really cared about these people." He dismissed the idea. "Minorities are interesting only when they pose a threat to majority rule."

Sherrill talked to Dinky. Here was a sole survivor, the kind of person his book was about, someone who could explain what it was like. Sherrill was buoyant; everything was working out. "What's it like to have an experience no one else can share?"

"I can't remember a lot of things I know I'll never forget," Dinky said.

"Did you talk to people about what had happened to your platoon?"

"I killed people but I'm not a killer. I'm walking but I'm dead. I don't even have to tell these guys, they already know."

"Did you try to tell people what you had been through?"

"If it wasn't on the screen they didn't want to know about it, and if it was on the screen, they already knew."

The patrol came in, and the men lighted heat tabs to warm their C-rations. At dusk they left a four-man ambush at the bridge, walked to the market place and scattered out choosing between the muddy street and the concrete walkways in front of the pavilions. Sherrill threw his poncho and liner on the concrete because the metal-patched tile roof offered some protection from the fine mist that filled the air. Belk lay beside him.

He had just gone to sleep when he was awakened. The ambush had come in. The squad moved quietly through the ville and were silently pointed into hootches. Sherrill and Belk were in an L-shaped hootch. A papasan and his family lay together on a plank bed at one end of the ell. Sherrill lay down on the damp, urine smelling, bare earth.

When he awoke a little girl was starting a fire with rice straw and wood shavings. For a moment she shivered in front of the fire, one hand folded in the other, then placed a pan of water over the fire to boil rice. Sherrill got up, found and lighted a heat tab and put the pan of water on it. Without speaking he knelt with the little girl before the fire and put his poncho liner around both of them.

"I had a little girl like you," he said. The child said nothing but her dark eyes were wide as she peered into the fire. He could feel the warmth from her frail body. He lighted another heat tab and placed his canteen cup over it to boil water for coffee. He watched the girl eating her rice and when the coffee was ready he offered her a drink. She took a sip, screwing up her face at the bitterness.

"Number one," he said, smiling. There was a trace of a smile on her face but she would accept no more coffee. Sherrill sipped his coffee, watching her. He tried to think of something he could wish for her.

What did he wish for himself? He wished to be with Jennifer and Marie. Everything else was decoration and delusion. Life was the only gift. The moment, the fire, the child. He searched his pockets for something to give her. He had nothing but cigarettes.

He realized that Belk was watching him. "This is better than bombing villages, but by being here don't the Marines make the ville a VC target? Did you see what the market place looked like?"

"The line units are supposed to keep pushing the enemy back while the CAP units fill in behind them, rooting out the VC in the ville and training the villagers to defend themselves. Eventually, all the fighting is supposed to be in the mountains, away from the populated areas."

"What's the conclusion?"

Conclusion? He couldn't think of an acceptable conclusion. Was it then meaningless repetition? Or was repetition the only conclusion, the only meaning? He was more confused than ever but meaning wasn't in conclusions; meaning was in revelations. Where then was the revelation? The insight? The vision?

"In twenty years they'll have cameras that film in the dark," Belk said. "I could have filmed you and that little girl, but until then I have nothing to say when the shadows get long."

"Prepare for the night," Sherrill said, surprising himself.

"What? It's morning."

"We have to prepare for the night."

Hearing others moving around, they slipped on their packs and flak jackets and went outside. It was dark and the rain was suspended in the air. When Sherrill looked back the girl was standing in the doorway watching him.

They followed the others through the ville to the highway where trucks were waiting for the troops. Taco claimed the puddles in the ville were the largest bodies of water he had ever seen. "Look at them white caps," he said. Over the combat base, which was under attack, flares drifted down through the clouds like slow, swollen, falling stars. The guns furnished lightning and thunder. Sherrill got in a jeep with Shivers and Psycho. Belk and the other reporters followed in other jeeps.

They drove up the paved highway, turned off on a dirt road where they were joined by trucks carrying Marines and PFs from other villes, and stopped when they reached a Vietnamese compound. The soldiers, living with their families in sandbagged bunkers just off the road, guarded a wooden bridge and kept the road closed until it had been swept for mines. They opened the wire to allow the Marines over the bridge.

On the opposite side of the bridge another wire gate held back a crowd of peasants, mostly women, waiting for the mine sweep to open the road to the market. For a few seconds

Marines and PFs carrying machine guns and rifles faced peasants carrying baskets of vegetables, firewood, geese, pigs, balanced on poles across their shoulders. In some of the baskets, beneath the vegetables, were mines and grenades. Each group was headed for the villages the other had just left.

There was no sun, no morning. Trees, hills, villes appeared out of the mist. A couple of miles past the bridge the trucks began dropping off troops at one end of the valley. Psycho pointed at a hill. "We'll take sniper fire from that hill and we'll drop a few mortar rounds on it. We'll take one or two WIAs and we'll get four or five kills."

By the time the jeep had stopped to let them rejoin Mother's squad, Psycho's prediction had come true, except that there were five Marine WIAs, four dead NVA. "People just don't act the same when they know they're being filmed," Psycho said. "We should have had no more than three wounded." He shrugged.

"Lights, action," Psycho yelled.

"Once more for the camera," his men responded.

Sherrill followed Psycho through a weedy field, across paddies, into a cane field, along a river bed. There was firing around him but Psycho knew what was happening before his radioman told him. They moved through a ville in which there was no sign of life—no people, no pigs, no chickens. "We call this 'No Nothing Ville.' On the maps it's marked as pacified," Psycho said. "We'll be ambushed crossing that paddy."

Two Cobra gunships passed low overhead and opened fire on a thicket to pin down the enemy while the Marines ran across the paddy and charged into the trees. By the time he reached the other side, the Marines had pulled seven NVA bodies into the open for the cameras. "Don't you have a camera?" Psycho asked. "How you gonna show?"

There was heavy firing to the right as they pushed through another woods, slipped down a high bank into a knee-deep stream. Bullets snapped overhead. A PF tapped Sherrill on the shoulder and handed him a canteen that had been dislodged by his slide down the bank. They worked their way along the river then climbed the bank and lay behind trees as a fire storm raged around them. Belk and his crew fell beside him. "They're not going to use this," Belk said. "We don't have anything on film."

They worked their way through the trees, firing, screaming, calling for corpsmen. "Taco's been hit," R.D. said. "This platoon has never rotated a man. Who's short now?"

"Rock in fifth squad," Punk said.

"Rock was zapped. That leaves Dinky."

"Dinky was hit."

"I'm dead but I'm not wounded," Dinky said.

"They're not going to believe this," Belk said. "This doesn't look real."

For some unaccountable reason the firing stopped. Nothing had changed, yet no one was fighting. They passed through the trees and into a ville. A handful of women and children squatted on the ground. One of the women was wounded and had been bandaged by the NVA. The PF honcho questioned them but the peasants had seen nothing. Bullets landed in the ville as the Marines followed a footpath out of the ville.

Around a bend in the trail Sherrill could see a broad valley of rice fields, broken by islands of higher ground thick with trees. Mountains rose on three sides. Psycho explained what was going to happen. "They'll keep pulling back, losing men as they go, until we have them completely out of the valley. On the other side of that pagoda, way back there, we'll run into dug-in positions. Then they'll come out of the mountains on both sides and try to overrun us. It never works."

"Never works for whom?" Sherrill asked, as Cobras passed overhead to soften up the entrenched positions before the Marines got there.

"Never works for nobody. Don't you love it? Too real."

They waded across a stream, along a trail. "Can't you do

something?" Belk shouted at Sherrill. "Can't you shoot at something? We're getting nothing on film."

They were receiving light, ineffectual fire. Sherrill saw that the television camera was on him, sucking at his face, setting him apart. He had to make it look real. He had to get his story together, to project his purpose. Who did he want to say he was? He hunched a little as though under heavy fire. He lifted his rifle higher, proud but not vain, steadfast but not stubborn, brave but not foolhardy, imperfect but not evil—

When he heard the click he knew it was the most momentous sound he would ever hear—of more consequence than Jennifer's protestations of love, of more significance than Marie's cries for life. And he knew he had been dreading and waiting for it all his life.

In that instant he hated himself for the fool he was, tricked not by his crimes but by his illusions, boobytrapped by his self-portrait. Then it disappeared in the ear-shattering bang that stunned, numbed, knocked his legs from under him, drove the breath from his chest and left him choking on the ground, gasping, unable to cry for help.

Through the pain, the ringing in his ears, he could hear cries, shouts, but he could not care about them, he could only desire breath. Just the legs, he prayed. Let it be just the legs. He could love, write, breathe without legs. Just breath. Fear rattled in his throat as his breath came back hard, laden with dust smoke blood stench of cordite. He wanted to cough, to throw up but was afraid to.

He fought to keep his mind numb, from searching out and touching that pain. Through the numbness, the ringing, he could hear someone speaking —a calm, deliberate voice— ". . .a corpsman is trying to reach him now, although there is the danger of other mines. . ."

Belk. The camera was on him, taking something that was his, something he needed. He wanted to hide his face but was afraid to move. He tried to set it, but could not. He opened his eyes and through the dust and smoke that hung in the air he could see Shivers. Fucking gunny, he needed a corpsman. Then he realized the gunny was clearing a path through the mines for the corpsman to follow and he was moved to tears. He tried to blink them back, knowing the camera would misinterpret them.

He wanted to explain, he wanted to describe what it was like to be wounded. One part of his mind was checking his reactions, trying to record what he felt. The smell of dust, cordite, blood, excrement, a kind of soapy gurgling, wetness, stickiness, nausea, something rising in his throat, weakness, heaviness.

When he looked down he could see bone. It made him queasy. It made him tingle. Hot then cold. He thought he was going to faint but he did not want to faint. He wanted to record, to remember. He didn't want to look but he looked anyway. He could see blood spraying in the air. He could see torn meat. He could see it quivering through holes in his uniform. He could see it quivering outside his uniform. This is my body, he said, feeling removed from it.

Someone was beside him. The gunny, the corpsman, he wasn't sure. "I'm sorry," Sherrill said. "Sorry, sorry." He wondered who he was apologizing to. Everyone. He was apologizing to everyone. How could he put them through this?

"No morphine," he mumbled, thought he mumbled. He could bear the pain and he did not want his perceptions clouded with drugs. "It's not so bad," he said. "I can take it."

Then the pain hit, sharp as orgasm. He held his breath, groaned through clenched teeth, giving himself to it. Too late he realized it was not pleasure, would not stop, went on, swelling, exploding in his head while his mind struggled to grasp it, to contain it, to escape it, refusing morphine even while he heard himself crying for it.

"You're going to make it," someone was saying to him. "Hang on to my hand. Grip it. Hang on. Open them eyes.

Goddammit, open them eyes."

He was afraid to pass out, afraid to close his eyes. He screamed or tried to scream while wetness welled in his throat. He could hear himself but could not understand what he was screaming. Morphine? Jennifer? He tried to convince Jennifer he deserved to live. He tried to convince God he knew what life was. Given time he would tell the world.

The gunny was in his face, saying something to him but he could not hear over his own screams. He did not know when the corpsman had given him morphine but the pain was not so sharp, leaving one little corner of himself, but he could not stop screaming. His mind slowly rose above the pain and he could hear R.D. saying, "You're going to be all right. I've made up my mind about you. You're going to be on your way home. Don't go to sleep. The bird is on the way."

The corpsman seemed to be pulling him together. Getting his shit together. He wanted to laugh. That was good; laugh for the camera. Jennifer would see him. Smile for Jennifer. Smile for Marie. He looked into R.D.'s face and what he saw there drove the smile from his lips. "Don't die on me," R.D. said from behind squinched-up eyes, twisted mouth, trying to prevent him from seeing his wounds. "You're on your way home. Back to the world. Just hang on."

He clung to the corpsman's words, dimly aware the gunny was trying to ease the grip Sherrill had on his arm. He knew he was squeezing so hard it was painful but he couldn't let go and the gunny couldn't break his death grip. "Death grip." That's what the words meant. How true they seemed; for the first time he understood them. Now he could write those words honestly. Let the critics call them trite, he alone knew what they meant.

". . .Dix Deveraux kind of hero, no one has ever questioned his heroism, his patriotism. . ." Belk was saying into the microphone.

"No," Sherrill said. "No."

". . .reckless devotion to a war that has gone on too long, trying to save the discredited military effort but failing to save himself. . ."

"No." He had done everything they wanted. Why hadn't it worked?

"Keep breathing," R.D. yelled. "In, out. Open them eyes."

". . .knows better than the rest of us the terrible price. . ."

"No."

"Guys like you don't die," the gunny said. "Guys like you get mad."

"In, out. Open. Open your eyes."

". . .representative of. . . "

"No." They were getting it all wrong. "No." He was on camera and they were stealing his story, they were stealing his spirit—

"Hang on, Goddamit, grip."

"In, out. Bird's on the way."

He felt a darkness coming over him. He wanted to cry, to plead, to beg but he was on camera, trapped in his own blood, urine, excrement. Brow furrowed with sorrow of thought. Mouth straight with reason and humor. Chin. . .not like this. Please God, not like this. Marie must not see him like this.

Alone. The corpsman, the gunny were so far away he could not touch them, hear them. It's true, he thought. He had always known that and yet not realized it before. Everyone dies alone. He and the camera. He did not want to die alone, the camera in his face. He tried to reach out. Tried. So many people. So many. "I love..." he said. Is that the way you treat people you love? Yes. Jennifer. Marie. Kelty. Some nameless child in Saigon. Some nameless child in a ville. All of them. He had faced that truth.

"Open them eyes. Wider. Wider."

When he opened his eyes he saw that it wasn't darkness of death upon him but the shadow of life. Over him loomed a monument. Jesus.